Married to the guy she met in college, *USA TODAY* bestselling author **Sara Orwig** has three children and six grandchildren. Sara has published 109 novels. One of the first six inductees into the Oklahoma Professional Writers Hall of Fame, Sara has twice won Oklahoma Novel of the Year. Sara loves family, friends, dogs, books, beaches and Dallas, Texas.

Zuri Day is the nationally bestselling author of two dozen novels, including the popular Drakes of California series. She is a winner of the RSJ Emma Award, the AALAS (African American Literary Awards Show) Best Romance Award and others, and a finalist for multiple RT Reviewers' Choice Best Book Awards in Multicultural Fiction. Find out more and stay in touch at zuriday.com

Also by Sara Orwig

Expecting the Rancher's Child
The Rancher's Baby Bargain
The Rancher's Cinderella Bride
The Texan's Baby Proposal
Expecting a Lone Star Heir
The Forbidden Texan
The Rancher's Heir

Also by Zuri Day

Sin City Vows
Ready for the Rancher
Champagne Kisses
Platinum Promises
Solid Gold Seduction
Secret Silver Nights
Crystal Caress

Discover more at millsandboon.co.uk

IN BED WITH
THE RANCHER

SARA ORWIG

SIN CITY
SEDUCTION

ZURI DAY

MILLS & BOON

First Published in Great Britain 2020
by Mills & Boon, an imprint of HarperCollinsPublishers,
1 London Bridge Street, London, SE1 9GF

In Bed with the Rancher © 2020 Sara Orwig
Sin City Seduction © 2020 Zuri Day

ISBN: 978-0-263-27932-0

0820

MIX
Paper from
responsible sources

FSC C007454
www.fsc.org

This book is produced from independently certified FSC™ paper to ensure responsible forest management.

For more information visit: www.harpercollins.co.uk/green

Printed and bound in Spain
by CPI, Barcelona

IN BED WITH THE RANCHER

SARA ORWIG

One

Driving north on the back roads of Texas, Wade Sterling was trying to get away from a storm.

He'd been on the Gulf, fishing, when the weather had cut his trip short. He'd received warnings of violent storms developing farther out in the Gulf and heading toward the coast. He had docked near Corpus Christi and was now driving north. When he had a little more distance between him and the coast, he would turn east to get onto Interstate 45 North into Dallas.

He had called home and told his mother he was safely back on land and he would be home in a few days, maybe even a week. He had learned long ago to overestimate how long he'd be gone or she'd get worried. He suspected he would be caught in rain driving home, so the trip might take longer than usual.

Now, however, the forecast called for possible flooding. To keep his mind off the weather, he thought about things he needed to do when he got home. Before he drove to Bar S Ranch, he wanted to stop at his condo in Dallas. He needed to go by his office because he had real estate holdings he should check on and other business matters to attend to.

He and his rancher cousins, Cal Brand, Jake Reed and Luke Grayson, had all contributed money to build a new arena in Fort Worth to replace a popular old arena that had burned down. The city wanted a grand opening and he and his cousins needed to agree on a date. He should get with his cousins and get that date settled.

Sadness gripped him when he thought about his cousin, Cal. Cal had been a rancher, as the rest of them were, but he wanted life on the wild side, too. He had done under-cover work for the government. He'd said two more years and he would retire to his ranch. When Wade contacted Cal about donating to build the new arena, Cal was en-thusiastic and sent more than they'd planned, saying he was sure the builders would find a use for the money. Two months later, his family received word that Cal had died in an accident on the Atlantic Ocean. The surviving cousins attended the memorial service held by Cal's family. Wade shook his head. He would miss Cal who was interesting, fun, and a good rancher.

Another of Wade's cousins had had a sad event. It was two years ago when Luke's wife and baby boy were killed in a car wreck. Luke no longer was as light-hearted as he had been before losing his family and Wade could under-stand why. It made him sad and he wondered if Luke would ever be the happy person he once was.

A deep rumble of thunder warned Wade he wasn't going to beat the storm.

His thoughts shifted to getting home.

Which led to thoughts of Olivia, and his need to break things off with her.

Though she was beautiful and exciting to be with, she was getting too serious. He didn't want to marry—not ever. Problem was, she did, and she made it obvious. Just the thought of marriage sent a chill down his spine. He never wanted to marry and risk having a kid like his twin. His identical twin. Identical in looks but not in temperament and personality. Not at all. Wynn had caused trouble as far back as Wade could remember.

Wade thought about the latest example. Last month, when he had stopped by his parents' home and waited for their return from the grocer's, their landline phone rang. He answered, in case it was a business call for his dad. Wade had just started to say "Sterling residence" when a woman's frantic voice cut him off.

"Wynn, this is Violet," she said in a nasal twang.

"I'm not Wynn. I'm—" was all he could get out before she interrupted him.

"Wynn, don't lie to me. I recognize your voice. You listen to me." Wade could hear the desperation in her tone as her words poured out louder and faster. "Your cell number has changed and I couldn't find you. Don't you dare hang up. We have a deal. You've been good about sending money, but it hasn't come this month. I need it, so get it to me. I'll keep my part of our bargain as long as you keep your promise and the money comes. I've stayed out of Dallas and no one knows about our child. If you want it to stay that way, get the money to me."

Shocked, Wade forgot about telling her who he was.

"It's in the mail, Violet," he said instead and hung up. He had given an answer and cut her off in the manner that Wynn would have done. She might learn Wynn had a twin and she had talked to the wrong brother, but he didn't think she would tell Wynn because she had given away his secret—Wynn had a child.

Stunned, Wade could imagine Wynn trying to hide the mother and the baby. Wynn's tastes ran to gorgeous, sexy women, but he didn't care if they were strippers in the worst nightclub in town or the cream of Dallas society. He always found the sexy beauties, but some of them he never took to meet the family. Violet, for one, he assumed.

He wondered about his folks not knowing their first grandchild. It might be just as well, and Wynn was paying regularly to bury the secret. He assumed Wynn had good reason to keep his baby a secret, so Wade would also, but it hurt to think there was a child out there that they'd never know and who would never know them.

He knew when his brother finally got around to marrying, it would be a dazzling beauty from a prominent, wealthy family. Someone like Olivia. Olivia would be a good match for Wynn because she could hold her own with him. Strong and bright, she would be a good influence on him.

For now, Wade would keep Wynn's secret. Wynn was a dad—that alone was an incredible shock. Another shiver ran down his spine. He couldn't imagine Wynn raising a child. He was still a child himself in many ways. But now he was a dad who probably had never even seen his own child. That wouldn't surprise Wade at all.

Wade thought about his own situation. He didn't want marriage or fatherhood at this point in his life, yet if he had a baby with a woman, he would want that child in his life. For just a moment he felt a pang and wondered if he would miss out on a lot by avoiding marriage. Then he had to laugh at himself. He didn't even have a woman in his life, since he was about to part ways with Olivia.

He kept his eyes on the road and pressed on the accelerator, trying to beat out the pending storm. But he couldn't outpace his thoughts. There was another problem, far more worrisome, on his mind. A few months ago his ranch foreman, Cotton Daniels, had told him that one of the cowboys was regularly receiving money from a man who drove to the ranch. Cotton happened to be taking out cedar trees when he saw the cowboy, Denny White, drive on a ranch road while a car came from the opposite direction and they parked facing each other. They didn't see Cotton because he was in a thick stand of cedars and his four-wheeler was out of the way. Initially he'd just passed it off as a gambling debt or some such, except the men were acting so secretive. The next month, about the same time, he saw them again near the gate.

Wade couldn't help but worry why someone was paying Denny.

Nor could he stop thinking this was another of the sneaky things Wynn was involved in. Wade had learned years earlier, if trouble occurred in his life, his twin was usually involved.

Throughout his life, Wade had never understood his twin's jealousy or his anger if Wade got something and he didn't. Wynn was their mother's favorite of her four children and he made certain he stayed that way. She was the one person on Earth that Wynn seemed to care about and went out of his way to keep happy.

Wade shook his head and sighed. When he got back to Dallas, he was going to have to deal with Wynn. He doubted if Wynn had delt with Denny face-to-face, but he felt certain that Wynn was behind whatever Denny was getting paid to do. Now he had to worry about that as well as Wynn's baby. His twin needed to tell the truth about his child. And he would have to wring out of Wynn if and what he was paying Denny to do. In the meantime he needed to give Cotton authority to fire Denny if he saw good reason. He trusted Cotton's judgment completely.

A clap of thunder brought Wade's attention back to his surroundings. The thunder rumbled ever closer. The bumpy county road had mesquite scattered on either side. To his left was a deep canyon with a creek at the bottom. It was a small stream, but in a storm, Wade knew how streams could become white-water rivers and flood the surrounding area. He didn't want to get caught in a storm on a back road that was unknown terrain.

He hadn't seen another vehicle since he left the coast. He didn't have to worry about traffic, so he sped up, hoping to get to the next town before the storm hit. In minutes, the first big drops splashed on the windshield and then a gray sheet of blinding, torrential rain swept over his pickup.

Once, when he glanced in his rearview mirror at the sprays of water going up in his pickup's wake, he thought he saw headlights in the distance behind him. The rain was too intense to be sure. He soon swooshed around a curve and a sea of water was in front of him. As the road dipped, he pumped his brakes, but it was too late to prevent driving into the water rushing over the road, and then he felt the pickup leave the road and he was floating, swept up by the water.

Frantically, Wade yanked off his coat. If he went into the water at the bottom of the canyon and had to swim, he didn't want to be wearing a coat.

As thunder boomed and the first drops of rain fell, Ava Carter saw a pickup in the distance ahead. The drops turned into torrential rain and she could barely see anything except red taillights. Frowning, she pressed the accelerator, trying to narrow the distance. She rarely saw anyone on this back road in the area where she owned a cabin for an escape from her busy life in Dallas. She had been in Persimmon, the nearest small town, and had attempted to beat the storm back to her cabin, but she wasn't going to do it.

In Persimmon, when she'd heard that the weatherman had updated his forecast for torrential rains, she'd grabbed what supplies she could and left for her cabin.

It had surprised her to see taillights ahead on the usually deserted back road. If that was a stranger, someone unfamiliar with the area, the driver needed to turn around, too, because in a downpour the road would be under water in minutes.

She wanted to catch up enough to flag the driver, but the rain was too intense.

A deluge of rain hid the pickup's taillights from her view. She leaned on her horn, hoping that might make the person stop, but the rain and thunder probably drowned out the sound. Seconds later, she knew it was too late when the pickup vanished as the road turned in a sweeping curve. At that moment, another bolt of lightning illuminated the entire area and she saw water gush over the highway and the pickup wash off the road. As it went over the edge, still carried by the stream of water, a man jumped from the pickup, hit the ground and rolled down the incline, disappearing from her view. Carried by the rushing stream of water, the pickup crashed into a tree and was then swept around it, continuing down toward the raging creek.

Frightened for the man who jumped, she felt compelled to help him.

Ava pulled to the side of the road, leaving her lights blinking, even though she was certain no one else would happen along. She couldn't drive away and leave someone lying on the steep slope to the creek in this terrible storm, which was predicted to get worse.

She jammed on a broad-brimmed Resistol hat and yanked on a rain slicker. With a deep breath, she stepped out and ran to the edge of the road, where she looked for the driver. Rain made it difficult to spot anyone, so she cautiously started down the slope that was becoming slippery and muddy where there weren't weeds and high grass. Then she spotted the man sprawled on the ground, his fall evidently stopped by the low-lying branches of a cedar.

Soaked and chilled, she inched down the treacherous, steep slope. When she reached him, the stranger was lying still. As she thought about what to do, she kneeled beside him. To her relief, he stirred.

"Thank heavens, you're conscious," she said. Because of a blow to his head, a knot had popped out high on his brow at his hairline and his skin was already bruising. A deep cut across his shoulder bled even as rain washed over it. He didn't have a jacket, just a torn shirt, jeans and boots.

Cold rain pounded them and nearby a tree crashed to earth, taking small trees with it and leaving thick roots sticking up in the air, reminding her to hurry.

"We need to get back to the road to my pickup." She took his wrist to feel his pulse, which was strong. Then she reached out and pushed the tangled black hair off his face. When she brushed his face, his eyelids fluttered and she looked into brown eyes that suddenly held her attention as much as if he had reached out and touched her. Her gaze locked with his, caught and held as if in a trap. In spite of the raging storm, the world closed down to just the two of them. Her awareness of him rocked her and she could only stare at him, stunned.

She shouldn't be feeling anything except the cold, drenching rain. Since her broken engagement to Judd Porter, she had been numb to men, not wanting to go out with any of them. Not even her male friends. Being around any man brought back the painful memories of Judd. So how, then, could this total stranger, with chilling rain pouring over both of them in a raging storm, captivate her and make her heart race?

A clap of thunder and then a sizzling lightning bolt brought her out of the brief daze and she realized every second they were out in the storm, their situation grew worse.

As if he, too, sensed the danger, the man sat up and she was relieved to see he could move.

"You're sitting, so how's your back?"

He shrugged and grimaced. "My back is okay. My head feels as if someone is pounding it with a hammer."

"We need to get to my pickup. If I help you, can you get up? And do you think you can make it back up this hill?"

"Yes, I can," he said as if there was no question about it.

"I have a cabin nearby. We have to get out of here before we get cut off by rising water. We can't go back to the last town now. Trees are falling and there's lightning. You're on an isolated back road. An ambulance wouldn't get here for an hour at best, and if the rain keeps up, an ambulance can't get here at all. I doubt if we can even get phone reception here. We can still drive to my cabin, I think." The whole time she talked, he gazed at her with such an intent look that her tingling response to him continued.

"Your cabin it is. Let's get out of here if you know a way."

"I do. It's not good, but it'll do. The weather predictions are getting worse."

"I'm ready," he said, standing without difficulty, and she realized he was fit and in good physical condition. She also noticed that he was tall, broad-shouldered and rather good-looking.

"Let me help you up the incline," she said, stepping beside him.

"I'll be okay," he said, as she thought he would. His shirt was ripped where he had fallen and been cut, the tattered, soaked material clinging to a muscled chest and a torn sleeve revealing a strong bicep.

"You'll have to look for your pickup later," she said.

"At the moment, that's not my worry."

"No, it isn't. We need to get to solid ground before some of this incline gives way and takes us down with it," she said. "Let's go."

The climb was slippery, mud constantly making them lose their footing as they gradually neared the road.

Seconds later, there was a crack of tree limbs breaking and then another tall oak fell. He pushed her away from the tree and not even the tips of leaves touched them, but chunks of ground broke off and slid downhill.

She slipped and he stepped close to put his arm around her as she grabbed him. "Thanks. I'm glad that wasn't your cut shoulder," she said, holding her hat on her head as she looked up at him.

As they steadied, he gripped a tree branch with one hand while he held her close with the other, her hip pressed against him. She gazed at him. Wind battered them and a sheet of cold rain swept over them, but she barely noticed it. Even with his injuries, he was strong, holding her tightly while his body heat warmed her side where they were pressed together.

As she gazed into his brown eyes, another sizzle made her forget rain, cold, danger—everything else except his strong arm holding her, his warm body against hers and those eyes that captured and held her gaze. Dark brown eyes that changed her world. When she saw the slightest narrowing of his eyes, she knew he felt something, too. She figured this primitive urge they both had was stirred by the danger from the storm. As if to confirm her thoughts, another big tree snapped and cracked, toppling to the ground.

"Let's get out of here," she shouted with a deliberate effort to break the spell. His arm tightened around her waist and, together, grabbing nearby limbs, they climbed the remaining way to the road. She pointed to her pickup. "You wait here and I'll come get you."

With a shake of his head, he took her arm and started toward her pickup. "Let's go."

When they reached her vehicle, he released her. As soon as they both were inside, she retrieved a first-aid kit from the back seat and handed him a thick gauze pad.

"Hold this against your shoulder. You're still losing blood."

He took the pad from her and placed it over the jagged cut on his shoulder. As he did, he reached out to remove her hat and toss it into the back, then he turned to take a long, slow look at her that made her forget she was cold and rain-soaked. All she knew was that his attention was on her and she couldn't get her breath.

"When I opened my eyes, you looked like an angel with your blond hair and blue eyes, but I don't think angels wear cowboy hats."

His voice was deep and he sat close while his dark brown eyes made her heart race. He had raked thick, wet black hair away from his face, but a few wavy locks had already slipped free to fall on his forehead. Regardless of his injuries and tattered, wet clothes, she felt another puzzling moment of heated, physical awareness. How could she feel intense awareness for a total stranger, and in these abominable circumstances?

She made an effort to break the eye contact and get her

mind back on their situation, which grew more hazardous by the minute.

She cleared her throat and dug out her phone. "I'll try to get info on the roads," she said with a breathlessness that she hoped he didn't notice. She focused on her phone for a moment and then shook her head and dropped her phone into a pocket of her jacket when she got no reception.

"My cabin is big, well-stocked and comfortable," she said, starting the pickup and driving back the way she had come. "We'll have to double back for a few miles to get there. If this downpour continues a lot longer, we may be stuck at my place until the storm is gone and water recedes. It's remote and isolated out here. As you can see, there's no cell-phone reception. No TV reception, either, so I don't even have a TV at the cabin."

"How many miles to your cabin?"

"About ten. There's a road I can take and it's on higher ground. It's a back road the ranchers put in across private property, but it gives about five of us a way around the low places when we have these torrential downpours. There are two bad things about the road—it's gravel and we have one creek to cross," she said as they continued on.

"A gravel road is okay. I remember a narrow road and a sign—'Keep Off. Private Property.'"

"That's it." She glanced at him because she noticed he was shifting and patting his pockets as he talked. "Is something wrong?"

Frowning, he looked at her. "I don't have my wallet. I must have lost it rolling down the hill. We can't go searching for it now," he said.

"No, we can't."

"No telling where my pickup has gone."

"There's no finding that now, either," she said, concentrating on her driving in the downpour. Thunder was loud and lightning lit up the area. "We need to get to my cabin before we're cut off from any shelter. There aren't many people who live out here."

"So I noticed."

"Yes, and it's not a good place to be in a storm like this. From here to the gravel road will take about five more minutes and then it'll be even slower traveling. We have one more bridge to cross." Her brow creased as a thought occurred to her. "If we can't get across that, I don't think we can get back to Persimmon. I'm sure the old bridge to Persimmon is under water by now." She shrugged it off. "Not to worry. If we can cross that last bridge, my cabin is on high ground. It's never flooded."

As she squinted through the rain-soaked windshield, she told him, "The road we're on is such a back road, it's seldom used even by those of us who live in this area. I have a close neighbor and we could go to his house, but he's nearer to the creek and that's probably already like a raging river. I wouldn't feel safe in his house in this storm."

She glanced at him. "How are you feeling?"

"My head is pounding, my shoulder still hurts and I'm thoroughly soaked. Otherwise, fair to middlin', I'd say. Thank you again for stopping to pick me up."

"Sure."

He didn't say anything else and she thought he might be tired of conversation and hurting. "Don't go to sleep in case you have a concussion."

"I don't think staying awake will be a problem," he remarked dryly and she wondered how much pain he was in. Or perhaps he was worrying about having lost his wallet and his pickup, which she suspected was downstream somewhere filled with water or smashed on rocks.

"I don't have my phone, either," he said.

"You can't use it out here, anyway." For a moment she

was quiet. "I think it's time we get introduced. I'm Ava Carter."

"I'm glad to meet you, Ava Carter," he said in a somber tone of voice.

They rode in silence and she wondered why he didn't introduce himself. When she glanced at him, he had such a worried expression on his face, she put her foot on the brake and turned to him. "What's wrong?"

"You don't know me at all, yet you know something is wrong."

She nodded. "You look concerned. Should I be worried about your identity?"

Shaking his head, he answered, "Well, yes and no, I don't think so. But that's just a feeling I have, because the problem is—" he hesitated only a moment as he stared at her "—I can't tell you my name. I don't know it. I can't remember who I am or where I'm from."

Two

She stared at him. "Maybe we should turn around and try to get to a hospital."

She grabbed her phone. "I'll try again to get through." But after a moment she put it away. "I can't get any reception. We're out of range." She debated what to do. He would get better professional care in a hospital, but she was certain the roads would already be closed. Sheets of rain still swept over them and wind shook her pickup. "I feel sure by now the roads to the nearest hospital are closed. Even if we could go back, Persimmon doesn't have a hospital."

"Does it have a doctor?"

"They have a vet and people go to him. But my close neighbor is a nurse. That sounds like the best we can do."

"Sounds good to me. Let's go to your cabin...unless you're concerned about my identity. I don't think I'm dangerous."

She looked into his dark brown eyes and he gazed back

at her. She couldn't understand her reasoning, but she felt okay about him. She hoped her judgment was sound. But then again, she didn't really have much choice. She wasn't going to leave him out in this storm to survive on his own.

Her gaze drifted over him, noticing again his expensive watch. His boots were covered with mud, but she could see part of them, as well as his belt, which looked hand-tooled and expensive. All meaningless as far as judging his character, however.

She shook her head and smiled. "I don't think so, either, although I trust you for reasons I don't understand. It's just that I feel a connection with you. Do you know what state you're in?"

"Texas. I saw the tag on your pickup so we can't make any judgments from that answer."

"Maybe not, but you gave me an honest answer. Do you know where you live?"

He frowned briefly and then shook his head. "Nothing comes to me. I have glimmers of things, but I don't know if they're from real life, television or friends of mine. I'm at a loss. I don't recall my parents, my friends, or where I live. Or what commitments I have."

"We'll assume you have some kind of family—parents, siblings."

"I don't have a wedding ring," he said as he looked down at his left hand. Then he turned his gaze back to her, shaking his head. "If my phone and wallet with all my info were in my pickup and it went into that stream, there's no telling if it'll be found, or by whom. Or maybe they fell out of my pockets when I slid down that slope. In all that mud and the rain, they may never be found."

He looked dazed and dejected, and thoroughly confused, and she felt the need to bolster him. "We'll deal with that later. Right now, let's talk." When he looked at her quizzically, she added, "You've had a head injury so you need to stay awake, and one way for me to know you're awake is for you to talk."

"We can both talk," he said. "Are you a rancher? Or in a rancher's family?" he asked her.

"No to both. I'm an occupational therapist and I have my own home-care business in Dallas. I provide caregivers. It's busy and sometimes I want to get away. I have someone who works for me who can take over when I come stay at my cabin. I did own a ranch that I inherited from my grandfather. I sold it to Gerald Roan, who lives on it. His wife, Molly, is the nurse I mentioned. I kept five acres—it's where my cabin is. I have three horses and a few head of cattle that Gerald takes care of. I wanted a cabin away from Dallas where it's quiet, in the great outdoors and there's a horse I can ride and a place to ride it."

She turned on the gravel road, slowing to a crawl. "Here's our private road." The road was rough and the rain was still a blinding downpour.

"This is a roundabout way to get home, but we only cross one creek and it has a strong bridge that hopefully will be above water. I've only seen it underwater once before, but this is a bad storm."

While she concentrated on her driving, he was silent. Night was approaching and she wanted to get to her cabin and out of the downpour before dark. With the storm it would get dark earlier than usual. After a few minutes, she stopped to try her phone again.

"There's a stretch here of fairly open country that's the highest point in the area, where I can sometimes get service. I want to try again to contact Gerald. He's got a four-story house on a hill, so that gives him a higher place to send and receive messages. At least his equipment works better than at my place, where I can't get any reception at all in this kind of weather."

She tried calling Gerald but got nowhere. Then she tried texting him. "Also, I'll try to text the sheriff in Persimmon to let him know about you in case he gets a missing-person's report." In minutes she shook her head. "I can't get through to the sheriff. I don't know if it's the distance or the direction or what. I did send a text to my neighbor and it went through, I think, but he hasn't answered." She was suddenly tense about going home with a stranger who didn't know his own identity. Worse, if the bridge was underwater, they would be trapped outside for a night in the car. She didn't want to think about that one at all.

In minutes, she got a text in return and Gerald offered to come stay if she was concerned and asked about the man's identity.

She sent another brief text to Gerald that the stranger had received a blow to his head and he couldn't remember his identity. Also, she relayed that his wallet and phone were missing.

Gerald wrote that he would drop by and she sent her thanks. She regretted that Gerald had to go out in the storm, but felt better about taking in a stranger who said he didn't remember anything about his identity and he didn't have any ID. Judging from the knot on his head, she felt he was telling the truth, but she was glad Gerald would come meet him. She drove forward.

"So what did your neighbor have to say?" he asked her a few moments later.

"I told him about bringing you home with me and he wrote back that he's coming by to meet you."

She glanced at the stranger and he smiled—a smile that made her heart skip beats. Another unwanted reaction, now more than ever. She didn't want to respond to any man right now, not when she was still getting over a broken heart, and definitely not one who had no memory of himself.

"It could make life easier temporarily if I take an assumed name just so you can get my attention or introduce me or whatever we have to do," he said.

"Of course. You're right. Pick a name you like."

"Bill Smith is easy," he said after a moment. "That sounds okay. It would be funny if it turned out to be my real name and that's why it sounds okay," he said and smiled again—another smile that made her heart skip a beat. She tried to ignore her reaction, but that wasn't easy.

"Okay, Bill it is. That's a good name," she said. They started downhill and she kept her attention on the road. "There goes the last time I can hope to get a text through. I'll always try if I need to send one, but from here on, I'm cut off from the world except for the people who live around me. Gerald and his family are close neighbors. The people who work for Gerald live on his property. Some of those people work for me, too." Concern for keeping him awake took a back seat as they approached the creek she had to cross. As she drew close, she gasped and slowed to a crawl.

"That's Blue Creek," she said. "I've only seen it like this once before. It's usually ankle-deep, but it's a river now. The bridge is supposed to be well-built and the water isn't totally over it yet," she observed, watching waves splash against the bridge. "I'm going to try to cross it. Otherwise we'll have to stay out here in my pickup all night. That's not a good alternative."

"If the bridge is as sturdy and well-built as you say, we should be able to cross without trouble." He unfastened his seatbelt. "Unbuckle. You don't want to be buckled in if the bridge collapses."

She unbuckled her seatbelt and drove cautiously, praying the bridge would stand. Holding her breath, she started across.

"You're doing fine," he said. "Nothing is shaking and that's a good sign. Not much farther," he added as they inched across. "Doing good. Across!" he announced, turning to give her a high five as he flashed a big smile. "Good job."

His irresistible smile sent a tingle to her toes while her heartbeat quickened. At the same time, every positive response she had to him stirred another instant negative response in a reminder that she should squelch any attraction she felt. She didn't want to be tempted by a man who made her heart race by just a smile. Especially a man who couldn't recall his own name.

The attraction felt more dangerous and a bigger threat to her well-being than the raging storm and rising water, which didn't make sense to her, but was true just the same.

She drove a few feet away from the bridge and paused to buckle her seatbelt again while he fastened his. "We're on this side now and there's no going back. That bridge will be underwater in minutes," she said. "Good news is we're close to my cabin with no more creeks or rivers to cross. Bad news is, with no reception, if your family starts looking for you and puts your picture on television or social media, we'll never know it until this storm is over and I can get to town or far enough back down the road."

"We can't do anything about that now."

He was right. "In addition to the tornado threat, Gerald mentioned that the storm has intensified."

As if to underscore her words about the storm, thunder boomed and a streak of lightning struck a tree, traveling down the trunk, splitting it in two and running a few feet along the ground as both parts of the tree crashed to earth. Knowing they needed to get to shelter, she continued driving.

They rode in silence until she turned on a paved drive. When she slowed in front of large black iron fencing, big gates swung open to let her enter. She glanced at him again. "You're getting a black eye below that bump on your forehead. Actually, the bump has gone down."

"That's good."

The gates closed behind her as she drove on. "Well, we made it to my place," she said.

"Yes, we did. You might have saved my life today, you know," he said in a solemn voice.

Startled, she glanced at him. "I think you would have survived if I hadn't been driving past. You seem strong and healthy. You got up to the road without any difficulty."

"I'm damn glad you came back to get me and I'm not out in this weather without a car or wallet or memory." He dipped his head and looked out the window. "AC Ranch," he said, reading.

"It's not really a ranch any longer since I sold it. I kept the AC Ranch sign because Gerald didn't care. He renamed his ranch Roan Ranch."

Though the rain was still steady, the lightning and thunder had diminished. They followed the winding road that ran between mesquite, all leaning to the north because of the prevailing winds, and then a few stretches of open space.

After going around a curve, they topped a slight rise and she waved one hand. "You can't see much for the rain, but there's my cabin. If you can make it out, you can see there's plenty of room for a guest."

"What I can see is not exactly a little log cabin. How many bedrooms do you have?" he asked, sounding amused.

"Six bedrooms—three are suites—and seven bathrooms. I don't have family now, but I do have friends and this is usually a relaxing getaway. There's a gym, too. I'll show you around."

"You're a long ways from a town. You take care of all this yourself?"

She smiled and shook her head. "Thank heavens, no. It's easy to hire help of all sorts from Gerald's ranch. Like I said, his house and buildings are close to my property."

"That's a good setup. But calling it a cabin doesn't exactly convey an accurate image of your getaway home," he remarked dryly.

She smiled. "True. But I love it here. My dream has always been to marry and have four or five kids to fill it."

He laughed and shook his head. "I don't have any idea, but I seriously doubt if I've ever taken out a woman whose lifelong wish was for marriage and four or five kids."

"Well, when you get your memory back, you might be surprised. I can say this, though—you probably have never taken out anyone who had no family."

"No family?"

She shook her head. "I don't have any family left. My mom and sister died from cancer. My dad moved away and remarried. My grandparents aren't alive." She shrugged. "So, essentially, I'm alone." When she saw his mood start to sag, she added, "But I'm okay with it. My work and friends keep me plenty busy."

"You said you're an occupational therapist with a home-care business in Dallas. It must be a booming business."

"We're busy, which is good. I have a much simpler place in Dallas, but I love this cabin and I built it for my future, for my dream home. Right now it's a vacation home, a getaway, so I don't have a landline or Wi-Fi. Just peace and quiet." She looked at the cabin and envisioned it without the torrents of rain marring its beauty. "Luckily I had this home when my mom and sister could still come out here to visit, before I lost my family. I'll bet you have siblings."

"I wish I could remember even one thing about my family."

"A family is wonderful. My sister was ten years older, so when I was growing up, she wasn't around. I love children and I love kids and I'm thinking about someday going back to night classes or taking online courses to get a teacher's certificate. I have a master's in occupational therapy. All I would need for secondary teaching would be the required education courses and student teaching. It's not a whole lot. Either that or I'll just volunteer for things that involve kids. Now I'm doing something that helps people, so I'm not ready to give up the home-care business yet. It's work I like."

He studied her with a thoughtful look and she wondered what he was thinking. He turned away. "That's commendable—helping people. I can't remember what the hell I do," he said.

"You'll remember eventually."

"Thanks again for coming to my rescue, Ava. I know you'd feel better if I could tell you who I am and what I do. Being friendly and grateful to be rescued aren't necessarily guarantees of a good guy," he remarked dryly. "With you being isolated out here—"

She cut him off. "I'm not really isolated here because of Gerald and his wife, the cowboys who work at Roan Ranch and their families, some of whom work for me. And Samantha cooks for me, although she's off right now because her daughter had a baby. Samantha is married to one of Gerald's cowboys. The wife of one of the cowhands, Margo, cleans, and Jonah and his crew do the yard work for me and for the Roans. I have people around all the time. Margo won't be here until next week because she was here yesterday. Oh, this is the first Monday in October in case you're interested."

"Neither the month or day means much to me right now. I don't know where I was going or where I had been. I don't know why I was where I was." He blew out a frustrated breath and raked a hand through his hair. When he turned to her again, he changed the subject. "You said your father remarried. Do you see him?"

"No, I don't. He divorced my mom when I was fourteen. He and his new wife live in California. I don't see him at all. They severed relations and he doesn't contact me."

Though it was sad that her father wasn't part of her life, she didn't feel sorry for herself. She had lots of good memories of growing up with both her parents. Which was more than this man sitting beside her could say right now.

She continued up the drive and turned off the main road that circled in front of the house. She took a branch road that veered around the house to a porte cochere along the west side.

"We're home," she said cheerfully as she put the vehicle in Park. Then she turned to see his reaction to the cabin up close, only to find him instead looking intently at her. Her eyes met his and suddenly it became another moment when she was conscious of him as a physically appealing male. She didn't know anything about him and she was about to take him in and let him stay at her house, under her roof, with her. And that thought made her heart race, but not with fear.

Breaking the spell that seemed to have fallen over her, a bright red pickup pulled in beside them and she smiled when she saw it was Gerald and Molly.

"Here are the Roans minus their kids. They have a sitter for them easily available—Gerald's grandmother lives on his ranch. Her house is close to Gerald's."

"It's weird to meet someone when you don't even know who you are," he remarked as he stepped out.

Even though they had both parked beneath a roof and were sheltered, the wind and torrential rain still blew through the porte cochere and Ava motioned for everyone to follow as she went ahead, opened the door and entered her house. The Roans were both bringing boxes and covered dishes as they hurried inside and set their packages on the floor so they could take off their wet coats.

As soon as they were inside the dark entryway with a terrazzo floor, she turned to face the Roans. "Let me help you get these wet coats off," Ava insisted. She turned to flip a switch.

"First, we don't have electric power because of the storm," Ava said, getting a flashlight from a shelf by the door. "I'll turn on the generators, but before I go, let me make the introductions," she said as she took off her rain slicker and hung it on a hook. When she turned, she noticed the stranger's gaze sweep over her and instantly she became aware of her tangled, long blond hair, her blue sweater and dark jeans. His gaze reached her toes and then went back up to meet her eyes, and she could feel the heat in her cheeks as they looked at each other.

To her relief, Molly was talking about dinner and Gerald had just finished hanging up their yellow slickers and hats, and he seemed distracted as he picked up boxes he was carrying when he came.

"We're calling him Bill Smith until his memory returns," she said to the Roans as she passed small flashlights to everyone.

"Bill, meet my neighbors. This is Gerald Roan," she said as Gerald balanced two big boxes he carried, stuck out his hand and they shook. Gerald was almost as tall as the stranger.

"Meet my wife, Molly," Gerald said easily, turning to his brunette wife, who only came to Gerald's shoulder in height. As always, she had a warm smile and Ava was once again thankful for them as neighbors. Molly held a stack of three covered bowls in her hands.

"Thanks for coming by," Bill said.

"I'm close and this is easy," Gerald answered, shaking out the rain. "Here's some clothes I don't want back," he said to Bill, indicating the top box he held. "I thought you might need something dry."

"Thank you," Bill replied, taking the box from him and placing it on the floor of the entryway. "That's good because all I have is what I'm wearing and this shirt is all ripped."

"Bill," Ava said, "I told you Molly was a nurse, so you might let her look at your injuries."

Smiling, Molly held up the bowls and a black bag dangled from her right arm. "I carry this for emergencies. I can look at your cuts. We have two kids, so I constantly practice my nursing skills."

"Thanks," he said, "to both of you." He nodded to Molly, then turned to Ava and flashed another one of those smiles that made her pulse jump. She glanced at Gerald and was relieved he hadn't been looking at her. She hoped her tingling responses to the stranger didn't show.

"Also, we brought dinner in case you two haven't eaten," Molly said, indicating the bowls. "We had a fish fry today and it was easy to bring some. I'll put all this in the refrigerator."

"Thank you so much," Ava said, smiling at Molly. "It smells wonderful. I'll admit, I haven't given a thought to eating or even asked if you had lunch today," she said, turning to the stranger, finding it difficult to think of him as Bill Smith. "I'll get the generators turned on and we can see what we're doing."

"I'll go with you," Gerald said. "This box goes to the kitchen," he said to Bill as he handed him the other box. "I know where your generators are and I can help," he said, and went off with Ava.

After getting the generators going, they walked back into the entryway. When they did, Ava and Gerald joined them.

"We put the food away," Ava said. "It's good to have lights again."

"Now that we have lights, before Molly looks at my cuts, I need to wash the mud off." The stranger turned to Ava. "I'd like a shower more than anything, if that's okay. It won't take me long."

"Go shower and when you're dressed, if you'll call me, I'll come tend to those cuts," Molly said easily.

"Gerald, you and Molly make yourself comfortable in the family room," Ava said. "I'll show Bill where he can shower." She turned to him. "Come with me."

"Gladly," he said. "I feel covered in mud, sticks and leaves." He looked at Gerald and paused. "Is there something you wanted to say to me?"

Gerald shook his head. "No. Sorry if I'm staring, but you look familiar."

"That's good news," Bill Smith said with relief in his voice. "If you recognize me or recall meeting me, that would give a clue to my identity. Whether it's good or bad, I'd welcome knowing because not knowing who I am and not remembering anything from my past is not a good feeling. Losing my wallet didn't help. It didn't occur to me to hang on to it even at a risk to my life."

"I might be wrong, but I think I've seen you before or

met you. I hope it comes to me," Gerald said. "I promise to tell you if it does."

"Thanks." Bill picked up the box of clothes and turned to follow Ava down a wide hall.

"I hope to hell he remembers and does know me or at least recognizes me, even if it was a 'Wanted' poster," he said and she smiled.

"You're wearing jeans, boots, a Western-style shirt. Gerald lives and breathes ranching. I'm guessing you're a Texas rancher and you've crossed paths before. Underneath that black hair that falls on your forehead, you have a pale strip of forehead while the rest of your face is tan. That pale strip indicates you've spent time outside and you were wearing a hat."

She stopped to take his free hand in hers and turn his hand over. As she ran her finger lightly over his palm, she noticed two things—his calluses and her reaction to touching him. Immediately she released his hand and started walking again.

"Whoever you are, you have calluses that indicate that you work with your hands. A lot of ranchers have calluses." She tried for nonchalance, but there was no denying she felt anything but. When she'd taken his hand she had been thinking only about his identity. The moment her fingers had wrapped around his warm hand, her physical awareness of him had intensified and she knew for both their sakes, she shouldn't have touched him.

"Want to look at my hand again and see what else comes to you?" he asked in a huskier tone of voice.

Startled, she looked up at him and realized he was teasing, actually flirting with her and she wondered whether it was because he was aware of those same sparks when they touched.

Smiling, she shook her head. "I think we better leave well enough alone when you know nothing about yourself."

"I know a few things about myself that I've realized since you showed up to rescue me," he drawled in a deeper voice that sent tingles up her spine and heightened her awareness of him.

"You're hurt, have amnesia, you're with total strangers…and you're flirting." Smiling, she shook her head. "You must be feeling better."

"I think you're causing the way I feel, and believe me, it's a dang big improvement over what's been happening."

She laughed. "You better cool it until you learn who you are."

"I don't think I can be held responsible for any innocent remarks I make right now when I don't even know who I am."

"They aren't so innocent and you know enough to realize what you're saying," she said, laughing at him and he grinned.

"Meeting you has been worth going through all that happened to me. At least, sort of, because I do want my memory to return."

"Cool it, cowboy. And I think I'm right—you're a rancher."

She turned into a room. "I'm down the hall but here's a guest suite you can use," she said as they entered a living area. Through an open door she could see the bedroom that had a blue-and-tan decor, like the sitting room. "You'll find packets of things you might need—comb, soap, toothbrush, that sort of thing—in the bathroom. There should be clean towels, too. There will be about two sizes of new pajamas on one of the chests. I'm glad Gerald brought you some men's clothes. On second thought, let me check to make sure the soap is there," she said, starting to turn away.

He stopped her with his words. "Go join your friends," he said. "I'm sure I'll have what I need. You sound as well-equipped as a drugstore. At least, I can remember what a drugstore is."

Before she could step away, he reached out to take her arm. The moment he touched her, she felt another tingle all the way to her toes. Her breath caught and she looked up to meet his gaze that was as sizzling as his light touch on her arm. Startled, she saw he felt something, too. He had a surprised look that changed to an intense focus on her, which made her pulse drum faster.

She should say something, move, do something, but she felt captured by a casual touch and a look. Only the touch hadn't been casual to her and it evidently hadn't been to him.

"Call me if you need me. It's Ava, in case you forgot," she said in a breathless voice that was almost a whisper.

"I can't remember my name, but I promise you, I remember yours, Ava," he said in a husky voice, still gazing at her with a curious look that kept her pulse racing. He released her arm and, with an effort, she turned to leave.

She hurried out, closing the door to his suite behind her. She stood a moment and gulped for air. She had never had such a reaction to a man. Never, not once. How could a casual, slight touch stir such desire? Especially by a muddy man who was a complete stranger?

After her breakup she hadn't been attracted to any man. She had turned down invitations, not wanting to date. She still didn't want to.

She was shocked by her reaction to this man. Especially now. Her heartbreak over Judd definitely had not healed and would never be forgotten. It still hurt to think about how he'd left her.

At this point in her life she didn't want to be attracted to any man. She couldn't handle another breakup.

So how could just a look from this stranger make her heart race?

He'd seemed as surprised as she was and she was certain it was every bit as unwanted a reaction to him as it was to her.

Telling herself to stop thinking about him, she hurried back to join her neighbors and thank Molly for bringing her nurse kit to tend to the stranger's cuts. Ava was relieved that she wouldn't have to do that task. The mere thought of taking care of his back or shoulder, or any other part of his anatomy where he had been injured, made her pulse race again. She banished the thought as she rejoined her friends.

"You're the greatest neighbors to go out in this storm to come by and meet him, in addition to bringing food, clothing and first-aid care. Thank you both."

"We're glad to do it," Molly said.

"I feel better meeting him," Gerald added. "I can't recall why he looks familiar, but I have a real strong feeling we've met before."

"That's good news, too," she said. "Right now he knows nothing about himself."

She looked out the window at the storm, which hadn't let up. "I hope your kids aren't afraid with both of you gone. That wind is fierce and the rain is still teeming." As if to emphasize her words, a streak of lightning lit the outside. Shortly, thunder boomed again and wind whistled around her house.

"The kids don't care. They're super good at entertaining themselves and, fortunately, both like to read, so they're either playing a game or curled up to read or comforting my grandmother over this storm," Gerald answered. "She's the one who will be scared out of her wits."

Thunder boomed and the sharp click of hail drowned out conversation for a moment. Gerald went to the window and then disappeared briefly. In a moment he returned. "Look at the size of this hail. This is slightly bigger than the other we had," he said, crossing the room to show them. "There will be roof and window damages with this storm."

Molly gasped, picking up a hailstone that looked the size of a golf ball.

"It's already let up," he said, taking the hailstones to the kitchen to toss them into the sink. "I think this storm will make the news," he said when he returned.

"Thank goodness the hail didn't last long," Ava said, looking at the window.

"Your dinner is in the fridge now," Molly reminded her. "And, of course, you know you both are always welcome at our house if you'd rather stay there."

"Thanks, Molly. I think we'll be fine."

She heard boot heels scrape the floor as Bill Smith walked into the room.

"I feel infinitely better after that shower," he said, entering the room, and Ava's pulse jumped. His hair was neatly combed. He wore jeans Gerald had furnished and his own boots, now with the mud scraped off and cleaned.

"Thanks again for the clothes, Gerald. I'm glad to get out of the others. Except for my shirt, which I threw into the trash, I brought my wet clothes with me in case I can throw them into a washer if you don't mind. I washed the mud off the clothes, so if you'll tell me where your washer is, I'll put these in."

He was bare-chested and he looked strong and fit with bulging muscles and tan skin. Thick black hair curled across the center of his chest. He still had the dark shadow of facial hair on his chin and jaw. She looked up to meet his gaze. Had he seen her looking so intently at him?

He held a hand towel pressed against his shoulder. "I'm sorry to bleed on your towel," he said to Ava and then turned to Molly. "If you want to look at my cuts, this is the time."

"Go into the kitchen near the sink," Ava said. "The light is good in there and you can pull a chair over or you can go back to his suite. It has a big bathroom."

"I know the way," Molly said, crossing the room. "C'mon. We'll put your clothes in to wash and then I'll see what I can do for you."

Ava watched the stranger leave the room. He had muscles, something else that might indicate ranch work. "I'm glad Molly's here to patch him up."

"If you're worried about staying here with him," Gerald said, "both of you can come stay at our house, like Molly said, or he can go home with us."

"I'll be okay."

"Once again, I honestly think I know him. It'll probably come to me in the middle of the night. With this storm and the area we're in, I won't be able to text or call you if I do remember, but if I know him, he's an okay guy. I don't know the other kind."

"A rancher seems likely. I saw his pickup when he jumped out of it. It was one of the big ones."

"I'll pick him up tomorrow and let him look at my horses. If he's a rancher, the horses might jog his memory."

"That would be nice if it works out, but if we're still having storms, don't come out."

He grinned. "I wish my horses would tell me that," he said and she smiled.

Soon Molly and the stranger returned. It was difficult to think of him as Bill Smith because that really wasn't his name. Now he wore a long-sleeved blue denim shirt that Gerald had brought. His arms were slightly longer than

Gerald's and his shoulders were broader, so the sleeves were short. He had the shirt tucked into his jeans and his shirt had the top three buttons undone. His injured shoulder was bandaged, with only a tiny part of the bandage showing. He was handsome and the sight of him, even with his blackened eye, forehead bump and bruises, still took her breath away.

"I feel better. Now if I just can remember who I am, life would be great." He turned to Molly. "Thanks for coming out in the storm to help and for tending to my wounds."

"Glad to do it," she said while Gerald put on his hat and coat and held out Molly's slicker for her while she slipped into it.

Bill turned to Gerald. "Thank you for bringing the clothes. I appreciate it. In this storm that's a big deal."

Gerald put his arm across Molly's shoulders. "I didn't want to wait for the rain to let up because from the predictions, we're supposed to have three big storms move through here. I think this is still storm number one." He turned to Ava. "We'll go, but if you want us for any reason, turn on your yard lights. We can see them and if it's late at night, turn them on and then step outside and fire three shots into the ground. The dogs will bark and all the ruckus will wake me. I'll hear them and come over."

"I think we'll be fine." She followed them out to their vehicle while her guest stayed behind in the house.

Molly turned to her. "I gave him instructions on things to do, take it easy, take care of himself. No alcohol. He shouldn't sleep right away. He has everything written so he can show you. Here's a short list for you," she said, giving Ava a torn piece of paper. "This isn't my area of expertise, but I think those are things he should do. He was interested and seems cooperative."

"Thank you so much for all you've done tonight. I wouldn't have known how to help him."

"You would have done okay," Molly said, smiling. "We better go."

Gerald paused once he opened the truck door. He looked back at Ava. "I meant what I said about firing some shots," he told her.

She smiled. "I don't think I'll need to do that. I think you're right about him being a rancher."

Gerald nodded. "I agree. I may remember who he is or at least where we met. We need to know and he needs to know."

She waited under the porte cochere until Gerald drove into the storm and his taillights disappeared in the darkness and the rain.

When she went back inside, once again, it was just the two of them. Her and the stranger. She was confident that Gerald knew him and would eventually remember how and where, and she wasn't afraid to have him as a guest. She was far more afraid of her own reactions to him, of the unwanted, fiery attraction she felt that drew her to him, a connection that was pulling her in.

Her worry was, alone with him, could she resist his charm and sex appeal?

Three

When she rejoined him in the large living area, he turned from the window and gave her a smile. And that's when Ava knew exactly how hard it would be to resist this man. Whoever he was.

"Ava, I can't thank you enough for coming back for me today. Not everybody would have done that." He walked toward her and his focus was intently on her eyes. "I'm very grateful."

Better he be grateful from a distance, she thought, sidestepping him and turning toward the kitchen. "No problem. How about that dinner now? Are you ready to eat?"

"That sounds great. Let me help."

Not only did she want her space, but she also remembered Molly's directions. "You should take it easy. I'll get everything on and you can sit and watch. Molly told me you shouldn't sleep right away and no alcohol. She gave me a list of foods good for you and, fortunately, what they had for dinner tonight is good for you—bass."

"Yeah, she told me when she worked on my shoulder that the bass is great." He flexed his shoulder a bit. "My shoulder doesn't bother me as much as my head and my memory loss. I hope she's right that the memory loss won't last." He followed Ava into the kitchen. "I can help you get things on the table, at least."

As she took dishes out of a cabinet, she said, "No way. You sit and watch." Only when she turned did she realize how close he had been standing behind her. She was caught again by those deep brown eyes as her gaze locked with his, and she was swamped by another moment of intense awareness. Another moment of desire. She should move, look away, do anything except what she was doing—standing immobile, barely able to breathe, her heart racing. But she felt trapped in his gaze. Her pulse drummed when she looked at his lips—he had a well-shaped mouth that took her breath away even more.

"I don't know why this happens." She thought she'd only said it to herself, until his eyes flared. "I—I think you should go sit across the room."

But he didn't move. He held his ground and held her gaze. "I don't know why this happens, either. But I'm your guest so I'll do what you want. But we may be missing something here by our restraint. After all," he said in a husky voice, "a kiss isn't a commitment. And this is a good night for a kiss."

His head lowered toward hers, but to keep him away, she placed a hand on his chest—a hard, muscled chest that did nothing to douse the desire that was burning inside her. "I think we should stick to restraint," she cautioned, making herself say the words. "We can't go wrong with restraint." She felt like she was lecturing herself instead of him. Her words were breathless. How could he ignite desire by just looking at her and standing close?

He paused a moment before he spoke. "Your call," he said, then turned and walked away. As he crossed to the table, she let out her breath. She watched him pull out a chair and sit to face her.

"I'll get dinner on," she said, aware her words were still spoken breathlessly. She was acutely conscious of his dark-eyed gaze following her as she got out dishes to set two places.

"I don't have any memory of my life. You, on the other hand, remember your life full well. So tell me about yourself. Is there a man in your life?"

"No, not at all."

"I find that difficult to imagine," he remarked dryly and she had to smile at him.

"I was engaged and we broke it off and I really haven't wanted to go out with anyone since that happened."

"May I ask why you broke the engagement?"

"Sure," she said, avoiding looking at him and trying to sound casual, busying herself with removing the containers from the fridge. "Actually, he broke the engagement to marry someone else. That was early last spring. I really haven't wanted to go out with anyone since then. That may change someday, but right now because I got hurt, I'm not ready for a relationship." She stopped to look at him and smiled. "Definitely not with anyone who doesn't know his identity. I'm sure you agree on that one."

"Oh, yeah—I don't want to have complicated my life in the meantime."

While the fish and vegetables reheated, she set a tossed green salad on the table, along with tall glasses of water for him and for herself.

His fingers closed around her wrist, stopping her and holding her near him. "This may not be the time to pursue it, but you can't deny there's something between us.

Something that comes out of the blue. I won't forget it, Ava, and I know there may come a time to explore it a little."

She didn't deny it, knew she couldn't, not when he could feel her pulse jump and race as she looked down at him. "I've never had it happen with a complete stranger," she whispered and he flashed that smile that made her heart pound and made her want to step closer to him. "I better move away right now," she said breathlessly without moving an inch. He stood, putting him even closer to her. Mere inches were between them and his gaze held hers and stole her breath.

"Damn, I wasn't going to do this," he said in a husky whisper. "We both just agreed we wouldn't, but I can't resist when you get me wound up with just a look. I know full well you don't even want to have that effect."

"No, I don't," she whispered. They stared at each other. She couldn't move or look away.

"You don't want to step away any more than I want to. Just say to hell with it," he whispered and closed the last tiny bit of distance between them. He paused just long enough for her to put her arms around his waist, then he took her into his arms and kissed her.

As if she was a puppet and someone else was pulling the strings, she turned her mouth up to his and closed her eyes.

When his lips brushed hers lightly, longing burst through her with a hungry need for more. While she tightened her arms around his waist, her lips parted. His tongue ran over her lips and common sense vanished.

As she pressed against him, her tongue slid over his and then his mouth came down hard and possessively. She had never been kissed this way in her life, nor had such an explosive reaction to a kiss. She wanted to kiss him the rest of the night. He leaned over her, his strong arms holding her. She felt his erection pressing hard against her as she clung to him.

She didn't know how long she held him and kissed him, until finally, reluctantly, she got her wits together and pushed slightly against him. He straightened to release her. They both gulped for breath as they stared at each other.

"We have to stop," she said. "Neither of us wants the problems kisses could lead to," she said quietly. "After what I've been through in my broken engagement, I don't want more stress or hurt in my life." Her words were a whisper and she didn't know whether she was telling him or herself.

With an effort she turned and walked away from him, leaving the room to put more distance between them. Her lips still tingled from his kiss. Every inch of her body wanted to be back in his arms, kissing him, being held tightly against his marvelous, strong male body. Desire was intense, but so was caution and memories of how badly she had been hurt not so long ago.

She crossed the hall to look into a mirror. "You are headed for more than a wagonload of trouble. Kiss him again and it'll be a trainload of trouble," she whispered to herself.

She didn't want to be attracted to him for too many reasons. He had no idea who he was. He didn't want to succumb to the attraction any more than she did—maybe a degree more because he was the first to give in to it.

But, oh, what a kiss. Her lips still tingled, her body was hot, she ached for his arms around her and his hard, muscled body against her.

"Sheesh, Ava," she whispered and made a face at herself. "Use your self-control. Do you want another broken heart? No, absolutely not. No, no, no," she told herself. So why couldn't she stop thinking that was the sexiest kiss she had ever experienced?

She threw up her hands. She should go down the hall to her suite, lock the door and not see him until tomorrow morning, when she would hopefully have forgotten his kiss. Who was she kidding? She'd never forget it, but she needed to resist kissing him again. The minute this storm was over, the water would recede quickly. As soon as she could get back to town, she would take him straight to the sheriff and let the officials take care of him and help him learn his identity. No one lived in a vacuum. And the stranger who had just kissed her senseless was no exception.

What she needed to worry about right now was keeping a distance between herself and him. She didn't want to think about his kisses that had made her heart pound with desire, excitement and a hunger for more. A lot more. She had to avoid him. She didn't want another heartbreak, didn't want to complicate her life. She looked at herself in the mirror. "Can you go back and eat dinner with him and keep away from him?" she asked her image. "I can. I have to," she replied. Taking a deep breath, she turned down the hall.

"I'm back," she said, getting the fish from the oven and getting their drinks and the rest of their dinner on the table.

Sitting across from him, she looked at him. "Kisses won't happen again," she stated firmly, telling herself as much as informing him. "I think you agree—that wasn't the smart thing to do. Neither of us wants another emotional complication in our lives at this time. Right?"

"I'm the one who lost it. I don't want to get into a relationship when I don't even know who I am." He nodded. "You're right."

"So, then, no more kisses. Let's just eat our dinner and move on," she said, passing him the platter with the fish.

"I apologize for losing control," he said as they shared the tossed salad, baked potatoes and carrots Molly had provided.

Ava looked into his midnight eyes and shook her head. "No, you don't need to apologize. It won't happen again, but believe me, you don't ever have to apologize for that kiss." She felt her cheeks flush and looked down because she was getting back on dangerous ground. She didn't want to think about the sexiest kiss of her life or that he sat only a few feet away.

Maybe it was because of the storm and all the events of the day that it just seemed that way at the time. The instant that thought came she knew better. She was tingly all over just thinking about their kiss. And it didn't have one thing to do with the storm or his rescue or the struggles they'd had getting out of the canyon.

"If you don't want to talk about it, we won't, but was your fiancé someone you had known a long time?"

"We'd been together more than a year," she replied, then paused to take a sip of her water. "We had a big church wedding planned, at least big to me—about two hundred guests. Two weeks before the wedding he told me he had met someone else and it was instant attraction and love."

"Two weeks? Maybe you're better off not married to a guy who would change like that."

She shrugged a shoulder. "Logically, I know that's true. I've told myself that, too, at least a hundred times, but it doesn't make the hurt go away or make any of it easier to accept. I had presents to return, letters to write, people to call. He walked and that was that."

"I see why you don't want any more complications in your life right now." They ate in silence for a bit and then he leaned back. "Well, tell me about how you entertain yourself out here without TV and internet."

Before she could answer, they heard the first ping of hail hitting the house. The hail came faster, the hailstones larger.

"Oh, damn, this must be the next storm coming through," he said. "Thank goodness we didn't have this before you came to my rescue. I'd—"

His words were cut off when a big hailstone smashed through a window on the south side of the room. As glass shattered on the floor, another hailstone broke another window, and she bolted. "I better get towels," she said, rushing from the room.

She could hear another window shatter as baseball-size hailstones struck the glass. She rushed back with towels and went to get a broom and dustpan to sweep up the broken glass.

When she returned, he took the broom from her. "Let me do this."

"I don't think you're supposed to exert yourself."

"I'm not. This is nothing," he said.

She started to argue, but one look at him and she turned away. "I have plywood that will fit the windows and we can fasten it to the window frames with duct tape to keep rain from coming in," she said. "It's on the other side of the porte cochere, in my workshop," she said as she pulled on a thick, tan jacket.

"I'll go with you," he replied, walking with her. She was intensely conscious of him close beside her.

"You may want a jacket because it's cooler out."

He shook his head. "I'm okay."

He was more than okay. He reached out to open the door for her and she smiled at him.

"Thanks," she said, glancing into his brown eyes and feeling as if they had made physical contact. And again, against every one of her warnings to herself, she was instantly conscious of him close by her side, aware it would be just the two of them at her house tonight and maybe several days and nights. The mere thought caused her insides to flutter.

As she passed so close to him, he caught a faint whiff of some enticing perfume. His pulse jumped and he longed to hold her in his arms again. He was very aware of her close by his side as they rushed to the garage without having to get out in the rain and then he followed her into an adjoining workshop.

"There are the sheets of plywood we can put over the windows so it doesn't rain in. I'll get the duct tape and the toolbox," she said and he barely heard her. His gaze went over her face, her smooth soft skin, her rosy mouth. Instantly, he thought about kissing her. Her kisses were hot, sexy, unforgettable. She bustled around him, getting a big roll of gray duct tape off a shelf, then picking up a toolbox. She put those things down and turned to the stack of thin plywood.

"If you can carry the toolbox and tape," she told him. "I'll take four of these boards just in case another window breaks."

"I'll take the plywood, you get the tools and tape," he said. He picked up the pieces of plywood, watching the sway of her hips as she walked past him. Watching her just made him want her more. He had to leave her alone, avoid hurting her. It was the least he could do, given that she might have saved his life. But it was impossible to stop thinking about holding her and kissing her. He almost groaned aloud.

When they went back to the kitchen, she set down and opened the toolbox. "One winter we had an ice storm and tree limbs snapped and fell. One broke through a window on this end of the cabin and another on the other side. Gerald has a man who works for him who's a good carpenter and they cut this plywood to fit my windows. It should keep out the rain until I can get new windows installed."

"Thank goodness you have it or we'd be floating by morning. Doesn't look like this storm is going to stop any time soon."

"I'm afraid you'll hurt your shoulder if you hold the plywood while I tape it to the window frame," she said as she helped him lean them against a kitchen chair. But he picked up one plywood board and carried it to a window where rain was blowing through the jagged opening.

"I'll be okay," he said as he rested the bottom of the plywood on the window frame. She cut strips of duct tape and stood there seemingly wondering how to get around him to apply the tape.

"Come here, duck under my arm and then you'll be close enough."

He raised his arms and held up the board and she stepped into the circle of his arms to apply the tape. She was as close to him as possible without being against him. As she moved, she brushed against him and he caught another whiff of her perfume. He was too aware that when she had the tape in place on two sides and he could let loose of the plywood, all he had to do to hold her was wrap his arms around her and draw her that last inch or two that separated them. Why was she so tempting to him? His head pounded and his shoulder still ached and he shouldn't feel all this hot attraction that she stirred constantly with no effort on her part. To the contrary, he suspected she didn't want to feel it at all.

She had a huge reason to want to resist any attraction

between them. She had been hurt badly. What a jerk she had been engaged to. She deserved better.

He was a total stranger to her and he'd lost his memory. In addition, he looked as if he'd fallen down a mountain, while she was heartbroken over her groom walking out at the final hour before the wedding. They had every reason to feel nothing, even more reason to avoid any kind of attraction. So why couldn't they resist each other?

At this moment, ignoring all common sense, he wanted her in his arms, close against him. He wanted to kiss her again. As he thought about their kisses, he could feel the sweat break out on his forehead.

She glanced at him over her shoulder and ducked under his arm.

"I'll finish taping this one because it isn't tight all the way around," he said, getting another pair of scissors to cut strips of tape. They worked silently and quickly, then moved to the next window and went through the same process again. And again he fought the same urges.

They had one more window after this one. As he stood trying to resist hugging her, he wondered if he would remember for the rest of his life opening his eyes to see a cowboy hat above big blue eyes and golden hair and a beautiful face leaning over him, and his first thought had been to wonder if she was an angel. But, as he'd told her later, angels didn't wear cowboy hats.

His memory was interrupted and he was back in the present as she bumped against him. He held the plywood with one hand while he steadied her with his other hand, placing his hand on her hip. He held her like that for a moment and looked down at her as she looked up at him, and he felt ensnared, unable to move, look away or release her.

His heart drummed and he knew what he should do.

Walk away. He also knew what he wanted to do. Tighten his arm, lean over her and kiss her again.

"I—I need to go," she whispered, breaking the spell she had on him. His hand nearly shook, a faint tremor filled with longing, but he released her.

She was breathing as hard as he was and the look in her eyes indicated she was fighting temptation as much as he was, which just made him want her more.

She shook her head, broke their eye contact as she stepped away.

When she returned, she taped the plywood quickly, working silently.

"There," she announced, then walked away and gathered up the duct tape and the toolbox. "We're finished and now it won't rain in. I'll just get the floor a bit more cleaned up. Thanks for your help."

All the time she had talked, she had looked at the plywood, at the floor, at the other windows on the east side of the room. She hadn't met his gaze at all and he realized she was making a deliberate effort to look away. Which was probably better, considering the sizzling attraction that seemed to flare between them with the least provocation.

He had no idea whether there was a woman in his life, but he was absolutely certain, without remembering anything, that there had never been a sexier kiss than Ava's.

"We'll put this toolbox away tomorrow," she said, setting it on the end of a long kitchen counter. "You sit and watch while I put the dishes in the dishwasher. It won't take long. Then let's go to the family room and turn on the logs."

"Sounds good to me. But let me help with dishes. I won't do anything that hurts badly or anything strenuous."

Working together, he was conscious of each time he touched her hands with his as he handed dishes to her.

He fought the temptation to reach for her and kiss her one more time, certain that there would be another time to follow. It was an effort to keep his hands to himself.

In a short time they went down the hall to a room with tan leather furniture and imitation logs that she turned on in a large stone fireplace with a high mantel. The room was cozy and comfortable with closed shutters, so they couldn't watch the storm, but they could hear the thunder, wind, rain and hail, and he knew the weather would keep him marooned at her place at least through tomorrow.

Above the mantel, he noticed a large framed photograph of horses running in a fenced pasture. "That's a beautiful picture."

"Thank you. That's one way I entertain myself when I'm here. I have a photography hobby."

"You're very good at it," he said, looking again at the picture. "I have no idea if I have any hobbies and I have no idea what interests I have. It's a weird feeling and a very uncomfortable one to not know anything about my life."

"I'm sure. Molly said to let the worries go and relax. Your memory will return."

"That's easier said than done, but I'll try."

"I'm worried about tonight. You have your own suite, but I don't want you to lapse into a coma and no one would know it."

"Oh, Ava, we can solve that one. You're most welcome to join me and keep an eye on me all night long," he drawled and she laughed, a faint sound, and gave him an irresistible smile. A smile that made him want to hold her and kiss her.

"You keep that suggestion to yourself," she replied, laughing again. "We'll not pursue it. What I had in mind is, since I'm the only person with you, I think we should stay awake a bit longer. I don't think you should go off alone yet and I don't think you should go to sleep yet."

He sighed and looked serious again. "Okay, doc. Let's continue to sit in front of the fire. That I can do if it makes you happy."

She smiled at him. "Good. I'm glad you're cooperative."

"For the pretty lady who rescued me, I can be very cooperative," he said to her in a husky voice that changed the moment completely.

"You're flirting again," she whispered as she shook her head. "We weren't going to do that when you don't know what ties you have in your life."

His smile vanished. "You're right. You're constant temptation, Ava," he said softly and lapsed into silence. Why was she such a temptation? From the first moment she had entered his life, and he was aware of her big blue eyes and her silky blond hair, he hadn't been able to keep from wanting to flirt, to touch her, kiss her. She didn't want him to because of the hurt in her past. He knew he shouldn't because he didn't even know his past. So why couldn't he see her as a stranger, a pretty face, a nice person—and nothing more?

He needed to get his attention elsewhere and keep it there. Think about other things and keep busy so he wouldn't be looking at her every second.

He knew that would be easier said than done.

Looking to keep him awake, Ava had an idea. "Want a short tour?"

"Sure," he said, standing when she did.

As they went downstairs to the basement, she talked about when the house was built. She showed him the gym, a big laundry room, the wine cellar, a huge closet with luggage, Christmas decorations and other holiday decorations. Finally, they went back upstairs and every step of the way, she was acutely aware of him. She showed him her library, and the dining room and her office with three computers, two with two screens. She had oak filing cabinets that blended with the oak paneling. Two large desks were at opposite ends of the room. While he looked at the rooms, she looked at him. He was handsome with thickly lashed midnight eyes and thick, black wavy hair. She remembered how he looked when he came back from his shower with his chest bare. And she knew how it felt to be pressed against that muscled chest.

No matter how much she knew she should, she couldn't stop thinking about him and noticing him.

"Looks like you bring your work here with you."

"Not often, but I don't want to have to work and not have what I need here. I did less work when my mother and sister could be here. We all brought friends when I first had this built."

"This is a great place to live, but out here all alone, don't you worry about being here by yourself? This is a big house."

"No. See the light switches by the door? Go flip the switch with the pale blue plate."

When he did, bright lights came on outside, making the yard almost as light as inside the house. Even with the rain, lights were on all over the yard and in trees, illuminating the surroundings.

"Well, I can see why Gerald told you to turn on the outside lights. He can easily see this. I'll turn them off before he gets into his truck and drives over here. But I get it. With these lights you can see what's happening, but you're still isolated."

"I have alarms that will ring at Gerald's. He's not really far away and some of his cowboys are up at all hours. Also, usually when I'm here, he brings over three dogs that I like and they stay with me. They stay in the house at night."

He smiled. "I guess you're not so isolated. Is he bringing the dogs tonight?"

"No, because you're here. You're a good replacement for the dogs," she said and he laughed. He had even white teeth and a dazzling smile.

"I hope that's the first time in my life a woman has told me that." He let out a small laugh and she smiled.

"Now, do you want the upstairs tour or would you prefer to just go back to sit by the fire?"

"Let's sit by the fire."

"Want a cup of hot chocolate?"

"Sure. I'll go to the kitchen with you," he said, walking close beside her to the big white-and-blue kitchen that had state-of-the-art appliances.

"Have a chair and I'll get our cocoa."

"I'll help," he said, following her to a cabinet and watching as she stood on tiptoe to get down white china cups and saucers.

"Let me," he said, reaching up to get the cups, standing close to her and making her think of being in his arms when he had kissed her.

"I know you're doing this because Molly told you to keep me awake. How long did she say to keep me from sleeping?" he asked, leaning against the counter and watching her as she got out the cocoa.

Ava was aware of his proximity and his gaze on her. He was close beside her, his voice a deep, enticing rumble.

"As late as I can," Ava answered, more aware of him standing close than their conversation. "She wasn't emphatic about it because she said this isn't her area of expertise, but she thinks that's what we should do."

"I'll cooperate with you, but I have to tell you, this has

been a day with both very good and very bad events. And damn exhausting events."

"I agree. I'm glad I could help, but the storm was terrible and I'm sorry for your injuries and the loss of your belongings. Your memory should return."

"Damn, I hope so. I don't like not knowing who I am or anything else about myself. On the good-news side— I'll heal. Molly said my injuries—the cuts, the blow to my head—shouldn't be too long-lasting or serious. I'll have a scar on my shoulder, though. She said as soon as I can, I should get a CT scan. That's routine, just to make sure my head is okay."

She picked up the cups and turned. At the same time, he turned to face her, and when she looked into his thickly lashed brown eyes, the moment changed. She could remember his kiss and her gaze lowered to his mouth. When she did, her lips parted while her heartbeat sped up. She looked up to meet his gaze again and could see his intent.

She couldn't get out the refusal that she knew she should say. She could barely get her breath. He took the cups from her hands and set them on the counter. His fingers closed on her wrist. The minute he did, she took a deep breath and forgot about the cocoa.She shook her head. "We shouldn't," she whispered, too aware of how close she stood to him. "We agreed we wouldn't."

"One more kiss won't change our lives and it's been a long day. Kissing you was the bright moment," he said in a husky voice. She shook her head, but she leaned slightly toward him and her lips parted again. It had been the best part of the day and she wanted to kiss again, too, even though she knew she shouldn't, that if they kept kissing, it would be tougher to deal with what was ahead. They had no future and she wasn't ready for any relationship. She wasn't ready at all. "I just can't," she whispered, but she stood rooted to the spot, unable to move away, unable to look away.

He leaned closer. "Ava, this has been a hell of a day except for you. If we can catch just a few minutes of bliss, I'm ready to go for it. You're the best thing in my life today. You looked like an angel when I first saw you—I still see you as an angel in my life. Maybe an angel with the hottest kisses. Come here, Ava," he coaxed in a deeper voice, drawing her to him, and she couldn't tell him no when she wanted desperately to kiss him. When his warm lips touched hers, her heart thudded.

His mouth covered hers, claiming her in a fiery kiss, while his arm circled her waist and she kissed him in return.

She finally raised her head. "We shouldn't—"

"Yeah, we should," he whispered, kissing her between words, "and we're not going to cause disasters because of one or two more kisses on a cold, rainy night." He wrapped his arms around her to hold her as he took possession of her mouth again.

She slipped her arms around him, and his hard, muscled body against her felt wonderful. Her heart pounded and she wanted to stop thinking, stop trying to do the smart thing, the right thing, and just kiss for the next hour.

Instead, she thought about how she would get hurt again. She had no idea what was waiting for him back in his real life.

Seconds, minutes, she didn't know how much time later, but she finally leaned away and he let her go.

Breathing hard, they both gazed at each other for a moment. She turned away from him so she wouldn't go right back into his embrace.

"We have to stop," she said. "I would bet my cabin and

land that there is a woman in your life." She took a deep breath and faced him again.

"We can still have cocoa and sit and talk," she said and her words were breathless while her heart still pounded. She wished she sounded light-hearted, just cheerful and friendly, instead of out of breath as badly as if she'd just run a marathon. She couldn't even stop looking at him. She didn't want him to know how she really felt, how attracted she was to him, though she suspected he knew full well.

He took her hand. "C'mon, skip the cocoa. Let's just sit by the fire and talk." He released her hand and she nodded. He left space between them as they went to the family room and sat in front of the gas logs.

She sat in a wooden rocking chair while he sat facing her near the other end of the hearth. Looking solemn, he sat with a lot of space between them.

From outside they heard the distant rumble of thunder and the pitter-patter of rain. It sounded as if the storm was letting up. But she didn't know if this was the third storm predicted, or if another was to come.

He cast his eyes toward the window. "Thank goodness I'm not sitting out on that slope in this weather in the dark with nothing. No shirt, no memory, no wallet or identity— even worse, no marvelous, sexy kisses," he said, and his voice had dropped deeper as he turned to gaze at her with a look that made her hot.

"Are you sure you don't want to come over here and sit by me? That'd keep me awake on this cold, rainy night," he said. This time his voice was lighter and she heard the hint of laughter.

"Thanks, but I'll stay seated right where I am," she answered. "It's safer that way. Especially since, like I said, we don't know if there's a woman sitting somewhere worried about you in this storm."

His smile vanished. "You're right. Well, we will try to do the smart thing so we'll sit by the fire with several feet of space between us." He settled back in his seat. "Go ahead and tell me about yourself. You've told me a little, but I'd like to learn more."

"I'm not that interesting. I've had an ordinary life in a lot of ways. I like helping people, so that's why I have the business that I do. I love kids and want kids in my life. Also, I like my independence, so I enjoy having my own business."

"You sound like a city person, but you have several horse pictures here. How did you get interested in horses?"

"My grandparents had this ranch, so I spent time with them when I was growing up. I've liked horses since I was young."

She talked and he listened, sometimes asking more questions. After a moment of silence, she focused on him. "When do ranchers put ear tags on calves?"

"When they're born. Why?"

"I just wanted to see how you would answer my question. The answer's not important. What's significant to me is you knew what I was talking about. You didn't have to stop and think about it to answer me. Try this one—what rodeo event do you like best?"

He looked startled and then smiled. "For the first time I remember something. Coming out of the chute during a rodeo. I was riding a horse. I'm glad it wasn't a memory of bull riding." He looked at her intently. "Maybe this is the beginning of the return of my memory."

"We'll hope so."

"Also, it's another small indication that I'm a rancher."

"I agree. If you remember one thing, you might recall something else. Remember, though, Molly said to just relax."

"I can think of some really good ways to relax if you want to help."

She smiled. "You're flirting again. We were going to avoid that."

"You bring it out in me. It's rather harmless so far and a whole lot more fun than trying to jog my memory."

"I think you've stayed awake long enough," she said, standing. "I'll turn off the gas logs, turn out the lights and we'll go to our rooms. If you want me in the night, just call."

One corner of his mouth curled slightly. "You can count on it, darlin'," he drawled. "I can tell you right now if that's all I have to do, you'll get a call."

She smiled. "Stop teasing. You know what I meant. If you have a problem—a real problem that has nothing to do with lust or kisses or crawling into bed together—then don't hesitate to call me. Otherwise, remember all the reasons we should keep our distance from each other."

"Aw, shucks. I thought maybe we would have a fun, memorable night. If it turns out that I'm single, I'm going to want to come back and do this night over."

She smiled again and he came to his feet. She was beginning to think he moved in the same level of society as her family and she wondered where his home was.

When they went to their suites, he walked to the door of his and turned as she started to walk to the door of her suite. His fingers closed lightly on her forearm. "Come here, I want to tell you something," he whispered in a husky, sexy drawl that stirred butterflies in her stomach.

"Whatever you have to tell me, I can hear you from here."

"C'mon, Ava," he coaxed in his drawl that kept the flutters going. "Soon, we'll go our separate ways and this night will just be an old memory," he said as he stepped closer. "It's been a bad time in some ways. Kisses help."

She could resist what he was saying to her, but she couldn't resist the look in his brown eyes. Or her memories. Taking her hand lightly, he drew her into his embrace and wrapped his arms around her. As he pulled her close, she didn't object. Her gaze was held by his and by the look of desire in his eyes. Earlier, she had tried to avoid another kiss, but now her heart raced, her lips tingled and she wanted to be in his arms. She wanted to kiss him and be kissed, to feel desired again after the devastating breakup that had made her feel so inadequate. His kisses made her forget the hurt and embarrassment, the heartache and pain, the colossal rejection.

Finally, she tilted her face up to his and his mouth pressed against hers. Her heartbeat raced while she held him tightly and kissed him in return. As his tongue stroked hers, she wrapped her arms around his narrow waist. He bent over her, kissing her into oblivion, into blazing desire, while she pressed her hips against him. Never had she known kisses as sexy as his. Or as dangerous.

They were playing with dynamite by kissing and everything could blow up in their faces. Did she want to get hurt even more than before? She knew the answer to that one. No, she did not.

Leaning away slightly, she looked up at him. "This is the biggest folly. Go home, find out who you are and what your commitments are. What your lifestyle is. Then we can think about kisses when you have answers about your life. Right now there are too many questions."

He was silent, as if fighting an inner battle. She fought her own battle, stating what they should do, but wanting to kiss him. From the start he had been a good guy. He had been kind, helpful, trusting and trustworthy. He had been considerate, grateful for what she had done and was doing for him. Her first feelings and judgments about him had been good.

His hand ran down her back, down over her bottom. His hand was light as it drifted over her, but she tingled with his touch. She wanted the barrier of clothing out of their way. She tried to cling to caution, again reminding herself silently that she didn't even know who he was. She shouldn't be kissing him until she knew whom she was kissing. And even then, she didn't want another broken heart.

She stepped away from him while they both were breathless. He looked as if he could devour her. She felt as if she wanted him to.

"I'll say good night now and I'll see you in the morning. And not before," she said, walking away and too aware he stood watching her. He looked as solemn as she felt. His teasing, flirting and ready smiles had vanished.

"You can come tuck me in and make sure that I'm doing the best for my injuries," he said in a deep voice.

Glad he was back to teasing, she turned to smile at him. "You're doing fine without my help," she said. "I hope you wake up tomorrow and remember your past and your current status. I'm glad I could help you today." She blew him a kiss. "Goodnight, stranger," she said, hoping to remind him of one big reason why the night had to end this way.

She stepped into her suite, closed the door and closed her eyes, momentarily remembering his kisses that had nearly melted all her resistance. He was far too good-looking and sexy. She knew as soon as Gerald got through to the sheriff, they might have answers about her new houseguest. A houseguest who had the sexiest kisses she had ever experienced.

How much longer could she guard her heart and continue to resist him?

Four

"Bill Smith," he said softly as he looked at himself in the mirror. But that name, or any other, didn't spark any memory.

He walked over to the bed, removed his boots and shed his shirt. Instead of lying back, he sat there, his hands on his thighs, thinking of the woman who'd just walked away. Ava had called him "stranger," to remind him of his status and why they shouldn't kiss. He didn't have any memories, but he couldn't imagine he had known any woman who was sexier than Ava. She set him on fire with her kisses. He wanted her—in his arms and in his bed for the rest of the night. But Ava had been hurt badly by the jerk who walked out on her, and he didn't want to hurt her further. Especially when she might have saved his life.

He could have been in bad shape out in the storm all night in a canyon, where trees were uprooting and falling and land was sliding down into the swelling creek that ran through that canyon. He wouldn't have had anything to eat and no potable water to drink. No way to defend himself against any sizable wild animals. There were probably coyotes, snakes and heaven knew what else out there.

Instead, here he was in this comfortable suite. Until this storm was over and the creeks and rivers went down. Thanks to Ava Carter.

Ava. Her big blue eyes captivated him and her silky blond hair made him ache to touch it. He knew he shouldn't, but he couldn't keep from wanting her naked in his arms.

But every bit of wisdom he could summon told him to avoid intimacy at all costs. He didn't want to hurt her in any way.

She was beautiful, capable, kind, intelligent and oh, so incredibly desirable and sexy. Just the thought of her made him break into a sweat and wipe his forehead. He could get hot, physically hot, hard and ready, just thinking about her.

He hoped that his memory would return soon. It couldn't be too soon to suit him.

Who was he and where did he come from? Who was in his life? The questions plagued him. Molly had told him to let it go. To relax and let nature take its course.

She said not to push it trying to remember. But he couldn't go on like this forever.

He looked at his hands. He had one small scar on the back of his left hand, and calluses on both. Because of that, they seemed convinced that he was a rancher. Or a cowboy. Plus, he remembered coming out of a chute on a horse at a rodeo. But how could he be certain?

Restless, he stood and paced around the room, then switched off the lights to go stand at the window. Constant lightning lit up the yard. She had lots of trees and landscaping in her fenced-in yard that probably hid rattlesnakes.

That thought surprised him and he didn't know where it came from. He had to be a Texan. Why would he think about rattlesnakes? His head still pounded and he reminded himself again that Molly had told him to try to avoid stress and worrying about his memory loss.

He sighed and wished Ava was here with him. A night together would surely keep him positive and relaxed. Oh, man, a night with Ava. What a thought. Not one conducive to sleep and peace of mind.

He walked back to the bed, propped up pillows and stretched out to watch the rain. He was physically tired, but his mind was whirring and he knew sleep wouldn't come for a while. He wanted to sink into thoughts about Ava and recall each breathtaking kiss that made him want one hundred more, made him want to get to know her. Really get to know her.

He closed his eyes, taking the memory further and envisioning her soft body pressed against him as he carried her to bed and made love to her for hours. Then, they'd sleep, and eventually wake up, and he would take her again.

He raked a hand down his face. Why was he torturing himself? He needed to leave her alone. He needed to get his memory back or use what wits he still had and get out of her life as soon as possible.

"Damn," he whispered in the silent darkness and wondered if she was doing as poorly at sleeping. He hoped with all his heart they weren't isolated, shut away in her cabin for days. If they were, could he exercise enough self-control?

If she changed her mind about sex, would it complicate his life terribly? There was no way he could say no to her. He tried to shift his thoughts elsewhere because that line of thinking wasn't going to help him drift off to sleep. He got up and walked over to the mirror, looking at himself again, hoping that his eyes or his hair or his mouth would remind him of who he was, where he'd come from. It was pure hell not to know what was going on in his life and why he had been out in the boonies in a big storm.

But when he looked in the mirror, he didn't have a clue about himself. He prayed he would wake up tomorrow and have some answers. Despite everything he'd forgotten about himself, he knew he would never forget kissing Ava.

"Leave her alone, buddy. Don't complicate her life or your own," he whispered, wondering if he was way too late for that bit of advice.

Ava woke to the tempting smell of coffee brewing and the sound of raindrops hitting her windows. Startled, she sat up and remembered her houseguest and the past day and night. It was still raining, so they would still be cut off from any communication with the outside world. Would this rain last all day? Two days?

She felt that each day that her houseguest couldn't try to contact someone or at least check with the sheriff of Persimmon, the stranger ran a risk of someone missing him badly.

When she recalled his kisses, her pulse jumped. Briefly, she was lost in memories of his strong arms holding her and his kisses demolishing the defenses she had kept around her heart. She had avoided getting involved with another man since her engagement crash. Until now. She'd taken foolish risks in kissing the stranger because he was exactly that—a stranger. He didn't know himself and she certainly didn't know anything about him. She stepped out of bed to shower and dress, and then she'd go and see if he was better this morning. Had any of his memories returned?

* * *

He was sipping the hot coffee he'd brewed and watching it rain when footsteps caught his attention and Ava walked through the door. When she did, his pulse raced.

Looking gorgeous, she was in jeans and a pink short-sleeved sweater that had two open buttons at the throat. Her straight, silky blond hair fell to her shoulders. She had on cowboy boots and she made his heart pound just looking at her.

"Good morning," he said, standing and smiling at her, fighting the urge to cross the room, wrap his arms around her and kiss her. He tried to remember the lectures he had given himself last night about kissing her and doing anything that might cause her more heartache. Intellectually, he knew what he should do. Physically, he yearned for her. "You look fantastic."

"Thank you. Another rainy day, I see. The coffee smells great," she said, entering the kitchen.

"You sit and I'll get your coffee. What do you want in it?"

"Just black, please," she said, sitting across from where he had been sitting.

He placed a cup of coffee in front of her and went around the table to sit facing her.

"You look a bit better than yesterday. Your black eye has improved slightly and that bump you had is gone. How's the memory?" she asked.

"A few random things that are insignificant. Not people, nothing that's really a help. Before you got up, Gerald stopped by. He said he might take me to Persimmon to the sheriff if we can get out of here. Judging from the pouring rain and what you've told me, I don't think we can get out."

"I know you can't and Gerald knows it, too. The rain has to stop and then the water has to run off and the creeks and streams go down. Just relax. We'll try to find something fun to do," she said, smiling at him and he smiled in return.

"May I make a suggestion?"

"I don't think so, unless it doesn't involve both of us and anything where we would touch each other."

"Well, you never want to hear my suggestions. They were good rainy-day ones," he said. "It would just put a bit of fun into our lives and I don't have to even know who I am to participate and have a great time. You don't have to do anything, but just be your irresistible self."

"I think we should avoid temptation and move on to other topics."

He sighed. "I know you're right and have spent more than half my waking hours since we last talked lecturing myself and promising myself I wouldn't do what I just did—tell you I want to kiss you. So much for common sense. I'll try to do better. We can talk about the rain or you can tell me more of your life history. I can't tell you anything. I'm a blank."

"Not really. You have ideas."

"Oh, yeah, do I ever," he said and smiled. "See what I mean? You bring that out in me." He tried to keep the conversation light, but that wasn't the way he felt. He wanted her in his arms and he wanted to kiss her. Right now, while he looked at her, his heartbeat was faster. They sat looking intently at each other and he realized she was fighting desire just the same as he was.

"What do you do to entertain yourself here?" he asked as he sipped coffee.

"Ride one of my horses sometimes, which is out now. I garden, which is also out. I have a gym and I exercise most days. I run on the treadmill each day. Sometimes I bake things to freeze and take back to Dallas with me. Or I get my camera and take pictures."

"If they're anything like the one over the mantel, they're good."

"Thank you. I have good subjects—my horses, Gerald's, too, a roadrunner who hangs out here in the summer, owls that are here year-round, a pair of cardinals. Once I caught a mountain lion going through." She stood and he came to his feet.

"I'll start getting breakfast," she said.

"I'll help. What can I do?"

"I'll scramble eggs and you pour orange juice," she said. She walked around the table and they both crossed to the kitchen counter and cabinets. He glanced down at her to catch her looking up at him, and when she did, he knew she wasn't thinking about breakfast.

He reached out to take her wrist, but her words stopped him.

"Breakfast, remember?"

"No, I don't remember," he replied in a deeper voice as he tugged lightly on her wrist to get her closer. "I can only think about one thing. Kissing you again." He drew her to him. "Even just a good-morning kiss."

She wound her arms around his waist. "You know we shouldn't. At the same time, you know I can't resist you," she whispered. She turned her face up to his and her big blue eyes were filled with obvious desire, making his heartrate quicken.

He leaned down to kiss her and with the merest contact, all his good intentions from last night were forgotten. He knew he shouldn't be kissing her now, but when he'd finally fallen asleep last night, he'd dreamed about her, and woke up wanting her. He knew she would be out of his life soon and he wanted as much of her as he could have when she was beside him. And kisses weren't binding.

Never breaking contact with her lips, he picked her

up. She put her hand on his good shoulder while he carried her to a chair and sat with her on his lap, holding her close against him with one arm, cradling her against his good shoulder. His other hand slipped beneath her pink sweater to push away her lacy bra and fondle her breast, her softness making him ache with wanting her naked in his arms. He caressed her lightly. Every touch, kiss and whisper made him want her more.

She moaned softly as she settled in his embrace. Her kiss was fantastic, blazing hot. Her hands fluttered over him, making him want all of her. His hard erection pressed against her hip as he held her tightly.

When his hand slipped down to unfasten her belt, she caught his wrist and sat up. She was breathing as hard as he was. He felt on fire with longing and need, for all of her, and wanted to carry her off to bed, her naked body against his. But he saw the determined look on her beautiful face.

"We need to have some space here," she whispered and he released her. She stood and walked away.

Pulling her pink sweater back in place, she turned to face him. "I think you know why I want to stop. I'll be back in a minute."

He stretched and took deep breaths as she left the room. He needed to think about something besides seducing her. Had he ever wanted a woman to the extent he desired Ava?

He looked out the window and tried to think about the storm. Was anyone out there somewhere, looking for him?

It was just lust, Ava told herself as she escaped down the hall. He was an incredibly sexy man—one who clearly wanted to make love to her. Her eager response to him was no doubt due to her being alone so much. And, she acknowledged, perhaps part of it was longing to stop some of the hurt over her broken engagement. It was a way to put an end to being so vulnerable.

She shut the door to her suite, and as she brushed her hair, she lectured herself to get it together and exercise self-control. When she heard a car, she looked outside. Recognizing Gerald's pickup, she went to greet him.

With his hat pushed back to reveal his thick blond curls, Gerald was already inside, talking to her guest, as she entered the kitchen. He looked strong and cheerful.

"We've got spotty showers predicted all day, so the water won't recede, but I thought I'd pick you two up and take you to my place. I'll show Bill some of my horses. You two can spend the day with us today."

When Ava started to protest, Gerald held up his hand. "We insist. Molly has already cooked a bunch of stuff, so get your raincoats, lock up and let's go. It's just drizzling right now so let's go while the rain is light. I can't go home without you."

She knew he meant it and they were sincere about the invitation. She was relieved because it was a constant, sheer temptation to be here alone with her guest. Going to the Roan house would work better and she wouldn't have to worry as much about what she was doing.

"Thanks, Gerald. I can drive to your place and then you won't have to come out again later."

"Naw, c'mon. I'll be out for one reason or another, anyway, so I'll bring you home. Do what you want here. I'll have a cup of coffee while I wait," he said, getting his coffee. The two men sat talking while she put away a few things. As soon as she finished, she went to get what she wanted to take with her and to put on her raincoat. She found an old slicker for Bill Smith. She still thought of him as a stranger, but she was beginning to feel that he was far from being a stranger to any of them.

"I'm ready," she said when she returned to the kitchen and held out the slicker and an old cowboy hat for her guest. He stood to put them on and the way he slid on the hat, catching his tangle of black hair that fell on his forehead, she had the feeling he had worn broad-brimmed cowboy hats before, and that strip of pale skin on his forehead indicated that, too. In minutes they were in Gerald's pickup on their way to Roan Ranch.

After a big breakfast with the family except the grandmother who had returned to her own house to catch up on her sleep, Bill Smith, Gerald and his seven-year-old son, Aiden, put on rain gear and left to go to look at the horses while Molly cleaned the kitchen and Ava read stories to their five-year-old, Megan.

The men and Aiden were back in time for a lunch of hamburgers, golden corn on the cob and homemade blackberry cobbler with vanilla ice cream.

"Well, Bill doesn't have many more memories, but I'm sure he's a rancher," Gerald informed them over lunch. "He knows horses and is familiar with ropes, tack, tools and barns."

"I have little glimmers of moments on horseback, moments in barns, but I don't recall anything significant or helpful beyond knowing that I'm familiar with those things." He addressed those remarks to Ava, then turned to Gerald. "I think you have some fine horses."

"You're right on that one," Gerald said. "I do. Fine, expensive horses," he added as he smiled.

After lunch the men left again and Molly, Ava and Megan had a quiet afternoon. Ava sat on the floor to play with Megan and her dolls while Molly got dinner ready. When Megan took a nap, Ava and Molly sat talking and later Ava watched Megan draw and color.

The men returned and while the kids went off to play,

the adults sat down with glasses of iced tea and some cheese and crackers.

"We drove back to the bridge over Blue Creek," Gerald said. "There's no getting across it today and probably not tomorrow, either. Water is over the bridge, and for about a quarter of a mile approaching it on either side, the road is underwater. Now it looks like a lake down there with roads running into the lake. Doesn't look promising for getting into town. Not until the rain stops and the water goes down."

That night, after a big dinner of baked chicken, mashed potatoes and gravy, home-grown okra and tomatoes, they sat in the family room and talked until about eight o'clock, when Ava said they should go. She felt they had imposed on her neighbors' hospitality long enough.

After goodbyes, Gerald drove them home.

As soon as they watched him drive away and they had stepped inside and locked up, her guest turned to Ava. "Once again, they're very good neighbors."

"They really are. The kids are cute and polite and fun. I love having them for my neighbors."

"I asked Gerald if he ever sold any of his horses and he said yes. I told him if it turns out I'm a rancher, I'm coming back to buy a horse. I may not have memories of living on a ranch, but I know he has some fine horses."

"He does. I think you are definitely a rancher. Everything points to that."

She studied the stranger who was becoming less and less a stranger to her, but she still couldn't think of him as Bill Smith. Somehow, the name didn't fit. She saw he was looking at her and wondered what he was thinking.

"They asked us to stay at their house tonight," she told him. "I didn't agree because Molly has worked all day to have us there, cooking breakfast, lunch and dinner for us, entertaining us. I felt we needed to give her a chance to catch her breath. That's why we're here."

And her first thought since she'd entered the house was they had another night to spend under the same roof.

The second was wondering if he would kiss her again.

Ava watched Gerald's pickup stop by the gate and her houseguest stepped out and talked to Gerald for a minute, then closed the truck's passenger door and headed toward the house. They had gotten through yesterday without a kiss, mainly because Gerald had come by to pick him up and take him back to Roan Ranch. Gerald thought if Bill Smith spent the day following Gerald around as he worked on the ranch, it might jog Bill's memory. Molly had said it wouldn't hurt to try if Bill was willing. He'd been very willing, so he'd left early and then stayed at the Roans' ranch last night because the rain had ended. Today they'd hoped to get across the creek and go to Persimmon to see the sheriff. Today was the first day Gerald could get through to the sheriff and he made an appointment for Bill and let the sheriff know briefly about Bill. Now she was eager to hear if there had been any announcements regarding a missing man.

With a sack in his hand, Bill Smith came up the porch steps two at a time. Her pulse jumped when she saw the unusual expression on his face. "What is it?"

"Come on, we can talk inside," he said, taking her wrist and leading her in.

The minute they stepped into her entryway, he turned to take her into his arms.

"There's only one thing I could think about all the way back here." As his mouth covered hers and he leaned over her, she pressed against him. His body was warm, all hard muscles and flat planes, and he felt perfect. While his strong arms held her, her heart raced. She clung to him tightly and kissed him in return, then stopped worrying about what she should or should not be doing.

At some point, he leaned away slightly and looked down.

"That kiss was the most important thing on my mind." Finally, he released her. "The next most important—I know who I am."

Five

"Sort of," he added.

She tilted her head to study him and frowned. "What do you mean by 'sort of'?"

"I have a name, but it means no more to me than Bill Smith. There's more news—we still can't get to the Interstate or much beyond Persimmon because part of the bridge was damaged by a tree floating down Blue Creek."

She waved away his latest words. "I don't care about the creek. For heaven's sake, tell me what your name is."

"Okay, I'll give you my name, but it'll mean as much to you as it does to me. I still don't have my memory, but at least the sheriff told me who I am."

She smiled. "So who are you?"

She looked into his dark brown eyes as he watched her. "I'm Wynn Sterling from Dallas, Texas. And it doesn't mean any more to me right now than Bill Smith, except it's my real identity and I do have a history and a family."

"Are you a Sterling of Sterling Energy?" she asked.

He nodded. "They said I am. That doesn't mean anything to me, either. I don't know Sterling Energy. But apparently I have a twin brother. His name is Wade and he was on television. That's how they found out who I am. The sheriff said Wynn Sterling disappeared driving back to Texas from a resort in Nashville. The storms we had here have been all across the Gulf coast and some worse than what we've had. They think Wynn Sterling might have been swept away in the storm. They said the twin brother, Wade Sterling, cut short his fishing trip to the Gulf coast because of the storm and returned home.

"The sheriff will contact the Dallas police. Gerald said we might not hear today because it's hard to get through on cell phones because of the poor reception out here in the boonies. Gerald and I agreed we weren't going to hang out at the police station all day to wait to hear. If I'm going to hang out, I'd rather be with you than the sheriff."

"That's flattering," she said, smiling at him. "Now you know who you are even if it doesn't mean anything yet. You have family, and a big one—a well-known Texas family. I have heard of the Sterlings. Wynn, you're a prominent Dallas citizen."

"So you say." He raked a hand through his thick black hair. "Damn, you remember and I don't. That's a hell of a thing."

"Patience. Your memory will return."

"Sorry. Don't stop telling me what you recall."

"I think you're single. I don't think you or your twin is married."

"That's good news."

"I've heard of your family, but I've never met any of you until now. Somehow I thought the brother named Wade was the rancher and the other one wasn't, but I really don't know that much about you."

"That's what Gerald said when we heard the news in town. He said he thought the brother he met was Wade. They met at a rodeo and they talked another time at the Fort Worth stockyards. Before Gerald left, he said he remembered that Wade Sterling and three of his cousins, Luke Grayson, Cal Brand and Jake Reed, contributed millions to build a new rodeo arena in the Fort Worth area. It was built to replace an old arena that burned down. I don't even remember having a twin. I have no memory of my sibling contributing to building a rodeo arena, but if I've ridden in a rodeo before and I'm from a well-fixed family, I don't know why I didn't contribute to building the new arena. More puzzles than answers, I guess." He smiled at her. "I'll tell you what I did do. The police helped and gave me the address and phone number of my parents."

"Did you call them?"

"I did and talked to my mother. It was a tough call. She was so happy I was okay that I don't think she worried about anything else and I couldn't tell her I don't remember her."

"You might have to tell her sometime."

"I hope to get my memory back before I see her. Anyway, I have my parents' address. That's where I'll go when I get to Dallas."

"Did you tell them you're coming home?"

"Yes, I did. I told them that because of torrential rains it might be a few days, that I would let them know when I start home."

"I need a car to get home, and I need a license. Not to mention, I don't have a clue where I live. I have my parents' address, but not my own."

"Don't worry, you'll be able to get directions from your

family and I'll take you home. We can go together. I'm not doing anything except riding out the storm and the worst of that is over, and the water will go down even more today. We can probably safely leave tomorrow if you don't mind waiting that long. We can try today, but there are still showers and the ground is soaked. I'd rather wait until tomorrow."

"I hate to impose on you to take me home."

"Not a problem. I'm eager for you to get home to your family and find out about yourself."

"Well, thanks. I'll go shower now. If you want to continue this conversation, I'd be more than happy to have you join me."

She laughed as she shook her head. "You don't stop trying, do you?"

He smiled in return. "Not with you, I don't," he said softly and she was conscious only of him and how near he stood. She forgot about his identity and the problems they each had.

His dark brown eyes conveyed blazing desire. It was so obvious it made her weak in the knees. She couldn't look away; she couldn't get her breath. His eyes narrowed just the tiniest fraction, and then he stepped the short distance between them to slide one arm around her waist.

Her heart pounded as she placed her hands lightly against his chest and slid them down around his waist to avoid hurting his shoulder. His dark eyes were filled with desire as his arms tightened around her. His mouth covered hers and their tongues met.

Holding her tightly, he kissed her with a deep insistence. As he did, he tugged her blue denim shirt out of her jeans. His hand went beneath her shirt to push away her bra and fondle her breast. Light touches by his warm, callused hand made her want more.

Clinging to him with her arms around him, she moaned softly as he caressed her. He picked her up to carry her to his bedroom, where he stood her on her feet while he kissed her.

Finally, he yanked the covers off the bed and began to unfasten her jeans. She put her hand over his and looked up at him with hooded eyes that didn't hide the desire consuming her.

"I've been hurt badly and where we're headed, I could get hurt again. I have to wait until you know more about yourself."

"Oh, damn," he said softly and turned away.

She left him, walking to her suite. She knew she was right and she was trying to guard her heart even if it was too little, too late. She couldn't fathom how important he had become to her.

She had to do a better job of guarding her heart or she would have another painful event to go through when they parted. Or was it already too late?

She groaned and paced the suite, trying to think about something aside from how badly she wanted to go find him and walk right back into his embrace. She wanted to go to bed with him and make love through the night. But that was the sure way to another ghastly letdown. She shook her head. She was already too involved, but she could get over the kisses. If they made love, she would go through heartbreak again because her emotions were invested in physical intimacy.

She had made one colossal mistake but couldn't make another.

If she would just stay out of his bed, out of his embrace and stop kissing him, she might be able to avoid more terrible heartache. That was just good sense, so why was it so hard to do?

She knew the answer to that one. He was incredibly appealing and sexy. She wanted to make love with him. And she knew he desired her. From their first hours, sparks flew every time they were together.

She groaned and changed clothes. Maybe she could slip down to her gym and work out, so she could get some of the longing for him out of her system. If he knew where she was, she hoped he had the good sense to stay away. If they avoided each other more, there wouldn't be that constant temptation to kiss. Right now, she needed to move around and get her mind off him. Wynn Sterling. From a wealthy old Dallas family. Beyond that, she didn't know much about him.

She rushed around the room, changing to shorts and a red T-shirt, then put her hair in a ponytail and peeped out of her suite. She hurried past empty rooms to the basement. She didn't know where he was, but she was glad they hadn't encountered each other.

She rushed into the gym and he was across the room from her running on a treadmill. For just an instant, she started to leave, but she needed a workout. Evidently he had the same idea and probably for the same reason.

She thought about Molly telling him to take it easy. Running on a treadmill was not "taking it easy." Well, she wasn't going to stop him. Right now what she needed more was to cool down her body. She still tingled from their kisses and his hands on her.

That thought did it for her and she rushed to get on a treadmill as far from him as she could get. In minutes she was running. Unfortunately there was no way to get him out of her thoughts.

Wynn Sterling. Tomorrow she would take him home and he would walk out of her life. She had no future with him even if he wanted one because she wasn't ready to risk her heart again. The pain from her breakup had been monumental, coming as it did two weeks before she was to become a bride. She wouldn't trust her heart to anyone again. Not at this point in her life. And if she could keep her wits about her for another twenty-four hours, she wouldn't go to bed with him because it would be much easier to say goodbye tomorrow.

After they parted she didn't expect to see him again. He had another life, a real one, and he was going back to it and out of her life forever, she was certain.

They'd been thrown together by a storm, but she needed to get a grip, resist his appeal and let him go because there could be only one outcome to seduction—heartbreak. *Her* heart. If only she could do the sensible thing—resist him. One more day and then he would be out of her life.

"Wynn Sterling," he said quietly as he ran. The name was meaningless to him. It didn't jog his memory, sound familiar or seem right. He was as blank as ever about his identity, except he had been told that was his name and he was a twin. Sheriff Ellison had recorded the TV clip with his twin and they had replayed it several times for him. They were identical twins. It was like looking in a mirror to look at Wade Sterling.

He had been lost in thought about the name and that it did not trigger even a tiny memory when the door opened and Ava stepped in.

He was surprised that she had also decided to work out because he thought she was going to avoid him.

But he sure appreciated the way she had dressed. She was in a clinging red T-shirt and tan shorts. Short shorts. She had long shapely legs that were to die for. The sight of her dazzled him. He wanted her and tonight would be their last night together unless more rain came.

When he returned to his real life, he knew he wouldn't see her. She didn't want an affair and he could understand why, at this point in her life. He wondered what his family was like and how he fit into the Sterling clan. Would getting back with them jog his memory? What kind of relationship did he have with his twin? He had no family memories, but he hoped they were close. Were they looking for him now? Were they worrying about him?

Right now he couldn't even speculate about the family that he might find at home. He couldn't keep from feeling he would do better when he was home with his family. It had to help his memory to be in familiar surroundings with people he had known all his life.

Out of the corner of his eye he saw Ava and the vision of her distracted him from his thoughts. She excited him and she had the hottest kisses he could imagine. She had him on fire now and he was going to run until he stopped thinking about kissing her. He had a feeling he was going to have a long run. Was that why she was here?

That thought wasn't conducive to forgetting their kisses, either.

He slowed and finally stopped, getting off the treadmill and moving to a stationary bike.

The bikes were behind her so he could watch her run while he pedaled and that was a delightful sight. She was a good-looking woman with a sexy ass, spectacular long, shapely legs that he could enjoy looking at for the rest of the day. He wondered if he'd get the chance to touch those gorgeous legs later and feel her smooth, soft skin. He shook his head as he pedaled faster. What was he thinking? He should leave her alone. Twenty-four hours and they would say goodbye.

He swore and tried to think of something else, but he

didn't have much in the way of memories. Instead, he was mesmerized by her blond ponytail swaying as she ran.

He groaned. He needed to get back on the treadmill because that view didn't stir sexual images like the one from the bicycle did.

Tomorrow she would drive him home to Dallas. That meant nothing to him. He couldn't envision his childhood home or where he lived now or any of his family. Instead, he had come to feel comfortable here with Ava.

As he ran, he remembered sitting on a porch and looking out over a fenced lawn. Beyond the fence was a drive and across the wide drive was a fenced pasture with horses. Did he own a ranch, too? Wynn realized he remembered something from his past and that pleased him and filled him with hope that his memory was beginning to return.

Before he could tell Ava, she left. Probably to go shower. That was not a thought to dwell on, either. It would mean more hours of running or riding a bike. Damn, he wanted her, but he didn't want to cause her more pain.

Finally he left to go shower and clean up. Tomorrow he would tell her goodbye. The more he thought about that, the less he wanted to do it.

They both lived in Dallas. Could they continue to see each other? But he had no idea what he was going home to and what commitments he might have. He couldn't keep from feeling that tonight would be his last time with her. Dejected, he left the suite to go find her and see if he could help with dinner.

When he walked into the kitchen, he drew a deep breath. She had changed into a clinging, short-sleeved red sweater that was tucked into the waist of her tight jeans. Her hair, golden and silky-looking, fell freely on either side of her face, and she took his breath away just to look at her. He wanted to walk up, wrap his arms around her and kiss her.

He wanted to carry her to bed. His heart pounded. She was watching the door and probably heard his approach.

He crossed the room to her and got a subtle hint of perfume, but he was lost in her big blue eyes. Her soft lips parted slightly as they stared at each other. "You look gorgeous," he said in a rasp. It took all his self-control to avoid touching her. He yearned to pick her up, carry her to his bedroom and peel off those sexy clothes so he could touch, kiss and make love to her all night.

For a moment they looked at each other. She took a step back as she continued to gaze up at him.

They gazed at each other as if caught in a spell that neither one wanted to break.

"You clean up rather well yourself," Ava finally told him, her heart pounding. His black hair was combed and still looked damp, a few unruly locks on his forehead. He wore clothes from Gerald—a blue denim shirt and jeans—and he looked incredibly handsome and sexy. Though she could look at him forever, she needed to move away, to stop staring at him and to stop thinking about tonight—the last night they would be together.

He followed her to the window. A steady light rain fell again. Any precipitation was enough to make a difference in ground already soaked and standing in water. "You may have to postpone leaving here," she whispered and turned to look up at him. He had walked up right behind her, looking over her shoulder. The minute she looked into his eyes, her breath caught. Desire filled his eyes, a hunger for kisses that she felt, too. She couldn't get her breath, couldn't move away or say anything. All she knew was that she wanted to be in his arms and she wanted him to kiss her. He reached out and placed his hand on her waist, then leaned toward her while his gaze lowered to her mouth, and she couldn't get her breath. She couldn't protest or step

away or look away. She could only look at his lips and remember his last kiss, which had dazzled her.

"We shouldn't," she whispered.

"I think we should," he answered. "Admit it, Ava, you
want to kiss me as much as I do you."

She couldn't deny what he said. His dark gaze devoured
her and she trembled, aching to lean a little closer, to feel
his arms go around her.

"It's our last night together," she whispered.

"To my way of thinking, it's a last chance for ecstasy,"
he said in a raspy whisper. His hand slipped around her
waist and he drew her to him.

She was going to regret telling him no.

She would regret saying yes.

Which regret did she want to have to live with?

She had to make a choice and take the consequences
one way or another.

"What will I have after tonight? I'm not part of your
family's world and you still don't know who you really are
or your obligations. You know I'll have regrets whichever
decision I make," she whispered to him. "If I say yes, I
may fall in love and get hurt. If I tell you no, I might regret
what I could have had." As she whispered her dilemma,
he dropped light kisses on her throat and ear, while he
also caressed her breast, slipping his hand beneath her
red sweater.

"Then say yes and live with those regrets," he whispered. "And, frankly, I think you've already made your
choice. I want you, Ava. I want you with all my being." He
showered more light kisses on her and tilted her chin up.
She opened her eyes to look into his and her breathing was
raspy. There was no mistaking the desire in his expression.

"Yes, I have made a choice," she whispered. "Yes," she
repeated as she wrapped her arms around his neck. "Want-

ing you outweighs the regrets I know I'll have. This is what I want." She ran her fingers through the hair on the back of his head and pulled him closer to kiss him.

His mouth covered hers and she was lost, spinning away on sensations that made her want all of him, made her want his hands and mouth all over her, made her want to kiss him from head to toe. "I don't know anything about fate and that sort of thing, but being here with you feels like it was meant to be. But, damn, I don't want to do one tiny thing that hurts you. You're a special part of my life, Ava Carter."

"One night isn't going to hurt me. I expect exactly the opposite of hurt tonight."

"Ah, baby, I want to kiss you and touch you for hours," he whispered.

As they kissed, he slipped his hand beneath her red sweater to push away her bra and caress her breast, each sensual touch intensifying her longing for all of him.

He swung her up into his arms and kissed her, walking out of the kitchen and down the hall to her bedroom. Beside her big bed, he stood her on her feet while he kissed her.

She pushed against him slightly, turning to open a drawer. She waved her hand at the packets that held condoms.

"I bought those for my honeymoon when I thought I was getting married. I didn't want to get pregnant on my honeymoon. So here they are."

He smiled and drew her to him to kiss her again.

Her heart thudded when she looked into his dark eyes, which were filled with purpose. When he picked her up in his arms, she cried out, "Your shoulder!"

"I'm fine," he said. He sat in a big comfy chair, holding her, and he kissed her, his tongue going over hers.

Her insides clenched and her heartbeat sped up while she held him tightly.

"I feel as if I've waited forever for this," he whispered.

"Good," she replied. "So good." And then she couldn't talk because they were kissing—wild, passionate kisses that made her want all of him. Kisses that gave her a feeling of being desired, loved. She wanted to experience his hands and mouth on her and hers all over him. She knew she probably shouldn't let down her guard with him, but for this last night, before she told him goodbye, she was going to make love and make more memories of him. He needed her to get him home, to take care of him tonight. She needed him to help her through a rough time and he was doing so beyond her wildest dreams. She shifted slightly to drag light kisses across his cheek and jaw, over his prickly beard to his ear.

"You're helping me get over some of the devastating hurt of my fiancé walking out on me," she whispered. "I hope I'm helping you get back into your regular life."

"You're giving me the sexiest kisses and most gorgeous body ever. I want to do everything I can to excite you, to take you to paradise. Come here," he said, drawing her closer and tilting her chin up to look into her eyes, and then his gaze dropped to her mouth and she couldn't get her breath.

"You are the sexiest man I've ever known," she whispered, meaning it, but unaware she had spoken loudly enough for him to hear.

He placed her palm on his chest and she could feel his pounding heart. "That's what you do to me," he said. His arms tightened and he leaned closer to kiss her, a slow, sensual, hot kiss, his tongue stroking hers, moving in and out, mimicking the sex act.

She held him tightly, her fingers going into his thick hair

at the back of his head while she kissed him and pressed against him. She wanted him with all her being and she had already made her decision. Wise or foolish, she didn't care. She wanted him to make love to her all night long. Why did she feel this closeness with him that she couldn't explain? She barely knew him, yet she felt as if she had known him always.

He was erasing the hurt in her life. She might get hurt by him, but she'd walked into this one, knowing what she was doing and what to expect and not expect from him.

She couldn't be in love with him when she had only known him a few days. This was lust and a hunger for happiness, to forget her broken engagement and shattered promises and hurt. He was strong, upbeat and sexy, and she wanted a night in his arms.

Six

Closing her eyes as they kissed, she clung to him. He shifted and his hand slipped beneath her sweater to caress her breast, sending tingles that rocked her and made her want more. So much more. And he obliged. He leaned back, his gaze on her, as he watched her while he took the hem of her sweater and drew it over her head.

Longing made her shake, but she, too, wanted the barriers of clothing between them gone. As he caressed her, she unbuttoned his shirt and pushed it off, taking care to lift it off his bandaged shoulder.

"Wynn," she whispered, touching his back. "Your kisses make me forget your shoulder. You may hurt it a lot worse—"

"Forget my shoulder. I'll tell you if we need to change something or stop. Don't worry about it." He slipped his arm around her waist to kiss her—another long, hot kiss that erased all her worries.

He had tossed away her bra and cupped first one breast

in his hand, then the other. His tongue drew wet circles on each sensitive nipple and she gasped with pleasure, while she ran her hands over his hard abs and slid them down to unbuckle his belt and reach for his jeans.

As his hungry gaze went slowly over her bare breasts, he moved her off his lap. He stepped away and when she looked into his dark eyes, her pulse jumped and raced. Desire was blatant in his expression. Standing, he yanked off first one boot and then the other and tossed them aside. He threw his socks on the boots and she moved to unfasten his jeans. She had stepped out of her shoes and there was no mistaking what he wanted. Her heart raced and she tingled, wanting him to take all night, to touch and kiss her into oblivion. She wanted him to make love and kiss her from head to toe, and she suspected that was one wish that would come true tonight.

Her gaze ran over his broad shoulders and desire overwhelmed her. Emboldened, she stood and peeled off lacy panties while he watched her.

The hooded look he gave her, the heat blazing in his eyes, nearly made her gasp. This was desire, the loving and fulfillment she had dreamed of, making her feel cherished, setting her on fire with longing.

When all their clothes were gone, he led her in front of a Cheval mirror and turned her to look into the mirror.

"You're gorgeous," he whispered. He ran his hand across her breasts and she shifted, turning to look at him over her shoulder. His thick erection was hard, ready for her now, but she wanted to take time. She rubbed her backside against him, closing her eyes and giving herself to sensations that aroused her more.

"Look at us in the mirror," he whispered, his tongue following the curve of her ear while his hands toyed with her nipples and she moaned softly. She was pale against his darker skin and black hair. He was all muscle, fit, ready to make love, his hands running lightly over her and slipping a finger between her legs to find what excited her most.

"You're incredible," he whispered, showering kisses on her nape as he held her close against him.

While his hands caressed her, his hard rod was between her legs, arousing her more, making her want all of him. She reached back to run her hands on his muscled thighs. His strokes rocked her as she moved her hips against him. She gasped with excitement.

"I want to touch you," she said, turning to face him in order to kiss him. She moved away and he let her go, stepping around her to yank back the covers on the bed.

When he turned, his hungry gaze swept over her entire body, then back up to meet her gaze. "You're beautiful. Stunning."

He picked her up again to place her on the bed. The only light was the small table lamp, turned low. It was a soft, mellow glow that highlighted his muscles and fit male body.

She held her arms out to him. "Come here," she urged in a throaty voice while her heart pounded. He was sexy and incredibly good-looking naked. She wanted to make love all night. She had made her choice and now she wanted to live it, enjoy every second of this last night with him.

He said she'd saved his life. Well, he'd saved her heart and was helping it mend. She would get over her broken engagement now. She would be able to let it go. And that was a gift from him to her. A gift along with the sexiest night possible.

He kneeled beside her on the bed and began to stream kisses on her thighs while one hand played lightly over her, caressing her legs, and the other hand fondled her breasts as he kissed her.

Moaning softly again, she spread her legs for him and he moved between them. He placed her legs over his shoulders, giving him access to her most intimate spot while he showered her with hot, wet kisses along the inside of her thighs, moving higher, kissing her intimately, making her cry out with her arousal.

She closed her eyes while her fingers tangled in his thick hair, her other hand knotting the sheet as desire built.

She grasped his arms and tugged. "I want you now."

"We're just getting started," he whispered. "I want to please you every way possible so you're way more ready than now. I want to kiss and touch every inch of you." And then his hot breath was on her and his tongue was kissing her intimately again, driving her wild with wanting him.

With a cry she wiggled to shift away and he let her go instantly. She sat up and pushed him down on the bed. "I want to kiss you the way you've kissed me," she whispered to him, slipping her leg over him to sit astride him and hold his thick rod, running her fingers across his chest and belly and then leaning down to slide her tongue over him.

He had the fingers of one hand in her hair. His other hand caressed her breast, circling her taut nipple lightly. "You're so soft," he whispered. "Beautiful and soft."

She glanced at him to see his gaze going over her and then looking into her eyes, and she wanted him more than she thought it was possible to desire someone.

She leaned down again to run her tongue over the satiny tip of his erection and then to take him into her mouth. He let her do what she wanted for a few seconds and then he pulled her up, putting her on his lap to sit facing him. She had her legs spread on either side of him and he could fondle her, touch her, shower kisses on her throat while his hands caressed and rubbed her.

"Love me," she whispered. "I'm so ready."

"Soon."

He sat up and put a hand in her hair to tug lightly and then he leaned forward to kiss her, another possessive kiss that made her tremble with wanting him. His arm tightened around her waist, holding her on his lap while he continued to tease her with light intimate strokes between her legs.

She closed her eyes against the overwhelming sensations. "I'm ready and you are, too," she told him as erotic longings streaked from his fingers between her legs. "Make love to me now."

"Just wait a little longer. You like this. You want my hands on you, don't you?"

"Yes, oh, yes," she said, gasping as he continued.

"It excites me to excite you," he said gruffly.

He looked down at her and she met his eyes. The hungry expression she saw there took her breath away. She had never felt so intensely desired.

This was sex beyond her wildest dreams because he was totally focused on giving her pleasure—and did he succeed. He gave himself to sizzling passion that heightened her need for release. She thrust against his warm fingers when he rubbed her soft folds, causing tension that rocked her. Her need for more of him grew stronger, undeniable.

She wanted to give back to him as much loving as she had received. She wanted to make him shake with longing as she did.

He wrapped his arms around her, drawing her to him, leaning over her as she clung to him. He kissed her, a thorough, passionate kiss that made her feel she couldn't possibly be more desired. If she didn't know better, she would have thought it was a scalding kiss of deep, mutual love.

She did know better, though, and realized there was no such thing between them.

And then she stopped thinking and gave herself to kissing him back as passionately as he kissed her. While he continued to kiss her, he picked her up and laid her down on the bed. Then he reached for one of the packets she'd put on the nightstand and opened it. When he returned to her, he kneeled between her legs to put on the condom.

Her gaze ran over him and her heart raced. She wanted him, this virile, handsome and sexy man. Tomorrow he would go out of her life forever, but she didn't want to think about that now.

He lowered himself, holding his weight off of her as he kissed her. Careful of his injured shoulder, she wrapped her arms around him, running her hands over his muscled bare back down over his narrow waist, then down farther over his trim, hard butt.

He paused, looking into her eyes, and then he entered her slowly and she gasped, closing her eyes and holding him tightly.

He pulled away and she moaned, tugging at his good shoulder. "Now…" she whispered. He thrust into her slowly again and she arched her hips to give him access. Sliding one arm under her to hold her, he began to move, slowly at first as she arched beneath him.

His thrusts started to come faster and she kept up with him, moving to his rhythm.

"Put your legs around me," he whispered and she did as he asked.

She was caught in a rising spiral of sensations and need, tension building as he moved deeper, pumped faster.

Clinging to him, she felt her world narrow to knowledge of only him, his strong body driving her wild, tension still building while she moved with him.

With a burst of ecstasy, she climaxed, crying out in her shattering release as waves of intense pleasure rocked her. He shuddered with his own climax as he continued to thrust, hard and fast.

Then, he slowed and stopped, letting his weight down slightly, and he put his mouth by her ear.

"You're marvelous," he whispered, his breath warm on her ear.

She felt swept away in ecstasy. They were united. He held her with his arms under her. Tightening her arms around him, she hugged him, loving every inch of their naked, warm bodies pressed together. His arm slipped beneath her to hold her while he rolled on his side and took her with him.

She stroked his muscled back, his skin damp with sweat. She lay with her eyes closed and let her breathing and pounding heart return to normal. He showered light kisses on her face and then just held her.

With his strong arms around her and his naked body against hers, she was wrapped in euphoria, filled with happiness.

"I want you here in my arms the rest of the night," he said quietly in his deep voice, sounding totally relaxed.

"I won't argue with that one," she whispered, running her hand over his smooth, muscled back. She didn't want to think about anything except making love with him. It was easier to keep her thoughts only on how sexy he was.

He looked at her and smiled. "I've been thinking," he said. "When I go home, I want you to stay with me at least several nights. If I don't have any commitments, then I'll be free to take you out at night and I would like that very much."

She was surprised because she had decided they would part tomorrow and he would go out of her life forever. She had told herself so many times that he was only in her life temporarily that she'd come to believe it completely.

"Thank you for saying that, but I suspect you're carried away by our lovemaking."

"I meant what I said."

After a few minutes, she sat up and scrambled around to pull the sheet up beneath her arms. "Here's what I'll do. We can drive to Houston and take a plane into Dallas and have a lot shorter traveling time."

"Look, I don't have ten cents—"

"I do and I'll get the plane tickets. You forget that. I have a car at the airport, so I can drive you to your home. I'll call right now and get our reservations."

"That part sounds like a plan," he said. "As long as you stay and have dinner with me. We're going to see each other again," he said in a deep voice.

He ran his index finger along the top of the sheet, his hand moving lightly and slowly over the curves of her breasts, causing tingles up her spine and igniting desire again. She moved his hand away and turned to reach for her cell phone. All the time she made reservations for their flight, he ran his fingers over her lightly. Finally, she finished. "We have a flight, no thanks to you who almost distracted me to the point of giving up my call."

"That call was about tomorrow," he said in the same husky tone he got when he was aroused. "Tomorrow is far away and now I have you in my bed and I want you back in my arms again."

"Gladly. I want you to be happy." They smiled at each other again as she scooted close once more and he wrapped her in his arms.

"You're one big surprise after another in my life," he said.

"I suppose I could say the same about you," she remarked dryly.

He hugged her. "That makes life interesting."

"Mine has certainly gotten interesting since the moment I saw the red taillights ahead through the rain. I tried to catch up with you. I honked, but with the thunder, you probably didn't hear me or paid no attention. You didn't stop or slow down. I know the road and I knew in storms like we had, water would be pouring over the highway and it would be impassable. I was going to turn around and go back, but that's when I saw your taillights. I thought if I could catch you and get your attention before you reached that curve, you would be able to turn around and follow me back."

"I'm glad you didn't catch me. I wouldn't be here with you like this."

"Maybe. You might have been and then you wouldn't have amnesia."

"True." He looked like he was giving that some thought. Then he spoke again. "I think we've talked long enough. Let's go shower."

"I don't know if I have the energy to stand."

"Well, there's a remedy for that," he said, stepping out of bed and turning to pick her up.

"Stop. Put me down before you tear your stitches loose and start bleeding. Don't you hurt?"

"Not holding you, I don't. I'm enjoying your warm, deliciously naked body too much to notice the aches. With you in my arms I don't care if I hurt and I'll bet Molly has me sewn up tight and those stitches will hold. You're a featherweight and it doesn't add to my aches to carry you."

She laughed as she wrapped her arms around his neck. "Okay, if that's what you want and it won't hurt you. I admit I like this better."

"I definitely like it better, too," he said in a deep, husky voice.

As they showered, his hands were all over her, just as

hers were all over him. They finally rubbed each other dry with fluffy blue towels and then he drew her into his embrace to kiss her again.

Each kiss seemed to have more impact than the kiss before had. She instantly wanted him again and she knew he wanted her.

He picked her up to carry her back to the bedroom.

"I can walk, you know."

"I can't stand you being that far away from me." He took her to the bedroom, placed her on the bed and turned to get a condom. As he did, her gaze ran down the length of him and her pulse drummed faster. Naked, he set her body afire. She was ready to make love again and again.

When the first rays of sunrise spilled into the room, she stirred. She turned to look at the man sleeping beside her. How many times had they made love last night? The bigger question was how much of her heart had she given him?

Until they made love, she could have walked away after telling him goodbye and her heart would still have been intact and unbroken.

Now she wondered how deep her feelings ran for him. One night shouldn't be everlasting love. But temporarily, he was part of her life and he was incredibly sexy.

She knew the risks when she'd agreed to go to bed with him. What was done was done and there was no way she could regret the lovemaking they'd shared. He was going to be impossible to forget. She hoped he had a nice family and she hoped his memory returned swiftly. And she hoped with all her heart she hadn't fallen in love with him.

She slipped out of bed and went to shower. When she returned, the bed was empty and she suspected he was in another shower. She left for her own suite to get dressed, but she couldn't keep him from invading her every thought.

He was going home to a big family and to discovering all about himself. Did he look forward to it…or did he dread it?

After she dressed, she entered the family room, immediately spotting him standing by the window. Wearing jeans and Gerald's blue-and-red plaid shirt, Wynn turned and his gaze swept over her and he crossed the room to her. Her heartbeat accelerated while she stood watching him, looking into his eyes and knowing he was going to kiss her. While her pulse raced, she felt a flash of desire.

"Remember, we have a plane to catch today. A commercial flight, so we'll have to be on time," she said.

"I'll remember, and this will just be a quick kiss. You look terrific, by the way," he said, taking in her jeans and blue sweater.

"Thank you. You look rather good yourself."

"When I get home, I'm going to give these clothes to charity, but I'll guarantee you, I'm glad to have them now because my own were in tatters." He stepped closer and slipped his arm around her waist.

"Last night was fantastic. The best," he said solemnly.

"I agree." She gazed up at him. "Are you going to kiss me or just keep talking?"

She saw his answer in his expression, and his arms tightened, drawing her into an embrace.

The minute his lips met hers, she wanted nothing more than to hold him, to have him stay with her. To strip off their clothing and cancel their flight. But she knew she had to let him go. He had to get back to his real life.

Finally, she stepped away, smoothing her sweater and trying to catch her breath and cool down. "We're running out of time."

For just a moment she thought he was going to reach for her again, but he let out a long breath and turned away.

"Yeah. We need to get to the airport. I need to go find my life and my past."

As she watched him walk away, she thought, *Yes, and I'm not part of either one except for the hours you spent in my cabin.*

Ava drove them to Houston to the nearest airport, parked and they flew the rest of the way into Dallas. They took a shuttle to get her car and then he gave her the addresses he had been given by the sheriff to his Dallas condo as well as his parents' home.

The whole time she tried to avoid thinking about telling him goodbye. They got her car, she put the address of his condo in her GPS and drove to a high-rise building overlooking downtown Dallas. As arranged earlier by the sheriff, Wynn got a key from security and they rode to the penthouse condo.

He was told he had a private entrance and they used it to take the elevator to the fifteenth floor where they stepped out into a hallway. He unlocked his condo door and entered. Sunlight spilled through a wall of windows as they walked through an entryway into a large living area. Walls, furniture and throw rugs were all white, with glass and stainless-steel contemporary furniture.

Wynn paused as he looked around and shook his head. "I don't remember one thing here. I'm not even sure I like it."

"Maybe you'll feel differently after you've been here a while."

He looked around and turned to her to place his hands on her shoulders. "The only thing that looks familiar in here is you. Come here. It's been a long time since we left your place and all I could think about most of the time was getting somewhere alone with you so I can kiss you."

He reached for her and she placed her hand on his chest to push lightly. "Whoa. One kiss only, because you don't have a lot of time. We need to allow thirty minutes to get to your parents' house. You told them you'd be there at five."

"We're wasting some valuable minutes here," he whispered, sliding his arm around her waist to draw her to him and kiss her. With every kiss now, she thought it was a goodbye, but then he found a time and place where they could kiss again. The real goodbye was coming tonight or tomorrow, she was certain. She stopped thinking about it because while his mouth was on hers she couldn't think about anything except his kiss.

While her heart raced, she pushed slightly and looked up at him. "You'll be late getting to your parents' for their family dinner for you tonight. You said you wanted to shower."

"Yeah. Want to join me?"

"You'd never get there for dinner," she answered, shaking her head.

"Okay. I'll go and I'll hurry. I don't even know where the shower is."

"You're a big boy. You'll find it," she said, turning to walk to the glass doors that opened onto a balcony.

She heard his boots as he crossed the room and then she was alone. She walked across the spacious room, saw an open door and walked into a large bedroom with black-and-white decor and an oversize bed with a mirror above the bed. She walked over to a glass table with steel legs. A picture in a silver frame was on the table and she picked it up to look at Wynn and a gorgeous blonde smiling into the camera. His arm was around the woman and she had her hand on his knee and was leaning against him. Her black dress was elegant and looked expensive.

Ava put the picture back. Looking at the picture, she

hurt inside, even though common sense made her question if there was a woman in his life.

She glanced around and walked out onto the balcony to look at Dallas spread below, but her thoughts were on Wynn and how tonight might be goodbye.

"I'm ready to go to my folks' house," he said, stepping out on the balcony minutes later, and her heart thudded. His black eye was gone and his bruises had almost faded away. His thick black hair was neatly combed. He wore a crisp white dress shirt, open at the throat, gold cuff links in French cuffs, navy slacks and his same boots, and if she had thought he was handsome before, it was nothing to the way he looked now. Her heart raced and she wanted to touch and kiss him and just look at him.

"Wow, do you clean up good."

"Dang. Now I really do want to call them and tell them I can't get there until tomorrow night."

Laughing, she took his arm. "No, you don't. No telling what they've been doing to get ready for your homecoming. Come on, handsome man, let's go. The sooner you go, maybe the sooner you'll get home."

"Yeah, right. I'm sure not the rancher brother—there isn't a pair of boots in that whole big closet that is filled with clothes. I don't know where or how I got these. I have to tell you, my taste in clothing must have changed with this bump on my head because there are some flashy clothes in that closet that I can't imagine wearing."

She laughed. "On you, I'm sure anything would look good, you handsome devil," she teased.

"I really would like to cancel tonight and go see your house and bedroom and shower."

"Maybe we can work that in later or tomorrow," she said lightly, but she hurt because she thought of the beautiful woman in the picture with him. She could easily be at his parents' home, waiting for his arrival.

As they rode down in the elevator, Ava couldn't keep from looking at him. He still had the shadow of short whiskers on his jaws and chin and the look in his dark eyes made her pulse continue to race.

"I can take my car and use the GPS."

"When you can't remember you parents, I don't think I should let you go on your own. I'll take you this time and I'll be happy to pick you up and take you back to my place or yours," she said, turning to smile at him.

"Oh, baby, I want to turn around now."

"No, your family is waiting. Let's go."

She drove to an older part of Dallas, where homes were mansions, set back from the street with landscaped yards, tall shade trees and well-tended beds of blooming flowers in the warm Texas fall.

"I'd like you to meet my family. Have dinner with me and my family tonight."

She wanted to say yes, but she didn't think she should. "Thank you. That's nice, but you're going home to your family and you don't know what you'll find. Your memory hasn't returned. You reacquaint yourself with your family. You may have a girlfriend here tonight waiting to see you and that could be awkward if I'm with you."

He rubbed the back of his neck and nodded. "I guess you're right. I'll be with you later tonight. By then I'll know my family and any friends they have join us tonight."

"Maybe seeing where you grew up and your family will begin to trigger memories."

"If it doesn't, I'll be sharing my time between a doctor's office and a home with a bunch of strangers who are my family. I don't even know what kind of work I do."

"I suspect you don't have to worry about it too much."

His family home had a circular drive and she took him to the porch steps of a sprawling three-story mansion with a wide front porch that had white Doric columns.

"Well, here's your parents' house," she said. "Your childhood home, from what we could learn."

While he unbuckled his seatbelt, he looked intently at her and her heart beat faster. Slipping his hand behind her neck, he drew her closer while he leaned toward her and his gaze went to her mouth.

The minute his mouth covered hers, her heart thudded. She closed her eyes and kissed him in return, slipping her hand to the back of his neck. It was a long, breathtaking kiss that made her heart pound and made this parting hurt more.

When he sat back, he looked at her solemnly and she wondered what he was thinking.

"Go get reacquainted with your family."

He glanced over his shoulder at his childhood home. "I'd feel a whole lot better about getting out of this car if you would agree to go out with me tomorrow."

She had to smile at that. "Why don't we discuss that when I pick you up tonight?"

"Tomorrow I'll have money, sweetie, and I can take you out to eat at the fanciest place we can find."

Laughing, she shook her head. "Just go find out about yourself."

"Okay," he said, smiling at her. She reminded herself he had no idea who was waiting in that big house for him. He'd had no past, no ties, and that was about to change completely and she could get a call from him later today canceling tomorrow's plans and telling her goodbye. She wasn't going to think about that until it happened.

"I can't wait for later," he said, giving her a look that made her tingle.

"Call me. You have my number."

He nodded. "Well, I hope I recognize my family and I hope this jogs my memory." He stepped out of her car, closed the door and went up the steps to ring the bell.

She drove away slowly, but looked in her rearview mirror as she went down the circle drive. He was standing at the door and she saw it open and a man greeted him as he stepped inside.

Hurting, she wondered if she had just kissed him goodbye.

Seven

Wynn stood on the porch and punched a button, hearing chimes play inside, and then a butler opened the door. "Ah, Mr. Wynn, welcome home. We were so happy to hear you're safe."

"Safe, but without any memory, so tell me your name. I don't even remember the house," he said, looking around. But as he studied the surroundings, he had a flash of memory. Walking into this entryway and hall and bringing a woman to dinner with him.

"Oh, my, they told me about your memory loss. I'm George Bolton, the butler. Let me show you to the great room and I'll tell your mother you're here. She and your younger brother, Jack, are home right now. Your sister, Lucy, isn't home yet, nor your dad. He gets in later tonight."

"His sister is home now, George," a cheerful voice said, and he looked down the hall to see a willowy, black-haired woman striding toward him.

"Lucy," he said, a memory coming of catching her when she fell off a horse when they were kids. And then another memory of her running to him when he set a high-school record as quarterback of the football team. And even though George told him, he remembered her name. "Lucy," he said again with more enthusiasm. She was the first person since the blow to his head that he recognized, and he was thrilled.

Relief filled him, along with a warm feeling for his younger sister. He was certain he had always been close to her. He started to hug her, but when he reached out, she shook his hand.

"Welcome home, Wynn," she said solemnly and he stopped, feeling surprised. She didn't really sound happy to see him. He shook her hand carefully and she turned away. "I'm going to my room. I'll see you downstairs at dinner."

"I'll tell your mother that you're here," George repeated and left, walking out behind Lucy.

Wynn looked at his sister walking up the stairs. What kind of dynamic did they have? Her cool greeting indicated she didn't like him, yet his memories of her were so positive. His reactions when he first saw her were warm and friendly. He wished he could tell all this to Ava. Ava was a good listener, with good ideas and clear thinking. Thinking about her, he felt a pang. He already missed her and that startled him. In spite of their intimacy, he barely knew her. And yet, because of their intimacy, she was on his mind a lot.

Now he was beginning to remember his life. Seeing his family and childhood home must have triggered the memories that were coming back to him full force. Relief that he remembered his life was overwhelming and he felt a rush of joy.

After Ava had pulled him out of that canyon in the storm, he hadn't had a clue about anything in his life or who he was. Ava had been the solid rock that had stabilized him, helped him, gotten a nurse for him and given him reassurance and hope. And then given him the sexiest night of his life. He wanted to be with her right now. That surprised him because he had just left her.

Thinking about her made him want her that much more. He wanted Ava in his arms, in his bed tonight. Making love to her was a recent memory and he had full recollection of every moment of that night. Total recall of how soft she was. How sexy she was. How fantastic she was in bed. No faded memories there. He was certain there had been women in his past, but he couldn't imagine any as sexy as Ava. Or as good a friend, even though they had known each other only a few days.

Was he in love?

That thought jolted him. He hadn't known her long enough to be in love. Suddenly another memory came. He didn't want to marry and he didn't want kids. He was as certain of that as he was that Ava had saved his life. And his reason for not wanting kids? He didn't want them because they might be like his brother. They might be like Wynn. They might be like his brother Wynn.

He ran his hand over the back of his neck as that thought struck him. *His brother Wynn.* "Damn," he said aloud, still standing in the hall by himself. His *brother* was Wynn. *He* was Wade. He closed his eyes as memories filled his mind.

"I have a ranch," he whispered. "I'm a rancher, just like Gerald said." And then he remembered his brother was a troublemaker in a lot of ways. And Wynn wasn't a rancher. He hated ranching.

"Damn." He was Wade Sterling, and he wasn't surprised

because he realized now that his brother had been impersonating him. And he remembered it wasn't the first time.

Memories tumbled through his brain. Wynn had done that over and over through the years. Wade felt certain of little snippets of memories, of fighting with Wynn because he had gone out with Wade's girlfriend in high school and told her he was Wade.

And now he remembered that he never wanted to marry and never wanted kids because they might be like his brother. Their dad had had his first stroke when he was fifty-two. Wade thought that was young and he blamed Wynn for causing their dad so many worries. He could remember all of that now. His whole life was coming back to him, pouring back in a rush.

Relief, joy and a huge longing to tell Ava filled him. He wanted to call Ava, so he just gave in to it.

She picked up on the second ring. "Wynn?"

"Ava, I need to talk to you." Without waiting for her response, he launched into the reason for his call. "My memory is coming back."

"Oh, that's wonderful!" He could hear the smile in her voice. "Molly said it would."

"Maybe the house triggered it. I don't know. But, Ava, I have a lot to tell you."

"I can't wait," she said breathlessly and he wondered if she was thinking about their kisses and making love. He hoped so, because he was.

"I'm not staying here tonight. I'll get a car and get back to your house."

"Just call me and I'll come pick you up."

"We'll see. Ava, I'm not Wynn."

"What do you mean? What are you saying?"

"I'm Wade Sterling."

"Wade? The other twin?" She sounded incredulous.

"But didn't you say that your twin was on television and he said he was Wade Sterling?"

"That's right. My brother has a warped sense of humor and we don't get along very well."

"Mercy," she said on a gasp. "You do have a lot to tell me later."

"Okay. Talk to you then." Before she could disconnect the call, he quickly added, "Hey, Ava, I miss you."

"I miss you," she said softly. "Really miss you," she repeated with a breathlessness that made him ache to hold her.

"I'll see you later," he said, then ended the call and put his phone in his pocket. He took a deep breath and stretched, relishing his memories of holding and kissing her last night.

He stood looking at the house, recalling more moments. He was Wade and his brother was Wynn. And his brother had periodically taken his place, not just in high school, but all through their lives. And he'd done it successfully. Wynn had been in all the school plays and was a good actor. As the years went by, he got better at acting and passed himself off as Wade.

"I'm Wade Sterling," he repeated. He thought back to the storm, to going off the highway in a flash flood, his pickup tumbling into the canyon. And he remembered…

"Olivia." He whispered the name. He'd been about to break up with her when all this happened to him. They moved in the same circles, but he had lost interest in her and he felt it was mutual. She seemed as ready to part as he was.

More recollections came back to him. He remembered he liked his younger sister, Lucy, and she had always liked him. The same with his younger brother, Jack. Along with Wade, Lucy and Jack had fought with Wynn all their lives.

Now he knew why Lucy had been so cool toward him—she had thought he was Wynn.

And then he remembered he and his cousins, Luke, Cal and Jake had contributed money to build a new arena in Fort Worth. The arena construction was complete, but they needed to plan a grand opening. He needed to call his cousins.

Suddenly his mom came rushing in and hugged him. "Wynn, I'm so glad to see you. My darling Wynn, I've been so worried about you. Dad and I have worried and hoped you'd get home okay. I thought you were going to see your friends in Nashville, so I thought you were safe and Wade was home with us." She hugged him. "My precious baby."

Wade had to laugh as he looked down at her. Her hair was a mass of black curls and her brown eyes weren't dark like his. He recognized the familiar perfume she always wore, year in and year out. "Mom, slow down. I'm fine. I'm home and I'm Wade."

"Oh, darling, you can't remember who you are. George told me you said you lost your memory. You're Wynn. Wade has been home in Dallas with us."

"Mom, I know you can tell us apart if you really look at us. Look at me."

She leaned away and stepped back. She put her hand against her cheek. "Oh, my heavens, you're Wade." He smiled.

"Oh, that naughty boy. Your brother just can't stop his pranks," she said, laughing. "None of us even noticed. We all thought he was you. He copies you well. Well, you're home and fine, so don't be mad at him and his games. I'm sorry you got caught in that terrible storm. Would you like a drink before dinner? The others will be here shortly. George told me Lucy just got here." She frowned. "Oh, dear, if you're Wade, and you are, Olivia is coming with Wynn." She patted his arm. "Now don't get angry with your twin. He likes his little jokes and no one was hurt. You didn't even know that he's been telling us he's you until you arrived here, did you?"

"No, Mom, I didn't know about Wynn's little joke." He didn't hide his sarcastic tone.

"Be nice, Wade. We'll have a party tonight."

"Mom, the woman who saved me and got me out of that canyon in a terrible storm lives here in Dallas. Actually not too far away. She saved my life. I'd like to invite her to dinner tonight and let the family meet her."

"That would be lovely. You should have just brought her with you."

"So you don't mind if I invite her now?"

"We'd be delighted to meet her. By all means, go call her."

"Thanks," he said.

"What about Olivia? Wynn is bringing her tonight."

"And he'll take her home tonight and that's fine."

"Oh, my. He'll have to tell her he's not you."

"Olivia will adjust," he said, certain Olivia already knew.

"Go make your call. If you want a drink, get one. I'm going to see about dinner. Oh, it's so good to have you home. To have all of you here." She laughed and shook her head. "Naughty Wynn. He just can't resist a little fun."

Wade watched her go, hurrying to oversee the Sterlings' first-class cook. His mother loved to cook and putter around in the kitchen and they had lost more than one good cook because of that. That was understandable, since cooking was her hobby. But he couldn't understand why she always forgave and excused Wynn. And if he quizzed her about it, she always said he was just like his uncle, Ethan

Sterling, their dad's younger brother. Wade remembered when he'd once asked his dad about their uncle and he said she was correct. Wynn was just like his Uncle Ethan and their mother had dated Ethan first. She had been in love with Ethan when he was killed in a motorcycle wreck.

Wade pulled out his phone and called Ava. His pulse jumped at the sound of her voice.

"Hi. We just talked, so what's up?"

"Mom wants me to invite you to come for dinner. I can't wait to see you. I feel like I told you goodbye hours and hours ago."

She laughed. "Are you sober?"

"Yes, I'm just wound up at the thought of getting you here."

"It'll take me a little while to change."

"That's okay. Text me when you're almost here and I'll go out on the porch and watch for you."

"That's a deal. See you in about an hour, okay?"

"Fine. An hour. And then when you leave, I'll go with you if that's okay with you."

"Of course it's okay," she said in a sultry voice that made him want to be with her right then. "I can't wait."

"Don't tempt me to skip out early. Mom loves having company for dinner."

"Goodbye. I'm going to get ready now."

"I am so ready," he said in a husky voice.

"Oh, my."

Wade smiled. He would be with her soon and with her tonight. All night. Images of their lovemaking last night flashed in his mind, but he banked them before he got aroused.

He tried to calm down and focus on the family and ignore his racing pulse and his eagerness to see her again. How important was she to him? That question startled him. But he had to admit she had become very important. He went upstairs.

He knew where he was and he wanted to go see Lucy if she was in her suite. Relief overwhelmed him that he knew his identity. He would get his life back and a lot more now because Ava was in his life. He looked down at the clothes he was wearing. Not his clothes. He wanted to get his own clothes and his boots.

He passed an open door and when he glanced inside, he knew it was Lucy's suite even though she wasn't in the sitting room. He crossed the room to straighten a picture that periodically slipped and became crooked and it was too high for Lucy to reach unless she stood on a chair, so often he fixed it for her.

He heard her behind him. "I'm fixing your picture. I wanted to talk to you—"

She stared at him and looked at the picture. "You're not Wynn. Oh, my gosh, you're Wade." She dashed across the room to hug him.

He blinked in surprise, then put his arms around her. "You didn't think so when I first saw you in the hall."

"No," she said, stepping back to smile at him. "I was distracted, but I can tell which one of you I'm with if I really look at you. And you straightened the picture, like you always do. Wynn never once has. Which is all right with me. On Dad's orders, Wynn is supposed to leave my things alone."

He wanted to reach out and hug her again, but she continued. "The whole family thinks you're Wynn. The whole family except Wynn, that is."

"Where is Wynn?"

"He'll be here and he's bringing Olivia." Her hand flew to her face. "Wade, Olivia thinks she's with you. You're the one she's been seeing for the past year. Do you think that's why he did this? He wanted Olivia?"

Wade smiled and squeezed her shoulder. "It'll be all right. Olivia and I were about to split, anyway. I'm glad she's with him."

"You really mean that, don't you?"

"Yes, I do."

Her lips firmed and she wrinkled her brow. "I know you won't lose your temper when we're all together. I worry about Dad getting upset. His doctors told him to avoid stress."

"Well, hell, that went out the window when Wynn was born. I'll talk to Dad and emphasize all the good things—I got home safely, I have my memory. At this point I think that's about all we can do." He shook his head. "I don't know why Wynn has to pull these childish pranks. He needs to grow up." He stopped. "Enough about him.

"On another subject, Mom told me to invite my new friend, Ava Carter. She saved my life in a terrible storm. She saw my pickup sweep off the road and saw me jump before it went down into a canyon. She climbed down to get me out of there, helped me back to the road and took me home with her. We had a hell of a storm that night and I really think she saved my life. I'd lost my memory—probably when I fell—and I didn't know where the pickup was, nor my phone, and I lost my wallet so I had no identification. To top it off, I was cut badly and bleeding."

"Oh, Wade, that's awful."

"I really owe her and I want all of you to meet her. She has no family. Her mother and sister died and she doesn't have contact with her dad."

"I'm glad she took you in, but with no memory—that's a little scary to take a stranger home when you live alone."

He told her about Ava's wonderful neighbors, including Molly, who had tended to his shoulder.

"How is your shoulder?"

"It's mending. I think it's fine. I'll go see our doc and let him check me over because of the head injury and memory loss."

"I'm glad we'll get to meet your friend."

"I'm glad you will, too. Ava is an occupational therapist. Well, sis, I'd like to say hello to Jack. I remember the house and where Jack's suite is located. I'll see you again shortly, probably in the great room."

"Sure. I'm glad you're home, Wade. Real glad."

"Thanks, Lucy," he said. "It's good to be home and beyond good to get my memory back."

She laughed. "Wynn had to behave himself to pose as you. What a relief it was."

"Well, he can be his usual ornery self again."

"I can't wait to meet Ava. If you like her, then I know I'll like her."

"You'll like her, I promise," Wade said, pausing at the open door. He smiled at Lucy and left to go see his baby brother and let him know about Wynn, the imposter.

He more than had a feeling Lucy's theory was right. In fact, he was certain Wynn did it to get Olivia. How long was she fooled? he wondered and smiled because he doubted if it was long at all.

At Jack's suite Wade knocked on the open door and walked in when Jack told him to enter. "Well, you made it back," Jack said with a glance as he pulled neatly folded black and brown socks out of a drawer.

"Looks as if you came home to get a few things."

"That and Mom twisted my arm to get us to come home to welcome you on your first night back."

"Being here in this house, seeing family members—I

don't know if that's what did it or if it was just a matter of time, but I have my memory back. I'm not Wynn."

Jack stopped what he was doing and whirled around to stare at him. "You're Wade?" his brother asked, doubt in his voice.

"I think I am."

"Dang. You are," he said, staring at Wade. "You sure are. I just glanced at you before, but I can always see it if I pay attention and really look. And that's the way you would answer," Jack said. "Wynn would have said, 'I know I am.' That damn Wynn, what did he have to gain other than to fool every—? Oh, wow," he said, suddenly quiet as he stared at Wade. "He wanted Olivia."

"I have no claims on Olivia. I do remember her now, but I'm not interested in settling down with Olivia. Frankly, that's how I realized my identity. The thought came to me that I haven't ever wanted to marry and Olivia was beginning to talk about marriage. I don't want to take the chance on having a kid like Wynn," he said, remembering being with Ava and thinking it would be good to have a baby with her. He looked at his brother. "Jack, that's exactly what ran through my mind and I realized I'm Wade."

Jack shook his head. "I should have caught on. At the time Mom just told me Wade was home and Wynn was in Nashville and I had no reason to doubt that."

"I understand, Jack. Don't blame yourself."

"But, Wade, about that no-kids thing—I've thought that myself sometimes. I don't want to marry someday and have a kid like Wynn. But I realize that isn't going to happen. Neither one of us would have a kid like Wynn, because we wouldn't tolerate his antics, unlike Mom, who thought he was cute and encouraged him."

"That's true," Wade said.

"While you were away he brought Olivia to dinner several times. I gotta say he knows how to impersonate you and it's actually too bad he's going to stop now because he's a whole lot nicer to have around when he's trying to pass himself off as you."

Wade actually laughed at that, as did Jack. He knew it was the truth.

His brother sobered quickly, though. "What about Dad? When this comes out, it may give him another stroke."

"Maybe I can get in touch with Dad and break the news that I'm Wade a little more gently to him."

"I think that would be good. You're perfect for that. Ah, now Wynn will just go back to being his usual rotten self." He shook his head. "I'm amazed Mom didn't fall all over you and cry with joy since she thought you're her darling Wynn."

"I'd already realized I'm Wade. When I told her he's been impersonating me, she just laughed."

"Speaking of Wynn, here he comes."

Wade saw Jack looking out the front window and walked over to watch. He saw his twin get out and circle the car to hold open the door and Olivia stepped out. Wade remembered her and was thankful again that he'd regained his full memory.

He also noticed that Olivia was stunning with her long straight blond hair framing her face. She wore a pale blue dress that clung to a curvy figure and had a short skirt that showed off her legs. The deep vee neckline revealed an ample bosom and a diamond pendant sparkled at her throat.

When he saw her, he could appreciate her beauty, but other than that, he didn't feel anything. Seeing her just made him think about Ava and wish they were through with dinner and he could leave with her.

"I don't know how you can keep from going downstairs and punching him out for telling everyone that he was Wade Sterling. Do you think Olivia will be angry?" Jack asked.

Wade shook his head. "Naw. I don't care to punch him and, frankly, I'll bet Olivia knows. I doubt if he could fool her. It's Dad I worry about the most. I'm not angry. Wynn solved a situation for me. I'm so relieved to have my memory back that I don't give a damn about what shenanigans he pulled.

"I didn't know I'd lose my memory, but I have it back now, so things should settle."

"Yeah, after Dad gets through blowing his lid over Wynn taking your identity."

"I'm remembering other times when he's done this, but he never involved the family in it."

"Yeah, he's never done it on this scale. You know he was actually on local television and all sorts of media as you?"

Wade nodded. "I'll get even with him someday."

Jack laughed. "I'm not holding my breath until that happens. He has a lot of luck and he has Mom's support."

When Wade heard the front door open and close, he said, "Let's go greet them." He walked out in time to catch up with Lucy.

"I want to see this," she said, falling into step with her brothers.

"It's just twins greeting each other, even if one has been posing as the other. Frankly, I'm not angry about it. I hope Olivia is happy with him."

They entered the great room and Olivia turned to greet them. The smile on her face fell and she looked startled.

"Hello, Olivia. Good news. I've got my memory back."

Her eyes widened and for a moment he saw her surprise, but then it was gone and she smiled, looking composed and amused. "I'm glad. I must say you have an interesting brother. I'm enjoying getting to know him better."

"'Interesting' is one way to describe Wynn, I suppose. Where is he?"

"In the library waiting for you to join him."

"I wish you both the best."

"You sound as if you really mean that," she said, looking intently at him.

"I'm sincere or I wouldn't say it. I think you'll be good for Wynn. You won't let him get away with all the stuff he does now."

She smiled. "You mean that, don't you? I'm glad," she added without giving him time to answer her. "I think it was over between us, anyway. Wynn does entertain me. He can be fun and exciting."

"I'm sure that's true."

"I wish you the best and I'm glad you're safely home."

"Thanks, Olivia. Have fun with Wynn."

She smiled and nodded at him as he walked away.

His affair with her was over—and all he felt was relief.

The library doors were closed so he knocked, then stepped inside and closed the door for privacy. He faced his brother, who stood by the fireplace looking neat in navy slacks and a white dress shirt that was open at the throat—looking the way Wade dressed. "Well, we look like the ultimate identical twins tonight, right down to matching watches. You have on my boots," Wade said and saw Wynn turn to look at him sharply and frown.

"I'm home again and I have my memory back, Wynn," Wade stated bluntly.

"Ah, there go my plans for the evening." He stepped away from the fireplace, a drink in his hand. "So you know I've been impersonating you."

Wade nodded. He expected Wynn to look guilty, embarrassed, something. But no emotion showed on his face.

Wynn walked to him and sipped the amber liquid in his glass, nonchalant and at ease. "Olivia is a beautiful woman," he said, spearing Wade with an intent look. "She knew the truth right away, but played along, anyway."

"Yes, she is, and if that's why you did it, well, you succeeded. I wish you both well. Olivia and I were over, anyway, as she probably told you."

"No, she didn't and I don't think she actually knew you were over, but I'm glad." He put down his glass on a nearby table. "So you're not angry?" Wynn asked, tilting his head to again study his brother.

In all honesty, he should be. But he was so relieved to have his memory back that he couldn't muster the ire at Wynn's antics. Still, he stood firm. "No. But you can't pass as me now, so that's over. How did you know I wasn't on my way home when you came home?"

"I keep in touch with Mom and she chatters and tells me where everyone is and what's going on and I learned they'd lost contact with you. I saw a chance for some fun so I cut short my Nashville trip and flew home. I called on the way. Everyone accepted me as you. I didn't know how long before you'd surface."

"Your days of impersonating me are over."

"How very civilized. I figured you'd be furious. Dad will no doubt take his usual dim view."

"Something just occurred to me. The sheriff of the little town who saw you impersonate me on the news made arrangements for me to get the key to my condo when I got back to Dallas. I realize now I have the key to *your* condo." He looked down at himself. "And I'm wearing your clothes." He reached into his pocket, retrieved the keys and tossed them to Wynn.

"Keep the clothes," Wynn said. "I just got those and the ones I'm wearing because they look like what you'd wear. I don't want them back." He put the keys in his pocket. "It never occurred to me that the sheriff would arrange for you to pick up the keys to my condo."

"Don't worry, I didn't disturb anything," he said, knowing if the situation had been reversed, Wynn would have gone through every one of his things out of curiosity.

"I don't know how you can tolerate the damn boots. I'll be even happier when this whole charade is over with."

Wynn's bland expression hardened. His jawline tightened and his eyes narrowed as they assessed his twin.

"You know, Wade, you always think you're better than I am, that I can't have what you have. But I've proved you wrong with Olivia. You're not getting her back."

"I can live with that, Wynn," Wade said, maintaining his calm. "And I don't always think I'm better. We're just different."

"Not too different, my brother. You've got the same blood in your veins as I do in mine. And guess what? Mom told me the 'big secret'—" his hands formed air quotes "—that I'm not supposed to share with you or anybody else, but I think this is the right time to reveal it. Dad isn't our real dad," he said, lowering his voice. His face flushed and his voice deepened as he continued. "Ethan got Mom pregnant, which makes Dad our uncle. Guess we'll have to call him Uncle Arlo now, huh?"

The news hit Wade like a semitruck. "You're lying," he said, staring at his twin.

"Oh, no, I'm not. And our real dad didn't know it because Mom was just barely pregnant when Ethan was killed. At the time he died, neither of them knew she was pregnant and she's never told Arlo. So live with that one," he said as he snatched his drink and looked at Wade as he gulped it. "Our so-called dad doesn't even know he's not our father. You may be his favorite but you're not his son." He looked smug as he added, "And you won't tell because that might give him a heart attack, so I know you'll keep Mom's secret."

As the revelation rumbled around in his head, he thought of his mother and the relationship she and his twin shared. And he felt sick to his stomach, disgusted and angry. "The one person on earth who is always good to you no matter what you do and you didn't even give her the loyalty of keeping her secret."

"I know you won't say anything to her because you won't want to hurt her." He pointed a finger at Wade and added, "Now you can think about that one and whose blood runs in your veins."

Wade wanted to punch his brother but he wouldn't stoop to Wynn's level. He took deep breaths and jammed his fists into his pockets, calling up every ounce of self-control. When he couldn't contain his anger, he turned to go, to get away from Wynn. Walking to the door, he stopped.

He turned around to see Wynn smiling because he knew he had gotten to Wade.

He crossed the hall to speak to them. "He knows I have my memory. I'm going to call Dad and break the news to him before he walks in and gets it from Wynn without knowing how well I am."

"That's a good idea," Lucy said. "It won't worry Dad nearly as much if he thinks you're okay."

"And it'll help for him to talk to you," Jack added.

"I'll be outside," Wade said and left, going down the steps and away from the house. He was stunned by Wynn's news, but he didn't doubt it was the truth. His dad was his uncle Ethan, a man who had been just like Wynn. So he and Wynn had Ethan's blood in their veins and not the blood of Arlo Sterling, the man he called dad. Wade hoped his father never found out.

Father. What was he thinking? Arlo Sterling was their dad—in all ways except by blood. He had raised them, taken care of them, showered them with love and guidance and wealth. He would always be the real dad to Wade.

But he couldn't get the blood inheritance out of his mind. Wynn's words echoed there. *Now you can think about...whose blood runs in your veins.* That just fortified Wade's determination to never marry and have kids.

That made him think about Ava. They weren't talking marriage, but still, he needed to warn her that he was definitely not a marrying man. He recalled his conversation with Jack. How much was Wynn like their uncle Ethan because of blood—or was it because their mother had always spoiled him and thought whatever he did was cute?

Wade stood with clenched fists, gulping air, trying to calm down. He didn't want kids because they might be like Wynn. He couldn't risk it. But was he making a mistake?

Ava wanted four or five kids, she had said. He thought about the odds on that. Four or five kids—if he married her and had five kids, two or three of them could be like Wynn. Hell, all five could be. What a thought.

As usual Wynn had once again stirred up trouble at a time when Wade had been happy and enjoying his homecoming. He had been filled with joy to have his memory back. He was even happy that Olivia and Wynn had found each other, and best of all, he had been filled with eagerness and joy because he would be with Ava later tonight. And then Wynn had thrown a damper on the evening. And broken a promise to their mother, but she would forgive him as she always did.

Wade stood outside in the dark, light spilling from the windows. As he called his dad, he again affirmed that Arlo would always be Dad to him. He listened to the phone ring and then heard his father's voice.

"Dad, I'm back and I'm fine. Good news—since I got home, my memory seems to have fully returned."

"Oh, son, that's great news." He could hear the relief in his father's voice.

"Look, we can talk more when you get home, but I'm so happy to be home and remember everything. I want you to know that I'm Wade. Wynn has been telling all of you that he was me." He listened to his father swear and hoped he hadn't made a mistake telling him on the phone.

"No one was hurt and I'm fine now that I'm home. Let it go because I'm okay and I don't want you to worry." The words nearly choked in his throat, but concern for his father made him force them out.

His father asked a few questions, his tone turning calmer with each of Wade's responses. "I think Wynn did it to get Olivia," Wade said, "and I'm glad because now she's happy and I don't have to go through breaking up with her."

His dad laughed. "I guess Wynn's good for something."

"Listen, Dad, I'm bringing a guest tonight. She got me out of that canyon and took me to her home. I can't wait for you and the family to meet her. But right now I better go back inside." Before he disconnected the call, he added, "I don't think I tell you often enough—you've been a super dad. I love you," he said and meant it. "See you soon."

He sighed, knowing that his father didn't deserve a son like Wynn. Which only made him more resolute in his decision never to marry and risk having a kid like his twin. He thought about Ava. At some point he needed to tell her how he felt. He didn't want to hurt her, but they'd been together only briefly. Surely both of them could walk away after only a few nights. Or was he fooling himself?

As quickly as that thought came, it was followed by another—he wasn't ready to say goodbye yet. He wanted her in his arms tonight, in his bed, and he wanted to kiss and make love for hours.

He looked at his watch and couldn't wait for her arrival. Twenty minutes later, Ava turned into the long circle drive and Wade went down the porch steps to meet her.

Eight

Smiling at him, she stepped out of the car, looking like an angel, her silky blond hair framing her beautiful face. Her black dress almost covered her knees and the scoop neckline was not cut low enough to reveal her cleavage, but he knew every curve of her body intimately. She took his breath away just looking at her. He wanted to walk up to her, take her in his arms and kiss her.

Instead, he waited as she walked toward him. "You look fantastic. And I can't wait to get you home," he said in a husky voice.

"Thank you." Her smile broadened. "I can't tell you how thrilled I am that you remember your past life."

"You know what I remember most of all?" he said, knowing his voice was deeper, something that happened when he was aroused.

"What?" she asked, looking up at him.

"Making love with you."

Her cheeks flushed. "I think we need to change the subject right now. Why don't you tell me the names of everyone I'm about to meet?"

While they walked to the house, he told her the names of his family. They went inside and he introduced her to everyone. He could see curiosity in Wynn's eyes, but his twin stayed at Olivia's side, merely giving Ava a curt wave. Lucy and Jack were happy to talk to Ava and hear about the storm and Wade's wreck. His mother stood talking to Wynn and Olivia. And then his dad arrived. He walked straight over to greet Wade, thrusting out his hand and then giving Wade a hug.

"Thank goodness, you're home," he said. "I've had business and wasn't home sometimes when Wynn was here as you. And the few times I was here with him, I just didn't pay attention. He's a good actor."

"Oh, yes. And he knows me well." Wade didn't want to talk about Wynn's charade. There was a more important reason to talk to his dad right now.

"I want you to meet Ava," Wade said, taking his dad's arm and crossing the room to where she stood with Lucy and Jack. "Dad, meet Ava Carter. She came to my rescue and I think she saved my life. Ava, this is my dad, Arlo Sterling."

"Mr. Sterling, I'm so happy to meet you. And I think Wade would have survived on his own, but I'm sure he had a better stay in my place out of the storm," she said, smiling at his father and offering her hand.

"I'm sure he did, too, Ava, and we're all grateful to you for what you did to take care of him."

As they stood talking, Wade studied his dad and realized he didn't look as good as he had only a couple of days ago. He wondered how much Wynn's constant annoyances had hurt their dad's health. His attention shifted to Ava and he wanted dinner to be over and for them to be able to go. He wanted her all to himself and it seemed far longer than just earlier today that they had last been together.

By the time dinner was over and they had visited for an hour, Wade felt they could leave. Goodbyes took time and finally he walked to Ava's car with her. She slid behind the wheel to drive.

"I keep extra keys in my dad's safe, locked away from Wynn," Wade said when he was in the car. "So now I have my condo key and my car keys. The pickup that went into the canyon was one of my ranch vehicles. Let's go to my place. That way I can get my car and I can entertain you."

"Sounds like a deal. I can't wait for you to entertain me," she said in a sultry voice, her eyes on the road.

"You shouldn't do that when you're driving because answers like that, said the way you did, tend to cause me to want to put my hands on you and kiss you and I can't while you drive."

"That'll just make you look forward to being home with me again," she answered.

"Ava, I've been looking forward to getting home again with you since I stepped out of your car this afternoon. You can't imagine how much I've thought about you since then."

"We better change the drift of this conversation because I need to keep my attention on the road. You're definitely distracting."

"And you are definitely sexy and hot."

Ava glanced his way for a second, then averted her eyes back to the road and sat up straighter. "You have a nice big family. Four kids is wonderful."

"Three of us are and you're changing the subject."

She laughed. "Oh, yes, I am before I throw myself in your arms and wreck the car."

"Next time, let me drive. I've developed the knack of driving and talking at the same time," he answered, amused, excited to be with her and aware his condo was closer than her house. He couldn't wait to get there.

"What part of what I said do you not get?"

He smirked, though he knew she couldn't see it. "I can't help it. You *are* sexy and hot."

"Stop," she said, smiling, but keeping her attention on the road ahead and city traffic. "How many more blocks to your place?"

"About another couple of miles. Want me to drive?"

"No, I don't. Your twin seemed charming tonight."

"Oh, he can be, especially to a beautiful, sexy woman. He can turn it on whenever he wants. He keeps on Mom's good side and she adores him. Believe me, you'll always see his good side."

"I've seen identical twins before and I could tell them apart, but I can't with the two of you. I can see how he gets away impersonating you—except you have a scar on your left hand."

"Didn't you see a band aid on his hand?"

"Yes, I did. I figured he cut himself."

"And that's what he would tell you, but underneath that band aid is no cut and no scar. He wears that so women who know me and know I have the scar think he has a cut where the scar is. He's devious and he's an actor. In high school he constantly passed himself off as me with girls I dated and only a few of them ever caught on. But he won't be able to do it so easily anymore."

"Why is that?" she asked.

"If you ever wonder if you're really with me, ask to look at my shoulder. Molly said I'm going to have a scar. And

Wynn isn't going to be able to do anything to match the way I've got my shoulder scarred."

"I'll keep that in mind," she teased him.

Wade continued looking out the window. "I recognize everything. Molly was right. My memory came back and it seems to be all there. All this is familiar like I never had a problem."

"I'm glad."

He turned to gaze at her. "Best of all, I can fully remember last night with you."

"I'm not even going to answer that and then you'll have to stop."

"That's okay if you don't join in my conversation. I'll just tell you about last night and how we showered together and—"

"If I wreck the car, you'll be sorry."

He laughed, enjoying teasing her and talking about sex. "You won't wreck the car. You're concentrating while I'm remembering the moments, holding you, kissing you—"

She began to sing softly and he laughed. Then he remained quiet because they were almost to his condo, six blocks off the busy highway.

He had a private entrance and the minute the door closed behind them, he turned to wrap his arms around her. He looked into her big blue eyes and felt his heartbeat race. "Finally, you're here and I can kiss you," he whispered. "I've waited forever for this moment."

Ava shivered as his gaze held hers and she could see his intent in his expression. She shrugged the strap to her purse off her shoulder and let it fall to the floor. There was only the soft light in the entryway, but she was oblivious of everything except Wade, who looked so incredibly handsome tonight.

Her heart pounded in eager anticipation as she wrapped her arms around him and kissed him in return, forgetting everything else.

He crushed her against him, kissing her passionately. She trembled with wanting him, feeling as much urgency as he seemed to feel. As he kissed her, his hands were at the zipper of her dress, slipping the zipper slowly down the back.

He raised his head for a moment and pushed away her dress. It fell in a heap around her feet. His muscled chest expanded as he took a deep breath, placed his hands on her waist and took a step back to look at her. While his gaze ran over her, she tingled with the need to kiss him again. "Wade," she whispered, tugging his forearms lightly.

Instead of reaching for her, he undid two buttons on his shirt and yanked it over his head to toss it aside.

Then he turned his attention to her remaining clothing. He unfastened her bra and dropped it. "You're beautiful," he whispered as he pushed down her lacy panties so she could step out of them.

After he shed his slacks and shorts, he sheathed himself with a condom and walked back into her embrace, and she could feel his thick manhood, hard and ready, pressing against her.

"I've thought about you constantly," he whispered between showering kisses on her throat and down to take first one nipple and then the other in his mouth. He ran his tongue over her and teased her with slow, wet strokes, his warm breath on her while he cupped her breasts in his gentle hands.

She gasped while each stroke of his fingers heightened her desire.Urgency built to make love, to have him fill her, to love her until she felt she would burst with her climax as only he could bring her to.

With a cry, she brought his head up. The desire she saw in his brown eyes made her stand on tiptoe and kiss him while she caressed his manhood.

When he picked her up, she locked her legs around him as he let her down slowly and entered her.

She gasped with an aching need for his loving.

As they kissed, he pumped hard and fast while she moved on him and held him tightly. Longing built, driving her. He went harder and faster while she clung to him and finally cried out with her climax, consumed by bliss. He thrust one more time and followed her into ecstasy.

When she finally lowered her feet to the floor, she was grateful for his embrace because her legs felt too weak to support her. Perhaps sensing it, he swept her up in his arms.

He carried her to his shower, switching on lights as he went. Unaware of her surroundings, she could see only him as he gazed down at her while he carried her through his condo. Basking in the afterglow of the orgasm he'd given her, she showered light kisses on his throat and his ear, as her hand played across his nape and she wound her fingers in his thick hair. He was a marvel to her, their lovemaking carrying her to heights she had never been.

"Sexy man, so, so sexy," she whispered.

He stopped walking, turning his head to kiss her passionately again while he held her tightly against him. Finally he raised his head and continued into a large bathroom with a king-size shower. As they showered together, she ran her hands over his exciting body. They dried each other with thick, fluffy red towels, then once again he picked her up and carried her into his bedroom.

In minutes they were in each other's arms in the bed with a sheet pulled over them and a low light on a table beside them.

"Ava, I've thought about you constantly since the last time we made love. You're special," he said, showering feathery kisses on her face. He leaned away to look at her. "I don't want to ever hurt you." She shifted so they were facing each other and he toyed with her hair, his brown eyes intent on her.

"You won't hurt me," she said, certain he wouldn't. He had been considerate of her feelings since the first time they were together.

With his fingers he combed long strands of her hair from her face and gazed at her seriously. "Ava, I want to tell you something right now. You've been hurt badly by your ex-fiancé. I don't want to add another hurt."

Suddenly Ava felt chilled and wondered what was coming because he looked solemn. Whatever it was, he probably hadn't remembered it until he got back to Dallas, to his home, and his memory returned. It couldn't be a wife, so she was puzzled, but she had a feeling that it wasn't going to be good news. He looked far too worried.

"You should realize now at least to a degree what my twin is like. He has made my dad's life miserable too many times. Dad has heart trouble and I told you that when he was fifty-two, he had a stroke. I blame Wynn for the worries our dad has had. Wynn made Jack's life miserable when he was a little kid, and he was mean to Lucy. He did stuff to me, too, but I'm his age and could beat him in a fight when we were kids. But he didn't stop when we grew up, posing as me, like he did now. I was going out with Olivia until I left for the fishing trip. I was planning to break it off with her, so I'm glad she's happy with him, but if I'd been in love with her, I would be livid with him now."

"I would think she would be because of his deception."

"Oh, no. He can be charming and she was through with

me, too. Wynn got what he wanted—Olivia. That was the whole purpose of this switch."

"I understand, Wade. I know you have no feelings for Oliva. If that's what you're trying to tell me—"

"No, Ava, there's more." He took a deep breath and when she saw the darkness shield his eyes, she braced for the bad news.

Nine

"What I'm working up to tell you is, because of my brother, I have never wanted to marry and I sure never want to have kids."

"Wade, you're not like your brother, and a child you raise wouldn't be like him. Your brother wouldn't have any great influence on your child."

"Influence matters, but genes—you have to live with them and you can't change some things that you inherit."

"You don't inherit a mean disposition when you're around nice people all the time."

"I'm very much like my dad who raised me," Wade said. "Wynn isn't like him one bit. We had the same dad raise us. We have the same blood in our veins, but there are qualities Wynn has that I don't have and vice-versa."

"Wade, you're cutting yourself off from so much joy. Family is everything. You have a brother and sister and parents that you like, right?"

"Yes, I do, but I've watched Wynn ruin my dad's health by simply worrying him constantly when we were growing up. He still does, for that matter. Look at this latest escapade."

"I don't think you're looking at the positive things. I'm alone. You have no idea what it's like to have no family. And you have a good family—all the other members. Lucy and Jack are friendly and nice. Your parents are warm. And Wynn—well, he's not a monster, Wade. I know he causes the family trouble, but he isn't dangerous. You seem to deal pretty well with him. And I don't think any child you'd raise would ever be like him. I don't think his jealousy, or whatever motivates him, is something a child of yours would inherit. You don't inherit jealousy."

Wade shook his head. "You don't know the whole story. We have two personalities that are alike in different generations."

"I'm not following you."

"It isn't just Wynn, Ava. My dad had a younger brother, Ethan. My parents and my older relatives have always said that Wynn is just like Ethan. So there's one like that in that generation and one in mine. Ethan and Wynn had different parents, different siblings, different influences in their lives, but they turned out the same way. I don't want to go through what my dad did raising Wynn. My grandfather had heart trouble and he died at sixty-three. I don't know if Ethan contributed to his health problems or not. I just told this to Jack today and he said he feels the same way."

"I can't imagine that you would have a child who would be like your brother. I think you're worrying unnecessarily."

"I might be, Ava, but I'm sticking by that, so I wanted you to know right now. I'm not a marrying man and I don't want kids. I'm not going to change."

Ava felt as if ice water had been poured over her as she listened to his declaration about marriage and kids. Then she tried reasoning it out. She thought how little time they had been together and what a short time she had known him. They weren't in love. This was lust and she knew that.

She looked into his eyes. They were in bed together, naked, they had made love, he was exciting, irresistible, handsome, sexy. Tonight she wasn't going to worry about his determination to stay single all his life and to avoid having kids. Tonight that wasn't a problem. Because she knew they couldn't be in love in this short amount of time.

She knew something else, too. Their relationship would have to be brief or she would be in love with him.

She wanted to make love, wanted his kisses, but she would have to guard her heart and tell him goodbye very soon. The realization hurt, but the pain would be easier to bear in the short term. Wade was a wonderful, sexy man, but she had dreams for a family and he would never give her that.

Sadness replaced the trepidation she felt when he'd started talking to her. "That's unfortunate for you, Wade, because you'd be a wonderful husband and dad. I can't imagine you'd have a son like your twin or your uncle. You're cutting yourself out of a family and children and to my way of thinking that's one of the biggest joys in life."

He lowered his gaze for a moment, then looked back at her. This time, his eyes shone with desire. "At the moment, I can think of another huge joy in life and we're letting it slip away from us," he said, starting to nuzzle her neck and then trail kisses on her ear.

His touch was like a balm. It turned her sadness and pain to longing and arousal. She met his kiss and felt that familiar yearning for his lovemaking. Tonight she wasn't going to think about his views of marriage and children.

She wasn't in love and he wasn't in love, and she was certain she could still tell him goodbye without being hurt. She let him kiss away all thoughts and even the worries he had just caused. For this night she would be in his arms.

She held him, running her hand over his smooth, muscled back and giving herself to his fiery loving. This time, words were nonexistent—everything was erotic feelings, with his hands and mouth all over her. She rubbed against him, kissed and stroked him with her hands and tongue, making him groan with desire. It seemed he'd never stop teasing and toying with her, never give her all of himself, which her body craved. Then, finally he had a condom and was on his back as he lifted her over him and she slid down for him to enter her. She cried out with pleasure, setting the pace as she rocked against him, then moving faster, as he caressed her breasts and pumped in her.

They climaxed together, his arms around her, with her sprawled over him, holding him tightly.

She didn't know how long her explosive climax rocked her, but finally she slowed and then lay quietly on him, his arm around her while his other hand caressed her back, sliding over her bottom, her thighs and up again.

"So perfect," he whispered, "so beautiful." He kissed her lightly. "So sexy. This night is a dream come true."

She held him, her ear against his chest, and she heard his pounding heart slow and finally reach a normal beat, and her breathing matched his.

At this moment, in his bed, in his embrace, lying on top of him, their warm, naked bodies together after fantastic sex, she tingled everywhere from his loving and she was satiated. At this minute, with him, there were no problems.

But with each calmer breath, the world, their lives and concerns and dreams, all began to come back. She heard his heartbeat, remembering his words. *I'm not a marrying man and I don't want kids. I'm not going to change.*

She chased the worry away. She hadn't known him long and they weren't in love. She could get over him. All they had between them were hours at her cabin and a few intimate moments.

Or was she kidding herself? Was she taking a big risk with her heart again to be with him?

She shifted to her side and slid off of him. He left for a few minutes to rid himself of the condom and returned to stretch out beside her. Drawing her tightly against his side, he held her close while she tangled her fingers in the thick mat of curly, black hair across his chest.

Each time she started to think about what he had told her, she tried to shut it out of her mind and focus on his body and the loving they'd already shared. There would be time later to think more clearly about his declarations of no marriage and no family.

"A kiss for your thoughts. I don't exactly have a penny with me," he said.

"I was thinking how sexy you are," she said in a lazy drawl. Tonight she was in his arms and she wanted to make love until dawn. She brushed kisses across his shoulder to his throat, then he shifted beneath her and his mouth covered hers in a hungry kiss.

He held her close. "Go to dinner with me tomorrow night, Ava. You took care of me after getting me out of the canyon and I want to take you out."

"Thank you, that's very nice," she said. Then caution reared its head, a warning light in the darkness, making her question the wisdom of continuing to see him. Dinner would no doubt lead to more lovemaking afterward and that would just put another link in an invisible chain that could bind her heart to him. Only he would never love her in return. She heard the firmness in his voice when he told her he didn't want to marry and he never wanted kids.

She did and she was certain she could never stay with a man who didn't want children.

It was just dinner, another part of her brain reasoned. A chance for Wade to show his gratitude for her kindness and hospitality. And didn't she owe him a note of thanks, too? Because of him, she was over her heartbreak with Judd.

She should be able to recover from whatever hurt she would feel when she and Wade parted later. Compared to the time she had spent with her ex-fiancé, she had barely been with Wade.

His arm tightened around her and his dark eyes searched hers. "What are you thinking? Will you go to dinner with me?"

Her mouth opened, her response surprising her. "Yes, I will. I need to go home first. I have calls, mail, things I should do. I'll be happy to go to dinner tomorrow, thank you."

"Good," he said, smiling at her. He kissed her lightly, wrapped her in his arms and held her. "Ava, I've seen your cabin, where you like to spend time and relax. I'd like to show you my ranch. We don't have to stay long. I just want to show you what I love and where I work. Will you go to my ranch with me?"

For a moment she thought about it. That would be more time with him, getting to know him better and seeing another part of his life. Did she want that risk to her heart?

"I'll have to think about that one," she said.

"I want you to see it," he said. "I haven't ever asked any other woman out to the ranch. You're very special," he whispered, showering light kisses on her throat and then down to her breasts. She wound her fingers in his hair, and all thoughts ceased as she was swept away by his tongue, his kisses and his hands on her.

It was noon when, showered and dressed, she walked into the living room to find him.

"I need to go home, get my mail and calls, do some things."

"Let's go to lunch and then you go," he said and she nodded. "And before we go to lunch, I'd like to take you with me tomorrow. My cousin Jake Reed called. My cousins and I donated money to build a new arena in Fort Worth this past year."

"That was in all the news," she said.

"My cousins and I haven't seen the building—they haven't seen it since the ground-breaking ceremony. I've seen it, but not recently and when I saw it, it was spectacular. Anyway, we have an arena board now and an arena CEO and other employees. We've been invited to come look at the arena. We're going to meet in the morning and tour, look at it. I'd like you to go with me."

She smiled. "I'd love to. I've heard so much about it on television. I'd love to go."

"Great," he said, laughing slightly. "I was in hopes when you said you'd love to go that you would add that you would love to be with me."

She laughed and rushed up to put her arms around his neck. "Of course, I'd love to go mainly to be with you," she said. They looked into each other's eyes and laughed and then the moment changed. Her heartbeat speeded and she tightened her arms around his neck and stood on tip-toe as he wrapped his arms around her waist, drew her to him while he leaned down to kiss her.

They had lunch together and he went to her car with her.

"I'll pick you up at half past six," he told her through her open window. "I have your address. I don't even want to tell you goodbye and let you go now."

She smiled at him. "I'll see you tonight."

He nodded and stepped away from the car. When she reached the corner, she glanced in the rearview mirror to see he was still standing, watching her.

"I shouldn't go out with you tonight or tomorrow or ever again," she whispered to herself. His announcement about never marrying and never having children came crashing back now, and this time she had to face the truth of what he had told her and how it affected their relationship. She should have said goodbye when she left, but she couldn't resist him.

It hurt to know a parting would come, and she feared that this one would be a whole lot worse than the first one.

In his jeans, red, white and blue plaid shirt and boots, Wade stepped out of his car. Lucy had asked him and Jack to look at her new house. She stood outside waiting and smiled when he was close, then hugged him lightly. "Thanks for coming to see my new home."

"Wouldn't miss seeing it," he said and turned to shake hands with Jack. "I'm glad you're here."

"I didn't invite Wynn and probably never will," she said. "Sorry. If I do, it'll be because of Olivia. I do like her."

"Don't apologize. Wynn caused you to feel that way. But I'm telling you, Olivia may bring about some changes for the better in our brother," Wade remarked and Lucy rolled her eyes.

"I'll believe that when I see it. I hear you're not coming to the family dinner tonight," she said as they walked to the front door of her house.

"No. I had already asked Ava to go to dinner with me

and I'm not joining the family instead, even if she is also invited, which she was."

"I don't know whether Wynn will really care or not. He does love an audience and I happen to know from someone else that he gave Olivia a huge diamond engagement ring last night and she accepted his offer of marriage. Can you imagine Wynn married?" Lucy asked, laughing while Jack shook his head.

"He's in love, believe it or not—the guy must be able to love someone besides himself," Jack said.

"Well, I know Olivia," Wade told them. "Our brother's met his match in her. Just watch. I predict you're not going to recognize Wynn. He will not be impersonating me ever again and I would bet the ranch on it."

"Wow," Lucy said, staring at Wade. "She can influence him that much? I can't imagine he wanted to marry her if she'll be calling the shots."

"She's perfect for him. She has old money. She's gorgeous. She can be fun. He'll find out what a strong, smart woman he married. I don't think he'll ever regret it, either. She'll keep him happy, but it'll be on her terms."

"Well, that is the best news possible," Lucy said. "I'm really impressed and I hope with all my heart you know what you're talking about. Our whole family will be happier if that's true about Olivia."

"Oh, damn right," Jack said. "That's fantastic news." He gave a whoop and laughed. "Ah, someone to finally boss Wynn. Even Dad couldn't."

"You watch how he changes," Wade said. "She has more money in her family than we do in ours and that will make Wynn think twice about crossing her. Trust me. I know Olivia. Believe me, our brother has met his match." He turned and looked at the front door of the house. "Well, let's see your new home, Luce." He stepped behind her as she unlocked the door and stepped inside.

The entryway opened into a great room that had a huge wood-burning fireplace, two walls of glass that overlooked a small yard, and beyond the backyard was a country-club golf course.

"Good view without having your own big yard," Wade remarked.

"I like your contemporary furniture," Jack added. Wade looked at the room. It was painted in a light shade, the furniture modern with open spaces and a polished hardwood floor. "Very nice," he said. He thought about what it would be like to have his own house with Ava and the idea held appeal.

"I like it and it should be relatively easy to care for," Wade said.

They looked at her office, which had a glass-and-metal desk, built-in file cabinets, a long glass table.

She showed them two bedroom suites and a third bedroom, a contemporary kitchen with floor-to-ceiling glass along one wall and light spilling into the room.

Finally she locked up as they left. "Thanks, guys, for your interest."

Wade hugged her lightly. "I'm glad to see your new home and I'm glad, too, that you're doing so well in the real-estate business. You're a young broker."

"I love it and because of my family, I have lots of good contacts."

"Have fun tonight," Wade said. "Both of you. And welcome Olivia into the family for me. I've already called her and told her I was sorry I wouldn't be there for dinner. She seems truly happy and she'll be a great addition to the family."

"I hope Wynn has half a dozen kids and they're all like

him," Jack said and then shrugged. "Well, maybe not if Olivia is a nice person. I wouldn't wish that on her." He let out a laugh. "This is one wedding I'm looking forward to. Hot dog!"

Wade laughed. "I'll second that." But as he drove away, all his thoughts shifted from his twin to Ava. He couldn't wait for tonight.

Excitement bubbled in Ava as she studied herself in the mirror. Her hair was parted in the center and fell straight on either side of her face. She wore a black sleeveless dinner dress with a deep V-neckline that revealed her curves, the skirt coming to midcalf. She wore high-heeled black pumps that showcased her legs and a diamond bracelet that echoed the small stones lining the neckline of her dress.

She was so eager for this evening with Wade that she nearly jumped when she heard a car door shut. She looked out the window to see Wade striding toward the house. In a charcoal Western-cut suit, a white dress shirt, gold cuff links in the French cuffs and black boots, he took her breath away. The breeze caught locks of his midnight hair and lifted a curl off his forehead. His injuries had healed and he was incredibly good-looking.

She wanted to run out and throw herself into his arms and kiss him while he carried her to bed. She also wanted an evening out with him because she had fun with him. It was exciting to be with him and she could look forward to coming back to share the rest of the night. She glanced around her house and her bedroom. She only had two bedrooms. Wade didn't seem to care what she had or didn't have. Then she forgot all about the house and furniture. Tomorrow she had already told him she would go with him to look at the new arena in Ft. Worth. She wanted to do that.

So for now, she simply wasn't going to worry about

the future or telling him goodbye. She was just going to enjoy being with him and hope she could hang on to her heart enough that she wouldn't be deeply in love with him.

He was the best-looking man she had ever known, she thought again as she rushed to open the door.

When she did, he had started to reach to ring the bell. Instead, he just wrapped his arm around her waist, stepped inside and closed the door behind them. He kissed her, an all-consuming kiss that made her feel as if she would melt in his arms.

Finally, he released her. "I promised you dinner and that's what we're going to do." Still, he didn't move toward the door, instead taking her in from head to toe. "You look gorgeous. You can eat and I'll watch you."

She laughed. "Don't be ridiculous."

"Come on. If we don't go now, we never will."

He took her hand and opened the front door. She set the alarm, picked up her small black purse and closed the door behind them, hearing the lock click.

He took her to a downtown private dinner club and she had a delicious steak dinner, but she could barely eat because all she could do was think about kissing him and making love again.

It would be a bittersweet night, but she wanted more time with him. And she couldn't keep telling herself it would only be one more time. Soon she knew she had to say goodbye and mean it or she might fall deeply in love with him. She would worry about that in another few days.

The early morning sun was bright in Fort Worth, the air crisp with a fresh smell. The city was still relatively quiet even though work-day traffic was picking up. She wore a frilly blue blouse, jeans and sandals and had her blond hair tied behind her head with a narrow blue silk scarf. She was happy to be with Wade, eager to see the arena.

When Wade and Ava drove into the Fort Worth parking lot there were already two pickups there. Two men stood talking, until he came into view and then they stopped talking and turned to watch him drive up beside their pickups. Dressed the same as he was, both had broad-brimmed hats, one gray hat and one black. Both men wore cowboy boots. They had on jeans and Western style long-sleeved cotton shirts.

"Are they your cousins?" she asked, certain they were.

"Yes, they are. Jake and Luke. I have other cousins, too."

"I feel like I shouldn't be here," Ava said. "I'll be the only woman here."

"Believe me, every man here will be glad you're here. Watch them try to get close to talk to you. It'll be nice for them to get to see the arena we donated money to build, but believe me, they will be more interested in talking to you. Luke, maybe just being polite."

"He's the one you said lost his family two years ago when his wife and baby were killed in a car wreck."

"Yep. He hasn't been the same since."

"I guess not. You couldn't ever get over that. That kind of loss makes a lot of other losses look insignificant. I'm surprised he can even get out of the house or that he wants to."

"You have to keep on living," Wade said. "Luke's a great guy. He's gotten very quiet, but you'll like him."

"I still don't think I should be here. This is a guy thing."

"No, it's not and we'll all enjoy your company and I'll do something special tonight to show you my appreciation that you came with me this morning. Believe me, I like it a thousand times better with you along." His gaze swept over her and she tingled as he smiled. After Wade parked, he grabbed his tan Stetson, put it on and stepped out to go around and open her door, taking her hand when she stepped down. She was aware of his warm hand closing lightly around hers. He looked handsome, strong and so appealing. He wore a navy shirt, jeans and boots. She was excited to be with him. She did feel slightly out of place, but she wanted to be with Wade and she wanted to see the arena. She knew it was a big thing for the city and the state and had cost millions, all donated by Wade and three of his cousins.

He extended his hand when he approached his cousins.

"Jake, it's good to see you," Wade said, shaking the hand of a man as tall as he was. They smiled as they shook.

"We were wondering when you were going to get here," Jake Reed kidded and they both laughed.

Wade turned to the other man and they shook hands. "Luke, it's good to see you. How're you doing?" he asked, looking intently at his cousin.

"Ava, I want you to meet my cousins. Cousins, meet Ava Carter. Ava, this is Jake Reed." He paused while Jake shook her hand and said hello.

"Ava, this is Luke Grayson. Luke meet Ava."

"I'm happy to meet you, Ava," Luke said, smiling warmly. "I'm glad you're with us this morning."

"Thank you," she said, smiling at Luke. "I'm glad to be here and get to see this new arena I've heard so much about. It'll be fantastic for the city and for the state."

"We hope so. The old arena was. We should get the grand tour," Luke said. He glanced at Wade. "How's Wynn?"

"Actually, maybe some slight changes. I think he'll stop impersonating me so that will be a relief." Wade glanced at Jake. "Jake, are you still fighting with your neighbor? Has either one of you taken the other to court this month?"

Jake shook his head. "Nope. We've had about eight months without a lawsuit or a big hassle. At least we don't shoot at each other like we've always been told the early day Reeds and Blakes did." As they all laughed, Ava was still looking over the new building.

"The facility looks wonderful from here," Ava stated and they all turned to look at the massive new building in a rich dark brown wood with glass along the center front running up to the roof. The first floor was the dark brown wood, but the upper floors had lots of glass to let in light.

"You'll like this arena," Wade said. He smiled at his cousins. "You two need to come to town more often and get off your ranches."

"As if you hang around Ft. Worth or Dallas," Jake drawled.

"It looks mighty good from out here," Luke said. "Course it should for what it cost."

"It's going to be great. It seats 11,360, there are 356 horse stalls. The building has a full service bar and an upper level cantina with catering," Wade said. "Our man, Bart Kingston will be here and he will tell you all about it," Wade said.

"You guys have seen it," Luke said. "It looks good from out here."

A black car turned into the lot and Wade paused. "Here comes Kingston. He's full of enthusiasm about this new arena. I think the arena board hired a very good guy for the job."

A tall, thin man with curly blond hair waved, parked and stepped out, hurrying toward them.

"Good morning. I got tied up in traffic held up by a

train. It's good to see you," he said, extending his hand to shake hands with Wade.

"This is my friend, Ava Carter," Wade said as Bart Kingston shook hands with Jake.

"Ava, this is Bart Kingston who will be in charge of this arena."

Wade turned slightly. "Bart, this is my cousin, Luke Grayson and another cousin, Jake Reed."

"I'm so glad to meet you both and thank you in person for your magnificent, generous donations that made this arena possible," he said as he shook hands with Luke and Jake. He smiled at all three men. "All of you, I want to thank you again for your very generous donations to build this new arena. It is a fabulous building and we are already booked for wonderful horse shows and events. It's a boon to Texas and to the city. Let's go look at it. You're in for a great tour."

"I'm looking forward to seeing the arena. I've heard about it," Luke said.

"Miss Carter, I'm glad you could join us. Let me lead the way and unlock the place." He headed for the massive front doors with carved horses in the wood. As he walked, he talked.

"We'll have the U.S. West Finals Rodeo this year. We've booked an Arabian horse show, an Appaloosa horse show, a Morgan show and Quarter horses. This is going to be big on horses. We have three rodeos booked. We'll have a National Teen Championship Rodeo this year." He paused to unlock big double doors. Luke, Jake and Wade all stepped forward to open the massive doors. Wade took Ava's arm lightly and she stepped inside a huge entry area with marble columns and a gleaming hardwood floor. She noticed an inviting faint smell of new wood.

"This is beautiful," she told Wade.

"It's great, but the big deal is the arena floor and the horse accommodations—their stalls, the facilities for taking care of them. There are cattle pens and a big barn behind this building even though we're in town," Bart said. "Just follow me. I hope you're already enjoying the first part of our tour," he said to Ava, who smiled as she nodded.

"I'm enjoying it very much. This is a fantastic building."

"We think so," Bart said. "It's beautiful, and it's going to be even more so when we get the paintings up and a few more things done. Now here is the arena." He led them out into the center of the arena and it was dazzling to her as she looked around.

"I don't know anything about what should be here, but this looks fabulous," she told Wade.

"It is fabulous," he said while she looked at all the box seats that looked luxurious and roomy with comfortable big cushioned chairs, tables to hold food. Beyond the box seats were cushioned seats that had ample leg room and wide aisles.

"The sound will be excellent," Bart said. He turned to point up. "We have a cantina with a full service bar, a seating capacity of 260, we have six concession stands in the building."

Wade stood beside her on her left and Jake was to her right. Jake looked over her head at Wade. "Looks like they spent the money well. This is going to be a great arena. Almost makes me wish I still was signed up for bull riding. Almost. I'm smart enough to know my limits."

"I agree," Wade answered as they looked around.

"Do you like rodeos or horse shows?" Jake asked Ava.

"Rodeos. I've never seen a horse show."

"What's your profession, Ava?" he asked.

"I'm an occupational therapist and I work for myself,

so I have what I want to do. I provide home care," she told him and he nodded.

Bart motioned to them to follow him as he continued talking while he moved on.

It was over an hour before they were through and had thanked Bart and finished talking to him. Wade held her arm lightly as they walked out with his cousins.

"It's going to be a great arena," Luke said.

"Yes, it is and we do have to pick a date for the grand opening, but the Board is going over the schedule and they have some new events to add, so we can't really get a date any time soon and we'll have to wait until Bart contacts us," Wade said and his cousins nodded.

"They still have to get their sign up with the arena name," Jake added. "It's going to be good when it's all ready. The Cal Brand Arena," he said. "The name is nice, but we'd all rather have Cal with us."

"Come go to lunch with us," Wade said.

"If Ava is going," Jake said, smiling at her and she smiled as she nodded.

"Yes, I am."

The cousins joined them and Ava found them to be fun and they were fun and happy being together. She felt a pang as she listened to them talk. Wade was so wonderful. The more she knew him, the more in love with him she was and it hurt. How could he not want his own children. He had wonderful cousins and they all had fun together. His children might be like his cousins instead of like his twin. Even though she heard what they were saying and laughed with them, she couldn't keep from thinking about Jake and how it was going to hurt to part with him. She had to do it and she knew it was going to break her heart. Today had just made her fall more deeply in love with Wade and his family.

She forced those thoughts out of her mind and then that evening when she was out with him, she had to try to bank the hurtful thoughts again. She enjoyed every moment of the wonderful dinner with him and every moment at his condo later and passionate, wild lovemaking all through the night and again in the morning.

When she woke, he wasn't beside her in the bed. But his scent lingered. She turned over and buried her face in his pillow, inhaling deeply and committing the scent to memory. Waking this morning, she knew what she had to tell Wade. And she knew that was their last night together.

Forcing herself out of bed, she showered and dressed in her black dress, the only clothes she had, and found him waiting in the kitchen with breakfast ready. Freshly showered, with damp hair, he was in jeans, a blue denim shirt and boots and he looked fantastic.

He walked up to kiss her, a long, sexy kiss that made her weak in the knees and wanting to hold back the words she knew she needed to say to him.

When she looked into his eyes, she saw him tilt his head slightly, a questioning expression on his face. She wondered if he knew what she had to say. But in a flash, his face changed and he pulled her close again. "You look gorgeous," he said, kissing her.

He'd fixed a delicious-looking breakfast of eggs, toast, strawberries, blueberries and hot coffee, but she couldn't eat more than a few bites. It was too difficult to get food down her tight throat.

He sat back. "I'd like to show you my ranch today. Will you go with me?"

She gazed at him and with all her heart she wanted to say yes. Telling her he had never asked a woman to the ranch before meant she was special to him. But was she special enough to change his views of life and his determination to stay single and childless?

She knew she should resist the invitation. But how could she when he had as much as said that she was more important to him than any other woman in his past? Yet they had no future unless he changed.

She argued with herself to go and take that chance on him changing. As she mulled it over, his new cell phone chimed. She knew he had bought a new phone to replace the one he lost in the flood. He answered, frowned and got up from the table to cross the kitchen. He spoke softly and she didn't care to eavesdrop, but she couldn't keep from hearing a few words and the concern-filled tone of his voice.

When the call ended, he turned back to her. One look at his face and she knew it was bad news.

Ten

"That was my brother Jack. Dad's in the hospital. They are putting in a pacemaker."

"Oh, Wade, I'm so sorry. I'll get a cab to get home. You go now to the hospital."

"No, I'll take you home, but I do want to go to the hospital now."

"Of course. But please let me call a cab."

He shook his head. "No. Your place is not out of the way," he said, raking his fingers through his damp hair.

"I'll get my purse," she said, rushing from the room, saying a silent prayer for Wade, his dad and his family. She hurt for Wade because it was obvious he was worried.

In minutes they were in the car and they made the drive in silence. At her house when he pulled up in the drive, she turned to him as she unbuckled her seatbelt. "Don't get out. Let me out and you go. Call me later, please, and let me know how he is. Call me if I can do anything. You and your family are in my prayers."

He smiled at her. "Thanks. I'll get back to you when I see how Dad is."

She stepped out quickly and walked to her front door as she heard him drive away. At the porch steps she looked over her shoulder to see his car disappear around the corner and she couldn't help the feeling that he was driving out of her life.

This heart attack would reaffirm his feelings on marriage and children, no doubt because he'd attribute it to the anxiety caused his dad by Wynn's antics. Wade would be far more determined than ever now to never marry, never have children. Sadness and hurt filled her.

No matter how much he wanted her to, she couldn't go to his ranch with him. She couldn't go out again with him. It was time to walk out of his life forever.

The pain was monumental, far worse than she thought it would be.

It was about two hours later when she had a call from him.

"Sorry to take you home so abruptly. My dad is doing okay so far and it wasn't as bad as the family thought at first. They've installed a pacemaker and said he will be here tomorrow for certain and then they'll see how he is. He's done well, thank heavens." Judging by how quickly the words tumbled from his lips, she knew he was stressed. And rightly so. She knew how much he loved his father. Before she had a chance to say anything, he asked her, "Will you go to dinner with me tonight? Nothing fancy, just go eat and be together. I don't want to be alone and I need to see you."

Her heart beat faster. She was hoping she didn't have to do this tonight, when he was so anxious about his father, but it couldn't go on. She had to say goodbye. "Yes,

I will," she said, hurting for him, and for herself, knowing what was ahead.

"Good. How's seven?"

"Seven is fine. Want me to meet you so you're free to go if you need to get back to the hospital?"

"No, he's doing well. I feel much better about him. I'll pick you up at seven and I can't wait."

"I can't, either," she said, though she could barely get her breath, her throat had tightened with so much emotion. If she was like this now, how would she get through tonight when she was with Wade?

"I'll see you then," he said. "Make it six thirty. That way we'll be through dinner sooner and we can go back to my condo if Dad is doing okay."

"That's fine," she said, hurting and wanting to be with him and have his strong arms around her.

"See you then," he said, adding a goodbye and he was gone.

After tonight he would be out of her life. She put her head in her hands and cried because that thought hurt so much. And that's when she realized that her biggest fear had come true. She had fallen in love with Wade, sooner than she had thought she would, more deeply than she had dreamed possible.

And tonight she had to say goodbye.

At six thirty that night, after she'd dressed for dinner in a red sweater and brown skirt, she wished she hadn't pulled her long, blond hair off her face in a low clip. Her heart hurt and knew the pain would just worsen when she saw Wade. How could she be this deeply in love with him in such a short time? She knew the answer to her own question. He was wonderful in so many ways. When his car came up the drive, she went to open the door.

He came up the porch steps two at a time and crossed the porch in long strides.

He wore jeans, another blue denim shirt and his boots. She opened the door and his gaze drifted slowly over her. "Whoa, look at you. You look better than any dinner possibly could," he said, stepping in and closing her door behind him. "It's been a hell of a day, but it's better now," he said, slipping his arms around her waist and leaning down to kiss her as he drew her into his embrace.

Her heart thudded and she forgot dinner and her resolution to tell him goodbye. She forgot everything except his mouth on hers and his arms around her and his hard, muscled body pressed against her.

She didn't know how long they kissed, but he picked her up and asked where the bedroom was and she pointed as she pulled his head down to kiss him.

He carried her to her bedroom and for the next hour he made love to her. Afterward, they lay in each other's arms as he lightly ran his hand through her hair, letting the locks slip and fall.

"You're so beautiful, Ava. I couldn't wait to be with you again, and dinner seemed insignificant, but if you'll throw on the same sexy outfit, I'll take you out to feed you."

"If you want something simple, I have burgers in the freezer. I can put them on the grill and we can eat here."

"Fine with me," he said as his arm tightened around her and he kissed her.

Soon they showered and dressed again.

"I'll get the grill and cook the patties if you want to do the other stuff," he offered.

"Sure," she said, taking him to her kitchen.

"Your house is nice," he said, glancing around a roomy kitchen with large windows that in the daytime would allow a lot of light on the yellow-and-white decor.

She showed him the grill on the patio that was under the limbs of big oaks. Through dinner she had no appetite for, they talked about his dad and the new rodeo arena being built.

"They'll have a big celebration when they have the grand opening next year. I'd like you to go with me."

She smiled at him, though his invitation brought her nothing but pain. "That's way too far in the future."

"So that's a no." It wasn't a question.

"It's a 'that's too far in the future,'" she said. Trying to defer further questions, she diverted his attention from the invitation. "Will you perform in the rodeo?"

"No, I won't. I haven't competed in a rodeo for several years. But I like to watch them." He looked down at her plate. "You're not eating. Is something wrong?"

She knew this was the time to tell him. "Let's go inside to talk. I'll get these dishes later."

"I can help right now and we'll be through in no time," he said, carrying their dishes to the sink.

She caught his wrist. "C'mon. Let's talk."

They walked into her family room, a room with lots of big windows that let in the east light and gave a view of her flowerbeds filled with roses that still bloomed.

She sat on the sofa and he sat facing her. "What's the problem, Ava?"

She hoped she could get through this without getting emotional. "Wade, it's been wonderful with you. I've enjoyed every minute. But this is one of those good things that has to come to an end. I don't want to get hurt again and this time I think I might get hurt worse than I did by my ex-fiancé."

"This is because of my views of marriage and children, isn't it?" he asked, looking intently at her.

"Yes, it is. You don't want marriage and you don't ever want kids. You're very firm about that."

"Yes, I am. I blame Wynn for Dad's heart problems. He's worried our dad to pieces."

"I imagine you feel more strongly about it after today and your dad being in the hospital for his heart."

"As a matter of fact, yes, I do," he said, looking somber.

"On the other hand, I want to marry and I want kids. I think I need to say goodbye and get out of your life now before I'm hopelessly in love with you and have to say these words and hurt way more. This isn't something where we can reach an easy compromise."

"No, it sure as hell is not." They gazed at each other in silence for minutes and she hurt more than she had thought she would. She stood to move away from him and his dark eyes that seemed to look right through her. She fought back tears and waited to talk until she could get her emotions under control.

She turned to face him. "I think we need to stop seeing each other completely. I can't take intimacy lightly. I've said what I need to say and tonight has to be goodbye." Clenching her teeth, she fought back tears.

He stood looking at her and after a moment he nodded. "I don't want to tell you goodbye, but I don't want to hurt you, either. I didn't want to hurt you this much."

"You let me know how you felt. I went out with you, anyway, so that's on me."

He said nothing for a moment, his eyes downcast, then slowly nodded his head. "I don't like it and I don't want to say goodbye, but I understand." His eyes met hers and she saw the anguish there that matched her own.

She watched as he turned to walk to the front door. Struggling more than ever to hold back tears, she went to the door right behind him. He opened the door, then turned to face her and he frowned.

"You've been wonderful and I've hurt you. I never wanted to do that."

"I know you didn't," she said. "It's no one's fault, Wade. We're just poles apart in our views of love and marriage and kids."

"We damn sure are, so this is best," he said gruffly. A muscle worked in his jaw and he looked tense. "You've seen my brother in action, so I hope you can understand where I'm coming from."

"Wade, I'll never understand. Family is the best part of life—love of a spouse, children, relatives. That's what I want with all my heart and I can't imagine deliberately cutting yourself out of a lifetime of joy just because of escapades by your twin. If you married, you're different from your dad. The woman you marry will be different from your mom. Any kids you have will have different influences in their lives. I know he's given your dad, your siblings and you grief, but that doesn't mean any child you would have would ever be like your twin." She looked away, clenching her fists because he'd made this a protracted goodbye and she couldn't hold back her tears. They spilled down her cheeks.

"Dammit, I've made you cry and that I never wanted to do." He reached out and cupped her face, wiping her tears with his thumbs. "I wish this wasn't goodbye, but you're a beautiful, sexy, smart woman and I know you'll get over me."

Would she? Right now she doubted it. He was a good man, accomplished, caring, so handsome and sexy. She knew now she should have walked away sooner before she got hurt. Before she fell in love.

Once again, she tried to get a grip on her emotions. She

shouldn't be feeling emotional over him. There had never been a declaration of love. They hadn't even known each other well enough or long enough to be deeply in love. She had to wipe away her tears and stand strong.

He tilted her face and looked at her. "I don't want it to be, but I guess this is goodbye," he said gruffly. He ran his fingers lightly on her cheek and lifted locks of her long hair away from her face. "You've been special," he said. "If you change your mind about the ranch or going out with me or just want to talk, you know how to reach me."

"I know." She brushed a kiss on his cheek and was going to turn and step away.

Instead his arm circled her waist and he held her tightly against him, putting his other arm around her and leaning over her, and he kissed her hard. A possessive, hot kiss that she knew she would remember forever. She shook in his arms and then she lost awareness of everything except his kiss, his mouth and tongue, his arms around her holding her tightly. While her heart pounded, she forgot all their problems because she was lost in the sexiest kiss of her life.

Finally he released her, both of them gasping for breath as they stared at each other.

"I'll never forget you," he said in a husky voice. Then he turned and went striding to his car.

She shut the door and stood there, unable to move. Tears streamed down her cheeks, but her silent, oh, so empty house reminded her why she had told him goodbye. She wanted a family man in her life, a man who loved babies and children, who would be a good dad.

It wasn't going to be Wade.

Putting her hands over her face, she cried because she was in love with him. So deeply in love with him. He was an ideal man in so many ways except the two most important things. She couldn't take life on his terms. He wouldn't take it on hers. Besides, he wasn't a man in love.

She had tried to minimize her feelings for him and what was happening in her life while he stayed at her cabin, but he had been too wonderful for her to guard her heart and resist him.

She sat in the nearest chair, placing her head in her hands, and let the tears fall freely.

"I love you, Wade Sterling," she whispered through her sobs. "I'll do everything in my power to get over you and forget you. I'm sure you'll forget me and you don't have to get over going out with me."

The worst part was, despite it all, she wanted to be in his bed, in his arms. She loved him. And she knew she would for the rest of her life.

Eleven

As Wade drove away, he hurt. He wanted Ava in his arms tonight. He wanted to make love to her all through the night and he wanted to take her home to his ranch tomorrow and show it all to her.

His feelings for her astounded him. She had gotten closer to his heart than any other woman he had ever known.

He still hadn't changed his mind about marriage and children, and he never would. But that didn't stop him from missing Ava.

All he could think about was Ava, holding her, kissing her. Fabulous kisses that set him on fire and made him tremble from head to toe. But he'd never kiss her again. Now he had only one thing he could do. Get over her.

He realized she was the first woman about whom he'd had to tell himself that. He had always been able to end affairs with his heart intact—Olivia, for instance—and he told himself this wouldn't really be any different. He wasn't in love and whatever he felt for Ava, he could get over it. He had to.

The next day he left for the Bar S Ranch. He'd stayed in town unusually long and now that he looked back on the days in Dallas, he realized part of it was getting back after the storm and seeing his family, but he realized he had stayed in Dallas because Ava was there.

He couldn't get her out of his thoughts as easily as he expected, and last night had been long and lonely. All night he'd told himself he'd get over her, that there would be someone else in his life, but right now, he missed her and he was going back to his ranch, where hard work would take his mind off her.

He drove another pickup he kept in Dallas to replace the one that went into the creek. It had been found and the sheriff called this morning about it. His wallet had been found,too, in the pickup, and they were sending the dried contents back to him. He'd have to get all new cards. The last thing he did before he left Dallas was place a large order of wild Alaskan salmon to be shipped to Gerald and Molly, as well as four cakes from a famous Texas bakery in a small town near Dallas, to show his gratitude. A similar order went to Sheriff Ellison.

He wished there was a way to show his gratitude to Ava, but their evening at the private dinner club would have to suffice. He wouldn't be seeing her again.

Opening the window of the pickup, he let the breeze blow away his memories of her.

At the ranch he poured himself into working outside. Sometimes he rode with the cowboys. He made repairs in the barn and he built a new dog house for a stray that had either wandered up or been dropped off.

The weekends were the worst and he tried to do enough

physical work that he would go to bed exhausted and sleep would finally overtake him.

He had some women friends who lived in the ranch area. On a weekend he'd called one of them and she could go out for dinner and a good time.

Or so he thought.

The first Saturday night he went out, he just thought about Ava and took his friend home early. At her doorstep she turned to look at him. "I had a fun time tonight, but I don't think you did. We've known each other a long time, Wade. I heard your dad has been in the hospital and I thought he was doing fine. Is that what's worrying you?"

"No, Nan," he said, smiling at the redhead he'd known for years. She was a good friend. "I've just had things in my life that didn't go the way I wanted."

She laughed and punched his shoulder lightly, leaning closer to stare at him. "Are you in love with someone who walked out? It had to happen someday, even to you."

He laughed. "I don't think so. I'm not in love and I'm not a marrying man and you know that."

"I know that, but your heart might not. It's hard to feel sorry for you, though, because you're the one who breaks hearts and you've never had a clue what that feels like."

He shook his head as he smiled. "Okay, enough on that subject. Sorry if I wasn't my best tonight."

She kissed his cheek. "I never thought I'd see this day come. Buddy, you're in love and you don't even know it, or else you don't want to be. Well, you'll get over it like we all do. Thanks for tonight. See you around, my friend." She laughed as she went in her house and shut the door.

He walked back to his pickup and drove to the ranch. A big furry dog met him when he stepped inside the fence. "Hi, Buster," he said, scratching the dog's back. "Want to go down with the cowboys or come in with me?" He held the gate open. The dog sat and looked up at him. Wade jerked his head and walked toward his house, letting the dog in with him.

The big ranch house was empty, and as he walked through it, Buster his only companion, he envisioned Ava here. Sitting on the sofa in her skintight jeans and heels, her feminine touches all around the room. He couldn't stop thinking about her, wondering what she was doing. Was she thinking about him, or seeing some other guy already? He couldn't count the number of times each week he'd pulled out his phone and had to force himself not to call her.

He stalked into the kitchen, the noise of his boot heels the only sound in the house. In the cavernous void, he thought he heard the echo of Nan's remarks. *You're the one who breaks hearts and you've never had a clue what that feels like.*

Nan was right about that. He'd always been able to say goodbye. But this time was different. This was the first time in his life he really missed someone. Not only did he hurt, but he also couldn't concentrate on work, which had never happened to him.

He'd worked long hours all week, coming in when it got dark and working in the barn or in his office until one or two in the morning. He hadn't slept well and he had no appetite at all.

He felt a tightening in his gut. Could Nan be right in her other assertion? Was he in love with Ava?

That thought shook him to the core.

"Damn," he said. He sat in a kitchen chair and scratched Buster's back, and groaned. How could she have gotten under his skin in such a short time? Especially when their views of life, love and the future were on opposite ends of the spectrum. He raked a hand through his hair and expelled a tight breath. He didn't know the answer to that, but he knew one thing for sure. If he had fallen in love, he'd get over it soon.

He pushed back the chair. "Time to work out, Buster. You want to come run on the treadmill? I tried to get her to come visit us, but she wouldn't. You'd like her and I'll bet she would like you. Damn, I miss her."

He left the room to go to his gym and work out until he could shake Ava out of his thoughts.

On a Sunday afternoon weeks later, when he was sitting at the table nursing a cup of coffee, one of the men called to tell him his brother Wynn just passed through the front gates. Wade thanked him and got his hat to walk out to the porch to wait. Wynn never came to the Bar S; he despised ranching, horses and everything about either one. Wade couldn't imagine why he was coming now. He wasn't going to try to guess. He sat in a white wooden rocking chair, put his feet on the rail and sat back to wait. Then Wade thought about their dad. Cold fear gripped him that something else had happened to his dad's heart.

He saw the plume of dust and then the bright red sports car speeding toward the house. Wynn hadn't changed since he was a teenager; he still liked fast cars. The car skidded to a stop, sending up a cloud of dust. Wynn didn't get out until the dust settled. He walked around the car and headed for the porch. His turquoise dress shirt was open at the throat and he didn't wear a tie. He had on charcoal slacks and loafers.

Wade's curiosity grew and so did his worry about his dad because Wynn definitely didn't look angry, he looked worried. Even if it was Dad, Wynn would have just called, he told himself, unless it was really terrible. Fear gripped him. "Is Dad okay?" he asked.

"As far as I know. That's not why I'm here."

Wade pushed out the breath he'd been holding, relieved. At least his dad was okay…but what did Wynn want?

"You must have an important reason to drive all the way out here," Wade said, assessing his brother. A muscle worked in Wynn's jaw and some emotion flashed in his dark eyes, but there was a hesitancy in his twin that Wade had never seen. Usually Wynn made his anger clear to all. Or his fear. Or his pleasure. He wasn't a subtle person and Wade's curiosity grew.

"Well, have a seat. We don't have to stand to talk," Wade said, sitting back in the rocker and turning it so he would face Wynn, who sat in another big rocker. Wynn sat on the edge of the seat and he looked nervous.

"You might as well say it," Wynn said. "You know I'm a dad."

"Oh, yes, I do," he said, briefly startled that the long-ago phone conversation was the reason for Wade's appearance.

"You didn't tell Violet it was you she was talking to that day."

"Violet? I did tell her, but she accused me of lying and we never got back to it. It was obvious you didn't tell her you're a twin, so after that first try I didn't, either."

They sat staring at each other and with every second, Wade became more and more puzzled because Wynn wasn't acting in his customary manner.

"You told Violet the check was in the mail and that's exactly what I would have told her because it was. That's how I found out you talked to her. She told me it was a good thing I wasn't lying when I said the check was in the mail."

"I was in shock and that sounded like what you'd say."

Wynn nodded, apparently accepting Wade's answer. He looked away for a moment, eyeing something in the distance, his hands toying with a rope that had been looped over the rocker.

Wade tilted his head, his curiosity growing. "You drove all the way out here for something. What's eating you?"

His brother finally looked at him. "You didn't tell the folks that they're grandparents. You haven't told anyone in the family. Why?"

Wade shrugged. "It's your secret and when I thought about it, I figured you were doing what you thought was best. I figured it might be better for Mom and Dad if they didn't know about this baby. It's really your call."

"I can't understand you. There was your chance for revenge for all the grief I've given you over the years. Real revenge. This could have wrecked my engagement to Olivia if you'd gone about it in certain ways."

"I'll be damned. You can't understand trying to do the right thing or the nice thing," Wade said, shocked that Wynn actually was puzzled why someone wouldn't do him harm. "Why in the hell would I want to deliberately hurt you? Damn, Wynn, to my way of thinking, life is a whole lot better and you have more friends being nice to people. You ought to try it sometime." He shook his head as Wynn continued to stare at him, obviously confused. "You're really at a loss about this, aren't you?"

"I know I've made you mad plenty of times. Absolutely furious."

"Yes, you have. That doesn't mean I'd enjoy doing that to you. I don't get a thrill out of being mean and I don't seek revenge, either."

Wynn dropped the rope and sat back, but he said nothing. He just looked at his brother.

"You know, Wynn, for the first time in my life, I feel sorry for you. You don't even know what you're missing." They stared at each other and Wade thought if a creature had appeared from outer space, he wouldn't have been any more puzzled. But this was his blood brother; he had to try to reach him.

"You know, Wynn, as toddlers and little kids we fought constantly and we really never outgrew that, which is sad. You and I should be brothers, in the deepest sense of the word.

"You're my twin and we don't understand each other or like each other. We can't even sit out here and enjoy a cup of coffee together before you go. We have no common ground and that's sad."

"I took Olivia from you. She's the perfect woman— every man's dream. You're not angry over that?"

Wade stared at him a moment in silence as he gave a slow shake of his head. "No, Wynn. Olivia's a wonderful woman, but she's better suited to you." They sat quietly a moment. "You know, it's not too late to become real brothers. Do you want a cup of coffee?"

Wynn's eyes widened with surprise and he tilted his head as he stared at Wade. "You're serious, aren't you?"

"Yeah, I am. If Lucy was here, or Jack, I'd make that offer to them and we'd sit and chat. I would with Mom or Dad, too. The rest of us all enjoy each other's company and like to be together. That's family at its best. It's not too late for us to become real brothers."

Wynn blinked and nodded. "I suppose I could try… Okay, we'll have a cup of coffee together."

"Just sit there. I have some brewed. I'll bring it out."

He left, wondering if they could tolerate each other for ten more minutes. He was back with mugs on a tray that also held cream and sugar, spoons and napkins. He set the tray on a table between them.

"Well, this is a first," Wynn remarked with sarcasm in his voice.

"Yeah. We might as well give it a try."

Wynn picked up his mug and took a sip. "I guess I should say thank you because it's a relief to me that you'll keep my secret."

"Sure, Wynn," Wade replied. "You might try life my way sometime," he said, "and I don't mean by trying to pass yourself off as me."

"Olivia made me promise I wouldn't do that anymore," Wynn said, sounding more like himself and making Wade smile as he shook his head.

"She'll learn." Wade leaned forward and held out a hand to his brother. "I think it's wonderful that you and Olivia are in love. I truly wish you the best."

"You mean that, don't you?"

"Yes, I do. I'm sincere about everything I've said to you."

Wynn accepted the proffered hand and shook it.

Wade smiled as he gave a playful punch to his brother's shoulder. "I can't believe my twin is getting married."

Married... At the mention of the word, his thoughts went to Ava. It'd been weeks, but still memories of her slammed into him. He couldn't seem to forget her.

Some men did—the guy that walked out on her. But he couldn't.

Wade drew a deep breath. He remembered how his heart beat faster and his whole body responded to just the sight of her. Her blue eyes melted him and if he saw her in the distance or across a room, desire consumed him. There was no way on earth he could see her the way he saw other women. She was gorgeous, special, unique. But she'd never be his, not the way Olivia would soon be Wynn's.

His brother's words drew him out of his reverie. "I may have to try life your way. I know how to act the part. Maybe I should try to live the part and see if I'm happier."

"You don't have to try to be like me," Wade said, focusing on Wynn again. "Just be considerate of your family and others. I think you'll find you have more people who like you. Life ought to be better. Start with your family and be nicer to them. As I just said, they bear the brunt of your anger and deceptions."

"They do. Anybody else would retaliate. Thanks again about the baby. I'll send her money until she's grown and educated. I'll do what's right."

"You're sure you don't want Mom and Dad to know their grandchild?"

"I'm sure. It's a baby girl, but no, I don't. Mom and Dad would have nothing in common with the baby's mother."

"They would have a baby in common, Wynn."

He frowned and shook his head. They sipped coffee and sat in silence for a few minutes, Wynn deep in thought. "I'll think about it, Wade."

"Good. You won't regret letting them know their grandchild. I feel certain about that."

"I never looked at it that way. I didn't think they'd be happy about the mother."

"They might not, but I'll bet they'll love your baby. They might be a good influence on the mother."

"Wow. Maybe I will. You sound very positive."

"I am. It's your baby and their first grandchild. They will be happy. I know Mom and Dad."

"Well, maybe I should." He was silent for a few minutes. "I asked Mom why she married Dad—I'll still call him dad," Wynn said finally.

"I'm glad because in every way except blood, he's been our dad, and to me, he's our only dad. Why did she marry him?"

"She said she was single, pregnant, didn't have money to raise a child by herself and didn't want to. Dad started dating her and in his own quiet way, he loved her and asked her to marry him, so she did, but she's never told him the truth about getting pregnant. And she said that he was such a good man that it didn't take her long to fall in love with him, too. She said she realized she had found the best father for her twins."

Wynn set down his coffee mug and leaned forward. His eyes met Wade's and there was sincerity shining there. "Wade, that woman you had at the folks' house—Ava. She must have been important to you. In fact, if I'm not mistaken, I think you're in love with her."

"I am."

The words fell out of his mouth before he could even think, shocking the hell out of him. But he wouldn't retract them. He couldn't. Heaven help him, but there was no denying the truth. He was totally, irrevocably in love with Ava Carter.

"Then you need to go get her."

There, Wade took exception. No way could he just go back to Dallas and claim the woman he loved.

"Hell, I didn't do it the conventional way, but I went after the woman I wanted," Wynn said with a grin. "And now I'm getting married. It still amazes me, but I love Olivia. I can't imagine being a dad—even though technically I am one. But the thought of actually possibly raising a child, being a real dad day in and day out, scares me."

"Why?" Wade asked, curious what Wynn would fear.

"I don't know little kids. I wasn't good to Jack. I thought he was a nuisance."

"I imagine brothers are different than sons," Wade remarked, unable to imagine Wynn as a parent with real responsibilities.

Wynn stood. "I guess I'll get going." He put his coffee cup on the tray and turned to Wade. "Thanks again for keeping my secret."

Wade stood. "Sure, Wynn."

"Well, we got through a cup of coffee together, maybe we can get through lunch together sometime."

Wade nodded. "I'm willing to try. I'll see you in town in about a week. Meanwhile, take my advice and try being nicer to the family and see what happens. After all, family is the most important part of life."

Wynn nodded.

"I'll call you about lunch next week."

"Sure." Wynn went down the porch steps and walked to his car. Wade watched him go and wondered if he would really change.

Could he marry and have kids?

He'd just told Wynn that family was the most important thing—family meant a wife and kids. And love between a man and a woman. He loved Ava. He faced that now, full on. He knew why he'd been living with hurt and loneliness, missing her for the last three weeks. He was in love with her. Deeply in love. Was it enough to marry and have kids? he asked himself again.

Kids with Ava… Right now that sounded good to him. Being a dad. He couldn't imagine himself being a father unless it was with her.

He'd knew he'd have to accept children if he wanted her in his life. After all, she had shut him out and said goodbye in order to avoid heartbreak months or years down the road when they separated. Well, there was a better way to guard against getting another broken heart and his way was a lot better than her way.

He pulled out his phone to call Ava and tell her he was coming to see her.

Twelve

Wade was coming over.

After three weeks, she was surprised he'd called, and she was still confused. He never gave a reason, just said he was coming. She wouldn't get her hopes up—after all, she was sure nothing had changed. She couldn't imagine that he had changed one tiny bit in his views. He was too set in them, and when his dad had had the last heart episode, Wade had become even more adamant that he didn't want to marry and have children.

She had gone back to work in Dallas as soon as she got home, and tried to keep as busy as possible because it helped to have less moments to herself, lonely moments when she remembered being in his arms, being with him. Nothing could stop her missing him and his vitality, his passionate lovemaking, his flirting. She missed him terribly and she loved him deeply, but she still would leave him the same way again. She might not ever love a man to the extent that she loved Wade, but she couldn't be in a relationship based on anything less than total commitment. And she would never give up her desire to marry and have children.

No matter the reason, he was coming to see her and she knew it wouldn't work out.

Even so, she had carefully applied makeup, put on a short-sleeved red dress with a V-neck and a full skirt that fell in folds below her waist. Her hair was tied back at her nape with a sheer red scarf and she had matching high-heeled pumps.

When she heard his car, she couldn't keep from going to the door. Her heartbeat raced. She tried to calm herself down because he could be coming for some ordinary reason and just be here minutes. When he rang the bell, she opened the door and her heart thudded.

He looked so incredibly handsome, so absolutely wonderful, dressed in a navy Western-cut suit, black boots and a white dress shirt with his usual French cuffs with gold cuff links. She wondered if she was going to love him the rest of her life and never marry because all men would pale in comparison. She wanted to throw herself into his arms and kiss him. Instead, she took a deep breath and, in a surprisingly modulated voice despite her pounding heart, said hello.

He looked at her. "Can I come in?"

"Oh," she gasped. She hadn't realized she was just standing there staring while she was fighting throwing herself into his arms. "Come in."

Smiling, curiosity in his eyes, he stepped inside, closed the door and turned to her. "You look gorgeous."

"Thank you. Come in and sit down," she said, walking into her front room. He followed and she turned to face him. "Have a seat."

"Thanks," he said, but he kept looking at her and didn't move. "I've missed you, Ava," he said.

"I've missed you, too." Her heart started drumming and she wondered what he had in mind. Why was he here? Why was he saying these things to her when he knew he was breaking her heart?

"Ava, I've been miserable without seeing you," he said so softly, she could barely hear him.

He took a step closer. "I don't know where to start. I've missed you. I love you. I'm miserable without you. You're the most important person in the whole world to me."

Her heart pounded but she couldn't give in to him again, no matter how much she wanted to echo his words. Not when their relationship had no future. She just stood there looking at him, seeing the desire in his eyes.

He stepped forward to wrap his arms around her. His voice was shaky when he spoke again. "I love you, Ava. I want to marry you. We can have kids. If you're their mother, they'll have to be wonderful."

Was she imagining this? For the past several weeks she'd dreamed every night that he'd show up at her door and say these things to her.

"Ava, did you hear me?" He gripped her arms tighter and it was like a wake-up call.

Her heart surged.

"Do you mean that? You really want kids?" She twisted away slightly to look up at him. Amazement shook her, as well as hope.

"I want whatever makes you happy," he said. "If you want kids, then I want kids."

"You're sure?" she asked, her heart pounding as she held her breath. "That's something you have to be sure about."

"I'm sure. I don't want to live alone or live the way I have been without you. It was pure hell. We'll have all the kids you want. I have to have you in my life. Kids and all. Will you marry me?"

She couldn't keep from crying as he was talking and holding her. "I've missed you and I love you and yes, yes, I'll marry you," she said.

He leaned back to look at her and wiped her tears. "Why are you crying? We can have kids. I want to marry you."

He tightened his arms, leaned over her to kiss her and she knew that the love of her life was holding her tightly, kissing her, going to marry her and they would have the family she had dreamed about.

"I'm so happy," she said, sobbing with relief and joy and amazement as she clung to him and kissed him.

She felt bereft when he stepped out of her embrace and went down on one knee. He dug something out of his pocket and looked up at her. "I love you, Ava Carter. I love you with all my heart. I can't live without you. Marry me and let's have all the babies you want. Ava, will you marry me?"

She was crying and laughing at the same time and she couldn't believe what he was saying, but she didn't doubt that he meant every word. Her heart pounded with joy. "You'll be okay with it if I want six kids?"

"I'll be overjoyed because I'll be with you. I love you, my darling, and I'll ask you again, will you marry me?"

"Yes, I'll marry you. I love you," she exclaimed.

He held out a box wrapped in white paper and tied with a pink bow. She took it and opened it, her heart drumming. She gasped and looked at him and then back at a gorgeous, huge diamond set in a gold band. "This is beautiful."

He stood and took the ring from her to slip it on her finger. She looked up into his dark eyes and she smiled. "I've missed you so."

"Not anywhere like I've missed you. I've been miserable. I was so scared I'd lost you forever. I love you with all my heart and want you in my life, in my arms always." He tightened his arms around her.

She looked down at her ring, then back up at him. "I've dreamed of this moment, I can't tell you how many times, but I never expected you to change your opinions on marriage and children. Why, Wade?"

"A man can change. Olivia has changed my brother, and you've changed me." He told her about Wynn's visit to the ranch and how he seemed like a different man when he left the Bar S. "I realize there's truth to what you've been saying all along. Family is the most important thing. And our kids will be good people, just like you. I love you, Ava, and I'll never tire of calling you my wife and the mother of my children."

He kissed her then, a long, passionate kiss that made her feel totally wanted and loved. She clung to him, her heart pounding with joy, with love for him, with happiness for their future.

"I have one request," she said when she could manage to speak. "I want a wedding soon."

He smiled. "We won't interfere with the date Wynn and Olivia have picked—December twentieth—but I think we can make it a quick wedding. And I'll take you anywhere you'd like to go for a honeymoon."

"How about a wedding in early November?"

"That's fine with me." He chuckled. "That was easy."

"It's easy for me to pick a date because I don't have family to worry about."

"You do now, Ava." He picked her up in his arms, kissed her and carried her to her bedroom.

She clung to him as they kissed. He stood her on her feet and held her tightly. She opened her eyes to look at him and at her ring that glittered in the soft light. "Ah, I love you and you've made me the happiest woman on earth."

He laughed. "Have you stopped to think a minute about the future? Can you live on a ranch?"

"If it's with you, yes, I can. I might get that teaching certificate because I'll bet there's a little country school somewhere near your ranch where I could teach."

"As a matter of fact, there is. There's a little town with a school. Great idea."

"I'll keep my place near Persimmon for a retreat. A retreat that maybe we can fill with kids," she said, smiling at him.

He pulled her close. "I can't wait to show you the Bar S."

"Do you have a guest house?" she asked as he showered kisses on her ear and neck and nape while his hands moved over her.

"Yes, I have three guest houses."

"I want to invite Gerald and Molly to visit us."

"You can have anybody you want," he whispered and leaned back to look at her. "You're beautiful and I love you and you really have made me the happiest man on earth now."

"Wait until we have a family. You'll really know happiness then. It'll be good, Wade, I promise."

He laughed. "You can't promise that. There are no guarantees in life like that."

"Want to bet? Watch me. You'll be happy."

He laughed again until she pulled his head down to kiss him. She held him tightly while her heart pounded with joy. She would have the love of her life and she would have a family.

* * * * *

SIN CITY
SEDUCTION

ZURI DAY

Life is an adventure,
often full of surprises,

Between the star-filled nights
and inspiring sunrises.

Ironic that those experiences
that are our hardest tests,

Are often the ones that lead us
into being our absolute best.

One

Clear skies. Light breeze. Bright sun. Firm snow. Noah Breedlove stood near the summit of the mountain and felt he was on top of the world. He was one opponent and a council vote away from closing his first solo business deal in a city that detractors had deemed off-limits to CANN International. Had they missed the meaning behind the company name, to have the skill, power or ability to do anything? That Breedloves could and did, every single day? Just as he'd vanquished almost every obstacle in the boardroom, all save that one lonely holdout, he now stood ready to conquer this legendary mountain in Manning Valley, two hours away from Salt Lake City. Hopefully the adventuresome trip down the mountain would clear his head and help ease the stress he felt at trying to close the biggest deal he'd ever done.

"You ready?"

Noah looked at Cole, the friend who'd introduced him to skiing, with a trademark Breedlove smile—twinkling eyes, winking dimple, sparkling teeth.

"Born that way."

"I know you're a pro, bro, but be careful," Cole said. "The speed of this mountain has felled lesser men."

Noah surveyed the terrain marked on maps by a double black diamond, a designation given to a resort's toughest runs. Narrow slopes, wicked turns and a virtual obstacle course of tall pines and craggy rocks loomed before him. Noah wasn't worried. He might look like a daredevil but really he wasn't. It was confidence in skill level and preparation that fueled his desire. Okay, maybe a tiny part of it was due to the thrill. If life weren't dangerous, it wouldn't be fun.

They pushed off, straight down the chute. Noah tucked his poles and flew like the wind. He slid around trees and jumped over rocks, his lithe, toned body soaring before landing with ease. Life was perfect! Couldn't be better!

They didn't see the thin white rope until right up on it. Cole managed to ski around it. Noah jumped it but his ski caught, causing a forty-foot tumble. His world went black.

Damaris Glen looked up as a bustle of activity interrupted an otherwise quiet evening. She was already halfway out of her chair when her assistant nurse and newfound friend, Wendy, stuck her head through the office door.

"What do we have?" Damaris asked, quickly checking for her stethoscope and stuffing a notepad and pen in her pocket as they sped toward the emergency department's lobby.

"Skiing accident. EMT's en route."

"How serious?"

"The patient's unconscious." Wendy's voice was casual, but her cornflower blue eyes conveyed a concern that was anything but.

"Dr. Noble?"

"Left an hour ago," Wendy continued at Damaris's questioning glance. She shrugged. "Slow night. He's on his way back now."

Damaris's heartbeat quickened. This was the first week not shadowing Ella, her supervisor. Her first night in charge of the team. Though she'd been extensively trained in how to receive and perform the intake and treatment on trauma patients, it was something nurses did only when a doctor wasn't present. Or on call. Like tonight. "Rarely happens," was Ella's answer when Damaris had presented this very scenario. Meanwhile "rarely" lay on a stretcher with an EMT beside him.

A calm settled around her shoulders as Damaris approached. She made eye contact with the EMT and gave a quick nod, but her first words were to the man lying prone on the gurney.

"Hello, are you awake? Can you hear me?" She placed a palm on his forehead, her other thumb on a wrist, taking his pulse. She was every inch the professional, but still, it registered that beneath the cuts and bruises was a very handsome man. Barely noted. Not acknowledged. Doing such was hardly a part of her job.

She looked at the EMT. "Has he spoken at all?"

The woman shook her head. "All of what we obtained came from the friend skiing with him. It's all here." She held out the report containing information gathered en route.

Damaris scanned the paper. "Vitals?"

"Stabilized," the EMT said.

"Do we know how the accident happened?"

"The friend who called 911 said a line of some kind was obstructing the trail, too thin to see until they were right up on it. He was far enough behind our guy here to clear the obstruction, once he knew it was there."

"Where is this friend?"

An obviously distraught man came around the corner and rushed toward them. "Is he awake? Noah!" He stepped toward the stretcher.

Damaris placed a hand on his shoulder as she spoke to the EMT. "We'll take it from here. Thanks."

She turned back to the harried-looking man still wearing skiwear and boots. "Are you the friend who called for help?"

He nodded.

"What's your name?"

"Cole." His voice crackled with emotion as he looked over her shoulder. "Is he going to be okay?"

"He's stabilized and we're doing all we can. The doctor

is on his way. I know this is hard but, please, try to calm down. We'll need you to tell the doctor everything you can remember," she continued, her voice low and soothing.

Cole nodded. "His name is Noah. Everything happened so fast! I called his family and they're on their way but we live in Nevada so it's going to take a while for them to get here. I'm the one who got him into skiing and if anything happens..."

Working as a trauma nurse was understandably difficult and dealing with the patients' loved ones was one of the hardest parts.

"We're going to do everything we can to help... Noah... right?"

"Yeah."

Damaris watched the distraught man gain control of his emotions, almost angrily swiping tears from his face. She gave his arm a comforting squeeze.

The sliding glass doors opened. A blast of cold air lifted the curls from Damaris's face. "Dr. Noble."

A thin man with wire-rimmed glasses and a friendly face walked over, his eyes on the stretcher. "Any change?"

Damaris quickly updated the doctor. The friend, Cole, now calmer, filled in the blanks not known by the EMT.

Dr. Noble turned to Damaris. "We need a CAT scan and a complete set of X-rays stat."

"Right away, Doctor."

The doctor left to check on other patients. Within minutes a technician arrived. Damaris directed the move to another room, where the patient was transferred to a trauma X-ray stretcher so that his spine could be viewed and analyzed while lying down. Damaris stayed beside the man she now knew as Noah, explaining procedures and offering encouragement even though he'd not moved. The technicians finished their work. Cole left to contact the family and give them an update. Damaris stayed, monitored his vitals and kept talking.

"Some believe that when our body shuts down and our mind closes out the rest of the world, it is so the body can protect itself, take an assessment of the situation and begin healing."

She watched his face for a twitch, a flutter, any movement to indicate he may have heard her. Nothing. Again, she was struck by the sharp, arresting features discernible beneath the bruising and scars. As she took a cursory examination of these facial wounds, she felt a stirring in her heart for this stranger that seeped into her soul, a stake so immediately and deeply invested in his recovery that it scared her. *I'm a caring, compassionate nurse, passionate about healing.* Healing, not heartthrobs, she told herself. Of course she'd care. It was her empathetic nature and when it came to the welfare of her patients she'd always felt this way. Hadn't she? Not really, but she forced herself to ignore this fact. There was no point in developing feelings for someone outside her faith. She'd done that once before and it had cost her. Big-time. She was still weighed down by the guilt.

"Noah, your friend Cole has contacted your parents. I'm sure they're on their way. My name is Damaris but that's a mouthful so most people call me Dee. I'm the lead nurse this shift and am here to keep an eye on you until the doctor returns and your family arrives. I hope you won't mind that I say a little prayer that by the time they get here, you will have regained consciousness."

Like many citizens of the Beehive State, religion was a central part of Damaris's family and very important to her. She believed in Western medicine and its power to heal, but felt it didn't hurt to add a little faith. Closing her eyes, she whispered a quick prayer. A strong sensation caused her to open them before she'd said amen. Staring back at her was the most beautiful pair of eyes she'd ever seen.

"You're awake."

She watched him swallow, attempting to talk.

"Do you remember what happened?"

He shook his head.

"You were skiing with your friend Cole and took a bad fall," she said, answering the question in his eyes as she reached his bedside and rang the nurses' station. "Your mouth is probably dry and you may be thirsty but I'm afraid I can't offer you water right now."

The intercom dinged. "Yes?"

"Wendy, can you tell the doctor that our patient is awake?"

"Sure."

Damaris returned her attention to Noah. "The doctor will be here shortly."

She noted that along with the large cuts on his forehead and chin, his lips were dry and cracked. "You've got a couple nasty cuts," she continued, crossing over to a set of drawers and retrieving several items. "I'll clean them out and apply medication that I hope will make them feel a little better."

He watched her every move. She knew it. Not because she possessed eyes in the back of her head, as her mom did, but because the intensity in those dark brown orbs felt like lasers at her back. No doubt he was in pain, probably confused, too. Still, he hadn't asked a question. Hadn't made a sound. Shock? Calm personality? Who knew? She'd be distraught.

After gathering cotton swabs, astringent and other medications, and a towel, Damaris filled a small paper cup with water and placed everything on a steel tray that she wheeled next to the bed. She dabbed a corner of the towel into the water.

"This will help the dryness a bit."

She reached toward his mouth. His hand shot up. The move was quick, unexpected. His eyes, searching, lips, moving, trying to talk.

"Is there pain?" Damaris asked.

He shook his head.

"Thirsty? Anxious?"

No on both counts.

She watched as he flicked his tongue against the lips she would have dampened, cleared his throat and uttered his first words since entering the hospital.

"I can't move my legs."

Damaris heard a mix of fear, panic and disbelief wrapped around those five words. She tried to address all three, simultaneously. "It's okay. Try to—"

"Nothing's okay. Didn't you hear me?" he continued, hoarseness coating the words he forced out with effort. "My legs. I can't move them."

"I'm sorry. What I meant was—"

"I hear we have an awakened patient," Dr. Noble said as he entered the room. "I'm Dr. Noble. You took quite a fall, young man. We're going to do our best to get you back up and running, okay?"

Damaris was grateful for backup. She moved the tray away from the bed so that the doctor could move freely around the X-ray stretcher, then hurried back to his side, ready to assist.

"My legs, Doctor. I've been trying to lift them, change positions, but nothing seems to work. I can't really feel them, either."

"There can be many reasons for that." Much as was Damaris's manner, Dr. Noble calmly chatted as he worked, examining the image on the X-ray screen before folding back the sheet from Noah's lower legs. "As I stated, you took a mean tumble. Your body is probably in shock, a state where the mind's call and the body's response have a hard time singing together, if you know what I mean."

A lover of music no matter the genre, Damaris understood the doctor's metaphor. She smiled encouragingly at Noah, who'd shifted those laser beams he had for eyes in her direction. His expression remained serious, almost haunting. Somehow she understood that, too.

She checked her watch. "Doctor, should I have another nurse make my rounds?"

"I think we're good here," he replied with a nod. "I'm going to perform a few tests and then we'll get you down for a CAT scan. All right?"

Noah nodded.

"You're in good hands," she told Noah, walking toward the door.

"You sure are," Dr. Noble agreed. "Dee is one of the best nurses in the building."

She smirked at the doctor, gave her silent, observant patient a wave and headed back to the wing she was in charge of. Checking in with the other patients, Damaris was efficient and friendly, giving them her undivided attention as best she could. But much as Noah seemed to be experiencing, and as the doctor described, her call and response weren't keeping the same tune. Her body went from room to room performing as needed. A part of her mind, however, remained back in the room with the accident victim who possessed a steely demeanor in the face of crisis, and a pair of intensely beautiful eyes.

Two

Images played across his mind like a movie reel. Snatches of moments from earlier that day. The flight into Salt Lake City. Meeting with council members and others to discuss his ambitious plans for opening the first legal casino in a no-gambling state. Climbing into Cole's rental car for the two-hour drive to Daredevil Mountain, sometimes called Death Mountain because fatal accidents had occurred on the extreme slope. Casual chitchat and laughter as they laced on their skis. Boarding a lift and zooming straight to the top. The whoosh of the wind as he pushed off from the ledge. Then…waking up and feeling disconcerted, an angel with curly hair and bright eyes hovering over his bed. What was her name? Delores? Naturally beautiful, at least in his mind. So much so she appeared otherworldly, made him consider the notion that heaven was real. He shifted, or tried to, and remembered something else, something he'd rather not think about. He couldn't move his legs. Which meant he couldn't walk. Could the angel he remembered perform miracles and make his legs work again?

A commotion in the hallway caught Noah's attention. Familiar voices drifted down the hall. Seconds later, the private suite where he'd been transferred to opened. His mom, Victoria, rushed into the room. Just behind her was his dad, Nicholas, one of his brothers, Adam, and Adam's wife, Ryan. The love and concern in all of their eyes felt like a warm blanket that covered him whole. His legs weren't responding but his heart felt plenty. He accepted his mother's hug and fought to control his emotions.

"Oh, baby. Look at you!" Victoria touched, then kissed the bandages that covered his facial injuries as though he were a child. "I'm so sorry you've been here this long without us. We got here just as quickly as we could."

"Mom! I can't move my legs."

"I know, son. The doctor said…" Victoria stepped back.

Her words had stopped with a quick shake of Nicholas's head. "Son."

Noah looked from one parent to the other. "What?"

Nicholas didn't answer. Noah's sister-in-law, Ryan, stepped forward. A naturopathic practitioner with a growing practice in Las Vegas, her bedside manner was gentle and comforting, with an air of authority that eased Noah's anxiety.

"Hey there, brother-in-love. The doctor spoke to us briefly just before we came into your room. He's not sure what's going on with you physically just yet. They're waiting for the results of the CAT scan. Until we know exactly what's going on, it's better not to speculate and for you to remain as still, calm and positive as possible."

Noah wasn't placated. "I know you mean well, Ryan, but that's hard to do. What does he think is going on? Does he think this situation with my legs might be permanent, that I'll never walk again?"

"Again, he doesn't want to speculate and neither should you. If something is strained, fractured or broken, keeping movement to a minimum will keep further damage from being done."

"Wait!" Noah's face brightened. "My body could just be in shock, right? The doctor said something like that earlier. My brain still feels jumbled from the fall, but I think that's what he told me."

"That's very possible," Ryan said. "Shock is one way the body protects itself."

The body protecting itself. He'd heard that earlier, too. Was it the doctor who'd said it? Noah's brow furrowed with the effort to untangle the thoughts in his brain.

"Son, are you feeling pain?"

Noah looked at his everyday-alpha father and was moved by the tenderness with which Nicholas spoke. "Only like I got beat up in a barroom brawl, then run over by a train."

Adam stepped forward. "But other than that, you're okay?"

Everyone laughed. The atmosphere lightened.

Victoria perched herself on a side of the bed and ran a hand over Noah's soft curls. "Your grandparents know about what happened and send their love. They wanted to be here but with Papa still battling a bout of bronchitis, Mama Jewel didn't want to chance him leaving the home."

"Where's Twin?"

"Christian and Nick are still in Africa, honey. Tomorrow morning, they'll take the first flight out."

As much as Noah wanted to see his twin, Nick, right now, the resort in Djibouti was his oldest brother Christian's baby. The first phase of the latest hotel construction was nearing completion. Christian should stay there and since Nick would be selling the pricey units, he needed to be there, too.

"Is that really necessary? My immobility is probably just due to shock. By the time they fly here from Africa, I may be released and beat them home."

"In that case they'll arrive in time for a celebratory dinner," Victoria said. "Once they learned about your accident, nothing else mattered."

"Yeah, man, I had to calm down your double," Adam explained. "Had he not been able to find a seat on an airline, Nick would have donned a cape and flown on his own."

The group kept up a lively chatter, until the door opened. A nurse entered that Noah didn't remember seeing before. His eyes remained on the door, subconsciously hoping someone else would walk in behind him. Her, the angel from yesterday. His heart dropped a notch when she didn't appear. The nurse checked his vitals and recommended he get much-needed rest. Within minutes of his family leaving, Noah fell asleep.

When he woke up, the angel had returned. Unfortunately, the happy mood generated by his family the day before had evaporated, replaced by a swirling of negative emotions over the very real possibility that he may never walk again.

"Good morning, Noah!"

"What's good about it?"

He noted the slightest of reactions, the merest widening of those gorgeous brown eyes, before Damaris responded, accompanied by another of her sunshine smiles. "My grandmother would say that any day waking up outside the coffin is a pretty good one."

"Was your grandmother paralyzed?"

Her smile fled faster than sprinter Usain Bolt leaped from starter blocks. "No." She took a breath. He could almost see a professional mask slip into place as she viewed the machines and began recording his vitals. Noah felt bad for snapping at her. She was only trying to make him feel better, seemed to be diligent in attending to him now and had nothing to do with why he was here. How the accident happened was something he was still trying to figure out.

"I'm sorry."

"I forgive you," she responded, almost before the apology was fully out. The warmth immediately returned to her voice.

"I've not been in your shoes and can't judge your reaction. To say it must be extremely hard is probably an understatement. But what we think about we tend to bring about so maybe thinking positive would be in your best interest right now."

"What we think about we bring about. Another quote from Grandma?"

Damaris shook her head. "I heard that one in college,

not sure who coined the phrase. Most of Grandma's quotes were from the bible. She believed in the scriptures and the power of prayer."

"Yeah, well, I'm not into scriptures and am not a praying man."

Their conversation was interrupted when the Breedloves arrived seven persons strong. Noah's skiing friend, Cole, was with them, too. Nicholas, Victoria, Adam and his wife, Ryan, who came yesterday, were joined by Noah's twin, Nick, brother Christian and Christian's wife, Lauren. They'd barely finished their hellos when Dr. Noble entered the room.

"I've got some good news and some that's a bit more challenging," Dr. Noble said after greeting the group and attaching several X-rays to a wall screen. "Which do you want first?"

"The bad news," Noah said.

"The good news," both Victoria and Ryan chimed at the same time.

Dr. Noble focused on Noah. "The challenging news," he continued, "is that the lack of movement in your legs is not due to shock. Had that been the case, you may have regained feeling and use already, at least in a limited capacity."

He pulled out a pointer. "Here's what's going on. These areas here are where major bruising occurred to your spinal cord, affecting the nerves controlling leg movement and other functions. The good news is that there are no fractures or breaks. With time, physical therapy and a positive attitude, you'll most likely regain full use of all your extremities."

There was that phrase again. Positive attitude. If heard for a third time Noah thought he might puke. "What kind of time are we talking?"

"Some take weeks, others months. It's hard to say."

"For now, though, I'm paralyzed?"

"You're suffering a temporary paralysis, yes."

For the second time in less than twenty-four hours, Noah's world went dark. A mental blackout this time but the results was the same. He'd recall very little of what was said after hearing *paralysis* come from the doctor's mouth, or what his family said as they tried to cheer him. He'd barely said ten words to his best friend, Cole, who somehow blamed himself for the accident, and dismissed the use of *temporary* to describe the condition, felt it a description that only prolonged the inevitable truth. He couldn't walk. Not now, maybe not ever again. With every thought of how not walking affected his lifestyle, Noah's outlook worsened. By the time his "angel" of a nurse arrived on the scene, once again, he was in a devil kind of mood.

He braced himself for her cheery good-morning, fully prepared to tear into her, and without apology this time. But as she approached his bed, she wasn't smiling. She caught and held his gaze. The compassion and empathy that fairly beamed from her eyes was intense to the point of being unnerving.

"I don't want your pity," he mumbled, but not low enough.

"Good, because I have none to give you." She began her daily ministrations in checking his health. "It's the last thing you need, especially now, when there is a chance that you'll walk again. It will not be an easy road, but at least you have one. My pity is reserved for the person who is told, without a shadow of a doubt in the doctor's mind, that they will never walk, or stand on their own power, or if quadriplegic, never again experience total independence."

She came back around to face him, meeting his intense gaze with one of her own. "What happened to you, Noah, is very unfortunate. And while you probably don't want to hear it, you need to understand how blessed you are to have been brought down Death Mountain on a stretcher and not in a body bag."

Her face softened, while her demeanor remained professional and authoritative. "The doctor will be in shortly, along with a physical therapist. They're going to perform a series of tests to try to determine the extent of the paralysis and what, if any, exercises you can begin to do right away. It's important to keep as many of your muscles as active as possible. It may be a fairly intense exercise so until then, try to get some rest."

With the merest of smiles she turned and walked out of the room, leaving Noah to digest what he'd just witnessed, someone who'd told him in no uncertain terms exactly what she thought of him and his behavior. He would never have guessed that the warm, bubbly person who'd entered his room was capable of being the strong, commanding woman who'd left it. Obviously, there were many layers to the nurse whose name he couldn't recall. He found the thought of discovering just how many an intriguing notion. Not the only thing he wanted, but a start. He wanted to walk again, too, preferably out of the hospital. And he planned to make it clear that building a CANN Casino Hotel and Spa in Utah wasn't just in the best interest of CANN International. But for those who opposed it, too.

Three

While attending to her other patients, Noah stayed on Damaris's mind. His ongoing negative attitude was not only annoying but concerning, as well. Attitude played a huge role in how quickly a person healed, to what degree they improved and sometimes whether or not there was any change at all. In giving Noah the highest and best treatment she possibly could, she felt it was her responsibility to share what she knew with his family and encourage them to try to keep his spirits high. Dr. Noble had his hands full trying to heal Noah's body. Damaris would focus on his mind.

Her chance came the next afternoon. She arrived for her shift and learned that Noah would soon be moved to the rehabilitation unit. Dr. Noble called together the family to discuss the proposed treatment and physical therapy regimen for the remaining two weeks Noah would be at the hospital and how to prepare for his return home. Once done and with their questions answered, Dr. Noble hurried to his next patient. Damaris watched the family head in the opposite direction, the parking lot most likely. She'd see less of them once Noah was moved to the rehabilitation ward and didn't want to miss the chance of speaking one-on-one with Victoria. She set her tablet on the nurses' station counter and hurried after the group.

"Mrs. Breedlove?"

Victoria paused, and turned. So did everyone else. Unrelenting gazes from curious faces all trained on her.

"Yes?"

Damaris observed the sophisticated, close-knit family, the runway-ready women and *GQ*-looking men, and became intimidated. She watched Victoria break away from the group and walk toward her. The trepidation increased. Who was she, a rather sheltered girl growing up in a small community outside Salt Lake City, to give advice to a worldly, sophisticated woman like Victoria Breedlove, one who—if what she'd overheard earlier was correct—belonged to one of the richest families in the United States?

You're a well-qualified, well-trained, well-educated nurse who knows what she's doing, came the response from something inside her. Damaris took a breath, smiled warmly at Victoria as she did so and continued to approach.

"May I speak with you for a second?"

"Sure," Victoria answered. She turned to the others. "I'll catch up, guys."

"We'll wait in the lobby," her husband responded.

"This is probably something that Dr. Noble has already done and is not officially my place as a nurse. But I saw such concern on your face regarding Noah. I wanted to offer some encouragement regarding his situation, and if you're interested, a little advice."

"That's very sweet of you," Victoria looked down to read her name tag. "'Da...'"

"Damaris," she said. "Most of my friends call me Dee."

"Dee is easier, but Damaris is lovely, as is your desire to help me navigate this process. I can truly use any and all the assistance available. My family has never dealt with anything like this. Noah's life has been relatively problem-free. He's a good kid—smart, hard worker, focused. I can't remember a time when he hasn't been fully in control of his life. Even as a child. Which has me deeply worried about how he'll rise to this challenge, not only the physical aspect but his mental and emotional frame of mind."

Bolstered by Victoria's words and made comfortable by her laid-back demeanor, Damaris suggested they cross the hall to a small seating area. Once facing each other on a love seat positioned across from a coffee table and two chairs, she continued.

"Though probably unlike Noah, the reactions he's exhibited are fairly typical of those who find their lives flipped upside down. If the person is strong-willed, independent and used to being in control of their life and circumstances, as you've described your son, it's especially difficult. Even with a temporary loss of movement, there's a grieving process that involves some of everything we've seen—anger, sadness, denial, depression. I haven't been in the field very long but, from what I've seen so far, most do come to grips with their new reality and make the necessary adjustments to have a productive life."

"As I said, Noah is very focused and determined. He's conquered everything that he's tried."

"Those traits will go a long way toward his healing. Another very important component is his overall attitude. Again, it's understandable that he's upset about life's prospects right now. It's important that the family be as upbeat and positive as possible, to not let him wallow in negativity or self-pity. Mind over matter isn't just a phrase. It is a real tool that can aid with his healing."

"You sound like Ryan, my son Adam's wife. She practices holistic healing, has a clinic in Vegas and can probably give more pointers along these lines. I'd like it if you spoke with her about this, too."

"I would love to speak with her."

"Good. I'll let her know." Victoria paused for a moment, then asked, "Do you think he'll walk again?"

"That's a question above my pay grade," Damaris replied with a smile. "With God, all things are possible. I'll pray for Noah's healing, and do everything I can to help him get better."

They chatted a moment longer. When Victoria requested Damaris's cell number, she didn't hesitate. Later, she'd have to examine the deep feelings she felt for her patient, the personal attachment to a positive outcome. She told herself it was because Noah Breedlove was her first solo intake, her first time treating a patient from their time of arrival through departure. It made sense that she'd want to chart the patient's progress, see him through to a successful end. That sounded reasonable, professional even. For now, she'd leave it at that.

A few hours later, Damaris returned to Noah's room. She'd gotten the call that a team from Rehabilitation was on their way over to transfer him. She'd need to make sure all of his charts were properly updated and ready to be passed on to the new crew. A sense of anticipation caused butterflies as she neared his room. The feeling surprised her and was unnerving, to say the least. Coming from a conservative, religious background, Damaris had been taught that engagement with the opposite sex happened largely after marriage. She'd had one serious boyfriend, Matthew, a church member she'd known since they were seven and eight years old. At seventeen, when he was eighteen, they announced their intentions to marry the following year. Her father didn't consider Matthew a "good Layman" and was opposed to the union. Eventually he demanded she end the relationship. It was the first time Damaris had defied her father. They planned to elope. Before that happened, Matthew was tragically killed in a motorcycle accident. It had affected her deeply, both his death and her deception, which is why nearly five years later, having just turned twenty-three, she was still unattached…and a virgin.

Even now, the guilt was palpable, with regret worn like a second skin. Noah was attractive, even with bruises and scars. But he was also her patient, a depressed, temporarily paralyzed accident victim. And he wasn't a Layman. She didn't have time for girlie emotions and sternly told herself to get those errant feelings in check.

She entered his room. The curtains were drawn, the

lights dimmed, Noah's face turned toward the wall. Remembering her advice of keeping the atmosphere around him as cheery as possible Damaris brightened the lights.

"Wake up, sleepyhead," she sang, while walking over to the curtains and opening them. "It's moving day."

"Close my curtains," Noah growled. "And get out."

"Sorry, no can do. Your charts have to be updated for the team on their way to get you. Travis, the physical therapist, is especially excited to get to work with you, get you up and moving as quickly as possible."

Noah snorted. "Yeah, well, good luck with that."

"Luck may play a small role," Damaris continued conversationally, as she checked his blood pressure, temperature and current weight. "But a lot of the improvement will depend on you."

"Here we go, another pep talk." He glared at her. "Save it. I'm not in the mood."

Damaris shrugged her shoulders. "Have it your way."

She said nothing else to Noah but began humming as she continued her work. It was a habit learned from her mother, Bethany, one she did without being aware.

"Will you stop it?" Noah demanded.

Damaris jumped, almost upending her tablet. "Stop what?"

"Singing. Humming. Making noise." He shifted and looked at the ceiling. When he spoke again his voice was calmer but demanding nonetheless. "If you must be here, try to be as invisible as possible, okay?"

Damaris counted to ten, then twenty. She wasn't accustomed to being yelled at, or rude behavior no matter what the injury. She bit her tongue against the desire to tell him just that and focused on finishing up her work as quickly as possible. His presence did funny things to her equilibrium, messed up the status quo and left her wondering about who he was before the accident. What his life was like outside the trauma unit.

"That's it for me, Noah," she said once done. "The guys from Rehab will be here shortly. You'll be transferred to their wing. The nurses I know who work over there are a pretty cheerful bunch," she continued playfully. "So I can't guarantee you'll get the bleak atmosphere you crave, but I believe there will be less humming."

From Noah? Silence, the deafening kind. His stormy countenance could have been cut from stone. Eyes closed. Brow scrunched. Lips set in a hard line. She blocked the desire to step up to his bed and administer a comforting squeeze to his bare, muscled arm or smooth away the creases that the frown created. To Damaris, his facial expression transmitted as pain. She didn't ask about it, and wasn't sure he'd answer anyway. Still, she made an additional note in her report and would be sure to share concerns with the doctor.

"Can I get you anything before I leave?"

"No."

Curt. Final.

"Then let me say it has been my pleasure treating you. I will continue to pray and believe that your body will recover, and that you will be up and walking in no time. Until then, please try to find gratitude in this simple truth. You're alive, which means there is hope."

A huff, as he adjusted his body away from her, a clear dismissal sign. He was right. She was done here and had other patients to see, ones who appreciated her visits and would never silence her hums.

"Goodbye, Noah," she said quietly, then walked out the door, ignoring the fact a part of her heart remained there. Her father would never approve of someone like Noah, who would likely have no real interest in a religious girl like her. The sooner he was out of Manning Valley Medical, the better it would be. For both of them.

Four

Noah wasn't known for angry outbursts, yet he'd had more in the past week than in his entire pre-accident life. Of the four Breedlove brothers, he was the calmest one, the most rational. It wasn't fair to lash out at the nurse. She'd been very patient through his mood swings, all kindness and sunshine when entering the room. Her sunny disposition was part of what irked him, all cheery when he could find no joy. He'd apologized the first time, though not all the way sorry, especially the more he recalled that exchange. Seeing the quiet, almost demure nurse turn into a spitfire made losing his temper almost worth it. Maybe that was why two days after leaving the trauma unit, Damaris was still on his mind.

I wonder what she's like in bed.

Noah banished the unwelcome thought as quickly as it came. As for now, nothing worked below his waist, or may ever function again. His mother told him to stay positive. Ryan said she'd do remote energy work, whatever that was. The angel nurse with the *D* name thought prayers might work and humming would make him feel better. It was all bullshit. From the waist down, he still couldn't move.

"You're alive." That was the parting reason she'd offered him to use as a lifeline. To be grateful because things could be worse. He could have come down from Death Mountain…well…dead. Noah now knew there were worse things than dying, like not being able to lift your leg, or get an erection, or make love again. For a man like him, one who cherished women, that was like not being able to breathe.

A light tap on the door to Noah's private room interrupted his musings. Probably the physical therapist he'd nicknamed Relentless on account of how determined he was to get Noah to move his noodle-like legs.

"Come in."

It wasn't Relentless. It was her. The nurse angel.

"Hello, Noah."

Her smile seemed forced but given their last interaction, commendable. "Hi."

"Remember me?"

"I remember."

"I know, I thought we were done with each other, too." She smiled to show she was joking. "As it turns out, the floor is short-staffed. I'm helping to cover shifts, which means you'll have to put up with me for a couple more days, though I promise not to hum."

"Thank you," he replied, his voice dripping in mock sincerity.

"Ha!"

Damaris began logging his vitals from the monitor into his chart. "How are you doing?"

"Last week I could walk. This week I can't. How do you think I'm doing?"

Her smile faded as quickly as a rainbow. "Still into the pity party, are we? That's not the kind of music I dance to, so I'll leave you to it."

Done with monitoring, she turned to go.

"Wait."

Her hand was on the knob. She didn't turn around, but she didn't open the door, either.

"What's your name again?"

"Damaris. Duh-mare-ess." She turned but made no move to come closer. Instead she leaned against the door. "Friends call me Dee."

"Only friends?"

"Mostly. I make exceptions. Your mother was one."

"Yeah, she's exceptional like that."

The merest hint of a smile flitted across an otherwise serious face.

"Can I call you Dee?"

"Definitely not," Damaris responded to Noah's surprise. "At this time you're still very much in the Damaris category."

Noah smiled.

"Actually," she continued, crossing her arms. "You're almost at the Nurse Damaris point."

His smile broadened. A chuckle almost escaped his mouth. That just happened, when, moments before, Noah wondered if he'd ever laugh again.

"Are you sure about that? If we're going to fight like siblings or arguing lovers, shouldn't we both be on a first-name basis?"

The most delightful shade of red crept from her neck upward. The thought of them being lovers made her blush? She smiled again, more genuine this time. *Ah, there's the sunshine.*

Damaris pushed away from the door and walked toward him. "About what happened the other day…"

"Don't even think about saying you're sorry. I'm the one who owes you an apology. Blowing up at the person trying to help me. Ignoring your presence when you said goodbye. Yours was the appropriate response to someone acting like a total jerk. I'm usually not so combustible. I apologize."

"Your apology is accepted, your mood understood. You're going through a lot."

Noah watched as Damaris approached him. She eyed the various machinery around him as she reached the bed, one especially designed for physical therapy. There were bars and pulleys, with weights on the ends. In the corner was more workout equipment. Beyond the bed was an expanse of window that allowed in abundant natural light along with views of rows of magnificent pine trees and the beautiful mountains of Utah. He saw none of that now, fixated as he was on the beautiful indoor scenery. She had wide, light brown eyes, surrounded by lashes that went on forever. Her nose looked natural, like it hadn't been reduced and sculpted by a knife. Beneath it were lips that were totally kissable, full and luscious, clear gloss-covered temptation. Her hair was thick and curly, her smooth skin the color of a caramel latte. He wondered about her heritage even as he knew it didn't matter. There was nothing to be gained from getting to know her better, except more pain at the thought that talking is probably all they'd ever do.

Damaris checked the intravenous fluid bags. "I see you're still receiving pain medication through the drip. How is your comfort level right now?"

"Better."

"The doctor felt that increasing the dosage would help. I'm glad you're experiencing less pain at least."

She was close enough for him to smell her cologne, something light and fruity, and to notice the slightest spray of freckles across the bridge of her nose. Again, Noah's thoughts turned sensual. He forced them in another direction as Damaris peeked under the bandages on his face.

"Where'd that name come from?"

The fingers lifting the bandages stilled.

"I didn't mean that to sound offensive. It's just that I've never heard it before."

"I get asked that a lot and am not offended at all." She studied his face with an unreadable expression. "Excuse me a moment. Your bandages need changing."

She walked out of the room. Noah's head fell back against the pillow. He'd never been a smooth talker when it came to the ladies, didn't possess his brother Christian's refined mannerisms, Adam's swagger or Nick's charm. He won over women with his intellect. His dark Breedlove good looks and healthy bank account probably didn't hurt, either. He was confident and well-spoken and couldn't figure out why with the nurse angel he was all kinds of verbal fumbles and mental snafus. Then he remembered. The fall on the mountain. Not only his legs had been affected. Something in his brain had jostled loose.

Damaris returned, carrying a small plastic box. She placed the container on a movable tray beside him and removed gauze, astringent and ointment from the container.

For a moment she was quiet, focused on treating his lacerations, the most serious of which was a cut above his right eye. The doctor figured it was from a rock or tree limb hidden just beneath the snow and would leave a scar that only plastic surgery could remove. Her hands were soft, her touch gentle as she began unwinding the soiled gauze from around his head.

"It's from the bible," she said, her voice soft, almost musical.

"Huh?"

"My name. Damaris. It's biblical."

"Oh."

Damaris laughed again. Noah decided he quite liked the sound.

"I gather that's not a book you read often?"

"It's one that I don't read at all."

"Most who do don't remember that name. It's only mentioned once, when the apostle Paul preached the gospel in Athens. She was one of only a few who converted, and as far as we know the only woman."

"So that's why you're named after her, because you're unique?"

"I don't know about me but the name sure is. I think my mom chose it because it was different, something I hated when I was younger."

"Why? I like that it's different."

"I'm a biracial Layman living in Utah."

"You're with the Church of Laymen?" Noah asked the question indifferently, a feat given that the influential religious group was the singular holdout in securing building permits for the biggest project of his professional life.

"Yes. All of the above and a Layman. That's already different enough."

Said in a tone that gave off all kinds of attitude and made him forget why her mere affiliation with his nemesis should squelch the physical attraction. It didn't. Again, Noah noted that flash of fire, a playful spark bursting through the modest image she displayed. He saw it and wondered if her hair was as soft as he imagined, and how wild her curly strands became when released from the band that held them locked at the nape of her neck.

"How'd that happen?"

"Being biracial? It's when two people of different nationalities get together and…"

"Thanks for confirming the details exactly as I imagined them. I was referring to your living in Utah."

"I was born here."

"And being a Layman? I'm not religious and know next to nothing about the church but the little I have read about or seen on television didn't involve people of color."

"There aren't many of us. My dad is a third-generation Layman who went rogue when he met and fell in love with my mom. Initially, his family was staunchly opposed to the union but then they met Bethany."

"Bethany, that's your mom?"

Damaris nodded. "She was a teenager when her family converted to the church. In time she eventually won my father's family over."

"Interesting."

"Quite."

"Any siblings?" Noah asked her, purposely making no mention of his connection to the casino her church opposed. Perhaps something she shared could help him break through the Laymen juggernaut that had proved even more difficult than he and the team had imagined. The less she knew about his business, the more of hers she might share.

"There are six of us—two boys, four girls."

"You're the oldest?"

"Youngest." Damaris paused. "You look surprised. Do you see a stray gray hair that I don't know about?"

She stretched a curl so that she could see it, feigning concern. And Noah would be damned but there it was again, that feeling he thought was gone forever—joy—subtle yet unmistakable.

"You're beautiful, so no need to worry about that." He watched as that now familiar blush slowly rose from her neck to her cheeks and became even more smitten. There was nothing innocent about the women that Noah dated. As for a woman blushing at hearing a compliment? He hadn't seen that happen in at least ten years.

"I guessed you were the oldest because of the way you take care of me, of all your patients probably, so naturally, like you've been doing it forever. I thought it maybe started when you were a kid, taking care of your brothers and sister."

"No, birds and other animals were my patients. My siblings had to fend for themselves."

"But you became a nurse instead of a veterinarian."

"I love conversing with my patients and don't speak bark or meow."

Noah laughed out loud, another first since the accident, and a rare reaction before then for this serious son.

"What about you?" Damaris asked. "When it comes to the sibling pecking order, where do you fall?"

"The youngest, by fourteen minutes."

"Ah, you're a twin."

"Yes, the fourth of four sons."

"Are you spoiled as is often the case with the youngest child?"

"Definitely not. Are you?"

"Definitely."

They shared another laugh. She was delightful! Her essence remained with Noah long after she'd gone. That all felt amazing. But there was another thought. She was a Layman, part of the church blocking the bill that would greenlight the casino project, and costing his investors money with every delay. That didn't feel good at all.

Five

By day five of Noah's hospital stay in Utah, a venerable team of experts had descended to work on his rehabilitation plan. Damaris found herself unexpectedly being one of his rotating nurses, due to a continued shortage of nurses on their ward. She told herself that volunteering to cover after working her shift had nothing to do with Noah. By the time she met Wendy in the cafeteria, she'd almost convinced herself.

They grabbed trays, made their dinner selections and found a table away from other diners. In addition to being her assistant, Wendy was also Damaris's friend. They'd both been so busy working there'd been little time for girl talk, or anything else.

Wendy reached for condiments to dress her burger. "He's gorgeous, isn't he?"

"Who?" Damaris said, shaking the packet of dressing that came with the chicken Caesar salad.

"Who," Wendy parroted. "You know who. The reason you snapped up that extra shift on Rehab. Breedlove. The rich boy."

"I took the extra shift because I could use the money and the floor could use my help."

Wendy chuckled. "Is that the story you're telling yourself? Because I checked you out while he was in trauma and observed something different."

"You observed me doing my job, because that's all that happened."

"What about that day I saw you talking with his mother?"

"I don't discuss patients with their family members?"

"All the time, but you seemed…chattier than with other interactions. Like you were spilling secrets and she was mopping them up."

Damaris shared what she'd told Victoria. "It's what I would have told any family," she finished, sitting back to take a sip of her soda. "The patient is always my focus."

"Calm down, girl. This isn't your employee review. Besides, I don't mind you using the mom to get close to the son. Get him to fall for you and your need of extra shifts will be over!"

"Wendy! I'd never do that."

"I know, and it's a shame. I went online, did a little research. That Noah Breedlove would be quite the catch. His family owns the CANN hotel chain."

Damaris frowned. "The casino?"

"Casinos, plural, housed in some of the most luxurious hotels in the world. Their hotel in Vegas is the only seven-star hotel in North America."

"Hmm."

The information Wendy viewed as exciting, Damaris found troubling as suddenly unrelated pieces of a puzzle now fell into place. His rugged good looks. Being from Nevada. A family able to fly to his bedside at a moment's notice. All of the questions about her faith. Noah Breedlove was a part of the family wanting to do the unthinkable—build a casino in Salt Lake City—something the Church of Laymen would never allow. Is that why he didn't tell her about the connection? Did he know that her father was one of his staunchest opponents? Is that the real reason he apologized for basically being a jerk?

In her faith, money was the root of all evil and gambling a major transgression. Utah, home to the Church of Laymen and where the faith had been birthed in the late nineteenth century, was one of only two states in the entire union where any form of gambling was against the law. Multistate lotteries couldn't muster up enough approval support, largely due to the church's well-lined coffers and powerful political influences. One of those powerful influences was Damaris's father, Franklin. What he lacked in money he made up in machismo. Fanatically devoted to the ministry, he'd campaigned tirelessly against every bill initiated and took pride in "keeping the devil out of the Beehive State."

"Want to hear something even more amazing?" Wendy asked.

Damaris wasn't sure that she did. Didn't matter, as it turned out.

"He has an identical twin named Nick. It's crazy, Dee. They look exactly alike! So—" she lowered her head and her voice "—you go after one, I'll snag the other and we can be sisters-in-law!"

"You know I'm a Layman. I could never go out with Noah, or anyone outside the faith."

Damaris continued to listen as Wendy fairly gushed over all that she'd learned of her patient. She had obviously spent quite a bit of time online researching the Breedloves and was a wealth of information. Over the next fifteen minutes, she went from describing Victoria's role in the CANN Foundation, the charitable arm of the for-profit corporation, to providing each brother's role in the multibillion-dollar enterprise. When Damaris returned to the rehabilitation unit to find Noah's room filled with family, she couldn't help but feel a little bit guilty, like she'd talked about them behind their backs, and, truth be told, been slightly judgmental, too.

"There she is!" Victoria said when Damaris entered. "We were just talking about you."

"All good, I hope." Damaris also hoped the smile she forced carried through in her voice.

"Absolutely," Victoria replied.

She motioned toward a couple looking out the window. The woman broke away and walked over.

"Damaris, this is Ryan, the family's naturopathic doctor I told you about."

Damaris held out her hand. "I find alternative medicine fascinating, Ryan. It's nice to meet you."

"Likewise."

"I told Ryan it would be wonderful if the three of us could have a nice long chat, later, when you're off duty."

"We're short-staffed and very busy," was Damaris's noncommittal reply. "In fact, I really should finish up here and head back over to Trauma."

"Of course," Victoria said. "I'm sorry to have delayed you."

"It's not a problem." And to Ryan. "I'm glad we met."

"Me, too. It would great to talk shop sometime."

Damaris walked over to Noah. "Hello, Noah."

"Hello, Dee."

In spite of her tarnished view of the family, she smiled at his use of her nickname. She also couldn't help but be reminded of Wendy's comment about Noah's appearance and admit he was a very attractive man. His twin, Nick, too, who, without the bruises Noah had sustained in the accident, would be a dead ringer for sure. She stole glances at the clan while performing her duties, her friend's descriptions of each one still fresh in her mind. She looked at the beautiful wives with the handsome husbands and wondered about the type of women in Noah's life. Her mind mulled the possibilities while tending to Noah's rapidly healing wounds.

"Don't bother her, Ryan," Damaris heard Nick saying when she came out of her reverie. "She's focused."

Damaris was totally embarrassed. "I'm sorry, what did you say?"

"When was your last trip to Vegas?"

There was only a second's hesitation before Damaris answered, "I've never been."

The whole room got quiet. Damaris felt the heat of the Breedlove stare.

"You're kidding," Noah's twin brother, Nick, said.

"Never?" Victoria asked.

Ryan looked at the man Damaris assumed was her husband. "Adam, can you believe that?"

Damaris focused on the machine recording Noah's vitals.

"You're a state away from one of the most popular tourist destinations in America," Victoria continued, "and you've never been there."

"Why not?" Ryan asked.

"The same reason it's taken our project so long to get off the ground here," Noah answered. "She's a member of the single entity blocking the casino being built."

"The Church of Laymen," Nick said, his eyes on Damaris. "She's a part of it."

"Exactly," Noah answered. "The group that wants us to build a hotel and spa only, no gambling."

"If there's no casino, it's not a CANN property," Adam said.

Nicholas, Noah's dad, turned his attention to Damaris. "Since you're a member of that religion, perhaps you can help us understand their zero tolerance for gambling. It's an activity that with the construction of a CANN hotel would boost the economy by more than 25 percent."

Damaris hesitated in giving an answer. While she was clear on the reasons the laws against gambling had been continuously upheld, she didn't want to speak for the church. She opened her mouth to say as much but there was no need. Victoria came to her rescue.

"Oh, no, boys. What we're not going to do is turn Noah's temporary residence into a corporate boardroom. The only focus here should be on helping Noah heal."

"Trust me, wife, him closing this deal would greatly increase that positive attitude you suggested was so important during rehabilitation."

The guys laughed. Damaris smiled. Noah commented,

"At just the thought of that deal going through, I feel better already."

Damaris was thankful for Victoria's intervention. It saved her from putting Noah in a very bad mood. Her grandmother had another saying: all money wasn't good money. As long as her father and others like him were on this side of the dirt, there would be no gambling in Salt Lake City, or anywhere in Utah. Period.

Six

Over the next week, Noah met with a group of spinal cord injury specialists, including two on the cutting edge of regeneration research. Because the damaged vertebrae had been crushed, not broken, they thought technology so new it had not yet been announced might work to repair the spine and help him walk again. That the institute was in Denmark gave Noah some concern. But to walk again, he'd travel to Mars.

When he wasn't going through physical therapy or sleeping off the rigorous routines, Noah conducted business on his iPad. His accident had made national news. It was important for his colleagues, employees and investors to know Project Salt Lake was moving forward. He was determined to succeed and driven to quiet the doubters, including his father, who said what he planned could never be done.

That didn't mean the continued delays didn't put a chink or two in his armor. The bill remained stalled within the city council, nowhere close to a vote by the residents. One of the major investors, a financial group based in Dubai, was threatening to pull out. Work kept his mind off his disability, the long road ahead to full recovery and the possibility that as hard as he tried, he may never walk again. For better or worse, focusing on the Salt Lake project also kept his mind on Damaris, a woman who became more off-limits with every facet about her he uncovered. That he didn't question her further after finding out she was a Layman, get deeper insight on the religion and the higher-ups that she knew, was unsettling. Again, he blamed the oversight on the jarring collision his head had with a rock.

When it came to Project Salt Lake, Noah had left the Church of Laymen up to Scott Robinson, a senior advisor on the team. Now, however, he was online doing his own research. He told himself it was because of the church's opposing viewpoints but honestly, it was to learn more about Damaris, too. By the time she arrived in his room an hour later, Noah had learned more than he ever thought he'd know about Laymen, and Damaris was even more an enigma.

"Did you know that until the 1970s, people of color weren't allowed in your church?"

Damaris, who'd barely stepped a toe into the room when the question was hurled, laughed softly. "Good afternoon to you, too."

"Yeah, hi." Noah found the history offensive and felt his question held no humor. "Did you?"

"Somebody's been online, I see." Damaris approached his bed and began her routine. "It's not quite as you've interpreted from whatever you read. People of color could not be ministers or hold leadership positions until the 1970s. But the Church of Laymen has always welcomed everyone."

"In separate services."

"Unfortunately, when the ministry was created, that was the way of life in our country."

As she talked, Noah clicked onto another site, and read from it. "'The Church of Laymen participated in segregated worship services, believing that people of color required a different, simpler form of instruction. Interracial dating was discouraged. Marriage between cultures, forbidden. These rules remained in place until the passing of Wayne Goddard III in 1974. Under new leadership, new policies were adopted and the practice of segregation in all areas of ministry was renounced.'"

Damaris continued her work, checking his vitals and making notations on her chart.

"Well?" he demanded after a pause.

"Well, what?"

"You belong to a church that doesn't even want you in it!"

"That may have been true at one point with some members. But it is not the case today and never was for a majority of the membership. When my mother joined, she was fully accepted."

She took a deep breath. "It is a given that there are areas in our history of which we're not proud. As I've stated, the practices of our church were in line with the times in which it was founded. In the late nineteenth century, segregation was law. As the nation evolved, so did the church."

Damaris made a notation on her tablet. "There's a slight change in your temperature. Are you feeling differently today than you did yesterday?"

"No."

"No dizziness or nausea?"

"None other than what reading about the history of your church produced."

The slightest of pauses and then she said, "If your symptoms continue, please ring the nurses' station."

Damaris turned to leave. Noah watched her quick retreat, could feel the fire she tried to keep hidden. With eyes like hers, that was impossible. When angry, the light orbs darkened, fairly blazed with the anger she felt. Her jaw had tightened along with her shoulders, before she took a calming breath and responded.

It might have been unfair to attack her in this manner. Neither religion nor politics were subjects for polite company. But the beliefs she and the church members held stood between him, the company's expansion goals and a town's economic well-being. In love, war and business, all was fair.

"Sorry to tell you, Dee, but your church hasn't evolved much."

She spun around, fire in her eyes. "Look, I'm living the life you just read about. No one knows better than me the problems we still face. Even so, the church has made strides in many areas. And while I'm sure it wouldn't seem like it to someone like you, some of the more conservative thinking has been amended."

"Really? Then why is the church still fighting one's right to gamble, a practice that is legal in forty-eight other states? Or even something as simple as buying a lottery ticket, something residents in forty-four other states can do? Why has it taken two years for our company to even have a member from your ministry sit at the bargaining table?"

"Because gambling is built on greed and gluttony," Damaris responded, anger beginning to leak through her professional facade. "And while it is my understanding that your family has lots of it, loving money is the root of all evil. People who crave it suffer and have no true faith."

Indignation caused Noah to lift his head off the pillow. "Money is evil? So you're working for free?"

"Right now, I'm not working at all. I'm arguing with you. But that's about to change."

She whirled around again, yanked open the door and stormed from the room. For a few seconds Noah stared at the door, as the electricity of their exchange continued to swirl around him. He flopped back, spent yet exhilarated. There was nothing like a good verbal joust to get the blood flowing. In Breedlove boardrooms that happened quite often. Heated arguments. Passionate debates. For the first time since he entered this place on a stretcher, Noah felt more like himself. He didn't need legs to hold his own in an intellectual conversation. Reinvigorated, Noah opened a Word document on his tablet and began writing a memo to his team. Damaris had relit his passion, stoked his determination. Building, winning, the Breedlove way; failure never an option. When it came to the CANN Casino Hotel and Spa being built in Utah, the fight was far from over. As for the conversation with Damaris about the Church of Laymen, or conversing in general, Noah wasn't finished there, either.

Seven

Damaris chided herself all the way back to Trauma, couldn't believe how she'd lost her temper and allowed herself to be goaded into a quarrel. Above all else, Noah was a patient. He deserved to be treated with compassion and care. What Noah thought about the church was of no concern, though his prodding questions raised her own. What his company did or didn't do with their casino hotels was none of her business, either. That was her father's arena. What did it matter anyway? In a couple days, Noah Breedlove and his wealthy family would leave the hospital where Damaris worked, she'd never see them again and the crazy feelings that bubbled up every time she saw the handsome heathen would quickly go away.

Two days later, Damaris sat at her desk trying to focus. She'd accessed Noah's files in the system and knew he was being discharged within the hour. For the best, Damaris told herself, then tried to believe it. From the first time their eyes met, her mind had been screwy. She'd even stooped to going online and learning more about him and his family. Everything Wendy had told her was true, and was just the tip of the iceberg. The pictures of them were glamorous, the guys looking decadent in full tuxedos, the girls hobnobbing with celebrities and sports superstars. Despite being a sensible, low-key kind of girl, she'd still sat back and wondered how it was to live like the rich and famous. To have everything you needed at your fingertips, where you could buy whatever you wanted. It was fanciful imaginings with no value whatsoever. With him back in Las Vegas, she could stop fantasizing and resume her conservative, predictable life.

She'd just begun a report for Dr. Noble when her intercom sounded. "Dee?"

Damaris pressed a button. "Hey, Wendy."

"Someone's here to see you. A... Mrs. Breedlove."

"Umm...okay. Can you escort her to the office? We'll be able to have a more private discussion in here."

"Sure thing."

Damaris disconnected the call, quickly opened her desk drawer and pulled out a rarely used compact and a tube of pale pink gloss. When the door opened, which missus would she see? Her first thought was Victoria, but she had Damaris's cell number. What could be so important that instead of calling, she'd come over in person?

Damaris stood as Victoria walked into the office, looking casually sophisticated in navy slacks with a matching tunic. Her short black bob was stylishly streaked with gray, and accented a flawlessly made up heart-shaped face. She wore a matching pearl earring and necklace set and stylish bone-colored heels. Damaris knew from Noah's chart that he was twenty-five, and from an earlier conversation that he and his twin brother were the youngest of four sons. That meant Victoria had to be in her fifties. Yet Damaris swore she didn't look a day over thirty-five.

"Hello, Victoria." She held out her hand.

Victoria grasped it with one hand and covered it with the other. "I was afraid that with it being a Saturday you'd be off work. I'm glad to have this opportunity to chat in person."

Damaris's curiosity was instantly aroused. Something was on Victoria's mind.

"Please, have a seat." Instead of returning to the seat behind her desk, Damaris sat in one of two matching chairs on the opposite wall. Victoria sat in the other one, a magazine-strewn table between them.

"Can I get you something to drink? Coffee, tea or a water?"

"No, thank you," Victoria said with a glance around the small office. "I'm fine."

Clearly not, Damaris thought, the way Victoria was wringing her hands.

"I understand Noah is scheduled to leave today. Have they already checked him out?"

"No, but he'll be ready to leave soon and frankly, Damaris, I'm terrified."

"That's completely understandable, Victoria. If I were a mother, my feelings would be the same. Noah appears to be a determined man, one who can accomplish anything on which he sets his mind and intention. As he gets better physically, his mood will improve."

"He's always been a brooder," Victoria explained. "The quietest of my children by far. He says he's okay, but he fears for his future. He's always enjoyed a very active lifestyle. This is a huge change."

Damaris's heart went out to Victoria. She could read worry all over the mother's face.

"I wish I could offer assurances for exactly how all this turns out or guarantee that he'll walk again. The truth is, all of you are facing unknown, uncharted territory. Uncertainty is scary. But from what I've seen, Noah has a strong support system, starting with you and the close-knit family you've created. He's got a team of international specialists charting his medical progress. It will be daunting and seem impossible at times. But you're a strong woman. You can do this."

"I hope so," Victoria whispered, her eyes bright with unshed tears. "If it were possible to switch places with him, I'd do it in a heartbeat."

Damaris reached over and placed a comforting hand on her arm. "Look, this isn't something I normally do, but you have my number. If you ever want to talk about the residue left over from his traumatic injuries, the rehabilitation process or just someone who believes it is possible for your son to get better, please give me a call."

"That's very kind of you, Damaris."

"Noah was my first intake as lead nurse on the trauma ward—a memorable experience. I'm happy to help."

"I believe you mean that."

"I do, absolutely."

"Well, I felt it out of place to ask this, but since you volunteered your continued assistance, there is one something you could do that would ease my worries considerably and I think help Noah, too."

"What's that?"

"Continue to help with his recovery."

"I'd gladly help if that were happening here, but as I understand it he's being released to the care of a team in Las Vegas, correct? And that Travis will be going with him."

"All of that's true. A brand-new duplex is being built, along with a customized rehabilitation workout room nearby to help Noah improve as quickly as possible."

"You built a whole house that quickly, in the short time that Noah's been here?"

"A whole two houses," Victoria said with a smile. "It took pulling in favors, a top-notch construction company and a small army working around the clock to pull it off. But my Noah has already been through so much. I wanted him to come home to a place where he could feel comfortable, somewhat independent, a place designed to meet his new set of needs. I get the feeling, though, that my son's mental and emotional recovery is as or more important than the physical aspect. You're a great nurse, Damaris, kind and compassionate and highly skilled. I've met a lot of people and can read them very well. I would love to have you as part of the team assembled on my son's behalf."

Damaris was stunned into silence, trying to absorb a request she couldn't possibly have heard.

"I don't see how that could be possible."

"You'd have to relocate, of course," Victoria said with a smile. "We'd match whatever salary and benefits the hospital pays you," she continued, leaving no doubt that indeed a job offer had just been made.

"And take care of the relocation, along with providing room and board."

The only reason Damaris didn't fall over was because she was already sitting down.

"You're asking me to move to Vegas?"

"It's a big ask but yes, for Noah. He's very sensitive about his...condition. But you were here from the beginning. He responds well to your treatment and care. He's talked about you when you're not around, how you've encouraged him and helped him believe that he could get better."

"He has?"

Victoria nodded. "That's surprising?"

"Absolutely. The reactions I've seen aren't ones very receptive to messages on the power of positive thinking. In fact... I just... Have you talked to Noah about this?"

"I wanted to ask you first. I didn't want to get his hopes up and then have them dashed if you can't accept the offer."

"You might want to run it by him. I'm not sure he'd want me on the team."

"Why not?"

"I'm a Layman, Victoria, part of the group opposing his casino plans. My views line up on the side of the church. I don't believe in gambling, either."

"I don't plan to put such in your job description."

"You'd still want me to work for you, given my position?"

"Absolutely. I want to do whatever it takes to help my son heal."

"I'm floored, honestly, and don't know what to say."

"Then say nothing. Think about it and give me an answer in a couple days. Oh, and please know that money is no object. If doubling the salary will help make your decision easier, then consider it done."

"Wow. I can't believe what you've just offered. It's a lot to think about."

"I know, dear, and I don't mean to push. But it's my son's life and emotional well-being on the line. I want to do everything possible to help him recover as quickly and completely as he possibly can."

Damaris walked Victoria to the elevator. Wendy followed her back.

"What was that about?"

Damaris closed the door, leaned against it and put her hands over her eyes. "I don't believe what just happened."

"What? Oh my gosh, Dee, spill it!"

"Promise you won't breathe a word of this to anyone?"

"Promise."

There was no chance of anyone overhearing but Damaris lowered her voice anyway.

"Victoria just offered me a job."

"What?" Wendy squealed.

"Shh!"

"Sorry." Wendy adjusted her voice to an exaggerated whisper. "What?"

Damaris appreciated her friend's humor. It took away some of her angst.

"Victoria asked if I'd relocate to Las Vegas and become her son's personal nurse."

"Stop lying."

"Cross my heart."

"Oh my gosh, Dee! That's amazing! When are you leaving?"

"What do you mean, leaving? I can't accept that job."

"You can't not take it. Living in Las Vegas as that hunk's personal nurse? It's the job of a lifetime! There's no telling what working with them could lead to, but it would definitely be something you couldn't get here. Don't you remember what I told you about that family? How they own a huge hotel chain and have properties all over the world? Don't be stupid, Damaris. It's a wonderful opportunity, plus they have more money than God!"

She didn't tell Wendy, who would surely berate her, but for Damaris, that was part of the problem. The other was her father. He'd absolutely hit the roof. To him, Las Vegas was akin to Sodom and Gomorrah, two biblical cities given over to debauchery and eventually destroyed with fire and brimstone. Could she move to such a place and stay true to her faith? The other question was did she want to?

Eight

He'd always loved the family estate, hundreds of acres encircled by mountains. Some landscaped, some wild, all beautiful. But the man who left two weeks ago wasn't the one who returned. That self-assured powerhouse no longer existed yet Breedlove, Nevada, a town cofounded by his father, and this, the land that was embedded in his DNA, hadn't changed. It still felt like home. Now, a day after arriving, he was trying to adjust to his new digs, an architectural miracle performed by an award-winning construction company and over a hundred hired hands. He was still checking out the four-thousand-foot, wheelchair-accessible wonder when the phone rang. He wheeled himself over to where he'd left both his business and personal cell phones on the table. He picked up the one for personal use and saw a number he didn't recognize.

"Noah Breedlove."

"Hi, Noah. It's Damaris."

His heartbeat increased. She didn't have to say her name. He'd know that voice anywhere.

"Your Manning Valley trauma nurse."

Only then did he realize he hadn't yet spoken.

"There's probably only one Damaris in this country, remember? I know who you are."

"Oh, okay. Good. How's it going, Noah? How are you adjusting to your new life?"

"How'd you get my number?"

"Your mother asked me to give you a call."

"Figures," he mumbled.

"If this is a bad time…"

"No, it isn't."

Noah's reaction was from knowing that Victoria Breed-love was a notorious matchmaker, always trying to line up the next wedding celebration. She'd been successful with his brothers Christian and Adam. She also possessed the uncanny ability to see romance blooming before the sons knew it had been planted. Noah had no intentions of continuing her winning streak with Damaris or anyone else.

"I know it's only been a few days," Damaris continued. "Which has probably been filled with a myriad of ways in which you're readjusting."

"That's an understatement. Everything is different. Almost every single thing I've ever done in life."

"I can't imagine."

Noah realized how good it felt to be sharing his feelings with someone who not only cared but, because of her profession, could possibly understand what he was going through better than most.

"Have you worked with other paralyzed patients?"

"Not in the capacity of a professional nurse. When in college, however, there was a little boy whom I studied with. His name was Trevor. He'd been paralyzed in a terrible freak accident where the industry-standard tractor his father used on their family farm malfunctioned when his dad put it in Drive and the machine went in Reverse. Trevor was standing behind it. His legs were crushed. It was horrific, to say the least. His family marveled that he lived, and even more at his spirit coming out of the chaos."

"Let me guess, his positive attitude," Noah replied, sarcasm dripping off the words.

"Not so much positive, as grateful. He was only seven years old at the time, nine now. But his perspective was so far beyond his years, very mature. He was happy to still be alive."

"Are you still in touch with him?"

"I am."

"Do you make it a practice of staying in touch with all of your patients?"

"No. Trevor is the only one."

"So, how did my mother convince you to call me?"

"She offered me a job."

Oh, here we go. Noah rolled his eyes. That was how she'd gotten her firstborn down the aisle.

"What could you do for me here?"

"Be a part of your medical team, same as when you were at Manning Valley."

Noah was shocked but not surprised. Many looking on would assume that their father, Nicholas, was where the Breedlove brothers got all their negotiation skills. That was true, in part. But calculated strategizing? That was all Victoria. The Breedlove family was her chessboard. She played for all to win.

"What do you think about that?" he finally asked.

"Not much, to be honest."

Her brutally forthright answer was refreshing. "Damn, girl. Say it like you mean it."

"I'm sorry. That wasn't meant to come off as a harsh statement. It's just that…"

Noah wheeled around so that he could see the home's perfectly landscaped backyard. A white peacock, part of a flock that roamed the Breedlove estate, strutted across the concrete surrounding the infinity pool. Once again, he was enjoying the verbal exchange with Damaris. He tried not to notice the way talking with her excited him.

"Go on."

"There are so many reasons I can't accept your mother's offer. Moving away from home and to Las Vegas of all places. Your company's stance on gambling, which is diametrically opposed to the faith that I practice. And yet…"

"Continue," he softly encouraged her. He watched as the sun began to sink behind a tall mountain as if it, too, was in line with setting a certain mood.

"Thinking of the offer from a practical and career-driven standpoint, it is certainly one that shouldn't be turned down outright. I'd work alongside some of the world's preeminent leaders in treating paralysis, and on the cutting edge of new technology to aid one's road back to a more normal way of life."

She paused, and Noah could imagine her actions. How she set her shoulders a certain way when needing mental reinforcement. He remained quiet, as he often did in business negotiations, where silence was often golden, and timing paramount.

"There's one very big problem, however," she said.

"And that is?"

"You."

"Me?"

"Us. Our last meeting didn't end on the best of terms."

"I'm sorry to have frightened you."

"Frightened? Excuse me? When did you think I was scared?"

"When you used being at work as an excuse to run away from our discussion."

"Being the youngest, you should know we never run away…from anything."

"Then you're considering my mother's offer?"

"Are you sure you want me to? I'm an überpositive, humming, religious nurse whose stance on gambling is not likely to change."

"And sometimes I can be an asshole. That's not likely to change soon, either. Plus, I'm going to keep fighting to build my casino. Given that knowledge, are you sure you want the job?"

"I probably shouldn't," she replied.

"Knowing Mom, I'm sure it's a generous and more than fair offer, so why not? Unless you're afraid."

"I thought you'd had enough of me here in Utah. I am sure there are any number of qualified nurses in Vegas, ones who love gambling and are ready to feed your ego in the quest to put slot machines all over the world."

"CANN International is about more than gambling."

"Prove it."

Now it was Noah's turn to get clarification. "Excuse me?"

"You said that part of the reason your company was fighting for a hotel in Salt Lake was to boost the economy, right?"

"That's correct." Noah sat straighter in his chair. Where was she going with this?

"Why can't you do that without the casino, with your company erecting a nongambling hotel and spa?"

"Because that is not the CANN brand, darling, an aspect of business I doubt you know much about. Your area of expertise is healing bodies. Mine is building casino hotels. I think this conversation will go much better if we stay in our perspective lanes."

"Agreed. That said, I'll let Victoria know that I can't take the position. I wish you well."

"That's no surprise. Only the best of the best can navigate our family's dynamics, and my specific set of challenges. Those who are weak in any area of their makeup need not apply, especially someone who lets an organization think for them instead of figuring out life on their own."

"Excuse me?"

"You heard me."

The response he received was a click and then silence. Damaris had hung up on him. Good. The last thing he needed was a gorgeous Goody Two-shoes around, one with soft curly hair his fingers itched to touch and a pair of eyes he could get lost in, though a little part of his heart had lightened at the thought of her coming to Vegas. He was focused on two things, walking and getting the casino bill passed, and not necessarily in that order. Anything else was a distraction, especially the angel named Dee.

Nine

Of all the pompous, arrogant, self-righteous posturing. The unmitigated gall! Damaris paced her room, about to burn a hole in the carpet of the upstairs room she'd called home for seventeen years before going to college and for the year since she'd graduated with a nursing degree. Who was he to insinuate that she was afraid to take the job? That she couldn't handle, what did he call it? Putting herself out there. How dare he suggest that she was a blind follower of faith unable to think for herself.

Damaris stopped, tapped the face of her phone and scrolled to Victoria's number. "I don't need to put up with this drama," she mumbled to herself as she pressed Victoria's number to make the connection.

Drama. Trauma.

Damaris hurriedly ended the call. The realization of the truth behind Noah's words hit her squarely between the eyes. She eased down on the bed, as the weight of the intuitive revelation settled on her heart. Noah's antics had nothing to do with her. His blustering was covering up what was really going on inside him. Fear. Not hers, his. Noah was the one who was afraid. Who wouldn't be? The world as he knew it had exploded. He'd landed unable to move his legs and didn't know if he'd do so again.

He landed in my care for a reason.

Damaris looked around the room, though the thought came from somewhere deep inside her. She went into nursing to help people get better, especially those dealing with trauma. Noah's experience was the sum total of all she'd learned, someone deeply troubled by an experience that had changed his world's paradigm. In that instant, what she needed to do became crystal clear. She again tapped a number on her cell phone, quickly, before she could think about what she was doing and change her mind.

"Damaris?"

Hearing her name caused an already rattled Damaris to search for words. "Um, yes, hi, Victoria."

"I recognized your number by the area code. You're my only Utah contact. Did you call just a moment ago?"

"Yes, that was me. I thought I disconnected the call before it went through."

"That's quite all right. I'm glad you called and hope it's to tell me you've accepted my job offer."

"Yes, I was calling to tell you that I'd take the job, though I'm not sure I should."

"Because of the gambling issue?"

"Because I just hung up on my patient."

Victoria laughed, much to Damaris's surprise. "I can guarantee you that doesn't happen too often. Did Noah deserve to be let go without a goodbye?"

"Given that I don't like being insulted, it was either that or say something that couldn't be taken back."

"Then good for you. I agree that it's exactly what you should have done. Now, I'll have my new assistant, Farrah, send over the employment agreement."

"Perhaps you should speak with Noah before we finalize this arrangement."

"I'll handle Noah. Meanwhile, please review the agreement carefully as it is legally binding. You've got what he needs—a determined attitude. Your arrival will be a perfect surprise."

Over the next several minutes, Damaris and Victoria ironed out the details of her employment, which would fall under a division of CANN International. Damaris voiced her discomfort in being connected to a business known for gambling. Victoria understood her concerns but assured her that wasn't a problem.

"Breedlove, Nevada, is twenty minutes and a world away from Vegas," Victoria assured her. "You'll live in an area where there is not a slot machine in sight."

Within hours, an agreement had been faxed over for Damaris's perusal and signature. Victoria wanted her to start right away. For her, having Damaris arrive the next day would have been preferable. But knowing the hospital was already short-staffed, Damaris gave her superiors a two-week notice and the promise to assist in finding her replacement. Before putting in her notice, she told Wendy. Her friend was ecstatic.

"Your whole world is about to change," she assured Damaris with a big bear hug. "Don't go all bright lights, big city and forget about us little people."

Telling her parents was going to be the hard part. Her father was an official consultant to the city council, and sure to know the Breedlove name. He'd object to her working for owners of a gambling enterprise or, worse, forbid her from leaving. Not wanting to again blatantly defy him, Damaris crafted a story that would not include the total truth but was not an outright lie, either. That night, during dinner, she broached the subject.

"I've taken a new job," she casually began, with her heart about to beat out of her chest.

"So soon?" her mother, Bethany, responded. "You were just assigned as head nurse in the trauma department. Where are they moving you?"

"It's not at Manning Valley Medical," Damaris said.

This piqued her father's interest. "They have the best trauma unit in the state. It's where you wanted to work."

"It is and I'm grateful to have been hired there. In fact, that position is what has led to an offer too good to refuse. I'll be working as a private nurse for a recent paraplegic, making twice what I'm making now and with similar benefits. I'll have to relocate for the position, but those expenses will be covered as part of the employment package."

"To where?" Franklin asked.

"Nevada." Damaris was careful not to say Las Vegas. Mentioning the state was tricky enough.

"Las Vegas?" Her father spat out the words she'd dared not utter.

"Oh, no," she hastily replied. "I made my stance on gambling very clear at the onset and was assured that where the patient lives, and where I'll reside, is far from that world."

"Nevada isn't a big enough state for it to be that far. Are they Laymen?" Franklin asked.

"No, but I've already gone online and found out that there is a church I can attend about ten minutes away. Have you ever visited the church in Nevada, Dad?"

"It's been years since I've stepped foot in Nevada but yes, I was there for that church's inaugural celebration. The pastor's name is Dean Sullivan. You know his grandfather, Pastor Joseph Sullivan, whose legacy goes all the way back to the founding members of our church."

Just great. Someone who intimately knows my father. While keeping that thought to herself, she said, "I saw that on the website and thought his name sounded familiar. He looks to have a lovely family—two boys and two girls."

"I think moving to a new location and a new congregation will be good for you," Bethany offered. "I'm sure there are fine young men in Pastor Sullivan's congregation. Ones who will get you thinking about marriage and starting your own family."

Damaris was glad the conversation shifted away from the Breedloves but not comfortable with its new direction. Especially since the face that sprang up when her mom mentioned marriage belonged to the handsome man about to be her sole patient. So what if even injured he radiated with confidence and swagger? Who cared if he was successful and ridiculously wealthy as Wendy had shared? None of it mattered, especially that. She was a Layman. He wasn't. He'd probably had sex. She hadn't. His family built casinos. Her family blocked them. They were polar opposites with only one thing in common—a desire to see Noah recover as quickly and fully as possible. She had two weeks to resolve any wayward feelings to the contrary once and for all. Over the days that followed she'd come to realize she needed every second.

The two weeks flew by in a whirlwind of packing, planning and searching for her replacement. Damaris was relieved when a nurse who'd recently relocated from the East Coast and had more than twenty years' experience sent in her résumé. She was interviewed that very afternoon and hired the next day. In between packing, there were several calls between Damaris and Victoria, who'd scheduled a meeting with Noah's team of caretakers the morning following her arrival. It was the first time Damaris would live outside her home state. The emotions she felt surprised her. However, with a farewell dinner that included her siblings, their spouses and friends from church, the Sullivans' phone number recorded in her phone and an admonition from her father to be at their church that Sunday, Damaris was dropped off at the airport the next day by her mother and boarded a flight into the unknown.

"Yo! Anybody home?"

Noah heard the front door open. "Where else would I be?" he yelled.

He reached the foyer just as Adam turned the corner. His brother removed his signature Stetson and brushed grass off his boots.

"You rode Thunder over."

"Yes, and realized there's something I need to add to your driveway. A hitching post."

"Great," Noah mumbled. "Yet another reminder of something else I can't do."

"Something you can't do today," Adam said. "From the looks of the physical therapist you hired away from Utah, the situation could look different as early as tomorrow."

Noah wheeled around and headed toward the kitchen. Adam followed him. "How's he working out?"

"Travis? He's cool. Strong enough to help do what I can't do myself. Missing a sympathy gene, which works in his favor."

Adam accepted the bottle of beer that Noah offered. "I heard that." He unscrewed the top and took a healthy swallow. "What else is going on?"

"Besides assembling the team to help put me back together? Not much."

"How's that going?"

"Mom's pretty much in charge. She hired a nurse who'll work closely with Travis and be a liaison to the specialists and the staff at the institute."

"I've heard the Nevada Institute of Medicine has some of the best. Still, it's too bad you couldn't get that PYT from the hospital in Utah."

Noah knew Damaris was the pretty young thing to whom Adam referred. "It's just as well. She's too holy for the likes of this place."

"Right, a Layman. That was a surprise."

"Why?"

Adam shrugged. "I guess I assumed that the women in a church like that would be wearing long dresses and bonnets."

"Maybe she does," Noah mumbled sarcastically.

"She could wear a burlap sack and still turn heads."

"Hey! Whose side are you on?"

Adam raised his hands. "Sorry, bro. Just saying. Hey, did you talk to her about Project Salt Lake? Maybe it's just the old guard resisting. Maybe Dee and the younger members could be the bridge between sides."

"That would be a negative, my good man. She doesn't want the casino, either. Believes the project should move ahead as just a hotel and spa."

"Damn! We're so close! You and the team have gone further than any of us imagined. When the mayor came on board…"

"He brought the rest of the business community with him. The Church of Laymen is our last holdout."

"And you've got how long to change their minds?"

"Probably not long enough. The council is going to choose a date at their next meeting—a special session to vote on this issue alone."

"Then I guess you're right."

"About what?"

"Dee the Layman not being the right nurse for you. Still won't hurt if whoever Mom finds is attractive. I think a sexy nurse is like a spoonful of sugar."

Noah cocked a brow.

"You know, helps the medicine go down."

"That was really lame," Noah deadpanned.

"True, though," Adam replied.

"Given what Travis told Mom, it will probably be a dude. He's got some business to handle on the East Coast in the next two weeks that will take him away for several days."

"What does that have to do with who'll be your nurse?"

"The physical capacity to help me do what until now I took for granted—walk, bathe, dress, stuff like that."

"Sorry, bro," Adam said with a hand on his brother's shoulder.

"Don't worry about it," Noah responded. "It is what it is."

Damaris thought she'd prepared herself to enter rich man's land. Wrong. As a set of massive wrought-iron gates opened and the car journeyed down a smoothly paved road surrounded by meticulously landscaped beauty, she realized two things. The pictures online of the Breedlove mansion did not do it justice and there was a level of rich beyond what she'd imagined. She wondered about the people who lived in what was described to her as a subdivision of Breedlove, Nevada, architectural wonders that sat on huge plots of land on appropriately named streets like Ace of Diamonds Alley and Royal Flush Road. As she worked to take in all that they passed—grazing horses, strutting peacocks, cows dotting the landscape behind what looked like a ranch—they turned into the circular drive of a stately mansion that appeared large enough to be a hotel. Damaris watched as the front door opened and Victoria walked out to greet her.

"Damaris!"

She stepped out of the car and into Victoria's welcoming embrace. "Welcome to Breedlove!"

Victoria hooked her arm in Damaris's and began walking them toward the door. "Don't worry about your bags. They'll be deposited at your new home. I hope you're hungry. I understand Noah's personal chef, Jermaine, has put together a scrumptious meal. In a bit, we'll head there for lunch. He's a new hire and I can't wait to try his food. Goodness! Listen to me ramble." Victoria took Damaris's hand and squeezed it. "I'm just so glad you're here."

They'd stepped through a set of ornately designed double doors and into a massive foyer straight off a Hollywood movie soundstage. The floor was slate tile. The ceiling was at least twenty feet high, dominated by a chandelier with a value that Damaris guessed probably exceeded some country's GNP. It was all she could do not to drop her jaw and gawk like a country bumpkin.

"How was your flight?"

"Thankfully, uneventful." They reached a hallway beyond which were paneless windows that showcased an expansive backyard. "Your home is stunning."

"Thank you. Making it and then keeping it that way is an ongoing labor of love."

They tied up a few loose ends regarding Damaris's employment, such as clarifying work hours and the days she'd have off. Victoria invited her to freshen up in the guest bath before they piled into her brand-new custom Escalade for the short drive to Noah's home. Again, Damaris was struck by the size and splendor of the homes that dotted the countryside. Before she had the chance to inquire about these neighbors, however, Victoria pulled into a driveway.

"Noah has no idea you've been hired," Victoria said, her eyes gleaming mischievously. "I can't wait to see his reaction."

"You didn't tell him?" Damaris wasn't sure surprising him was the best idea.

"No, but he'll be happy with my choice. Trust me," Victoria said, as she reached for the door handle. "A mother knows."

They walked up a ramp leading to a wide wraparound porch.

"Noah!" Victoria sang out, as she reached for the door. "Where are you? I'm with the newest member of your team!"

"In the dining room, Mom. Ready to dig into this feast that's…"

As Victoria came around the corner with Damaris in tow, his words died.

"Hello, Noah," Damaris said in a voice lighter and softer than she'd intended.

"Dee," he replied, his face devoid of emotion. "What are you doing here?"

Ten

Great. Just what he needed. Noah laid down his fork and plopped back in the chair—his appetite fleeing along with his smile. He'd spent the better part of the morning debating those with her mindset, people who felt it was their right— no, duty—to determine how and where other adults spent their money. And here one comes, invited by his mother no less, right through his front door.

"I asked you a question," Noah said. "Why—"

"Please, forgive my son's lack of manners," Victoria interrupted, gesturing toward a cushioned seat while seamlessly gliding over the awkward moment. "You remember Damaris, darling, from Manning Valley Medical."

"I remember the Layman," he snapped. "The one who'd never before been to Nevada. It's still Sin City," he taunted. "Do you think anything's changed?"

"I was hoping you had," Damaris calmly replied, meeting his steely gaze with her own. "It is clear there is more work to do."

"And you think you're the one to do it?" He asked this in the same brusque tone, even though inwardly he thought her flippant reply was sexy as hell.

"Victoria does."

Victoria reached for a pitcher of lemony tea and began filling their glasses. "I met with an agency, Noah, and considered their recommendations. In my opinion, Dee's attributes will best complement the rest of the team and lead to what we all want, for you to fully recover."

Noah reached for his glass, his eyes on Damaris. "What do you think?"

"I've studied hard, worked harder and am confident in my skills. But the team and I are only half of the equation. The other half involves desire, determination, attitude, belief. I think those intangibles as much as any medical procedure go a long way to aiding recovery. Can you walk again? I think so. But will you, and how long will that take? That, I think, is entirely up to you."

The room fell silent, even as a tension heightened by mutual attraction fairly crackled in the air.

After a moment, Victoria asked, "Well, Noah, do you agree that Dee will be an asset to your medical team?"

"I do," he replied, somewhat begrudgingly. "Just can't believe she accepted your offer."

"Your mom drives a hard bargain," Damaris said, as she took the tongs Victoria offered and placed a helping of beef on her plate.

Offered a lot of that evil money, he wanted to say, but held his tongue. Before starting another argument, no matter how stimulating, he needed to at least wait until her bags were unpacked.

Victoria lifted the lid of a serving bowl, releasing the fragrant aroma of roasted vegetables with the steam. "I was quite persistent," she admitted.

"You didn't have to be."

Noah placed a freshly baked roll on a saucer and reached for the herb butter beside it. At her answer, his hand stilled.

"This is a rare and unique opportunity to work with specialists who are at the top of their fields. I can learn so much during the time that I'm here, then apply that knowledge while working with other trauma patients when I return to Manning Valley Medical or wherever I'm hired."

He resumed eating, chagrined that his thoughts had drifted toward the impossible. What did he think Damaris was going to say? That she found him attractive, and came here to date? That they were fresh out of gamblers, not to mention paraplegics, in Utah so she thought to give this Breedlove a shot?

"Damaris has already provided valuable input regarding your overall treatment," Victoria was saying when Noah tuned back in. "Over the past week, she and Travis have begun mapping out a game plan that will coincide with what's done at the rehab center and through the doctor's recommendations."

Noah was stunned. "You were hired over a week ago?" No answer. "What else have you two been plotting behind my back?"

"Only the plan to get you better," Victoria answered, after finishing a bite. "Which will have to include a good amount of exercise if Jermaine keeps fixing meals as delicious as this one. Don't be shy," she said to Damaris. "Help yourself to more food."

"Everything's delicious. I've never eaten such tender beef."

"Repeat that the next time you're around Adam," Noah said. "You'll become his friend for life."

Over a lunch filled with some of the best foods Damaris had tasted, the three put Noah's health aside and chatted on more casual topics. Victoria and Noah plied Damaris with tales of growing up in Breedlove's Wild West, with Sin City in the background. Damaris shared being raised in a conservative enclave where life revolved around church and family. Noah was amazed at Damaris's lack of knowledge when it came to pop culture, from popular music and video games to the latest blockbuster films. He was equally impressed of her love for the outdoors; how her family camped, hunted and went skiing on a regular basis. Noah could tell Damaris was initially nervous and liked how she grew more animated the more she relaxed.

Lunch ended with a light dessert of strawberries and vanilla cream over shortcake biscuits. Shortly after the last forkful, Victoria looked at her watch.

"I have a foundation meeting before Nicholas and I leave for a dinner engagement. Noah, would you be kind enough to give Dee a tour of her home, and make sure she gets settled in for the night?"

"That's no problem."

She turned to Damaris. "Your pantry is stocked, and Noah's new chef, Jermaine, has placed a couple days' supply of fresh frozen dishes in your freezer. We didn't know if you cooked or not and wanted to make sure you didn't starve."

"I do cook but it's nice to have something already prepared."

"Breakfast at the main house is at eight. You're welcome to join us. Our meeting begins at nine in the same place we met earlier."

Victoria said her goodbyes and sailed out of the room.

"Well," Damaris began, watching her exit, "were you really as shocked as you sounded when I walked into the room?"

"Even more than that." Noah began wheeling himself from the room. Damaris followed him. "You had my number. Why didn't you call?"

"I'd already given notice at Manning Valley Medical and didn't want to take the chance of getting fired barely after being hired."

"Ha! Can't say I blame you. Given our last few conversations, that chance was real."

"Exactly."

"Even though during our last conversation, as I recall, you hung up on me."

"As I remember it, the call got disconnected."

"Yeah, by your finger."

Damaris suppressed a smile. "Perhaps."

* * *

Damaris admired the furnishings as they passed through the living room and down the hall to the front door. Unlike the main house clearly stamped with Victoria's signature, this decor was simple, masculine, a blending of rustic and modern that Damaris guessed was quite like the man who lived here. She assumed the van outside was wheelchair accessible and that was what they'd be driving to her home. Instead of heading down the ramp as she'd almost done, Noah continued down the length of the porch to another front door that mirrored the one she'd just closed.

Noah stopped his chair just to the left of the entrance. "Welcome to your new home."

Damaris's eyes flared briefly. "My home?"

"Yes."

"I'm staying here?"

Noah nodded. "This is a duplex. The architects did a brilliant job of disguising that fact."

Damaris worked to process Noah's simple revelation, to juxtapose it over the humble abode she'd imagined would be hers as part of the Breedloves' household staff. She tried to hide her shock but judging from the smirk on Noah's face, she wasn't totally successful. Shock gave way to mortification at what her family would think of her living arrangement. That she would be a single woman living alone, next door to a single man. Any normal person would conclude that a man paralyzed from the waist down posed no sexual threat to his daughter but for Laymen there were sins that could be done with one's hand. Or mouth. Or mind. She was about to voice an objection when another thought occurred. Surely this entire place wasn't for her. She hadn't considered that the entire staff would share quarters but given the size it shouldn't be a problem.

"Do Travis and your chef live here, too?"

"No, Dee. This is all yours." Damaris stood staring at the

still-closed door. "Unlike mine, this door isn't automatic. You have to open it manually to go inside."

Still trying to figure out how to graciously refuse such trappings, she opened the door and stepped into a type of fairy tale. She expected a layout exactly as she'd just seen next door, but its design was totally different, and decidedly feminine.

"Mom usually only provides the basic furnishings for guest homes," Noah explained as he came up behind her. "She likes whoever stays to be able to make it their own."

"It's...big."

Damaris crossed the foyer to a wide hall that led to an open-concept area. Beyond it was a kitchen and dining area with a bar counter running between them. Large, bare windows let in tons of light, along with sweeping views of the land around them. The grass was a vibrant green even as snowcapped mountains loomed in the distance.

"Is that a lake?"

"Yes."

"Man-made?"

"Designed by my father, Adam and another trout-fishing enthusiast."

"It adds to the beauty of the landscape."

The glistening water, tinged blue by the sky along with the verdant greenery and white-capped mountains was a breathtaking site. Utah was beautiful but Damaris had to give it to the Breedloves. They'd taken their land and fashioned a bit of paradise.

But she couldn't live here. That point was made plain moments later, as the tour continued.

"This is the master," Noah said, rolling into a suite the size of a small apartment. It was on the back side of the home, offering that glorious view of lakes and mountains.

"Go on in, take a look. If you're anything like the women in my family, you'll really love the closet. It's huge."

Damaris stepped into a sitting area separated from the

actual bedroom by a half-wall bookshelf. There was a fireplace! In her bedroom! Leaving would be harder than Damaris first thought. Perhaps she was being silly to make such a big deal of living next door to Noah. Even though being alone in the home of a man who was not a relative, a man whose handsomeness awoke parts of her she didn't know were sleeping, was not Layman appropriate.

He's your patient. Get a grip! Her inner voice spoke with authority and gave her the courage to continue the tour, which included a guest bedroom, hall bath, the magnificent kitchen with everything stocked as Victoria had said and an outdoor sitting area that was enclosed and private.

They returned to the hallway. Noah pressed a hidden button. A portion of the wall lowered to reveal an electronic panel that worked everything from lighting to sound. He explained the intercom, video and security systems and then nodded toward a tray in the foyer that held a set of keys.

"A car for your use is in the garage. There's a walkway between our homes, through the garage, so that during inclement weather or when it's a million degrees you won't have to go outside."

He stopped, looked around. "I guess that's it."

"Thank you for showing me around. It's a beautiful home."

"If you need anything, just, um, hit me up on the intercom."

"Okay."

Noah made no move to leave. "Would you like to have a drink or something? I'd like to learn a little more about your role on the team."

"Sure."

Yes, let's talk professional. The more their conversations stayed focused on business the easier it would be for Damaris to remember why she was here, the only reason.

"Shall we see how well that kitchen is stocked?"

"Okay." Silly, but the simple statement made her nervous.

She and Noah in her temporary home felt, well, too homey. In looking at him it struck her that this was the first time except for Matthew, or work, she'd ever been alone with a man who wasn't family.

"It's your place," Noah said, motioning for Damaris to go ahead of him. "After you."

They entered the kitchen. Damaris opened a panel of the double-door refrigerator that had been stocked with organic canned drinks. Next to it, a counter boasted a Keurig machine, and a wooden box holding a variety of coffees and teas.

"What would you like?"

Before the sentence was finished, Damaris realized the double entendre she'd thrown out. "To drink," she added.

Noah smiled, confirming that he'd totally caught it. "Whatever you're having."

She pulled two colas from the fridge and glasses from the cabinet. She filled them with ice, poured the drinks and began walking toward a patio door.

"It's not that cold and I noticed a firepit. Let's sit outside."

The seating area held a table and two chairs, the perfect height for Noah.

"I can't believe I'm here," she said, leaning against the chair's back. "How are you, Noah…really?"

"I'm okay."

Those eyes again, black, piercing, caused Damaris's stomach to flip-flop and made her mouth go dry. She took a long drink of cola, appreciating the burn as it went down her throat.

"This land, your home is beautiful. Everything here is like something you see in movies."

"It went up as fast as some do on a set. This place wasn't here two weeks ago."

"Your mother told me about the superfast build. I would have thought that impossible."

"Almost anything becomes possible when you stack the

coins high enough. Dad and my brothers got together with a leading West Coast construction company who hired additional crew and had this built so I could get around in a wheelchair and…have help nearby."

"It's hard to believe that all of this was just built. The decor, furniture, everything seems cozy, so right for the room, as if lived in for a while. And outside, the lawn, all of the landscaping is impeccable."

Noah sipped his soda and surveyed the land. "My mom's vision, mostly, along with incredible architectural, interior design and landscaping teams. Not much happens beyond the gate without being put past her first." He sipped his cola and looked around. "Thanks for that, though. Nice to appreciate the land through a newcomer's eyes."

"Is she a part of the neighborhood association?" Damaris was eager to learn about the other families who lived here.

Noah frowned. "Huh?"

"We passed several homes before reaching the duplex. Do all of the owners participate in what decisions are made?"

"No, my mom pretty much runs things." He paused, smiling. "It's all Breedlove property, Damaris. The homes you passed belong to family or are guesthouses. The ranch is Adam's. He breeds that delicious beef you ate."

"Your brother is a rancher? He doesn't work in the family business?"

"All of us brothers work in the business. The ranch is a side hustle."

One that, according to Wendy's research, had made several million dollars last year. Damaris couldn't imagine making that much money per year working one job full-time, even two. Noah continued to watch her intently, making Damaris realize she'd stopped talking. Casual conversation was hard. The guy did things to her insides and made her want to squirm. She returned to the safe topics of medicine and healing, hoping to break the spell.

"I'm surprised at how quickly your facial injuries are healing. You can hardly see the cut on your forehead."

"Yeah, Ryan and a friend at the spa brought around their miracle potions. Looks like they're working."

"I look forward to visiting her practice one day. It includes a spa, as well?"

"The spa is part of our hotel."

"Oh."

Again, conversation faltered. She glanced at Noah from beneath her lashes, watched his fingers beat a silent rhythm on the arm of his wheelchair before finishing his drink. He was tense, too. After another few seconds of silence, they both spoke at once.

"I should really—"

"You probably want to—"

"Go ahead," Noah said.

"I was thinking to call my family and let them know I arrived safely."

"That's a good idea." Noah headed across the shared patio to his sliding glass doors. "No worries. I'll see you later."

"I'll come over to do a quick checkup—temperature, blood pressure, stuff like that."

"Only if you think it's necessary. Otherwise, it's okay if you take the rest of the day and get settled. I think I'll live until tomorrow."

"Okay, thanks, Noah. Verbal feuds aside, I look forward to helping in your healing journey."

His gaze intensified in an unreadable expression. "Me, too, Dee. Me, too."

Eleven

"There's a meeting at corporate tomorrow," was Nick's greeting the next morning after Noah opened the door. "You need to be there. This house is cool, so much so that I'm thinking about using that construction firm when I get ready to build. But you can't hide out forever."

"Who says I'm hiding?" Noah spat over his shoulder, wheeling himself through the living area and onto the patio beyond it.

"I'm saying it, bro." He followed Noah outside. "Not that I'm trying to be insensitive."

"Yes, you are. Dee would probably applaud the comment. I probably need a good kick to get off my pity pot."

"She's the more informal Dee now, huh? How's the pretty nurse working out?"

"Pretty well."

"Mom seems to like her."

"Mom likes every potential daughter-in-law."

"True that. From what I've seen so far, you could do much worse."

"Definitely couldn't do any better, not now. I can't imagine any woman in our circles wanting to spend their life pushing a chair around."

Noah's eyes narrowed. "Sounds like you need to expand your imagination. You're a good man, Twin, same as you've always been. Legs didn't make you and they will not break you."

"Easy for you to say. You're standing on yours."

Nick sighed as he sat on a patio chair. "I felt you that day, when it happened. It was late night in Africa. Chris and I had just left from having dinner with our hosts and were being driven home. We were riding along and something hit me. Bam! Like I'd been punched. Out of the blue. Ask Chris. He saw it and thought I was playing around. I wasn't. When we got the news about you a short time later, it wasn't a total surprise."

Nick stroked his chin as he looked over the land. "I hate what happened to you, man. It kills me, for real. I can't imagine you spending the rest of your life like this, so the only thing I can think of to do is encourage you to get better, to force life back to the way it was. I know it's only been three weeks and you're working hard to recover physically. It's your focus. I get that. I just know how much you love the business, how much that world is your normal. Makes your blood flood and your brain tick, just like me. I'm also a bit familiar with your type A personality and am not used to seeing someone else run your show."

His twin was right. When Noah returned to Las Vegas, he hadn't wanted to see anyone. He'd been in the news and knew everyone was wondering what exactly had happened. That his peers were curious as to the severity of his injuries. He couldn't stay hidden forever. He just hated the thought of being viewed by the public as that guy in the chair and pitied because of it. The thought of being labeled disabled was something he was loath to admit bothered him. But it did.

"You know what, bro? I'm an asshole, okay? Don't worry about showing up tomorrow. We'll videoconference you in if we need to. Just focus on getting better."

"Don't do that."

"What?"

"Start coddling me. Right now I need the asshole who cuts me no slack. Got it?" Noah held out his hand for a fist bump.

Nick leaned over with an outstretched fist. "Got it."

"Now, what's going on that I don't know about?"

Nick hopped up from the chair, walked over to a fridge in the outdoor kitchen and pulled out a bottle of beer. He held it up to Noah, who shook his head.

He returned to his seat and unscrewed the cap. "Dad didn't want me to say anything, at least not yet."

"About what?"

"The extent of your injuries is about to be made public."

"What? How?"

"Someone leaked the story to a major publication. We don't know who and Sandy won't name his source."

"Sandy is breaking the story?"

Sandy Lebowitz was a business reporter and longtime associate of the Breedloves. He'd done articles on them and the CANN organization for more than a decade.

"If he doesn't, someone else will. At least he had the decency to call the office, tell us what he had and give us, you specifically, a heads-up."

Noah spat out an expletive.

"I know. It sucks. But given how many people it took to get you here and the money a story like this could net, it was bound to happen."

A thought caused Noah's heart to almost stop beating. "Do you think it was Dee?"

"The nurse?"

"No, the groundskeeper."

"Whoa! Where'd that come from?"

"From the list of possible suspects."

Nick shook his head. "She doesn't seem like the kind of person to do something like that."

"I didn't think she was someone who'd take a job behind my back, either, but she did."

Noah could tell he'd shocked his brother. "You didn't hire her? Mom hired her without your input?"

"Yes and no. While at Manning Valley Medical she'd

bring her up, asked me if I was satisfied with the level of care she provided."

"Are you?"

"Yes, but... I don't know. I guess that since she's a member of the conservative Church of Laymen, I'm just surprised she took the job. Unless..."

Nick leaned forward. "Unless what?"

"Unless she had an ulterior motive for coming here."

"What kind of motive? Money? Fame? She's a nurse, dude, and while I wasn't around her all that much at the hospital, I'm a pretty good judge of character and she didn't give off a gamer kind of vibe."

Noah wasn't listening. He was already halfway to the patio door. Once inside, he went straight to his phone and tapped the face.

"Mom, I need to see Dee's résumé." He paused, frowned. "I don't have time to explain right now. Can you email it to me ASAP? I need to check something out, that's all."

He disconnected the call, turned and took in Nick's questioning gaze. "The Church of Laymen is the only reason the hotel bill is stalled in council. My paralysis becoming public could call my very competence into question and make it easier for those still deciding to be swayed back to the church's side. You feel me?"

"Not really. Dee didn't have to accept a position here to do that. She could have blown your cover while you were in Utah, had photographers snapping you on the stretcher, or inside the hospital. She could have tipped someone off when you were leaving so you'd be snapped in the chair. If she was the one who leaked what happened to the press, I think coming here and sleeping mere yards away from the person wronged is the last place she'd want to be."

Noah eased back against his chair. "You're probably right."

His phone dinged. He tapped the mail icon, downloaded the file Victoria had sent and opened it up. At the top of the one-page document in bold letters, all caps, was her full name: Damaris Glen.

One glance and Noah's hackles were raised. "No, can't be," he whispered. He did a quick internet search and confirmed the impossible. A major opponent to the bill, Franklin Glen, and Damaris Glen were not just related. Damaris was his daughter.

He went into his office and retrieved the tablet he'd placed there. "She's up to something."

"You're still talking about Dee?" By the tone of Nick's voice, he was clearly confused.

Noah's fingers flew over the touch keyboard. He used his forefinger to scroll down several pages until he found the information he wanted. "'Franklin Glen, Associate Pastor/ Business Development, Church of Laymen.'"

"Okay." Said as a question, or statement, or both.

"She's his daughter, Twin," Noah said, fuming. "Damaris is the daughter of my toughest opponent, the guy fighting the hardest to keep gambling out of Utah and the casino bill from going through!"

"One more time. What could she gain from coming here to work for you?"

"I don't know," Noah said, heading toward the front door. "But she's good at keeping secrets, I know that. She accepted the job from Mom behind my back. Discussed gambling and Project Salt Lake City without once mentioning her father!" The more Noah remembered, the angrier he got. "So I don't know what's going on in that head of hers. But I sure as hell am going to find out!"

"Twin!" Nick hurried to catch up with his fast-rolling brother. He grabbed the handgrip just as Noah neared the door. "I understand you wanting clarification and more information. But go over there like the brother I know, the one that's too cool for school. There might be a logical explanation to whatever you're supposing. You don't want to offend the very person who's upended her life and relocated here to help you."

Noah took a breath. "You're right. Thanks, bro."

"The last time you got this heated over a woman, y'all were dating."

"Don't go there." Thinking about his corporate-ladder-climbing ex was the last thing Noah needed.

"I won't but you might. Damaris is fine."

He opened the door. Noah stuck up his middle finger as he went toward Dee's house. He could hear Nick's laughter as he reached the door and pressed the bell. Nick pulled out of Noah's drive and gave a honk as he drove away. Noah waved, and waited. Two minutes, longer. He rang the bell again.

Is she trying to avoid me? Does she have a feeling that her cover is already blown and she's coming up with a story?

Too cool for school began to feel like heat in the street as five minutes later, he was still on the other side of the door. He rang the bell a third time, then opened the screen, about to bang on the wooden interior door when it jerked open.

"Noah! What is it? Is there something wrong?"

At that moment all kinds of wrong happened, starting with the thoughts that ran through Noah's mind as he took in Damaris's freshly showered appearance. Her hair wrapped in a towel. A short silk robe hastily tied. Bare feet with toenails painted a lickable shade of coral pink. His eyes took a slow crawl from her feet to her face, one that eyed him questionably even as a blush dusted her neck and crept up her chin, making her even more attractive than seconds before.

"That's what I came to find out!" He took a breath and added more softly, "I'm sorry. I should have used the intercom."

"Why didn't you? What's the matter? Are you experiencing some type of physical discomfort?"

But for the fact that he couldn't feel below the waist, Noah was sure he'd be in the stiffest kinds of pain.

"How I feel physically has nothing to do with why I'm upset. We need to talk."

"I can dress and be over to your house in ten minutes."

"This can't wait," Noah countered, working to keep his anger in check. "We need to talk now."

She eyed him for a moment. "Okay, come in."

He entered the house, feeling justified though a bit embarrassed at how he'd almost been ready to beat down her door. How he acted around her wasn't like him. Damaris stirred something in him, a simmering fire. Crazy thing was, Noah wasn't sure he wanted it to be put out.

"Give me a moment," she said when they entered the living room. She left Noah alone with a chance to gather his thoughts, returning moments later with skinny jeans beneath the now properly tied robe, still-damp hair in a high ponytail, and feet bare.

She sat on the couch and pulled her legs beneath her. "Okay, what do we need to talk about?"

"Your father, Franklin Glen."

She'd almost contained any reaction, but Noah was an expert at people reading. He'd noted the slight widening of the eyes and stiffening neck.

"What about him?"

"Why didn't you tell me?"

"That he was my father? You didn't ask."

"So you lied by omission?" Noah asked.

"I didn't lie at all," Damaris replied curtly. "And I resent you insinuating that I did."

"You didn't lie and didn't come clean, either. All of the discussions about gambling in Utah, the Church of Laymen being the only reason the bill hasn't passed, and the thought to mention your dad's intrinsic involvement never came to mind?"

"It did, but obviously I decided against it. His position on gambling has nothing to do with my work as your nurse and my assisting the medical team. Keeping those two worlds separate seemed sensible then and, given your reaction, an appropriate decision."

Noah watched as Damaris leaned against the couch, the flash of anger gone from her eyes. She'd sounded sincere. Noah almost believed her, *almost* being the operative word.

"Are you sure there isn't more to the story? Given your unexpected arrival and the plans with my mother of which I was unaware, I think my question is *appropriate*." He repeated with emphasis the word she'd used to describe her decision. Her crossed arms signaled it irked her, as he knew it would.

"What exactly are you asking?"

"Are you here on his behalf?" Noah asked just as directly, believing a straightforward conversation was the best one to have.

What happened next was totally unexpected. Damaris cracked up. Not a polite chuckle, or a sexy giggle meant to tickle his senses. A full-out, head-thrown-back, gut-busting guffaw.

"You're kidding, right?" she finally asked.

"You know how hard we worked to keep the severity of my accident private, right?"

Damaris sobered a bit. "Yes."

"Well, someone leaked it to a major publication. The story is going to run next week."

"Oh, no. I'm sorry, Noah. Wait." The humorous gleam in her eye disappeared. "You think I had something to do with that?"

"News of my…situation…could negatively impact Project Salt Lake."

"And you think I would disregard the hospital's privacy policy, ignore my own integrity and expose my patient's medical condition to somehow help my dad?"

"Business is a dirty game—"

"I'm not in business. I'm in health care. And I take strong exception to the implication of what you're asking. If I was going to expose you, why would I accept Victoria's offer? I was the second medical to see you after the EMTs, had full access to your records from the day you fell and ample opportunity to bring out the paparazzi or whoever covers people in the public eye. No, Noah. I haven't and would never talk to anyone outside the hospital about any of my patients, under any condition. Understand?"

He'd been properly chastised and damn if she didn't look delicious while doing it, especially since in her hand-gesturing, her robe had loosened to provide him the merest of glimpses to the fullness of a lovely breast. She followed his eyes and pulled the fabric together.

"Sorry, natural reaction." Noah looked away. "I admit to coming over with the preconceived notion that your father's position against our building a casino in your state may have something to do with you accepting this job."

Damaris's eyes slid from him to an arrangement of exotic flowers on a table across the room, then above them to the large living room window and the world beyond it. The look on her face combined with her silence made Noah feel foolish. Nick was right. Damaris wasn't the conniving type. Noah wasn't normally one to go off half-cocked. Then again, nothing in his life had been normal since he fell off a mountain.

"Why didn't you tell me that Franklin Glen was your father?"

"As I said before, you didn't ask. The names of my parents never came up in my conversations with Victoria and listing them on my résumé never crossed my mind. I assume you met him at one of the council meetings?"

"Assume? Given he's the church's primary representative at those meetings and acts on their behalf, you were probably sure of it."

"He doesn't discuss the church's business with me, but I

felt there was a chance that you two had met. Dad is practical, pragmatic and honest. Everything he's seen about the impact of gambling has gone into his staunch opposition to your casino. Information I shared openly, by the way, while still in Utah. What made you think CANN could achieve what no one else has done? Legalized gambling in any and every form has been proposed and promoted over and again. No matter the package, each time it has tried and failed."

"No other method would bring as many jobs to the city as our casino hotel. It would attract tourists, who would then spend money at other businesses. There's a reason why your church is in the minority. A strong enough force to slow the progress, for sure, but not enough to stop it."

"If a better economy is your goal, why not do everything you've planned except without a casino? There would still be jobs and a reason to visit. Your hotels are known all over the world."

"Because without a casino, it wouldn't be CANN."

Damaris gave his comment some thought. "Let me give you some advice that you didn't ask for. There's no way a bill to build a casino in Salt Lake will ever pass. A large majority of its residents belong to the church. That said, and for the record, I'm not here for my father. I'm here for you, as your nurse and caretaker. The only fight I'm waging is one where you will walk again."

Undoubtedly, she meant those words. It showed in her eyes. His mother was almost always right. This time was no exception. Damaris was a great addition to the team.

"I believe you." He held out his hand. "Truce?"

She made a face and moved her hand farther away. "I don't know," she said, her voice coated with mock doubt.

The unexpected reaction made him laugh. "Come on, don't be like that."

She slowly stretched out her arm and placed her hand in his. Their eyes locked and held as she softly replied, "Truce."

He meant to release her hand, but the next thing he knew he'd pulled it to his lips and kissed it.

"Thank you."

"You're welcome."

So soft, Noah thought as, not wanting to let go, he turned over her hand. He resisted the urge to trace her lifeline with his tongue and instead used his finger.

"What are you doing?" she whispered, gently pulling back her hand.

It was a question to which Noah had no answer. He shrugged.

"I'm glad we cleared the air," she said.

"Me, too," Noah said, although to him the air was heavier than it had ever been, filled with unspoken words, hidden desire and the allure of something impossible, and off-limits.

When Noah left a short time later, the stormy encounter had given way to calm waves of understanding. Damaris didn't know it but their talk had also given Noah a new dose of determination. To say that something could never be done made him all the more resolved to do it. Unwittingly, she'd given him something else. The first inklings of another possibility for a way to make it happen.

That idea, however, would have to wait. The most pressing issue was to get ahead of the story that would break in a few days. A meeting was hastily called involving Nicholas, Noah, the brothers, the company publicist and key staff members from CANN. Later that night, Noah posted a video on the company website, which was later sent to the major news networks and business publications. They couldn't keep the extent of Noah's injuries a secret. But they could somewhat control the narrative.

The shot was filmed in Noah's home office, a masterfully blended design of casual and contemporary. He sat behind one of his favorite furniture pieces, an antique mahogany desk rumored to have been owned by one of the state's founders. His stylist had suggested a business casual look and paired a tailed black suit coat with a pin-striped shirt and no tie. His hair was freshly cut. Though the suggestion was made to camouflage it with makeup, Noah decided not to hide the scar on his forehead. It gave him a roguish air. The camera crew set up a teleprompter and after several revisions and run-throughs, Noah delivered the message that he hoped would limit any potential damage to his prospective business deals once the news of his paralysis was out.

"Good evening. I'm Noah Breedlove with CANN International. Several weeks ago, as was reported on many news outlets, I was involved in a serious skiing accident on Daredevil Mountain near Manning Valley, Utah. What was not reported at that time was the extent of my injuries. Fractures occurred along my spinal cord that have rendered me temporarily paralyzed in my lower extremities. A team of world-leading specialists believes that I can and will make a full recovery. I'd hoped to already be walking, which is why I chose not to share this before. I disclose the challenge at this time not only because of the inevitable leak that is forthcoming but also as an otherwise healthy young man, a corporate executive who can put a somewhat public face on a disability that is experienced by thousands of people in this country and all over the world. I have a new appreciation for the brave men and women who experience what I have and still have the courage, strength and determination to live full lives, who do so whether they recover fully or not. My legs are temporarily out of commission, but my mind is still very much intact. I'll continue to kick butt, take names and make deals. To all of the CANN family and the customers we serve, thank you for your support."

Onscreen he came across as strong yet caring, successfully navigating the unexpected circumstances of his life. Inside he'd been a bundle of nerves. His mother assured him it didn't show.

"You were marvelous, honey. I'm so proud of you."

His dad, Nicholas, and all of his brothers praised him, as well. But it wasn't until the next morning when Damaris arrived to take his vitals and deliver his morning medications that Noah truly felt what he'd recorded had truly delivered.

"I watched your announcement," she said, pausing from her work to look at him directly. "I was moved to hear you share your heart, and relate to others, most without your resources, who are battling this same challenge. Noah, you'll never know how many people you helped."

"Let's just hope that my words prove true, your prayers work and my paralysis is indeed temporary."

"Either way, I think what you said was pretty amazing."

Noah hadn't realized how much Damaris's opinion about his taping mattered. But it did.

Twelve

That day after Noah left her house, Damaris didn't sleep much. She lay awake reexamining all of the choices and events that lined up to bring her here to work as Noah's nurse. She thought about the kiss, Noah's lips on her skin. As a woman, not a nurse. She allowed in memories that hadn't been revisited since Matt died. Too painful. Once shameful. The closest intimacy she'd experienced with a man because, until married, doing so was against the rules. The thing was, Damaris finally acknowledged, at least to herself, that she didn't agree with that rule, and many of the others she'd been taught as truth. But what was she going to do about it?

The woman she was becoming was a different person from the little girl her parents raised. Admitting that to herself was one thing but what did that mean? To go against the church was to go against her family. To leave one meant being shunned from the other. Were Damaris's beliefs strong enough to withstand those consequences? Even if the impossible happened and Noah's playful flirting developed into something more, if they actually began dating and developed feelings for each other. Would the Breedlove family and their love be enough? Could she ever gain enough to cover the loss of her family?

Last night, she'd seen a different side of Noah. She'd gotten a peek inside the heart of the man she nursed and had seen the sincerity and compassion just beneath his steely facade. Her father had labeled the Breedloves evil because of their business. Yet so far, she'd seen a kind, hardworking, close-knit clan that, ironically, in some ways resembled her own. Were they truly responsible if an adult came into their establishment and chose to gamble? How much of her viewpoint had been shaped by the church and her father? For the next couple days, while adjusting to her new environment and schedule, she pushed the matter aside. But she couldn't keep putting it off. She had to speak with her dad. There was no way she'd let him be blindsided with the news about Noah, then put two and two together and figure out that he was her new boss.

She waited until Thursday evening, just past dinner, when she knew her parents would be in the study enjoying a cup of tea. Her mother would be reading or working a crossword puzzle while Franklin enjoyed his one vice, a hand-rolled cigar. She reached for her own cup of chamomile as the call connected. Bethany picked up on the second ring.

"Hello, honey."

"Hi, Mom."

"How's it going, Dee? Ready to quit the job and come home yet?"

Damaris smiled. "No, Mom. It's going well. There is something I need to discuss, though. Is Dad with you?"

"He's right here."

"Can you put me on speaker?"

"Sure."

Damaris heard mumbling as Bethany covered the receiver to speak to Franklin and then muted background noises when she hit the button.

"Okay, Dee. Dad's right here."

"Hi, Dad."

"Damaris."

He was still upset with her decision. *No bueno.* It had been made, however, and there were new developments.

Just because something was unpleasant didn't mean it could go undone.

"As you know, I don't usually share much of my work with you guys. The whole doctor/patient privilege, hospital confidentiality and all that. However, Dad, I recently learned that you know my patient, and that his already public profile is about to get more exposure."

"As long as you're not working for anyone who promotes gambling, there won't be a problem."

"My patient is Noah Breedlove."

"You will end that job tonight." Franklin's response was immediate and definite, made after the slightest pause. The call was going worse than Damaris thought it would, and she'd thought it would go really badly.

"That's not possible, Dad."

"Don't you sit there and tell me what you can't do. I will not have my daughter working for the devil and those Breedloves are his next of kin."

"Franklin," she heard her mother murmur in the soft tone that seemed to always soothe him. "Perhaps we can at least hear her out."

Damaris gave a succinct recap of what happened with Noah, from the time he was brought into Manning Valley's emergency trauma center until Victoria asked her to relocate and become his personal nurse.

"I went into nursing because I felt it was my calling," she finished. "Victoria told me that she needed my help, specifically, at a very dark time for their family. If I can bring in a sliver of hope, a ray of light, I felt it my duty to help her."

"I appreciate your passion, honey," Franklin said, from an obviously calmer state. "I really do. But there are plenty of local nurses with your same qualifications."

"Technically, yes, Dad. But she didn't ask them to come work for her. She asked me. I signed a six-month contract that is nonnegotiable. Noah's mother put in this special clause because the world as her son knew it was upended.

She wanted a team that could provide consistency in what we all know is a very difficult time of rehabilitation. I felt I could do that and agreed to commit. I have to honor my word."

"If that family thinks they are going to use an employment contract to sway my mind on their casino operation by having my daughter become a part of it they can think again. They're using you, Damaris. Don't let a slippery serpent's tongue lead you astray."

Damaris chuckled. "You and Noah may have more in common than you realize, Dad. He made the same accusation about you, that somehow I'd taken the job to sabotage him."

Franklin persisted, undeterred. "What about the faith, Damaris? How can you work for a family that promotes evil?"

Damaris hesitated before giving an answer. She'd asked a similar question of herself. "I am not working for the family, Dad, or have anything to do with the corporation that builds casino hotels. I was hired by Victoria as a caretaker for her son who was injured while skiing near where I work in Manning Valley. The only gamble is whether or not the team they've assembled and that I'm a part of can be successful in helping Noah heal."

"Not a gamble," Bethany said. "But a conviction, a belief. I understand your father's concerns but personally feel your heart is in the right place. I'll be praying for Noah, and for you."

"I don't like it," Franklin admitted. "I wish you'd spoken with your mom and me before signing the contract. I'm sure you didn't because you knew we wouldn't approve."

"I made the decision quickly, Dad, but not lightly, and understand your concerns. I've spent four years of college and time on the job around people who believe differently than we do. I can handle it."

"That's what you think. During those times, you were

here in Utah, in close contact with your family and surrounded by faith. I'll call Pastor Sullivan," Franklin added.
"To tell him you'll be in church on Sunday and joining their
ministry while away from home."

Damaris didn't resist her father's antics, trying to control her life from four-hundred-plus miles away. She probably would have visited the church anyway, out of habit if
nothing else. Truth be told, though, Damaris had started to
question some of what the church taught as absolute truth.
At school and work, she'd met amazing people who weren't
Laymen, and knew of church members who were not saints.
At some point she'd have to make her own choices. Noah
had accused her of not doing enough of that.

The next night when Damaris's phone rang at 7:00 p.m.,
after working hours, she guessed it was either her parents,
her friend Wendy or Pastor Sullivan's wife, Ruby, calling
about her attending Sunday's service. Travis was on the
clock with Noah. When she picked up her phone and saw
the therapist's number, she felt instant alarm.

"Hi, Tee," she answered lightly, using the nickname he'd
created, his Tee to her Dee. "Is everything okay?"

"Hope so. I need to ask a favor."

"About you leaving next week to handle a family matter? Noah already told me."

"Kind of, except needing to leave tomorrow instead."

"Really? Is something wrong?"

"Yes and no. My dad died last year—"

"I'm so sorry."

"Thank you. Anyway, Mom's downsizing and selling
the home. We thought it would take a few weeks to close
but the buyers are paying cash and need to move ASAP. I
promised Mom I'd help her so…"

"No, of course. How can I help you?"

"I already have a guy from the rehab center covering my
days off next week and someone to carry out his morning

exercises. If you could execute Noah's nightly rubdown and get him ready for bed, I'd owe you big-time."

The request caught Damaris off guard, as did the image that Travis's bedtime request unexpectedly provoked, one not fit for Sunday services.

"I know it's on your days off and hate to ask. I tried to find someone else from the rehab center but it's late and they didn't have an extra body to spare away from the clinic. I don't know if Noah would be open to doing the work at the center instead of private sessions. I guess if push came to shove..."

"Don't worry, I'll do it. What time?"

"His evening rubdown? In half an hour. I wasn't planning to fly out until next week and my flight leaves at 6:00 a.m."

"Got it."

"The table is in the rec room. Clothing changes are in the chest of drawers just inside his massive closet. Thanks for helping me out. I'll see you when I get back." Tee ended the call.

She had less than a half hour to put on her game face to spend time alone with a man, albeit a patient, who was not a family member. After a few minutes of indecision on what to wear, she donned the black jeans from earlier that day, pulled a favorite faded T-shirt out of a stack in her third drawer and slid her feet into a pair of sandals. She forced her mind to remain professional, recalling what she'd learned in an advanced class involving massages for musculoskeletal and spinal trauma. The one and only time she'd performed the task was during her senior year and a week's training at a nursing home. Her patient then was a spry, quick-witted seventy-nine-year-old. Something told Damaris that working on the body of the young, strapping Noah Breedlove would not be the same. At all.

Thirteen

"No worries, Travis," Noah said while rolling from the office to his bedroom. "Focus on your mom and the family. Everything here will work out."

He ended the call and continued inside the same massively designed walk-in closet that Damaris enjoyed. Other rooms of the duplex differed in design, but the bedrooms were identical. He went to a horizontal chest of drawers that spanned a short wall and pulled out a change of workout clothes, the baggy shorts and loose-fitting, sleeveless T-shirt he usually wore for Travis's nightly rubdown sessions. Tonight, though, it wouldn't be Travis. It would be Damaris. No big deal. She was his nurse, not his next hookup. Even so, he grabbed a pair of black linen drawstring designer duds and paired it with a black T-shirt that was tighter than the ones he wore with Travis. He removed his business shirt and undergarment and pulled the T-shirt over his head, then slung the shorts over his wheelchair arm and continued to the bathroom, where one look in the mirror reminded him that he hadn't shaved. Oh well. Too late for that. After washing his face and brushing his teeth, he picked up then put back a bottle of cologne on the counter. *Get it together, Noah. This isn't a date!* Somebody should have told his heart because as hard as it began beating a few minutes later when the doorbell rang, it surely felt that way.

He looked at the home security screen and pressed the intercom button. "It's open, Dee. Come on in."

Was it him or had he just added a bit of bass to his voice?

He headed down the hall to meet her. "Hi."

"Hi, Noah. I guess Travis told you I'd be covering for him."

"Yeah, I got off the phone with him not long ago."

"It has to be hard making a lifestyle change like that, for his mom I mean."

"I'd imagine," Noah said casually, while reading everything about Damaris like a bestselling novel. She was nervous, which surprised him given her profession.

"Are you okay with taking over for Travis? Because if not…"

"I'm a nurse, Noah. This is part of my job. Of course I'm okay with it."

Noah hid a smile at the physical change in her demeanor, the tight lips, squared shoulders and quiet resolve that she'd turned on and displayed in her answer.

She nodded at his slacks. "We need to get you changed out of those."

He lifted the shorts from the chair arm, turned around and threw over his shoulder, "Follow me."

They entered Noah's master suite. Damaris stopped just inside the doorway. "No way!" She continued inside and over to the contraption near Noah's bed. "You have a bod-riser! Those aren't on the market," she continued, eyeing both him and the device a bit incredulously. "I've seen a couple prototypes in industry mags but these aren't due out for at least another two years."

Noah stopped beside her. "I guess it depends on who you know."

"You'd have to know the inventor to get…" Realization dawned. "You know this person." Said with arms crossed, a side-eye and attitude, like *really, dude?*

Yes. Really.

"I don't but Dr. Woo does. Dr. Okoye, the man behind this marvelous wonder, is one of her colleagues."

He watched as Damaris inspected the machine with an

almost reverent wonder. The Body Lift Assistant, nick-named the body riser and shortened to bod-riser by the few lucky test users, was created by Nigerian Dr. Israel Okoye after a former college roommate was paralyzed in a diving accident. During a visit the friend complained of how men-tally debilitating it was to be totally dependent on another, unable to do tasks as simple as using the restroom or dress-ing oneself. Dr. Okoye returned to Africa consumed with the desire to help his friend. Nine short months later, the first prototype for the bod-riser was presented at a medical conference in Switzerland. Dr. Woo saw it there and from that meeting came the connection that allowed Noah the opportunity for a modicum of autonomy.

"How has it worked out for you?" Damaris asked. "Are you able to handle certain tasks completely, yet?"

Noah shook his head. "I still need assistance getting from here—" he tapped the arm of his wheelchair "—to there." He nodded at the device. "After that, I'm good to go."

"Great! Let's get you transferred."

He saw what appeared to be a wave of relief come over her face, glad, Noah imagined, not to have to totally help him undress. He didn't know much about the Church of Laymen but couldn't imagine a church that banned gam-bling would be too allowing of flaunting one's nakedness with the opposite sex.

She positioned herself in front of him and with a strength that surprised Noah, lifted him out of the chair and into the riser.

"I'm impressed," he said. "You're stronger than you look."

"Thank you. It's all in the technique," she said, with a wink, her eyes taking in the surroundings. "Travis men-tioned a recreation room?"

Noah frowned slightly. "He did?" A pause and then, "Oh, the rec room. For recovery, not recreation."

"Or maybe both since our goal is to re-create your ability to walk."

"I never looked at the word like that."

"Me, either, until now."

"Sounds totally appropriate. The re-creation room is on the other side of the great room, first door on the left. I don't think it was set up the day you arrived."

"I'll go check it out, then. See you there."

"Not so fast, lady. I can change into these shorts but haven't mastered jumping from here back into the chair."

"Oh. Sorry."

That delicious blush that he'd come to expect and appreciate began a slow crawl from the base of her neck.

"I'm messing with you. Step into the hallway if you'd like. It'll only take a minute."

It took seven minutes, a considerably shorter time than the average paraplegic could perform the same task, usually from a prone position. Noah did not take this fact lightly. He knew how fortunate he was to be a man of means, with money, connection and power. He wasn't one of those who professed that life was fair and the playing field was level. It wasn't. If that were the case, he'd be walking.

Damaris's professional yet friendly disposition, more relaxed than when she'd first entered, calmed Noah, too. She chatted casually while assisting him from the chair to the table, again using technically advanced wonders that made for an easier transition. He pushed a button that lowered the table. A lever reclined his chair and a harness allowed Damaris to handle the transfer without additional aid.

She placed a hand on Noah's leg. He knew because he saw her do it, yet a part of him swore he could feel her flesh—soft, warm—against him. It was phantom and fleeting, an impossible desire. He hadn't felt anything there since that day. He watched as she gripped portions of his legs, manually gauging the bone density and muscle tone much as Travis had once done. She wasn't Travis. Every inch of her reminded him of femininity, the strong type, like iron covered in velvet. She paused, pushing in an area of his lower thigh, her brow knit in concentration, her luscious lips pursed in thought. He imagined how it would feel to kiss them, then closed his eyes to blot out the image.

"You're in good shape," he heard her say dispassionately, her total focus seemingly on his lower extremities. "It's good you were so healthy and worked out regularly. It makes recovery—"

"Re-creating," he corrected, opening his eyes once more.

"Yes, re-creating, much easier."

Something shifted between them while something else developed. It was a small shift, the merest of changes, but he saw it in Damaris's eyes when she smiled at him, and again, felt it in the touch that he couldn't really feel.

"How do you take your massages? Soft music and dim lighting or brightness and rock?"

"Rock? Ha! That must be a new type of therapy. Actually, neither. Travis just goes to work on me. We chat a bit. He asks questions. I answer them. Or vice versa. Otherwise, it's silent."

"Hmm. I wonder what your sister-in-law would think about that?"

"Ryan?"

"Yes, the holistic doctor."

"Good question."

"Glad you think so. I'll ask her. Meanwhile, I'd like to play something soft and relaxing. Some circles teach music as healing. I believe there is truth to that. Would you mind?"

"Not at all."

Noah instructed her on how to operate the panel in the main hallway that filtered music throughout the house and various rooms. He waited to hear something ethereal and heady such as the New Age music Ryan sometimes played in their home. Instead, the soft strains of a classical piano piece interrupted the silence, the reverberation of the lower chords quieting his soul. Without a word, Damaris returned to the room and began to work. He watched as she placed delicate yet strong fingers around his foot and began slow, firm circular motions from his foot to his shin and the area beneath the knee. Against the background of Debussy's "Clair de Lune," she stroked and kneaded his muscles, bones, flesh, spirit. She deftly pressed areas where, unbeknownst to Noah, knots had formed or tendons had tightened. He closed his eyes and allowed himself to be transported by the motion of the melody to another place, another time. He imagined his former buff body instead of the broken one, and that the massage being given was more sensual than standard therapeutic fare, albeit by a beautiful nurse. Riding the waves of relaxation, his mind wandered from thoughts of work and family to nothing at all. He felt good, more at peace than since the accident happened. Almost normal. In that moment, he didn't feel like a disabled patient. He felt like Noah Breedlove, and uttered a whispered gratitude to Damaris for the gift her hands had brought.

"What did you say?"

"I said…" His eyes fluttered open to find Damaris's head bent low to hear his whisper, those luscious lips mere inches from his own. Pure instinct took over. He raised his hand, placed it behind her neck and pulled her face closer.

"Thank you," he finished before raising his head to erase the short distance between them.

Her lips were even softer than he imagined, her touch, tentative. He expected her to pull back. Instead, something amazing happened. She increased the pressure, following him as he lowered his head back to the table. That simple act of acquiescence was like a starter gun at the Kentucky Derby, his passion like a Thoroughbred shooting out of the gate. His hand slid from the nape of her neck into her thick tresses at the same time his tongue pressed through her slightly parted lips. Their tongues met and danced—

slowly swirling, tasting—in a leisurely, unhurried get-to-know. Just as he raised his other hand and placed it on her back, ready to gently press her lovely orbs against his chest for even more contact, she ended the kiss.

"Noah," she murmured. He felt her body straighten and then heard, "Oh."

It was a soft exclamation, a quick intake of breath, unnoticeable except for a lull in the music. He opened his eyes and met Damaris's unreadable gaze. She quickly broke contact and said nothing. But her skin was talking, a light blush across her entire face as she moved to the other side of his body. He was confused until his eyes fell and he glimpsed an erection—long, thick, undeniable—begging for attention. There was no room for embarrassment. Hot damn! Kissing Damaris made his dick work! The knowledge that what his grandpa Will called their third leg was in this small way functioning normally gave him hope that the other two would someday do the same.

He looked up to apologize but the lips still tingling with excitement and desire couldn't form the words. He wasn't sorry about anything that had happened. From Damaris's expression he didn't think she had any regrets, either.

Fourteen

The placid professional mask Damaris slipped into place hid a torrent of emotions. What the heck just happened? The kiss was something she'd later unpack. But why had a simple erection unnerved her? She wasn't unfamiliar with the male anatomy. She and Matthew had honored the church's mandate to not have intercourse until marriage but they hadn't exactly remained chaste. They'd explored each other's bodies. One time, Matt had even asked her to kiss him "there." She'd been filled with guilt afterward but in the moment, the act was exciting.

That her patient had gotten and seemed to be maintaining a healthy erection should not have surprised her. From advanced studies she knew this could occur and the reasons behind it. What bothered her were the less than professional feelings swirling around her heart. Why was she having such difficulty maintaining control of them? Damaris prided herself on being able to remain compassionate yet emotionally detached from each patient she tended. Her mentor had assured it would benefit her long-term. Easier said than done. Even harder when her eyes traveled from his groin to his face to find him silently watching her. She willed the floor to open up and swallow her whole. When it didn't, she tried to mask her nervousness with a medical explanation.

"What you're experiencing is most likely a reflexogenic erection," she said calmly, as though talking about the weather. "The nerve endings controlling tumescence remain intact."

"Tumescence?"

"The, um, instrument becoming engorged."

"My penis?"

Was that a gleam Damaris detected in Noah's eye? She squared her shoulders and lifted her chin. She would not be intimidated. She was a professional. She could do this!

"Yes, Noah, your penis."

"What did you call it? A reflex..."

"Reflexogenic reaction."

"Not usually the way my body responds to a simple kiss."

Simple? Seriously? There was nothing simple about it. Damaris remained quiet and tried to control the oncoming blush but felt her face grow warm. Instead of feeling more in control by facing what had happened to her patient head-on, Damaris had gone from the frying pan into the fire. A part of her wanted to flee to the sanctity of her home. But Damaris wasn't a quitter. When she started a job, she finished it.

"If the nerves are working, why can't I feel it?"

"That is probably a conversation best had with Travis, or one of the specialists." She began bending Noah's legs, performing the exercises Travis had detailed in the email he'd sent. "I'm sure that is only one of several questions you have regarding how the paralysis will affect your life in that area."

"I apologize if the question made you uncomfortable."

"Accepted."

Damaris wanted to say that she'd not been bothered at all but lying could lead to more questions. Instead of talking she focused on the exercises Travis had outlined. The massages, he'd explained via the messages, were designed to stimulate circulation and improve the patient's overall health. Blood was definitely circulating, Damaris thought, willing herself not to blush again.

For the next two days, Damaris was spared from performing Travis's duties by the therapist who worked at the rehab center and helped out on weekends. Neither brought up the kiss. Damaris tried to forget it happened. Still, something had shifted. Noah felt it, too. Their conversations were stilted, forced, almost too polite. At times she caught him looking at her and wondered if he did the same, then chided herself for fantasizing about dating him. His girlfriends were probably rich runway model types. It was silly to think someone like Noah would ever look romantically at someone like her. A conversation with her mother on Saturday night put the matter to rest.

"Dee, I'm worried about you," her mother, Bethany, said seconds after Damaris answered the phone. "I know you think you're strong enough to withstand that town's temptations but you've never been this far from home before, away from your family and church. Have you spoken with Pastor Sullivan, or Ruby, his wife?"

"No," Damaris said, remembering the unknown caller she'd seen and ignored a couple times. She told her mother about them and added, "I probably should listen to my voice mail messages. I've been really busy."

"Not too busy to remember your faith, I hope. You must remember your place there, as an employee, nothing more."

"I know, Mom." Except her heart didn't.

"Be sure you do. Men like the one you work for might take liberties with a pretty girl like you but if and when he marries…it will be to someone whose values equal his. Clearly, yours do not. Correct?"

"Correct." The weight of her mother's truth caused Damaris to plop on her couch.

"Good. Your father spoke with the pastor and asked the family to look out for you. He has a daughter, Lori, who's close to your age. She's looking forward to meeting you at services tomorrow."

"I'll be there."

After Bethany's call, Damaris listened to her voice mails.

Indeed, the pastor's daughter, Lori, had called. Damaris texted to let her know she'd received the message and would see her the following day. A restless night gave way to a rainy morning—a perfect match to Damaris's mood. She rolled out of bed determined to shake the doldrums, had just finished a quick breakfast and was headed to the shower when the phone rang. It was the house phone, not her cell, which meant one of two people were calling—Victoria, or her mom.

She quickly crossed the room. "Hello?"

"Good morning, Dee. It's Victoria."

"Good morning."

"I just realized I've been remiss in showing some good old Breedlove hospitality. You've not been invited to our legendary Sunday brunch and I'd be delighted for you to join us. Any time is fine but the meal officially gets underway at ten."

"Thank you for inviting me, Victoria, but I have other plans."

"Oh?"

"Yes. I've been invited to church by the relative of a member back home. I was headed for a shower when the phone rang."

"Okay. I hate that you won't be joining us but wanting to be in familiar surroundings is understandable. Have a wonderful Sunday, dear. I'd love for us to chat soon, perhaps lunch next week?"

"Of course."

"Great. I'll be in touch."

Damaris went to church. She met Lori, two years older, married to a man named Philip Bolton and expecting the couple's second child. She sat with them and Philip's best friend, "an upstanding Layman" named Steve. The sermon seemed tailor-made for Damaris, could have been written by her father. Pastor Sullivan admonished the congregation to avoid sustained interaction with outsiders, resist temptation and cling to the faith. When Lori invited her to dinner in their home later that week, Damaris accepted. It was the right thing to do. She sang familiar songs, recited familiar phrases and returned home feeling more conflicted than ever. She was still torn the next day as she headed to her final session with Noah before Travis returned, a swimming exercise like the one she'd briefly watched the week prior before administering a round of medication. That day she'd watched from a distance. Today she'd be in the pool.

Damaris reached the main house and followed the drive to the infinity pool at the back of the home. Globed lighting outlined the pool against an inky black sky, dotted with a thousand stars. The shiver that ran down her back as she spotted Noah already in the pool had nothing to do with the chill in the air. Nick and his father, Nicholas, were seated at a nearby patio table, chatting as Noah lay on a floating device, with additional floaters around each biceps. They stood as she reached them and, after exchanging greetings, beat a hasty retreat.

Damaris tilted her head toward the retreating figures, made her voice light even though upon seeing Noah her heart beat wildly. "Was it something I said?"

"They were just keeping me company until you arrived."

"Are you ready to begin?"

"Sure."

Damaris slipped off her sandals and walked toward the pool steps.

"What are you doing?"

"Getting in the pool," she responded, well aware of why the question was asked. Not having packed a swimsuit for her time in Nevada was only one reason she'd planned to conduct the session wearing an extra large T-shirt over a sports bra and knee-length baggy shorts. Modesty was another. Fear of inciting further attraction or arousal, by either party, was a third.

"Where's your swimsuit?"

"Don't have one. Besides, the temperature is dropping and I'm cold-blooded by nature. My getting sick won't improve your health."

Noah used strong strokes to guide the float toward the pool's edge. "The pool's heated, Dee."

She dipped a foot in the water. The temperature was perfect, no cover-up needed. She began descending the pool steps.

"You need a suit," Noah replied.

"It's one exercise for thirty minutes. I'll be fine."

"Not acceptable," he said as she waded through the water to reach him. "There's extra swimwear in the pool house, purchased specifically for unprepared guests. Go get changed."

Damaris eyed Noah's broad chest and rock-hard abs. Instead of joining him in swimwear, she wanted to give him an oversize T-shirt. This outsider was too much temptation. "This will do for now. Come on, let's get started."

"Street clothes are not allowed into the pool," he replied with a calm authority and an expression that conveyed the word *no* wasn't an option.

Damaris huffed but didn't argue. Clearly, Noah was used to having orders followed. She was his employee. How could she argue? Plus, she felt this was another test—Noah purposely seeing how she reacted when pushed out of her comfort zone. She was determined to prove to both him and herself that she could resist the unspoken yet growing attraction between them. Once inside the pool house, Damaris continued to a room that looked more like a boutique. She quickly spotted a conservative black one-piece with matching cover and in less than five minutes was heading back out the door. The image that greeted her once back outside stopped her short. Noah, resting on the floater. God help her but his body was gorgeous.

Back outside she quickly shimmied out of the cover-up and into the pool. Beginning the exercises were more for her than him. Total body stretches. Knee-to-chest pull-ups. Intensive core work. Noah's abs were like stone. Muscle retention resistance. Noah put 100 percent into the workout and looked amazing while doing it. Had Damaris completely flummoxed and confused. Utah was full of great-looking guys. Some of them went to her church. What was it about Noah that caused her insides to quiver and certain body parts to pebble and pulse? Seeing him now was not that different from every night when she massaged his shins, thighs and buttocks and applied the ointment Ryan made to prevent blisters and sores. She should be used to seeing his bronzed body by now. Only she wasn't. That was a problem. Crushing on a patient was so not cool.

They finished the last exercise thirty minutes later.

"I think we're good," Damaris said. "What do you think?"

"We're finished with my workout. What about yours?"

"Trust me, I'm fine." As long as she didn't look at the lips she longed to kiss again.

"What, you scared to lose to a guy with no legs?"

Damaris's eyes narrowed. "Don't do that to yourself."

"Let's line up." Noah eased himself along the pool's edge to the shallow side of the pool.

"You're serious?"

"You tell me to think positive, right? I believe I can beat you."

Damaris was dubious but appreciated his moxie. "Okay." She waded through the water to the side of the pool. "Ready, set, go!"

She waited a beat before pushing off from the wall. In that instant, Noah was several strokes ahead of her. Even without the use of his legs, he went faster than she thought he would. After pushing off the wall, she used powerful freestyle moves in an effort to catch up. About midway through, she got even with him and then started to pull ahead. She kept going, not wanting it said that she'd "let him win." She was just a foot or so from the wall, ready to touch and claim victory when…

Whoosh!

Damaris was pulled back and underwater by a powerful force. The move was unexpected and caught her off guard. She did a flip underwater and pushed off the swimming pool bottom to rise to the surface. In the process the band she had around her hair came undone. It took several seconds to catch her breath and remove a blanket of wet hair from her face. When she did, it was to find Noah balancing himself on the winning end of the pool, laughing his head off.

"You!"

"I won!"

"You cheated!"

"I didn't say how I'd finish first, only that I would."

Damaris swam over to where he was gloating. She reached him and with no warning, splashed water in his face. Taken aback, he coughed and sputtered before returning the favor. The water fight was on, each splash getting bigger and more forceful than the next. A drenched Damaris made a move to get away. With one hand gripping the lip of the pool, Noah caught her leg with the other. His strength surprised her. He pulled her to him, then quickly let go of her leg to grab her waist.

"Now who's fighting unfair?"

"Let me go!" Damaris squirmed, trying to break Noah's viselike grip.

"Promise not to splash me again."

"I promise nothing!"

"Then I can't let you go."

Damaris stopped squirming and looked Noah in the eye. In that instant the mood changed. Their close proximity, his hard frame and lean fingers gripping her waist, those hypnotic eyes, all hit her in an instant. One small move, and she could kiss his wet, smiling lips. She felt restraint slipping. "Let. Me. Go."

His eyes became darker, dropped down to her lips. "Say please."

She licked her lips. "Please."

"I like your freckles," he said, still holding her, his eyes shifting to her mouth. "Your lips, too. I want to kiss you again."

Damaris eyed his lips also—full, wet, experienced—and imagined hers pressed against them. Her head lowered of its own accord as control began slipping away. Just before their lips touched, her mother's words came to mind. *Men like the one you work for might take liberties with a pretty girl like you...* She placed a hand on his chest and pushed to get away. His hard muscles and wet skin made her fingers tingle. She felt conflicted with desire and forced away the feeling.

"We need to get you out of the water," she said in a voice more breathless than she would have liked.

"Are you sure?" Noah asked, his intense gaze searing her soul.

"Yes," she managed, on a shaky breath. *No!* her body cried.

"Isn't a—" he thought for a second, then continued "— reflexogenic reaction good physical therapy?"

"Physical therapy is over, Noah," she replied.

He released her. She felt the loss, keenly. Now they were headed to his house for his nightly rubdown before preparing him for bed. With her luck he'd probably get another erection. *Just great*, Damaris thought as she exited the pool and pulled on the cover-up. *That's. Just. Great.*

Fifteen

Both personally and professionally, Noah's decisiveness had always been an asset. If he wanted something, he fearlessly went after it. Until now. The injury changed everything. He was attracted to the pretty nurse who'd captivated him from the moment they'd first locked eyes, but the possibility of rejection haunted him. There were many questions that needed answering, starting with why Damaris had rushed out of the pool.

He waited until they'd reached his home and once there, he informed Damaris that tonight he wanted a simple rubdown in his bed instead of on the massage table.

"Why?" she'd asked, as he knew she would, which was why he had an answer.

"I'm tired. Plus, less work for you. Once done I can say good-night and roll over."

Damaris considered his answer. "Works for me."

After exchanging wet swim trunks for a pair of comfy drawstring pants, Damaris helped him into bed. For a moment, he watched her work, while trying to exercise mental control and not allow errant thoughts to wake his snake. Considering what he was getting ready to bring up, there were no guarantees. In fact, the very opposite could occur.

"I want to ask you something," he began. "As a woman, not my nurse."

A quick look and slight brow raise were Damaris's only reactions. She finished rubbing down one leg and shifted to the other.

"Back at the pool, why didn't you kiss me?"

Her hands stilled for the briefest of seconds, before the kneading resumed.

"You wanted to," he told her.

"I did," she answered.

He wasn't surprised at her honesty. "Then why didn't you?"

"You have to ask?" She spoke without looking away from her task.

"We kissed before."

"That was a mistake."

"Says who?"

"Propriety. What happened the other night was inappropriate, and unprofessional."

"What we're discussing is personal, isn't it?"

"Not for me."

"Because you're my nurse."

"That and also because it's how I was raised."

"You were taught to ignore your feelings?"

"I was taught to follow the rules," Damaris finally said.

"Whose rules?" Noah shot back. Her short, simple answers were irritating, as was the emotional shield she hid behind. Noah was convinced that a blazing heat smoldered beneath her cool, aloof exterior. He wanted to be the one who stoked it, brought her to the type of erotic rapture he was sure she'd never experienced before. He wished certain body parts were working that would allow him to claim her completely. But there were other ways in which he could satisfy her. Noah knew them all.

He changed tactics, deciding on a less combative approach. "Was I mistaken about what happened the other night, and was almost repeated in the pool? Do you not find me attractive?"

"I find you very attractive," she admitted.

"Then is it because of my injuries, because I'm in a chair."

"Of course not!"

"Then you'd date me?"

"No," she quickly replied. Then, "I don't know," in a softer, less sure tone.

Noah shrugged. "I can't imagine the women I know dating a disabled guy."

Finished with the rubdown, Damaris washed her hands before reaching for a digital body reader. "What does your girlfriend think about it?"

"Is that your way of asking if I have one?"

"Never mind. That question wasn't professional, either. Quiet while I take your blood pressure."

Noah did as she instructed, watching her intently. He appreciated the command she exhibited in going about her duties, taking care of him, helping him get better. Being only twenty-five he'd never given serious consideration to what he'd want in a long-term relationship, or a marriage. He decided that some of the traits he saw in Damaris should be on the list.

"I don't have a girlfriend," he offered, when she was done. "Were you seeing anyone back home?"

"No," Damaris said after a pause.

"Were you dating?"

She shook her head.

"Why not? You're a beautiful girl."

"I was engaged. My fiancé was killed in a motorcycle accident. Placing all of my energy and focus into nursing helped me get past the loss."

"That had to have been difficult. I'm sorry."

"Thank you."

"Are you past it, the tragedy?"

"That's a good question," Damaris answered.

"How will you know?"

"I guess when my heart opens up to let someone new inside."

Their eyes met. He held the gaze. Damaris looked away.

He wanted to kiss her again, longed to pull her into his arms and see if doing so produced another erection. He wanted to be able to feel that erection, to do what came naturally when such occurred. Instead he reached up and caressed her arm.

She stood abruptly, made a final notation on her tablet, then placed it in the tote she'd brought into the room. "I'm all done here. Is there anything I can get you before calling it a night?"

Plenty, Noah thought, but now was not the right time to ask. Instead he lowered the top portion of the bed to a fully reclined position and pulled up the cover.

"Sweet dreams, Damaris," he said.

"Good night, Noah."

It was a long night. Noah spent most of it trying to forget how good Damaris had felt during those few but precious seconds they play-fought in the pool. How softly yet firmly her hands massaged his immobile limbs. The way she avoided his eyes while doing her job. It was clear she'd been uncomfortable with the subject of dating, but she hadn't backed away. His disability would take him out of the running, for most women he knew anyway. But could someone like Damaris be interested, even if he never walked again? Would he be interested in someone like her, unworldly, conservative and sexually immature, if not for the chair? Did it matter, considering her religious stance against gambling when his family owned one of the largest casino operations in the world?

The next morning, Noah was up and out of the house an hour and a half before Travis was due to show up and drive him to the office. He dressed with minimal assistance, wheeled himself to the van and, ten minutes later, was headed to the main estate. Last night he'd sent a group text calling for a family business meeting to be held ASAP. Grappling with his feelings for Damaris and her father's direct opposition to them doing business in Salt Lake City had led him to an idea he felt could be total trash or pure genius. He needed his family's help to decide.

As he entered the home, greeted his mom and continued on to his father's study, he mulled over the plan, knew it could work, had to work. Noah knocked, then opened the door. His father was there, behind the desk, looking like the big baller shot caller even in a silk robe. Christian was there, too, enjoying one of the family chef Gabe's legendary cinnamon rolls. It didn't surprise him that Nick wasn't there yet but that he'd beat Adam to the meeting hadn't been expected. His rancher brother was usually up with the sun.

He walked in and gave a hug and handshake to the men in the room. "Where's Adam?"

"On the way," Nicholas said. "An overseas client called just as he was heading out the door."

"Problems?"

"No, thank goodness," Nicholas said, the relief clearly evident in his voice. The Breedloves had banded together to help Adam overcome a very challenging situation, one that could have cost him his ranching business, the family, even more. They did not want to ride that pony again.

Christopher reached for a napkin. "Where's your twin?"

The door opened. No knock. "Who's asking?" Nick strolled in and headed straight for the coffee, Adam two steps behind him.

"Who called this early-ass meeting," Nick mumbled, "and what's it about?"

"I did, bro," Noah replied. "Your second question will be answered shortly. Morning, Adam."

"Morning, family!" In direct opposition to Nick's appearance, Adam was showered and dressed in a tailored suit, his eyes bright as though he'd risen with the dawn.

Noah gave Adam a shoulder bump as he watched a disheveled Nick add three helpings of espresso to a caramel latte, then walk over to a leather recliner, plop down and lie back. No one had to ask how he'd spent his night. The only question was the one Adam asked.

"Who was she?"

"No time for that," Noah interjected. He pulled a folder from his briefcase and passed a one-page document to his brothers and dad. "After careful consideration, I'd like to make a few slight revisions to the Utah casino proposal."

"Like not building it in the first place, as was my suggestion?" Nicholas asked, without looking at the paper. "As it is, we've got about a half dozen investors ready to pull out."

"And another half who are unlikely to trust us again," Christian added.

"Thanks, bro, Dad, for your continued support."

Noah added a half smile and put up a hand to ward off further comment. He appreciated his dad's and brother's honest opinions. They removed any trace of nervousness and allowed him to get straight to the point.

"I'm more convinced than ever that ours should be the first gambling operation in the state of Utah."

"In Manning Valley?" Adam asked, looking up from the paper. "Besides those who run the Daredevil Ski Resort, do people live there?"

"Not many, which is why it's the perfect alternative to building in Salt Lake. Manning claims about ten thousand residents, with about a hundred thousand living in surrounding towns. Manning Valley Medical is the single biggest employer and, aside from ma-and-pa businesses, the only one. A CANN hotel would help grow the town, which officials want to do."

"That's not a minor revision," Nicholas said.

"It's a necessary one, Dad. The Church of Laymen's reach doesn't extend that far south. The town is struggling. It would be a win-win. The other revision will not only yield higher profit margins but get us past the religious argument against gambling in their state."

"Virtual machines." Noah pulled out another sheet of

paper. "I've analyzed research and crunched the numbers." He looked at his siblings pointedly. "That's what I do, better than anybody."

A statement no one tried to dispute.

Instead, Nick asked, "How much of this has to do with the pushback from the church and your interest in one of its pretty members who just happens to be your private nurse?"

"It has everything to do with her."

The honest answer sat the twin straight up.

"Well, damn," Adam drawled.

Christian, too, looked surprised. But no one was more taken aback than Noah. He'd never admitted this truth to himself, let alone considered saying it out loud. But he had. Nothing to do but push forward, even more confident. In for a penny, in for a pound.

"While there are a growing number of politicians, lawmakers and businessmen becoming more open to legal gambling in Utah, even in the face of staunch opposition, the church's pushback and amount of power wielded there was underestimated, especially in Salt Lake. The size of the city, its proximity to Provo and Park City, and the infrastructure already in place made it the obvious choice. A conversation with Damaris, however, led to a broadening of my perspective and along with it the amount of available possibilities to get this done."

"Outside the CANN model, too," Christian said, looking up from the paper he held. "A virtual casino, bro?"

"Exactly, in Manning Valley, with customized luxury buses that pick customers up from the airport, and stop at other towns along the way. They'll be brought to a place that looks very similar to an actual casino except all of the gambling is actually done online, and the payouts, too."

"I don't like it," Nicholas said. "People go to a casino because they want to gamble. If they only want online games, they can play those from home."

"People go to a casino for the experience," Noah said. "Most slot players are already using digital screens."

"What about table games?" Christian asked. "I can't see gamblers getting too excited about virtual cards for poker and blackjack and rolling dice from a screen."

"I agree. Table games will happen in a different section of the casino, one where membership is required. This will be incorporated into our club rewards program and handled when the customer applies to get discounts and points.

"Technically, it is the exchange of money that defines gambling and is not allowed in Utah. By making ours a cashless casino, where players use cards containing money held in another state, that law is averted. The card will work as cash, usable wherever credit or debit cards are taken. Later this week, I've got a meeting with United States Capital, the largest bank in America and one we've used almost since this company's inception, to talk about how they can handle the financial component."

Nick, clearly intrigued, sat up in his chair. "But why Manning Valley instead of a town closer to Salt Lake?"

"As I explained, fewer Laymen," Noah answered. "Our research shows that residents there who belong to the church number less than fifty percent. Plus, it's a growing community eager to expand. The amount of jobs our project would create, along with the complementary businesses that could grow as a result, is very attractive to the city execs. Finally, we could buy twice the amount of land in Manning Valley for less than what we've budgeted for the state's capital."

"Son, I've been hesitant on this project from the beginning. But with this brilliant new concept, you're about to change my mind."

"That gives me hope, Dad. If I can convince the man who's mastered the hotel casino game and landed us at the top, maybe I can get those naysaying Laymen to play, too."

For the next hour Noah further laid out his vision for touch screen slots and bingo, horse race and sporting theaters and the elaborate financial system that would deliver winnings directly from a bank outside Utah to casino debit cards, with no direct cash exchange happening within the state. By the time he left his father's office, the family was on board. With their wind of support beneath his wings, Noah was unstoppable.

"Twin!"

Noah hadn't noticed Nick trailing behind him. "Hey, man."

"Let me catch a ride to the office."

Noah eyed him suspiciously. "Something wrong with the Lamborghini?"

"Not as cool as your tricked-out van," Nick replied.

"Get in. I'm going to swing around and pick up Travis. Not sure I'm ready for the freeway just yet."

Minutes later they were heading out of Breedlove. Nick kept up a running dialogue during the twenty-five-minute ride to the Strip. Noah was glad for his brother's company. It kept thoughts of the moment's significance at bay and with it, Noah's whirling emotions at being able to return to work at all. As the van turned into the entrance, he took in the familiar sight of the CANN Casino Hotel and Spa sign sparkling against the waterfall backdrop. He forced down the complaint that jumped to his throat when the physical therapist parked in a handicapped spot. Nick hopped out on the passenger side. Travis opened the side door and patiently waited as Noah maneuvered the chair onto the lift, then pushed the button, lowering himself to the ground. Travis reached back inside and retrieved his briefcase.

"Are you sure you don't want me to go in with you?" he asked, as he handed it over.

"We've got this," Nick answered, confident that together there wasn't anything the twins couldn't do.

Noah appreciated his therapist's concern. "We're taking the private elevator and won't encounter many people. Just be back to pick me up around seven tonight."

"That's almost nine hours," Travis protested. "It's your first day back, Noah. You might want to take it easy."

"That's what I've been doing for the past few weeks."

"The long day concerns me but you know your body. Just call if you need anything, or if you want me to come back earlier."

"He won't," Nick said, offering a fist to bump. "But thanks for looking out for my brother. You do a good job."

They headed down an outer hall leading from the parking lot to the interior. Nick's cell phone rang. Noah watched his brother listen to the caller, then glance at him.

"Um, sure. But can I meet you in a half hour or so? I want to get my brother settled—"

"Who is it?" Noah interrupted, and stopped moving.

"Hold on a minute." Nick muted the call. "It's Tiffany. She's here and wants to meet for breakfast."

"Go."

"I will as soon as—"

"You don't have to babysit me, bro."

"Doesn't matter."

"I know this building like the back of my hand, and I know how to wheel a chair. Plus, I know how Tiff has you wide-open right now so...go meet your girl."

"Are you sure?"

"Positive." Noah could tell his brother wasn't convinced. "I want back my independence."

"I can understand that. All right, bro. See you at the conference."

They entered the hotel. Noah watched his brother walk in the opposite direction, toward a set of public elevators that would land him in the south tower, closer to the hotel's boutiques and restaurants. He continued to the executive elevator and pressed his thumb against the scanner.

He took a breath, tried to relax muscles that were suddenly tense. It was his first time out of Breedlove, the first time he'd been without Damaris, Travis or a medical professional. Outside the estate, this was the first time he'd been alone in his chair. It was foreign, unsettling. He felt isolated and vulnerable but refused to give in to the fear. Everyone in the company had been very supportive. Noah began to relax.

The elevator arrived. So far, so good. Rolling into the car, he scanned his thumb for the floor available only to the top executives. The elevator doors opened to the gleaming CANN executive offices foyer and the smile on the receptionist's face lit up the room.

"Noah!" she cried, before jumping up, racing around the counter and offering a crushing hug. Smiles, tears and heartfelt greetings continued from there to his office and on to the boardroom, where he entered to a standing ovation and thunderous applause. Within seconds, all of Noah's trepidations about returning to the workplace fell away. Except for the fact that his chair now had wheels, it was just like any other day as a CANN executive. He allowed only a brief update on the article regarding his paralysis and the video produced as a result before taking control of the meeting and outlining the innovative new direction and location for the Utah casino, an idea spawned from his and Damaris's gambling debate. The pushback was expected, the voiced concerns valid. Noah listened. His counterarguments were sound. He went home exhausted yet more determined than ever to get his life back on track all the way around.

A ringing landline greeted Noah as he unlocked the front door and wheeled himself in. He reached for the one on a desk in the foyer and checked the ID.

"You must have seen the van," he said to his mother, placing the call on speaker.

"Good evening, son."

"Good evening. I'm fine. The day went great. Yes, dinner has been prepared. No, I'm not hurting. I have twenty minutes to eat and unwind before exercises with Mr. Relentless." Victoria's increased laughter as he continued answering the questions he assumed she'd called to ask made Noah smile. "Anything else?"

"Actually yes, dear. One, can you conduct your business from Denmark for the next couple weeks and two, does Dee have a passport?"

Sixteen

Damaris headed toward dinner with Lori Bolton, her husband, Philip, and their kids, with a growing sense of unease in the pit of her gut. How would the new Dee she'd just embraced interact with the old ideals she was sure to encounter around tonight's dinner table? She'd tried calling Wendy just to hear her thoughts out loud but her friend was doing a double shift and wouldn't be off until midnight. So here, just minutes away from a certain interrogation, Damaris grappled with a headful of clashing speculations on her own. When her phone rang and interrupted them, she was grateful.

"Hello?"

"Dee. Noah."

The mere sound of his voice made her squirm. She did her best to keep the excitement she felt out of her voice. "Hi, Noah. What's up?"

"Do you have a passport?"

Damaris frowned. "No, why?"

"Mom was wondering. Says she tried to reach you earlier, but it went to voice mail."

Only now did Damaris remember seeing Victoria's missed call. "I saw that and meant to call back but time got away. I'm having dinner with someone from the church but will call her afterward if it's not too late."

"I'll tell her."

"Why was she asking about a passport?" Damaris asked,

exiting in Henderson, Nevada, as she followed GPS directions from a staid male voice with a British accent.

"Because the team wants to use treatments and products that won't clear customs because they don't have federal approval. They want to bring the patient to the potential cure instead of the other way around."

"They want you to fly to Scandinavia?"

"Yes, said I'd probably be over there a couple weeks. I'd want to maintain the already established regimen, of course, and bring you with me."

Damaris was too shocked to give a quick reply. She'd always wanted to travel out of the country but would never have guessed taking the job with Victoria would have been the way to do it. Would have never dreamed that first trip abroad could be with a man like Noah. An arrangement that the old Damaris wouldn't have considered at all but had the new Dee throbbing in unspoken places.

"Dee, you there?"

"Oh, yeah, sorry. I was just thinking, digesting that news. It sounds wonderful, but that you'd want me to come along is a surprise."

"Dr. Woo and the team thought it best. Travis will come over initially, as well."

"Oh." Adding that little tidbit made his reasons for asking crystal clear—business, not pleasure. Good. It would be okay for her body to fly in the clouds but she didn't need her head there, too.

"Tell me more about these treatments."

"I only got briefed by Mom, who says that while I was at work and unavailable she was on the phone with them for well over an hour. What they have is a new and largely untested form of treatment involving laser surgery on parts of my spine that were affected by the fall combined with these stimulators attached to various nerve points through fiber-optic braces."

"Robotics."

"I guess."

"Bionic legs!" Damaris's excitement grew as she reached Lori's neighborhood and followed the Brit's directions to a block of complementary homes covered in various shades of stucco and sporting red tile. She pulled into the two-car drive and parked behind a white Ford truck.

"Wow, Noah, that's fantastic! I remember reading something about this being developed during my junior year at college. The design was these sleek rubber sleeves that looked natural under clothes and are far less cumbersome than their steel counterparts. Did you see them?"

"I did."

"And you're not excited? It's a radical form of treatment that, once perfected, may revolutionize the industry and allow all paras and quads to walk. People like you, Noah, might walk again!"

"In theory, yes, but it's not definitively proved."

"That's what the testing is for, correct?"

"Yes. That's why they want me to fly to Denmark."

Damaris turned off the engine. "Why don't you sound excited?"

"I'm cautiously optimistic. But work is here, with major projects on the table. It's a critical time."

"Your health should be your main focus," Damaris said. She looked up to see Lori waving from the steps, a mini-me clutching her pant leg.

"Noah, I have to go. How do I get a passport?"

"We'll take care of all that. My assistant will send over the paperwork right away. Return it ASAP, later tonight if you can. This process usually takes anywhere from a few weeks to a couple months, but I have a contact in DC who can push the application through."

"Okay. I'll fill it out and return it tonight. Bye, Noah!"

Damaris exited the car with a big smile on her face. She hurried up the walk and hugged her host.

"Come on in," Lori said, eyeing her keenly. "Wow, some-one looks happy."

"I am," Damaris gushed. She mussed the hair of the little girl beside her before walking through the door Lori held open. "I'm traveling out of the country…to Denmark!"

"What's over there?" By her tone Lori was clearly not as excited.

"Innovation," Damaris replied, in a tone more subdued. "Something smells good," she added, going for safer ground.

"Nothing fancy," Lori said. She led them into the dining room, where Philip sat chatting with another man. They stood when the ladies entered.

Damaris recognized the guy at once, Philip's best friend. She should have guessed their invite on Sunday wasn't just about dinner. The uneasy feeling from the drive over returned.

"Hello, Damaris," Philip said, his hand outstretched. She shook it as he spoke. "You remember my good Layman brother Steve. I hope you don't mind that we asked him to join us."

Would it have mattered, was her inward thought. Outwardly she smiled. "Hi, Steve."

He took her hand in both of his, eyes shining with open admiration. "Good evening, Damaris. It's wonderful to see you again."

She gently pulled her hand from his grasp and took a seat as Lori directed, working to hide her chagrin at being set up. Not even five minutes inside and Damaris already knew. It was going to be a long night. Small talk ensued as the first course, a simple salad, was served. Once church news and weather observations ran out, the conversation became all about Dee.

"I hear you're a nurse," Steve began, reaching for his glass of soda.

Damaris nodded.

"That's what brought you here?"

Another nod, around a bite of lasagna. The thought came to keep her mouth full and chew her way out of more detailed explanations, but one look at Steve and she knew that ploy had little chance of working. He was obviously smitten, the Boltons matchmaking. That this was a marriage mission couldn't have been more blatantly signaled if they'd put that message on a balloon tied to the back of her chair.

"Not at a hospital, though," Lori said.

"Your father tells us you're working for those billionaire Breedloves." Philip didn't try to hide his disgust. "I couldn't believe that as a Layman you'd accept their employ, or as his daughter, Glen would allow it."

Damaris took a moment to wipe her hands with a napkin, then enjoyed a sip of tea. She owed no one an explanation, yet briefly explained how she'd met the family and Victoria's request that she help Noah full-time.

"They are not Laymen," she concluded, "but living among them I've witnessed the kind of love, mercy and compassion that our scriptures describe."

"Wolves in sheep's clothing would be my guess," Steve said. "With riches gained through the misfortune of others. Have you seen their casino? It's the jewel of the Strip—shining bigger and brighter than all the rest. The kingpins of gamblers and thieves."

"Sounds like you've been inside," Damaris replied.

"Only to better understand the wiles of the enemy and better win the lost."

Damaris worked to not roll her eyes. Were these truly the beliefs that until now she'd wholeheartedly embraced? Steve sounded less like her dad and more like her grandfather.

"But that job's only temporary, right?" Lori asked.

"It's a six-month contract," Damaris replied.

"Six months and you get a vacation?"

"No."

"You said you're going overseas."

"Yes, but not on vacation. As part of my job. There are medical options not yet available here that might give Noah, and other victims of paralysis, the chance to walk again."

Philip leaned forward, as he listened intently. "You're planning to travel with an unmarried male?"

"I will be traveling with my patient, along with members of his family and other medical staff."

"Your father is okay with that?" Steve asked.

"I'm an adult," Damaris snapped. "My father doesn't control my work, or my life."

"Steve doesn't mean to upset you," Lori said, in a caring tone. "He, we, are all concerned about the short-and long-term effects of you working so closely with non-Laymen. Your father spoke at length with Philip. He's beside himself with the fear that you'll lose your way."

"Or find it," Damaris mumbled, chagrined but not surprised that she'd been a topic of conversation between Philip and her dad. She cleared her throat. "I appreciate your concern and will speak to my father. But I assure you, who I am and what I think are products of my own mind, developed through my own reasoning. I think Laymen could benefit by spending more time with the other—" she emphasized with air quotes "—people like the Breedloves, before being so quick to judge them."

The dinner conversation never fully recovered. Later, when Steve asked for her phone number, Damaris told him flat out that she wasn't interested. When Lori mentioned seeing her at church the next Sunday, she made no promises to attend. Driving back to Breedlove, Damaris realized that what her dad, the Sullivans and the Boltons had tried to do might have backfired. Instead of their talk pulling her closer to her Laymen roots, they'd highlighted how quickly and dramatically Damaris's views had changed. Instead of running from that truth, she decided to embrace it, explore it and see what happened. Which meant no longer ignoring her attraction to Noah. Perhaps by giving in and allowing him those liberties her mother feared, his spell over her would be broken and they could both be free.

Seventeen

In less than a week, Noah and a small contingent boarded a private company plane for an almost fifteen-hour nonstop flight to Copenhagen, the capital of Denmark. Adam and Ryan were the only family on board. Victoria would arrive tomorrow. Nicholas, a week later. With time running out and investors antsy, his brothers had all turned their focus to Utah, and put other projects on the back burner to help Noah's plans succeed. Noah felt secure with those who'd accompanied him. Damaris, Travis, Noah's personal assistant, his friend Cole, Roy, his therapist, and his executive secretary, Lydia, who'd have to coordinate work, rehab and sleep schedules for him to successfully work across continents and time zones. The schedule would be crazy. He knew that, and was prepared.

Noah had visited more than two dozen countries, but this was his first trip to Scandinavia. He was excited, not only for the possibility of walking but because it was Damaris's first time out of the country and, as he was quickly reminded by her gasp as she entered it, her first time on a private plane. The CANN jet had been pretty impressive before its nose-to-tip upgraded renovation last year. Now its interior rivaled the wealthiest of royalty and corporate execs.

"You like it?" he asked, while leading her past a set of seats and down the wide aisle to the open-space living room, where his chair could be both accommodated and locked in place.

"I never knew something like this existed. It looks and feels more like a home than a plane."

"Exactly what my mom and the designer were going for," Noah replied. "Later, after dinner, I'll give you the full tour."

Dinner service began just minutes after the plane leveled off and just before a magnificent sunset announced the end of the day. Damaris's joy was contagious, making Noah feel light, almost boyish as he experienced the life he took for granted through her virgin eyes. He delighted in watching her try new dishes, like the trio of mini-appetizers that began the meal—caviar on pita tips, truffle-laced mac-n-cheese poppers and oysters Rockefeller. A glass of vintage pinot further relaxed her. Conversation flowed as smooth and easily as the wine. He flirted and teased, delighted when instead of meeting a wall of resistance, she flirted back. When the entrée arrived and Damaris moaned with the first tender bite of medium rare chateaubriand, Noah imagined his manhood twitched, as he focused on the sultry experience generated by a voyeuristic journey deep inside her. By the time dessert arrived, a decadent slice of triple chocolate fudge cake, the two entered a new type of intimacy while sharing gooey bites of heaven from the same plate.

Damaris accepted Noah's invitation for the last bite of cake. "That's the best meal I've ever eaten in my entire life," she exclaimed, then fell back against the plush leather seat. "Now all I need is a comfy bed and a thick, soft blanket and I'd be off to dreamland in five seconds flat."

"I was just thinking the same thing," Noah said. He reached for the buckle securing the chair and unlocked it. "Come on."

Damaris looked at him through sleepy eyes. "Where are we going?"

"On that tour I promised."

She got up and followed him toward the front of the plane where the other passengers lounged. Travis and Noah's personal assistant sat at a table playing chess. Adam and Ryan were watching a movie.

Adam looked up and paused the video. "Hey, you two." The couples chatted briefly before Adam said, "Do you ladies mind if we talk business real quick?"

"Not at all." Ryan unbuckled her seat belt and stood. "I'd love the time to chat with Dee anyway."

Noah watched Ryan pull Damaris to a couch on the opposite side of the plane, then turned his attention to Adam. Meanwhile Damaris, who rarely imbibed, gratefully accepted a liqueur-laced cup of coffee from the flight attendant.

"Enjoying the flight?" Ryan asked Damaris, after they'd been served.

"It's beyond incredible," Damaris replied. "I have no words."

"I didn't, either, on my first private flight. Couldn't believe people really lived like this."

"I'm glad Adam was able to come over with Noah. He's been fairly fearless through a life-changing event that would have felled stronger men. But he keeps a lot inside him, too, including the vulnerability and uncertainty that he certainly feels."

"Mom and Dad are coming, too," Ryan said, referring to Nicholas and Victoria.

"They've been extremely supportive, which is invaluable to a patient's recovery."

"I've never seen a more tightly knit family," Ryan admitted. "Before Adam, I didn't know this type of closeness existed. Meeting him changed my life."

"How did you two meet?"

"Adam and my brother Dennis went to high school together. He introduced us."

"Was it love at first sight?"

"Ha! Hardly. On the surface, Adam and I were as different as night and day."

"Really? To see the two of you now, I never would have guessed that."

"It's hard for me to remember those days because now, I couldn't imagine my life without him."

Funny, but at this very moment, Damaris couldn't see her life without a certain Breedlove brother in it, either. She was about to ask Ryan more questions when she heard Noah laugh before turning to come toward them.

"Enough talk about health and healing," he joked. "It's time to finish our tour."

"Talk more later?" Damaris asked Ryan.

"Absolutely! Maybe you can go with me to see the home of Hans Christian Andersen. So far, Adam is less than enthused."

"Didn't he write 'The Ugly Duckling'?"

"That and other wonderful fairy tales."

"I heard about that story as a child and would love to go."

They started down the aisle.

"Be careful, Dee," Adam teased. "Noah might try to show you more than the plane."

Damaris blushed at the bold comment, while wondering if and how Noah's earlier flirting might play out. It was the first time he'd shown that kind of interest since Travis returned and the massages ended, causing her to think she'd waited too long, ready to act on an attraction that Noah no longer felt.

Noah took the lead as they passed the area where the two had eaten dinner and showed her how all of the sleek sofas doubled as beds.

"Wow, how many does this plane sleep?"

"Comfortably? Ten or so, but up to twenty or more if we have to and include floor space. This is an Airbus that in its original design could carry a hundred and sixty passengers, so the designers had a large layout to work with."

He pointed out a deluxe full bathroom with a shower, tub and sauna stall, touting platinum fixtures gleaming against marble in subtle shades of gray. The next section of the plane held a formal dining table with seating for twelve, one that could be lowered into the plane's belly, turning the room into a theater. He showed Damaris a dedicated bedroom, a second smaller room used as an office/workout area and the master panel that allowed passengers to control temperature, lighting, window shades and entertainment devices without leaving their seats. They continued down a short hallway to a closed door.

"Now," Noah said, looking back at her, "this next one is my favorite room on the plane."

Damaris followed Noah into a master suite that defied description. While easily half the size of the one in her guest home, it was many times more luxurious with every amenity and convenience one could imagine or ever need.

Noah quietly watched Damaris take a turn around the room. She peeked into a doorway. "Another bathroom?"

"One of three," he said with a nod. "There's another one at the front of the cabin."

"I could easily live here," she said, sitting to test out the bed. "This mattress feels as good as or better than the one back home."

Noah yawned as he rolled to the side of the bed. "Yes, and I'm getting ready to take full advantage of it."

"It has been a long day. Would you like me to get Travis to help you get settled?"

"No, Damaris, if you don't mind, I'd like your help with that."

Noah's voice held a tenderness that brought Damaris's nipples to instant attention. She looked down, thankful the reaction remained hidden behind a padded bra.

"How can I lift you?" she asked, using her tongue to moisten suddenly dry lips.

Noah nodded toward a closet. "The portable bod-riser fits on that hook."

She looked up and noticed the gleaming stainless steel fixtures. "Portable, huh?"

"Dr. Okoye had a prototype specifically made just for me."

She walked to the closet and pulled out the compact, collapsible device and wheeled it over to Noah. Focused on its novel design and ease of function while helping Noah undress, Damaris's professional mask barely slipped at seeing the strong chest she remembered and his tanned, sculpted legs. The bulge in his black boxers, however, could not be ignored.

"Do you feel that?" she asked, in a voice she hoped sounded dispassionate.

Noah looked down, then smiled. "No, but I wish you would."

Damaris grew warm, everywhere. Being ready and acting out a desire were two different things.

"The seat detaches," Noah said, focused on the lifter. "Through the stainless steel snap hook on the side. After sliding the leather beneath me you reattach it here. The harness works just like the one at home." He returned his gaze to her, eyes bright and intense. "Think you can handle it?"

He spoke of the lift, but her eyes slid to his crotch. "Sure."

Damaris pulled back the covers. Noah removed his shirt and T-shirt. She eased him into the lift and expertly transferred him into bed, adjusted the pillows and pulled his legs beneath the covers.

"Sit," Noah commanded, patting the space beside him. She did. "Touch me."

Damaris took a breath before turning her body more fully toward him. She grabbed the elastic top of his boxers with both hands and pulled. His erection sprang up like a just-released cobra, swaying slightly as though moved by her charm. She was the one enchanted. Turning off thought she let feelings take over, taking him in her hands with a gentle squeeze.

"Do you feel that?" He shook his head. She dropped her hands and then stroked him from base to tip. "Anything?"

"No," he replied while gently rubbing her back.

She repeated the move, her fingernail accidently flicking his perfectly mushroomed tip. His already engorged shaft further thickened in her grasp. She looked up expectantly, Noah's eyes on it, too. "Anything?"

He shook his head. "Damn." Noah's head fell back against the pillows.

He looked so defeated. Damaris's heart fell. "It's okay," she whispered, climbing into bed beside him, a move that was totally unplanned. She kissed him then—deeply, passionately—as her fingers splayed across his hard abs. Noah caressed her face before deft fingers eased over her top, and then beneath it. He lightly brushed them across her skin. Goose bumps followed in their wake. Her nipples tingled, longing for the same experience her back had just enjoyed. Her hand slid to his toned, muscled arms with a reassuring squeeze of silent consent to go beyond the bra to her breast, heart and soul.

Noah stopped, and with a finger raised her chin to see her eyes. "Take off your clothes. I want to feel you, however, wherever I can."

It was a reasonable request, one her hardened nipples straining against soft cotton gladly welcomed. She sat up, removed her top and bra, then shifted to lie upon him. Their bodies touched. Noah moaned, buried a hand in her hair and drove his tongue into her moist cavern.

"Pants, too," he whispered, once they came up for air. "Take off everything. I want to…satisfy you."

Caught up in the moment Damaris quickly obeyed, without one shred of shyness. She removed her slacks and underwear, felt the dew of excitement and wonder spring between her legs. Her inexperience caused a moment of worry. There was no need to fear. Noah was in control and an expert teacher. With his tongue and fingers, he played her body like an instrument and created a melody so beautiful it almost made her cry. He stroked and caressed her, plunged his deft finger into her core. She writhed against him to stoke the heat he created, wanting more of a sensation she'd not felt before. He encouraged her to give in, let go, enjoy the ride. She did, gasping at the force of her release, amazed at the revelation of what all had just happened, and how at that very second she fell completely in love.

Utterly spent, she reached for the sheet as she slid down and cushioned her head on his chest. Noah's heart beat strong and steady against her ear. She rubbed her hand across his stomach, and lower, brushed it against the now-flaccid member. She waited for guilt to creep up and consume her, but it didn't.

Noah eased tendrils of damp hair away from her face. "You okay?"

She nodded against his chest.

"Are you sure?" he continued. "How do you feel?"

"A little embarrassed. But other than that…amazing."

He chuckled then, a low, satisfied sound that warmed her insides.

"How do you feel?" she asked, looking up to see his expression.

"Happy that I helped you come out of your shell. You have a beautiful body."

"So do you. It's the first time I've lain beside a guy totally naked. Since meeting you, it's been the first time for a lot of things."

"What do you think about that?" she prodded, when he remained silent.

"I'm thinking that I want to continue being your first when it comes to experiencing pleasure."

"But you still didn't feel anything?"

"I felt something. I want this to continue on a regular basis, until I feel more. Are you okay with that?"

Damaris didn't answer, just nodded and cuddled beside him. Later, when the glow wore off, she might feel like a heathen. Right now, though, she was okay with all that had happened…absolutely everything.

Eighteen

Once Noah and the gang reached Denmark, everything changed. His plans for one-on-one physical therapy with Damaris were put on hold. Wanting to take advantage of every moment of his time at the center in hopes of seeing definitive results, they were taken from the airport directly to Forskning and met by Drs. Filip Sondergaard and Yonni Virtanen. The team was excited about having the prototype they'd worked on for over five years tested out in a human. He was x-rayed, given several physicals and prepped for a procedure made fairly noninvasive using specially designed implant needles and topical anesthesia. A series of stimulator electrodes were inserted along his spine's injured vertebrae, designed to work in conjunction with a formfitting pair of knee-length rubber shorts, similar to scuba gear, threaded with electrical current to activate the mini wonder discs.

Eight hours later, an exhausted bunch piled into a van and headed to the home they'd rented just outside town. While Noah had been in surgery, Damaris and his Nevada team had been given in-depth instructions and taken through the initial training of the program for his recovery. Noah was asleep before they'd driven out of Copenhagen's city limits. Between the rigorous schedule planned by the doctors and the ever-changing, fast-moving project back home, he was going to need all the rest he could get.

The next day, after an early-afternoon appointment with the doctors, a light workout with his bionic pants and absolutely no private time with Damaris, Noah settled into the home's airy office handling last-minute preparations for an upcoming videoconference. A constant flurry of emails and text messages had gone back and forth between team members. His brothers had rearranged their schedules to help implement the revised plans and keep the project on schedule. Clearly, everyone believed the Laymen problem had been solved and were moving quickly to implement the changes. Copenhagen was nine hours ahead of Las Vegas so just before six that evening, he sat in front of a large TV screen to head what would be a 9:00 a.m. meeting with the team back home.

A chef had been rented out with the house. She entered the home office, where Noah had set up shop. A breath of fresh air, otherwise known as Damaris, was just behind her.

"Hello, beautiful."

"I know you're busy," Damaris responded with a glance toward the chef, obviously uncomfortable with his public praise. "I saw her coming this way and decided to check in, make sure there is still no soreness or pain."

"There's a little pain," he said, eyes low, voice sexy and filled with innuendo. He nodded toward the portable monitoring device she carried. "Nothing that can't be fixed."

He smiled at the telltale rosiness of unease that crept up from her neck. He loved pushing her buttons. No time for that, though. The chef, who'd picked up an empty dish from the silver serving tray and set down a fresh pitcher of lemon water and a clean glass, stood silently by.

"Alma, correct?" Noah asked.

"Yes," the middle-aged woman replied. "Excuse me. Can I get you anything else, sir? Some juice perhaps, or another cup of tea?"

"No, thank you," Noah responded. "The salmon was delicious."

"Thank you. Please, if you need anything just ring the buzzer above your desk."

Noah nodded, his eyes on Damaris as the chef quietly left the room. "Your turn."

"Oh, okay." Damaris set the device on the desk, ready to take his temperature.

"Not for that." He pulled Damaris onto his lap. "It's your turn to ask if there is anything you can do for me."

"Oh. Well, is there?"

A flicker on the screen caught Noah's eye. "Dang it, not now." He gave Damaris a quick peck on the lips before easing her off him. "I've got to handle this meeting, but definitely want time with you later."

He watched her retrieve the device and checked out her sexy exit before turning his attention back to the countdown clock on the screen. When the computer's appointment clock hit zero, the picture came on, revealing an executive conference room. Guys from the department waved and shouted out greetings.

"That's a great office, Noah," one of the junior execs noted. "But is IKEA the only store in that place?"

"Hey, it's good stuff," Noah replied, laughing off the comment.

Sidney Beck, VP of Expansion under Noah, held up an oversize coffee mug in greeting. "Don't let my wife hear you talk bad about it," he admonished the junior. "Half of our house is furnished with their products. I should buy stock in that store."

Personally, he appreciated the sharp, clean aesthetic of the Scandinavian designs. How they seamlessly blended functionality, minimalism and style. The casual chat continued as the chairs around the conference table filled. Once the select group of key players who'd been invited had arrived and taken their seats, Noah officially began the meeting.

"Good morning this evening," he began, then got right down to business. "I understand the Laymen have received word of our Manning Valley purchase?"

"Absolutely," Sidney responded, his startling gray eyes boring into the camera. "To say they are displeased would be an understatement."

"*Pissed* would be more accurate," Nick said. "*Shocked* and *befuddled* work, too. Moving the project out of their county and therefore out of their direct control is a move they hadn't expected."

Noah had learned how to navigate the real estate business from the best of them, his father. Using the art of the unexpected was one of his foundational rules.

"Any direct communication?"

"No, but my Layman insider said they called a special meeting to discuss what to do next, that they're thinking about trying to block this on the state level."

"How, with the Supreme Court?" Noah asked.

Sydney shrugged. "I'm sure they'll use whatever legal means are at their disposal."

Noah's brother Christian leaned back in his chair. "Don't worry, Noah. Our attorneys are already on top of it. They've retained a guy who's an expert on Utah, the Laymen and the history of gambling in that state. He was born and raised there and used to be part of the church. Our guys say he has a personal ax to grind."

"What's his name?"

"Thomas Riley."

Noah typed the name into his notes.

"And get this," Nick said, a gleam in his eye. "He grew up with one of the project's fiercest opponents."

"Who?"

"Franklin Glen."

Noah's brow rose. "You're kidding me."

"Seems confident he can get Glen to back off. Says he knows something about the elder's past that would tarnish his image, lessen his influence with the Laymen community."

Sydney cleared his throat. "Get him to fold, and the rest of their contingency will crumble."

Noah thoughtfully stroked his chin as he absorbed this news. What could be so detrimental to Glen that he'd end his objections? Given his growing feelings for Damaris, would he want to be the man to expose it?

"This isn't personal, it's business," Nick said, as though reading his mind.

Another team member nodded. "Remember, business negotiations are no place for being nice."

"I agree," Sidney said. "Whatever it takes to get this project moving and calm down our investors. These delays and legal battles have cost enough as it is."

"Lydia, set up a phone call for me with Thomas Riley. If he's set to potentially assassinate someone's character, I want to know what type of bullets he's using."

The call lasted another hour, and left Noah drained. Being reminded of the ongoing opposition from Damaris's dad caused him to consider the possible consequences of a continued romance with Damaris. That she was inexperienced was something he didn't take lightly. If the procedure made it possible for him to have a sexual relationship with her, could he, if required, condone also taking down her dad?

For now, there was too much going on to worry about it. His physical condition hadn't improved. There was no time to spend with Damaris alone. When not at the prestigious research center just outside Copenhagen, he was back at the house handling what was now called Project MV, for Manning Valley, while being further analyzed by researchers, scientists and the medical team.

A week passed with no change in his condition. Noah tried to remain optimistic, had been told not to expect results overnight, if at all. He thought he'd prepared himself for the long haul. Now that the plans for the casino in Manning Valley were progressing, it was important for him to closely oversee everything that was happening. A responsibility handled much easier if he could walk!

He removed his shirt and buzzed for either Roy or Travis to help him remove the rubber shorts. Having seen no physical progress made an intense day longer. He rolled over to a window that looked out on a lake. A fresh snow sparkled under a bright, full moon. Stars dotted the inky blue sky. In spite of his will not to entertain them, thoughts of doubt ticked the edge of his mind. Doubt that what the doctors thought foolproof was truly innovative. Doubt that he'd ever walk. He heard the click of the automated door and breathed a sigh of relief. He wanted to get out of the constricted rubber and more, didn't need to be alone right now.

"About time," he said, whirling around. The rest of the comment died on his lips. "Dee."

"Hello, Noah."

She wore a loose, flowing maxi, the kind Ryan liked. Her hair was down, and damp, as though just out of the shower. She looked soft, sweet. Noah imagined tasting every inch of her skin.

"Where's Travis?"

"I told him and Roy that I'd take care of you."

"Why?"

She reached him, then boldly sat on his lap. "Because it almost feels as though I'm being avoided. Then I told myself to stop being selfish and remember how much you have on your mind."

She reached over, caressed his face. Her smile filled the room, her eyes shone with desire. She kissed his cheek, then slid her lips along his jaw to his ear.

"I know you don't believe in such foolishness," she whispered, before outlining his ear with her tongue. "But I've been praying for you. I have a good feeling about you walking again."

Noah was set to object but just then she shifted, her luscious backside pressed against his crotch. Even through the rubber he imagined he felt it, and responded. Damaris felt it, too. She eased off his lap, skimmed his rubber-clad thighs with her fingernails. "I know they serve a purpose, but do you want me to help take these off? You've been in them for hours."

She didn't wait for an answer. Just wheeled him over to the lift, slid the holster under his body, got a grip on the sides of the shorts and pulled. He was naked beneath them. She slid the pants to his ankles, then worked to remove them. When she straightened, it was to the sight of Noah's dick—hard, waving—like a welcome sign. A slight widening of the eyes was her only reaction, before maneuvering the holster over and lowering him into bed. She sat down next to his hip, causing Noah to wonder what happened to the bashful church girl and who was this take-charge vixen?

"Do you feel anything?" she asked, pointedly eyeing his penis.

"No."

She reached over and wrapped her fingers around it, rubbing up and down. "What about now?"

A shake of the head was all he could manage, watching incredulously as she lowered her head. There was no way. It couldn't be. She wasn't going to... "Ah!"

Forget about walking. The feel of her soft, wet lips on the tip of his dick made him feel like he could run out of the room! He gripped the chair with both hands, watched in shock and awe as she nibbled, licked and kissed it. Then he closed his eyes, leaned back his head and focused on the moment. It felt so good. She felt so... *Wait a minute.*

"Dee."

She looked up, smiled and continued to please him.

He reached out, put a firm hand on her shoulder.

"Damaris."

"Yes?" Her eyes filled with concern.

"It's… I feel something. I can feel you!"

Needless to say this new development changed the vibe. Damaris hurried from the room, raced back to cover his nakedness, then ran out again. She returned with Travis and Roy, Victoria not far behind. They called the doctors, who suggested he note any further changes throughout the night and come in first thing the next morning.

Filip and Yonni were there when he arrived.

"Good morning, Noah," Filip said. "Your phone call was quite something."

Yonni nodded, his excitement restrained. "Indeed. What happened? Tell us everything."

It took effort for Noah to not look at Damaris, the only one who would ever know all that occurred.

"I'd just gotten undressed when I felt…a sensation. That's when we called. Later, there was tingling and other sensations, a muscle twitch, or similar."

The doctors exchanged a look. "Let's get you into the lab."

A short time later, Noah was in a private hospital room surrounded by Victoria, Damaris, Travis, Cole and a team of specialists. X-rays were taken and tests were performed for nerve detection from waist to toe.

"There are definitely signs of improved feeling in parts of your lower extremities," Dr. Sondergaard concluded, as some of the special equipment used to work on him was wheeled out of the room. "I don't want to speculate prematurely, but what we'd hope might happen could in fact be occurring right now."

"The bruised area of my spinal cord is healing?" Noah asked cautiously, even as sparks of hope burst in his brain.

"We shouldn't get ahead of ourselves, but your improved ability to feel is indicative of nerves now responding that previously were not. You've also regained some flexibility in the lower area of your back. Minimal, but even so an upgrade from what I saw earlier this week. We'll have more information for you in an hour or so. Until then you have some family members that are probably pretty anxious for an update."

Noah left his private room at the research center feeling cautiously optimistic. His wishes and the pretty nurse's prayers may get answered after all.

Nineteen

Damaris looked up from her cell phone and gazed out of the window as the plane flew past the Breedlove estate and the landing strip came into view. A return to Nevada was a return to reality, when she'd have to unravel her feelings and deal with her father, who, given the voice mail messages she'd just heard, was upset that she'd left in the first place. Her feelings were jumbled, the line between professional and personal totally shattered. She took full responsibility. What happened wasn't Noah's fault. She just needed to know what this was that had developed between them. And she needed Noah to tell her. As if prompted, he materialized beside her.

"A lot different than in Denmark," he remarked with a nod to the view.

"Totally."

He locked his chair into position, then pulled out his phone. "You ready to be back in the real world?"

"Not really."

Noah stopped scrolling and looked up.

"I turned on my phone a little while ago. There were several messages from my family, my dad. He's upset that I flew to Denmark without telling him. I told my mom," she added.

"Any regrets?" he asked with an unwavering gaze.

Her eyes held as she gave her answer. "None."

The plane landed. Everyone was exhausted. The entire team was given the night and the next day off. Damaris shared a quiet ride in the van with Noah, but, after a brief hug, walked to her unit and pulled her luggage inside. She'd just filled the tub and was about to strip and enjoy her first bubble bath since moving there when her home phone rang.

"Hello," she mumbled.

"Damaris?"

"Yes."

"It's Walter, the guard at the front gate."

"Yes, Walter. How can I help?"

"Your dad wants to speak to you."

"My dad? Why did he call you when they have both my home and cell numbers? Wait, how did he get yours?"

"He's not on the phone, Damaris. He's at the gate and says he's not leaving until he sees you. Should I let him in?"

Shock added to Damaris's already sapped mind, rendered it totally blank. Hearing her father's raised voice in the background, and the guard's calm replies, gave her the jolt needed to move.

"I'm coming out," she blurted. "Tell my dad to give me five minutes. I'll be right there."

Damaris hurriedly pulled on a pair of jeans and the sweater she'd just thrown in the hamper. Her dad, here, in Vegas? And not just Vegas but the town of Breedlove, at the gate of the family's estate? She slipped into a pair of ankle boots, grabbed her coat and car keys and ran toward the garage. Seconds later she was speeding down the picturesque private lanes. Currently unable to formulate a complete sentence in her head, Damaris had no idea how she'd talk to her father.

She arrived at the gate. Her father stood pacing outside a rental car, his face a mask of worry and pain. In that moment, her thoughts shifted. Had something happened to someone in the family? Had they been trying to reach her for an emergency when she'd purposely been unavailable? She got out of her car and walked through the gate, shivering against the cold.

"Dad! Why… What are you doing here? Did something—"

"What am I doing, Damaris?" Franklin countered, a bit too calmly. "What are you doing? That's what I came here to find out and I'm not leaving until I get an answer."

The guard approached them, just as another member of security pulled up in his car.

"Is everything all right, Ms. Glen?" he asked her.

"I'm her father," Franklin stated, agitation raising his voice.

"Dad, please, this is private property that is heavily guarded with cameras as well as personnel. You can't just show up here."

"How else was I supposed to speak with you, Dee, when you don't return my or your mother's calls?"

"You both know I've been out of the country. We just got back, not even an hour ago. Mom knew I had no international plan and would communicate by email or Skype."

"Did you?"

"No," Damaris belatedly realized. "The schedule was so intense over there and combined with the time difference I just… I'm sorry."

The guard cleared his throat. Damaris hadn't realized he still stood close beside them. "Would you like to use the guardhouse, ma'am? It's warmer in there."

"Thanks, Walter. We'll talk at my home. Will you please open the gate?"

She returned to her car and braced for confrontation, too tired for anything but truth. She was no longer Daddy's little girl. She was a woman, a nurse, performing a legitimate job with an amazing family. She'd developed feelings for a man outside the faith. She felt bad doing so would disappoint her father but knew that what she felt for Noah was not wrong. Hopefully she'd put whatever concerns her dad had to rest, send him on his way and take the bubble bath she'd dreamed of.

She drove slowly, her dad following in his rental, seeing

the grounds anew as through her father's eyes. Would he appreciate the jaw-dropping beauty of a landscape that fed her soul, or would he perceive the opulence as evil?

She pulled into the driveway, not the garage. Her father parked behind her. He got out, his eyes taking in everything around him, including her house, before finally falling on her with an expression she couldn't read.

"Who lives here?"

"I do, Dad. Let's talk inside."

"I want to know who all I'll be dealing with, and prefer not to interact with outsiders."

"It'll just be us. Come on." Damaris opened the door and led her dad into the living room.

"You live here alone?"

"Yes. There are guesthouses for some of the people who work here."

"Everyone gets their own home, not their own room?" He shook his head. "Such waste and extravagance when people are homeless."

"Not everyone."

Frank crossed his arms. "How did you qualify for such high living?"

"It's because I'm Noah's nurse, Dad. He lives next door."

"He what?"

"Dad, please, can we discuss this calmly? I'm sorry for not keeping in touch with Mom or returning your calls but it was a strenuous, exhausting trip. I don't want to argue."

"Don't you have regular hours?"

Damaris smiled. There was nothing regular about the Breedloves. "My job doesn't come with set hours, but I love it." She walked over to the couch. "Join me?"

He did, on the edge of the cushion, as though cooties covered the back.

"I feel that I'm making a positive difference. A bath followed by a good night's sleep and I'll be okay."

"You are not okay. You're changing and don't even know it. Look at you! Look at your hair."

Damaris had forgotten about Ryan flat-ironing it while they talked on the plane. "It was just to try something different. You don't like it?"

"You look worldly. Like them."

"You're right, Dad. I am changing."

"I knew it." He shook his head sadly. "I knew that once you left us, you'd lose your way."

"That's how it may appear to you." Damaris spoke softly, aware that their relationship would be forever altered after this. "To me, it feels like I'm finding it. Who I am and how I really feel about myself, the church and its beliefs. Not everyone outside the faith are the monsters I expected. The other people I work with here, for instance, are gracious, and compassionate, and kind. I've grown to respect the Breedloves, and admire their close-knit family. They're not evil people, Dad. They're—"

A sound interrupted her explanation, before Noah's voice came through the intercom.

"Dee, you okay?"

"I'm fine. Do you need me?"

His voice changed, lowered. "Of course."

"My dad's here." Said too forcefully, too quickly and too late, according to her dad's raised brow.

"Your father, Frank Glen? He's at your house right now?"

"Yeah. I forgot to keep in touch with Mom while overseas. He came to check on me."

"Hello, Mr. Glen. Noah Breedlove. We met, briefly, about a year ago. I head up a project for the CANN—"

"I know who you are."

"Excellent," Noah responded, not missing a beat. "I'd love to talk with you. How long are you here?"

"Just long enough to get my daughter packed up and back home."

A sustained pause, and then, "Dee, you sure you're all right?"

"She's fine."

"It's okay, Noah. I'll call you later."

"You may call him once we're back in Salt Lake. But you're leaving with me, tonight."

Damaris turned off the intercom. "Dad, this is my job. I have a patient. I can't just leave!"

"This isn't up for discussion, Damaris. I refuse to lose my child to this place." He stood, his look one of a made-up mind. "It's clear they have the resources to replace you ten times over. I'll pay to have your belongings shipped, or replaced."

"Dad." Damaris stood, too, the combination of exhaustion and strong emotion putting her near tears. "I'll come for a visit soon, I promise. But I can't leave now."

"Then you have no reason to come back at all. You can choose to live in disgrace here, with this family. Or you can come home to the people who love you, who truly have your best interest at heart. Weigh your decision carefully, daughter. Because you can't have both."

Twenty

Resisting the urge to barge through their shared door almost killed him. Of course, he couldn't. He had no right. Franklin was her father. It was her home. She could invite in whomever she wanted, even the bane of his existence for the past twelve months. To take his mind off the conversation happening next door, he picked up his phone to have one of his own.

"Yes, son."

"Hey, Dad. I'm not sure whether or not I thanked you for joining us in Denmark. I appreciated having you there."

"There's no need to thank me. It's what dads do. I'm so glad to have gotten there in time to meet all of the people working on that device, who put everything together to help you walk."

"I'm not there yet."

"You will be."

"That's the plan. Hey, Dad, I'm checking out the property in Manning Valley next week. You should join me."

"Chris told me the team had put in an offer. He said it's about forty acres of prime real estate."

"Backed up to the mountains and close to the freeway. Most important, it's out of the county where the Church of Laymen rule. We close in two weeks."

"I gotta hand it to you, Noah. You're doing the impossible. I'm proud of you, son."

"Thanks, Dad. We've cleared a major hurdle but are still far from a done deal. You know better than me what all can happen during these kinds of negotiations. Don't pop the cork yet."

The doorbell rang. Noah checked the security monitors. "Hold on, Dad. Dee's at the door."

He put the call on hold and tapped the intercom button. "Hello."

"Noah, it's Damaris."

"I can see that." He watched her eyes scan the doorway and light on the lens. She wore no makeup and her hair was wet, probably just out of the shower. His body responded, despite her forlorn expression. He pushed a button. "Door's unlocked." Then, "Let me call you back, Dad."

"Is Dee okay?"

"That's what I'm about to find out."

He met Dee in the living room, looking small and vulnerable, totally unlike the ray of sun that normally shone whenever she was around. He remembered the woman who took care of him right after the accident. The cheery demeanor and confident assurance that all would be well. That he would walk again. He was determined to make her situation better now, the way she did his back then.

She walked in and sat on a couch by the wall.

"What, no kiss or hug, nothing?"

Only then did he notice her too-bright eyes, and the tears that threatened.

"Baby, come here. What did your dad say? I'm worried about you."

She shook her head. "I'll just start crying again. I've done enough of that already."

"Talk to me, Dee. What's going on?"

"I have to go home."

"When?"

"Now." Damaris shared with him her father's ultimatum.

"I don't agree with him at all. But they're my family, Noah. When I ask myself if standing in my truth is worth it, if I can live never seeing or speaking to them again, the answer right now is no."

"Didn't you sign an agreement?"

"Yes, and not honoring it breaks my heart. I was totally blindsided, had no idea he'd come here. But I have no choice. Once I explain the circumstances, I believe Victoria will understand."

Noah could now imagine how Franklin felt when he learned they'd pulled the build out of Salt Lake City. He wanted to demand that Damaris stay and honor her contract. But this was already painful enough.

"I've spoken with Travis, who'll contact the rehab center. They have a roster of highly qualified on-call nurses. She'll have no trouble finding a replacement."

"What if I said I was happy with the nurse I have and didn't want to interview another one?"

Damaris stood and walked over to where he sat. She knelt down and placed her hands in his. "There are no words for how sorry I am, how I'm ashamed of my father's actions and am heartbroken that I won't be able to finish my contract. But I'm proud of you and so very happy that because of the new technology your walking again is just a matter of time."

"I appreciate that."

"I'll never forget the time I spent here in Breedlove. This beautiful land. Your family. My first time traveling out of the country. The only thing more beautiful than the Danish landscape and the city of Copenhagen is my experience of being there with you."

"The trip of a lifetime?" he said, his voice much lighter than his heart.

"Close," she said after a beat. "Hawaii would be the trip of a lifetime."

"You've never been there, either?"

"No, and that's my true dream vacation. Maybe someday." She rose up and hugged him. "I care for you deeply, Noah, and will miss you every day."

She stood and hurried to the door.

"Dee."

"Yes?" she answered without turning around.

"I agree that family should come first, but only when they put you first, too."

He watched her shoulders rise and fall, her hand still on the knob. The moment stretched on until he thought maybe she'd change her mind about leaving altogether. Finally, she opened the door and closed it softly behind her.

Noah swore the sky darkened and the room lost air.

The rest of the week he buried himself in Project MV and learning to walk again. The rubber shorts were replaced with a set of customized braces that also worked in conjunction with the implanted discs. The braces allowed him to stand upright, and then take his first step since falling down the mountain. He couldn't walk far, and only with assistance, but he was out of the chair. The word of his ongoing recovery spread fast within the company and the town's inner circle. Women who'd not called him once since the fall now texted and left voice mails. But his conversation was reserved for the pretty nurse who'd always believed he'd walk again, and whose view of him stayed constant no matter his posture.

That Sunday, he pulled into the main estate's circular drive and parked the van. Instead of going to the front door, he wheeled himself down the drive and toward the chorus of voices drifting from the large patio out back. He rounded the corner and took in a beautiful tableau—a dozen of his favorite people, family by blood or by choice, enjoying beautiful weather, incredible food and each other.

He reached an empty space at the table, parked his chair and, with no greeting, reached for a pitcher filled with a drink he hoped contained alcohol.

"Still no word?" Victoria asked.

Noah shook his head, a slight smile appearing when

Adam retrieved a decanter from the bar and poured more vodka into his Bloody Mary. "Thanks, bro."

"She feels terrible about what happened, son. I can't imagine the position she's in."

Nick turned to his twin. "I'm still waiting to hear exactly what happened."

"It's a long story," Noah said. "Christian, pass the menu."

He spent the next few minutes focused on brunch selections, not so much because he was hungry but to avoid the inevitable interrogation headed his way. Knowing he couldn't avoid them forever, he tapped a customized app on his phone and sent his order to their chef.

"We're not going to stop hounding you, bro," Nick said. "Mom wouldn't tell us—said it was your story. You might as well get it over with now, while we're all here. That way you won't have to repeat it."

Noah took a swallow of his drink, and grimaced as the strong liquor hit his throat then made its way to his stomach. He took another, smaller sip and set down the glass.

"Dee's father surprised her, flew down from Utah. He was here when we got back from Denmark."

"What'd he want?" Adam asked.

"In a word? Dee. Wanted to rescue her from the evils of gambling, including our family."

"How does he know about us?" Lauren asked.

Christian answered his wife. "He's a member of the Church of Laymen, the most vocal and powerful opponents to Noah's project in Utah."

"And you hired his daughter to work for you?" she asked Noah.

"That part wasn't planned." Neither was developing the strong feelings for her that he'd tried to ignore.

"He only found out later about their connection," Nick added. "And that Noah had met him in the project's early days."

"Yikes," Lauren said. "That's a sticky situation."

Christian rested a hand on his wife's chair, studying Noah. "This appears to be about more than an employee, no doubt an excellent nurse but one who can be replaced. Was there more going on? Did you develop feelings for her?"

Noah shrugged. "I don't know, man."

"He knows," Nick countered.

"You've never let anybody intimidate you or call the shots," Christian continued. "And if I remember correctly, you've got a business trip planned for next week. So what are you going to do?"

It took Noah a few days to come up with an answer. When he did, he booked a flight to Salt Lake City. It was time to confront his feelings, and Dee's dad.

Twenty-One

Dee sat across from Wendy at their favorite coffee shop, one week after leaving Nevada, nursing a cappuccino and a broken heart.

"I've ruined everything," Damaris quietly admitted. "Made so many mistakes. Coming back home instead of following my heart has been the worst of them."

"Come on, Dee," Wendy countered. "It can't be that bad."

Damaris fixed her with a stare. "It can't be worse."

Wendy reached across the table and squeezed Damaris's arm. "Tell me what all happened, friend. You were always so busy. We've barely talked. Start at the beginning."

Damaris launched into a recap of her time with Noah, from the time she arrived at the guesthouse until her dad showed up at the gate. Wendy listened intently. She asked questions for clarification but otherwise said little else.

"The problem was all the secrecy," Damaris surmised, after taking a break and finishing the coffee that had long grown cold. "I should have been truthful from the beginning—told Dad about the job offer and Mom about my feelings for Noah when they started to grow. Maybe I never should have taken the job. Had I never gone to Vegas, I wouldn't be sitting here hurting so much."

"You're in love with Noah," Wendy said. "That's why you're in so much pain."

Damaris shrugged. "I don't know. He's only my second serious relationship and it's been so confusing. I'm not sure I know what love is."

"I think you do know."

Wendy became quiet. Damaris looked up to see Wendy staring intently. "What?"

"I want to ask you something. Have you ever stopped to consider what Matthew has to do with everything that's happened?"

"Matt? He has nothing to do with it. He's dead."

"Exactly, and not only did losing him in that horrific accident tear you apart but that you'd continued to date him against your father's wishes filled you with guilt."

"I don't think—"

"Wait, Damaris. Please, hear me out. I know how much you love your family and can't imagine how the possibility of being cut off from them feels. But I wonder if you left Nevada and Noah because of that threat, or so as not to once again defy your father."

"Probably both." Damaris rubbed her arms against an inner chill. "I'm tired of talking about something that cannot be changed. What's up in Trauma? Think I can get hired back on?"

With that, Damaris effectively changed the subject. She listened to Wendy's colorful recap of the hospital shenanigans, even laughed a time or two. But with her return home came the shroud of misery that had covered her world since leaving Breedlove. Wendy's statement returned, too. The one she'd denied at the coffee shop but that had played in her head nonstop since. Had all the barriers she'd created when it came to loving Noah come from the fear of losing her family, and especially again disappointing her dad?

Noah gazed out of a window with the peaks of Daredevil Mountain visible in the distance. He'd chosen the nearby restaurant on purpose, to discover how his body and mind would feel back at the place that changed his life. His muscles grew stronger every day and with technology's help, he was standing. One day, after regaining their full use and getting his ski legs, he'd go down the mountain again.

For now, though, he was content to sip the hot tea that had just been delivered and eye it from a distance. They'd made a bid on the land that shared the same mountain range. He'd met with Manning Valley's city leaders. There were two stops left on the agenda before boarding the plane, one for a conversation that was long overdue.

A punctual Thomas Riley walked up to the table. "Noah Breedlove?"

Noah stood to greet him. Thomas's jaw dropped.

"I thought you were…"

"I was. Still recovering." Noah held out his hand. "Nice to meet you."

They sat. "Would you like to order something? I don't have much time but…"

"You're a busy man. I won't take much."

Straightforward. To the point. Noah liked that. "I understand you grew up with Franklin Glen?"

Thomas nodded. "Knew his whole family. We lived on the same block."

"My understanding is that his family has always been Laymen."

"Back several generations."

"I can't imagine someone so deeply entrenched in the faith would do actions that went against it."

"Every religion has rules. Laymen among them. Some of the rules they deem righteous seem cruel to the average man."

What Noah learned in the next ten minutes changed his itinerary. He still planned to have a conversation with Damaris. But first he had to speak with her father. Acting purely on instinct, he called the church, made an appointment and directed his driver to the address the receptionist provided. Once there, Noah reached for the cane he'd been given to aid mobility and made a slow, determined walk to the executive office's entrance. Thankfully, the receptionist was just inside.

"Mr. Wright?" the kindly receptionist asked, after viewing her watch. "Mr. Glen is waiting for you. Please, go right in."

Noah approached the closed door and after a slight knock, opened it. Frank stood near a window with his back to the door. He turned around with a cordial smile that lessened slightly as he came forward with an outstretched hand.

"Mr. Wright?" he queried with narrowing eyes.

"No," Noah replied with a firm grasp of Frank's hand. "I'm Noah Breedlove."

Frank pulled back but Noah held the grip. "I apologize for deceiving your secretary, but it was imperative that I speak with you. For as much as we differ, we do share one common interest. Damaris."

Only then did Noah release Frank's hand and watch the elder man's head-to-toe perusal.

"My daughter claimed you were paralyzed."

"I sustained a crippling back trauma, yes, and, for a while, was immobile. Only recently have I been able to walk short distances, with the help of braces, this cane and technology still being tested. I am not yet healed, sir. In fact, it took considerable effort, almost all that I had, to walk through that door to face you like a man. It is painful standing here now." Noah nodded toward a chair. "May I sit down?"

He could see the wheels turning in Frank's mind, but correctly guessed he would be hard-pressed to deny a chair to an injured man who needed one. He motioned for Noah to have a seat, then took one behind a desk.

"What do you want?"

"Again, my apologies for making the appointment under an assumed name but I felt it was the only way you'd see me."

"As my daughter is no longer employed by you, how is this about her?"

I love her. That was the answer that immediately came to Noah's mind but since he'd not yet shared that with Damaris or processed it himself, the timing didn't appear right to let Frank know.

"Damaris is an exceptional nurse and was very happy in Breedlove. By the time she left, our relationship had grown beyond that of patient/nurse."

"Then my timing couldn't have been better."

"If you'll forgive me, sir, your timing sucked."

Frank stood. "Nothing good can come from this conversation. I knew you'd be a bad influence on Damaris and I was right, just like I am about the moral decline a company like yours will bring to Utah. So if you're here to talk about either of those subjects you're wasting your time. You cannot date my daughter and that casino you think belongs here will never be built."

"Decisions arrived to based on your faith?"

"Absolutely."

"Yet you continue to visit your brother, even though that, too, is against the rules?"

Noah said this while staring at Frank and noted the look of utter shock before Frank regained control, schooled his features and came back around the desk.

"I don't know what you're talking about."

"I understand why it would be almost impossible to totally abandon Frederick, or Freddy as he's called. I know because, see, I have a twin, too. No matter what Nick ever did or didn't do, I could never turn my back on him."

Frank slowly sat down. When he spoke, his voice was low and raspy with emotion. "How did you find out about him?"

"That doesn't matter as much as knowing that with all of your loyalty to this institution, there is still a part of you that has a heart for someone who, according to the rules, should be put away and forgotten."

Franklin regained his stern composure. "What do you plan to do, try to blackmail me or Damaris with the knowledge of a crazy uncle she's never met?"

"I believe the politically correct term is *mentally ill* and no, I'm not here to blackmail you."

"Then why are you here, to try to get me to endorse the casino? To back down because you've changed locations? To get me to accept you and allow Damaris to return to Las Vegas? Neither will happen. You're wasting your time."

"I no longer need the church's endorsement to begin building. Regarding your daughter, I'm not here so that she can return to work. I'm here to tell you that my intentions are honorable. I care about Damaris. You've raised a beautiful woman."

Frank stood once again and spread his hands on his desk. "Let me tell you something, Breedlove. Your money might buy you everything else, but not my approval. You may have fooled her but I know your kind. You will never build a casino in Utah and you will never date my daughter."

He watched Frank walk over to the window, then joined him there. "As she is a grown woman, Mr. Glen, don't you think she should be the judge of that?"

"Obviously, her judgment is way off. Otherwise, she would have followed the rules."

An easy smile covered Noah's growing frustration. "You underestimate your daughter, sir. Dee strikes me as an excellent judge of character and a woman very much capable of making up her own mind. As for rules, there are exceptions, such as the one you make for your brother."

"That's different."

"How?"

"I don't have to answer your questions."

"Then I hope you'll answer mine, Dad," Damaris said, as she quietly entered the room. "And once he and I are done talking," she continued, her eyes narrowed and now on Noah, "I'll have some questions for you, too."

Twenty-Two

The shock on her dad's face was no less than what Damaris had felt upon hearing Noah's voice coming from his office, what was being said and that he was standing unaided as he spoke.

"Iris wasn't at her desk and I heard voices…"

Frank looked from Damaris to Noah and back. "Is this your doing, Damaris, having him come here?"

"No, Dad."

"Not at all, sir—"

Frank whirled on Noah. "You. May. Leave."

The room became quiet. Nobody moved. The air fairly crackled around them. Finally, Noah turned toward Damaris. "Will you be okay?"

"I'll be fine."

He walked over to her. "Call me later?"

Damaris didn't respond.

"What about meeting me in an hour, at the Inn by Northwest? Please, Dee, we really need to talk."

After a curt nod from Damaris, he turned to Frank. "Mr. Glen, thanks for your time."

Had the daggers her father threw at Noah's back been real, she would have needed her nursing skills. Given what she'd overheard, however, she doubted even those would be enough to stitch up the wounds between them.

She crossed over to her father. "What happened?"

"That outsider manipulated Iris by lying to get an appointment. It was a waste of time."

"Was this about the casino?"

Frank snorted. "I think he's beginning to understand that that pipe dream will never happen. This negotiation was about you. But I shut it down."

"Dad…"

"We've had this conversation, Damaris. Your time with those people is over. I'm not changing my mind."

Damaris took a deep breath. "I've changed, Dad, and it has nothing to do with the Breedloves."

"I'm not going to talk about this anymore."

"Then will you talk about the man I heard Noah refer to as your brother?"

"No," Frank said. He sat and began rearranging papers on his desk, a clear sign of dismissal. "I'm not going to talk about that, either."

One look at the hard set of her father's jaw and Damaris knew he meant it. She left his office and dialed home on the way to her car. No answer. She tried her mother's cell phone. It went to voice mail, too. Who was this man Noah referred to as her dad's brother? Needing answers, Damaris started the car and drove over to where she could get them.

The Inn by Northwest, a chalet-inspired boutique hotel located on the outskirts of town, sat nestled against a set of towering mountains and next to a lake. Damaris had heard of it but never ventured inside, probably because a night's room rate was more than an average apartment's monthly rent. Once inside, the lobby took her breath away. Gold chandeliers against rich burgundies and dark woods gave the place an unexpected yet sophisticated old-world charm. After peeking into the quaint restaurant's dining area and seeing no familiar faces, she texted Noah, who replied with a room number. Her first thought was to demand that he come downstairs and meet her in public. The second one was that given what he might share about her father, privacy was needed. Either way, Damaris didn't plan to be there long. She crossed the lobby. Beside a small elevator tucked into the corner, a grand staircase led to the two upper floors. She walked down the richly carpeted hallway to the last door on the right. She knocked. Her heart raced.

Within seconds Noah stood before her, handsome as always, a steely resolve to his countenance, the merest hint of vulnerability in his deep, dark eyes.

"You're walking."

"Yes." He took a step toward her, then stopped, as though unsure if he'd get a caressing hug or a cursing out. "Would you like to join me for dinner or…"

"No."

He hesitated, but then erased the distance between them and pulled her into his embrace. Damaris cut the hug short. She was ecstatic about his improved health. But they needed to talk. What he did was not okay.

He grasped her hands. "How angry with me are you?"

"On a scale of one to ten, I'd say eleven." Damaris pulled her hands back. "Why didn't you tell me you planned to meet my father? You had absolutely no right to do that, Noah, without letting me know."

"You might have asked me not to, and I wouldn't have wanted to go against that. But I was determined to speak with your dad."

"So you lied? Made the appointment in someone else's name? That after snooping around to dig up painful facts of his past?"

"I learned something rather interesting about Franklin, and yes, wanted to ask him about it."

"For what? To use against him in the push for your casino, to try to get the upper hand and possibly ruin his life in the process?"

"I have no desire to hurt your father, you or the church, but everything that's happened is what I felt I had to do."

"Which is?"

"To let him know how I feel about you, open the door for some type of dialogue, maybe reach an understanding.

I care about you, Dee, and didn't want it to feel as though I was sneaking behind his back to date his daughter."

Damaris raised a brow. "You didn't want to sneak behind his back, but it was okay to sneak behind mine."

"As soon as that meeting was over, you were my next call."

"I should have been your first one."

"Perhaps you're right."

"But I wasn't. And what was that about my father having a brother?"

"Maybe you should ask him about that."

"I'm asking you!"

"If he wants it known, he should tell you."

"So not only did you lie but now you're keeping secrets, too?"

"Dee—"

"Did you or did you not lie to get in to see my dad?"

"He never would have seen me otherwise." Noah leaned against the wall and sighed. "Babe, I didn't come here to upset you and I'm sorry that you're angry. But I don't regret the actions taken to meet with your father. I did what I felt I had to do."

Damaris walked over and stood in front of Noah. "You know what? I believe you. I'm sure you thought everything you did was perfectly fine, the same way my dad justified showing up at my door unannounced and issuing the ultimatum that brought me back here."

Her voice fell to a near whisper. "I didn't like feeling manipulated then. And I don't like it now. It's understandable why you can't get along with my dad. You're too much alike."

She whirled around and headed for the door.

"Dee, wait!"

"What?"

"Don't leave angry."

"Leaving is the only chance my mood will get better."

Noah pushed away from the wall and came toward her. He tried to hide the effort it took to walk completely unaided. Damaris noticed. A twinge of guilt hit her heart. Like Noah, she hid her pain, too.

"I don't leave until tomorrow," he said, as his hand gently clasped her arm. "Stay with me?"

Damaris shook her head, then opened the door. "I'm thankful to see that you're walking, Noah. But I can't stay. Goodbye."

Damaris drove home in a daze. Once there, she went straight to her room. She was right to call Noah out on his manipulative actions. But why did she feel so bad?

A soft knock at the door disrupted her thoughts. "Honey?"

"Yes, Mom."

"Franklin told me about Noah. May I come in?"

Seeing Bethany almost brought on the tears that threatened. Damaris swallowed them and told herself to be strong. Face the truth. She and Noah were over.

"I don't want to talk about him," she informed Bethany, shortly after her mother had taken a seat on the bed. "I want to talk about my uncle, Freddy, and why I'm just now hearing his name."

Over the next half hour, Damaris learned about her father's twin, Frederick Allen, a troubled young man who'd been diagnosed with a mental illness shortly after turning eighteen. A fraternal pair who'd been pitted against each other and therefore never close, who were further distanced by a stigma Franklin tried hard to avoid. By the time they turned twenty-one, he'd become a youth leader in the Church of Laymen, who believed mental illness was brought on by lack of faith and disobedience. Those diagnosed as such were to be avoided at all costs.

"With the more visible position, Frank totally changed his social circle and cut off all contact with Freddy. When their parents died, he placed him in an assisted-living facility and the secret visits began.

"He loves the church and his brother," Bethany finished. "It's been one of his greatest burdens."

Damaris absorbed the news in shocked silence, realizing her dad had asked of her something that he himself could not do—cut someone she loved completely out of her life. It was a burden she wasn't sure she could bear.

The following week, needing space away from family and time to think, Damaris moved out of her childhood bedroom and in with Wendy. She went back to Manning Valley Medical—working, and miserable. Though still upset about the stunt pulled on her father, she missed Noah more than a fish missed water and hadn't accepted his calls. Hearing his voice broke her heart. Not being able to see him was even more painful. But her father had made his position clear. If she went back to Noah, he would disown her.

"Hey there."

Damaris looked up from a tray of uneaten food. "Hey, Wendy."

"Are you losing weight?"

"Probably. Not much appetite."

"Why don't you go back already?"

"Because I don't like being lied to or feeling manipulated."

"Noah tried to talk, but you wouldn't listen."

"I'm a grown woman. He should have come to me first."

"Maybe he didn't for the same reason," Wendy quietly responded. "Because he's a grown-ass man.

"Call him, Dee. Hear him out. Life won't be the same without knowing the whole story."

"How will it be without my family?"

"If they really love you, they'll come around."

March snows gave way to April showers. Though still distant with her father, Damaris and her mom talked almost every day. Bethany worried about Damaris and agreed with Wendy that if her daughter truly had feelings for Noah, avoidance was unhealthy. The two needed to talk. Damaris knew she had to go one step further. She needed to see Noah. It was time to return to Las Vegas.

"Good morning, babe," Noah answered the next day.

"Good morning."

"I'm headed to a meeting and only have a couple minutes. What's up?"

"We need to talk."

"About?"

Damaris heard the pain beneath the anger in his voice. "I shouldn't have left so abruptly when you came to Utah. Yes, I was angry about your visit with my father. But you deserved the chance to tell your side."

"And you deserved to not have been blindsided by my visit. I'm sorry about what happened, babe. Looking back, I could have and should have handled that situation differently. Not including you in something involving your family, not telling you about my plans or your uncle was wrong. You should have been the first person to know everything. Believe me, if given the chance, something like that would never happen again."

Noah finished his meeting, then called Damaris. They talked for three hours that night and every day afterward. Both were delighted that Noah's mobility continued to improve. By the time the end of the month rolled around, Damaris stopped fighting the inevitable and booked a flight to Las Vegas. She hoped Wendy was right and her family's love would prevail because Damaris wasn't returning for a simple visit. She was moving back to Breedlove…to live.

Twenty-Three

Over the summer, Noah was busier than ever. The bill for virtual card-cash gambling in Manning Valley finally passed, a first for the state. On top of the continued travel back and forth to Utah were monthly trips to Denmark for the as yet non-USA-approved electrode treatments. He'd developed another passion: revolutionizing an industry to help those with spinal injuries. He and his twin, Nick, had formed a company, Breedlove Bionics, and become investors in the robotics company that helped him walk again. Then there was Damaris and their budding relationship. She was back in Vegas, adjusting to a new job, schedule, life. Fall arrived, then winter, with her still estranged from her family, still battling mixed feelings about leaving Utah. Noah encouraged her to take as long as needed to be comfortable with her choices. He was a patient man, supporting her no matter how long it took.

One Breedlove constant was the family brunch, where he was set to meet Damaris before spending a day enjoying her favorite new pastime, riding horses. As he turned the corner onto the estate's outdoor living space, he spotted Nick and Damaris with their heads together standing by one of the bars. She burst out in laughter, then noticed him approaching and tried for a straight face.

He offered a brief hug and kiss before asking, "What is he telling you now?"

"Blackmail material," Nick answered. "In case you get out of line."

Noah and Nick shared a shoulder-bump hug. "That's your job."

"You seriously tried to build a spaceship in seventh grade?" Damaris asked.

"I'm still trying to build one," was Noah's quick response. "If I get cleared for space travel, will you go with me?"

"Um…let me think about it…no." Said quickly, all of the words running together, which suggested her answer took no thinking at all. "The search for E.T. is all yours."

The rest of the family arrived. More than the delicious food and extravagant atmosphere, the Breedloves enjoyed each other. They all marveled at Noah's continued improvement and medicine's technological advances, which dominated early conversation.

"How many treatments are left, bro?" Adam asked, before biting into a double-decker sandwich.

"If my body continues responding the way it has, they might be over by the end of the year."

"After that you'll be totally healed?" Lauren asked. Of all the wives, she was the least informed on Noah's journey.

"I'll be able to walk without the aid of robotics," Noah said. "Whether or not one ever completely recovers from a back injury is hotly debated. That I'm walking at all is a miracle, and that there doesn't seem to be any lasting restrictions of my lower extremities is more than the doctors could have dreamed. If a little pain here or there is the price to pay for that freedom, I'll take it."

Nick sat back down after a second trip to the buffet. "My question is when do you think you'll be able to ski again?"

"That's not happening," Victoria chided.

"He should go as soon as possible," Nicholas countered, one of the rare times he and his wife weren't in total agreement. "The best way to get over the fear of a fall is to fall again."

The topics jumped from medicine to sports before centering on business and Project MV.

"I can't believe how quickly the bill passed once the location moved." Nicholas looked at Noah. "Why didn't that idea occur to you sooner?"

"All of the research done led us to Salt Lake City. It seemed the soundest economical choice. Insiders who thought they could sway church members fell through. We'd already bought the land, applied for permits, hired subcontractors. I had tunnel vision," he admitted. "Focused on a battle instead of the war."

"It takes strength to admit that," Victoria said. "You should also acknowledge the real reason you moved the operation to Manning Valley, why the bill was passed and you're set to begin construction." Everyone waited for the answer.

"Dee, of course! She's the one who pushed you to think outside the box and when you did the results were brilliant."

Noah reached for his glass. "You're absolutely right, Mom. To you, Dee."

The table joined him. "Hear, hear!"

About an hour after brunch ended, Noah, Damaris, Adam and Ryan saddled up and took a leisurely ride. Conversation was good but minimal, with everyone content to enjoy the beautiful surroundings and the unseasonably cool day. Noah noticed Damaris being especially subdued. Later that night, after they'd returned to his home and were enjoying mugs of hot chocolate by the patio's firepit, he asked her about it.

"Come here, babe." They were sitting across from each other. Noah invited Damaris to sit on his lap. "What's going on?"

Damaris looked at him. "What do you mean?"

"Don't do that. I'm becoming fluent in Damaris. You were extra quiet during the ride. Why?"

She sighed, leaned her head against his shoulder and

looked at the changing sky, a dusky blanket of turquoise turning to indigo, revealing thousands of stars. "It's my favorite time of year."

"And that makes you sad?"

"It might be the first one without my family."

"Do you think your dad would seriously forbid your family from coming to visit, and they'd listen?"

"Dad is going through a lot right now. I'm not sure what he'd do. You're lucky, Noah. I watched your father, and can see how much he loves you, how proud he is of all his kids. My dad still refuses to speak to me. Mom said he feels I've befriended his enemies and blames me for the bill going through."

"You know that's not true, right?"

"With my head, yes, but not with my heart."

Noah would have bet money that Damaris was wrong, that no way would her dad allow the holidays to pass without her. But when Thanksgiving rolled around, that was exactly what happened. She talked and video chatted with Bethany and a couple her siblings but Franklin made it clear that Damaris wasn't welcome back home and Bethany couldn't visit Las Vegas. The day was filled with turkey and the usual trimmings but for Damaris, little joy. Later, when the tears came, Damaris allowed them. Noah held her, and wiped them away. Each felt like acid and fueled his resolve. This would be the last holiday Damaris spent without family. He'd do whatever it took.

Twenty-Four

"Hawaii, darling? That's terrific!"

Damaris had just finished packing her bags for the week she and Noah were going to spend in the Aloha State over Christmas vacation. They'd be returning on the thirtieth, in time for the Breedloves' annual New Year's Eve bash. She knew that Noah had planned the trip to lift her spirits and that she should be super excited. But the truth of the matter was that in addition to Christmas, she'd just had a birthday. None of her family had been there. She missed them, and no amount of sea and rainbows could replace her mom and dad.

"Aren't you excited?" Bethany asked. "You've always wanted to go there."

"Yes, but I always imagined it would be with my family."

Bethany quietly replied, "Maybe someday."

Time to change the subject. "It's almost cookie season. Have you guys begun making the dough?"

"All we're preparing for is the birth of your niece. Your sister has four weeks to go and is as big as a house. Everyone believes the child will come early."

"I can't imagine not being there to help out. Baking cookies for the local shelters, military and single dads has been a tradition since before I was born. I wish Dad…"

"Me, too, Damaris. Know that I'm slowly, continuously trying to change his mind. It was easier for me. I don't agree with your current lifestyle, but I do believe your heart is in the right place. I also like what I hear about your young man, Noah. It took courage for him to face Franklin and admit how much he cares for you. These kinds of changes take time, but they can happen. Trust in that, okay?"

"Will you take lots of pictures for me, and maybe sneak a video call in sometime during the day?"

"I'll do what I can, sweetheart, but you're the one who needs to take pictures so I can visit that beautiful place through your eyes."

The doorbell rang.

"That's probably Noah, Mom. I need to go. Our plane leaves in about an hour."

"All right, sweetie. I love you."

"Love you, too."

Damaris went to the door and opened it. Instead of Ryan it was Elvis, one of the family's drivers.

"Noah asked that I come for you," Elvis explained. "He's tied up handling some last-minute business before your vacation begins."

A feeling of loneliness threatened. Damaris pushed it away. She was being selfish and ungrateful, focused on what wasn't happening instead of the blessing that was right in her face. Her wonderful, thoughtful boyfriend had planned a trip to Hawaii because he knew it was her favorite place and wanted to make her happy. There were worse ways to spend Christmas than having a dream come true.

Noah couldn't remember ever being ruffled. He was the brother with ice in his veins. But right now, while overseeing this latest project, neither *cool*, *calm* nor *collected* could be used to describe him. He could feel every nerve in his body and they all were abuzz.

He glanced over at Damaris, still sleeping beside him in the master suite of his brother Christian's private plane. Poor baby. He'd kept her up for most of the night and should have felt guilty. He didn't. The lovemaking had been too good. When she shifted and exposed a soft, toned thigh, he figured another round would be the perfect distraction.

He eased back the covers, slid his body down and kissed the tempting limb. He looked up. Nothing. He kissed it again, ran his tongue up to her hip. She frowned, turned away and partially exposed a silk-panty-clad cheek. Perfect. He ran his lips over her lusciousness, before lifting gently shifting her legs and settling his face between them.

Damaris gasped. "What are you doing?"

Noah's grin was mischievous. "Remember when you used your lips to help me feel? I'm returning the favor."

Noah ran his tongue between her folds—quickly, expertly—she could barely respond. He suckled and nibbled until her pearl became moist and words failed her completely, until her thighs shivered with the first orgasmic wave. Hard, thick and ready, he lifted himself and slid inside her, filled her completely and set up a slow, throbbing pace.

"Baby," she moaned, running her hands over his hard butt before lifting her hips and swirling them against him, in time to his beat.

"That's it, sweetheart," he encouraged. "Let your mind go, let your body be free. Let's make beautiful music together."

A couple hours and a powerful orgasm later, Noah felt infinitely more relaxed. He left Damaris in the shower, dressed quickly and reached for his phone to text Victoria.

We're almost there. All set?

No!

Victoria's response was immediate and not at all what he'd expected. The nerves returned full force. His mother

was the queen of last-minute parties, could pull off one for
a crowd of hundreds in less than a day. What was going on?

His phone lit up again. Last-minute changes to guest list.

Noah's heart dropped. Damaris's family? Were they not
able to come?

Sorry, honey. Delay an hour, at least. Will text when coast
is clear. Don't worry. It'll be fine.

Damaris finished dressing. They'd be landing soon and
took seats up front. Noah placed an arm around her as he
looked out the window. He could imagine her thoughts
around this holiday season. Family. And her not with them.
A part of him knew he was doing the right thing, no matter who did or didn't show up. The other part wasn't sure.
Franklin seemed unmovable, willing to lose his daughter
for the sake of the church. The celebration he'd planned for
her had cost him a fortune. He knew she'd be pleased. Yet
all of the money in the world couldn't buy the one thing
Damaris wanted the most—unconditional love from her
dad.

Noah couldn't imagine being estranged from his father.
Was it right for Damaris to lose a relationship with hers
because of him?

No way. The decision made, and his heart breaking, he
tapped his mother's smiling face icon once again.

This whole thing is a bad idea, Mom. Tell everyone that
something came up. Put them on planes tomorrow. I'll arrange for Dee and I to stay at one of our Maui houses, and
show her the island once everyone's gone.

Victoria's response came screaming across satellites.
ABSOLUTELY. NOT.

I can't come between Dee and her family, Mom.

The pause was longer this time, but she finally answered. You already did, son, the moment she fell in love with you. Don't give in to doubt. Follow your heart. It will always take you home. xoxo.

Not so easy, Noah wryly thought. Said heart was already in his stomach. By the time they landed it would be on the floor, on his feet or just beyond them. When Damaris turned to face him, he pulled himself together enough to present a real smile.

"Excited?" She nodded. "Good. We're about twenty minutes from touching down."

"It's beautiful."

"It is."

"And very green."

"Yes."

"We'll be staying at one of your family's properties, right?"

"A CANN property, yes, with all of the amenities of one but not a hotel. It's a series of houses located on a private island, for the vacationer who wants to get away from it all."

"Like cooks and housekeepers and a concierge?" Noah nodded. Damaris sat up, obviously intrigued. "How does that work?"

"We have a network of employees that work to ensure the comfort of every guest. There is a chef for every home along with housekeeping, laundry, gardening and other staff. There are no cars allowed on the island but there are ATVs and UTVs, scooters and carts, a boat for quick access to the main islands and a variety of vehicles for water sports."

"It sounds incredibly expensive."

"It is. Fortunately there are people in the world with tons of money and nothing to do but find ways to spend it."

"I can't imagine it," Damaris said.

Noah smiled. *Soon you won't have to.*

The pilot announced the plane's descent into Honolulu. Noah and Dee fastened their seat belts to land. Moments later they walked off the aircraft, Damaris's eyes bright as she walked down the stairs.

"I've always considered Utah one of the most beautiful states in the Union," she said. "But those mountains are incredible. The clouds are so close I can almost touch them."

Instead of responding, Noah reached for her hand, content to listen to the ramblings of an excited first-timer taking in paradise. He also used her preoccupation with the new surroundings to exchange a few discreet texts with his mother and Nick. He also texted Bethany, hoping she'd found the strength to defy Franklin and attend her daughter's party after all.

Damaris's banter continued as they entered the airport. She squealed when presented with an exquisitely designed lei, and breathed in the fragrant smell of orchids.

"Thank you," she said as the young lady smiled.

"Aloha."

The next flight was on a smaller aircraft and took just over half an hour. They neared the exit. Damaris stopped. "Wait, where's our luggage?"

"Someone is handling that for us. Your clothing will be at the house when we arrive."

"Ah, part of the private home amenities." Noah nodded. "I could get used to this."

Instead of the usual town car, a tricked-out Jeep sat idling at the curb, with tinted windows, a fire-red leather interior and rims so gleaming Damaris could have used their reflection to put on her makeup.

"This is cool!"

"You like?"

"I love."

"I can see you tooling around Breedlove in one just like it."

A middle-aged man with curly black hair and gleaming brown eyes approached them. "Good afternoon, sir. Dale Tana."

"It's just Noah, man. Nice meeting you, Dale. Thanks for the wonderful weather."

The driver smiled, revealing bright white teeth against his weathered, tanned skin. "All my doing, Noah. You're welcome."

The easy banter continued as the Jeep sped along the road, Dale barely slowing along hairpin curves. Soon hard-packed dirt was traded for a well-paved road, seemingly carved inside a dense jungle of flowers and trees. They rounded a curve. Noah heard Damaris's sharp intake of breath. She'd seen it, the wide expanse of crystal-blue water behind La Damaris, the mansion bearing her name.

"Is that the ocean?"

Noah nodded. "The one we just spent almost six hours over, the majestic Pacific." He watched a myriad of happy feelings play across her face. To know he'd helped to put them there made him feel like a superhero. Life only got better when they arrived at the gate with *La Damaris*, a wrought-iron work of art, written in cursive, starkly contrasted with the bright white posts that held it.

"Noah, look! My name!"

"Well, what do you know."

"I never, ever see my name. But it's there, on the fence. How'd that happen?"

His eyes twinkled. "No idea."

"Wait… You?" Noah watched Damaris's gaze become misty as reality dawned. "You had them carve my name on the gate?"

"You like it?"

"I think it's the coolest thing that's ever happened to me. But why?"

He kissed her. Twice. "You ask too many questions. Let me show you the house."

A welcoming veranda surrounded the three-story wonder. Dale let them out at the front entrance, then continued on around back where the sound of another engine reached them.

"Part of the staff?" Damaris asked.

Noah shrugged. "I guess."

"It's just you and me, and only for a few days. How many people could that possibly take?"

Instead of answering, Noah opened the door and stood back to let Damaris enter first. Scents from a five-foot floral arrangement in the vast foyer wrapped around the couple like a welcoming hug. Deep bluish-gray paneling gave relief to the stark white silk-covered walls that flowed seamlessly into a great room that was more like magnificent. The furniture was high-end yet inviting—white leather couches, chairs upholstered in raw silk, mixed with accents of deep blue, onyx and sage. Modern art blended perfectly with restored antiques. Large paneless windows let in an abundance of light, the greenery of the meticulously landscaped yard and an unobstructed water view.

"This is so pretty," Damaris said, her voice a whisper. "Don't pinch me if I'm dreaming. I don't want to wake up."

Sounds of muffled laughter floated from the rooms beyond them. Damaris eyed Noah, her look slightly chagrined. "How many people have been hired to help us this weekend?"

"I'm not sure," Noah said. "But it sounds like more than I've paid for. Let's go have a look."

They passed through a library, then walked across an expansive dining room with a movable wall of pure glass. Noah slid the glass open. The sound of noises increased. They walked out on the patio, turned the corner and heard a chorus of voices.

"Surprise!"

The look on Damaris's face was easily worth the money the party cost him. That the Breedloves were there could be explained. They owned the property. But when she saw Wendy, and a few friends from Utah, tears formed in her eyes. The crowd parted. A beaming Bethany held out her arms.

"Mom?" Damaris made like a missile and flew into her arms. "What are you doing here?"

Bethany smiled at her daughter while wiping tears. "Your sister couldn't travel all this way by herself."

Damaris whipped around. "Stephanie's here?"

Stephanie laughed, coming out from behind a pillar. "Last time I checked." The sisters hugged. "This place is crazy," she whispered, "and has your name on the gate and everything. That's pretty cool."

"There's one more surprise," Bethany said. Damaris's eyes widened with hope. "No, not him," Bethany said. "Your brother, Charles, came, honey. He's changing out of wet swim trunks and will be down soon. Happy birthday, sweetheart."

Everyone who heard her echoed, "Happy birthday!" With that, the party was on.

Much later, around midnight, feet bare, hair gently moving with the breeze, Damaris stood on the balcony facing the water, and gave gratitude for her life. A sound startled her, before familiar arms wrapped around her from behind. She luxuriated in his embrace.

"Hey, handsome." She turned around. "I want to tell you something."

"What?" Noah kissed her cheek, her forehead, her lips and neck.

"You're pretty amazing, you know that?"

"I try." His hands slid up her arms. One finger flicked at the outline of a nipple, now clearly visible beneath the short silk robe she wore.

"How'd you do it?"

"Your family?"

"How did you contact them? What did you say to get Mom here without my father? There's no way he approved of their trip."

"I have a feeling your mom is stronger than you think, but it wasn't me who reached out. Mom contacted Bethany."

"Victoria. Of course."

"She knew I wanted this day to be special. That couldn't happen without some of your family here."

"It was great seeing Cole, too."

"He's been busy with a new job on the East Coast. But he wanted to be here, for both of us."

"I can't think of a way big enough for me to thank her, or you."

Noah wriggled his thick, black eyebrows. "I can think of a way." He kissed her. "Maybe two."

Damaris tried her sexiest moves as she took his hand and led them to the bed. For the next several minutes she let her lips do the talking. So did Noah. Their tongues, too. They nibbled and swirled and sampled each other, growing hotter by the second, each moan louder than the last.

"Baby." Noah placed a hand on Damaris's chest, and pushed her back gently. "Wait."

"I don't want to wait. I want to feel you inside me."

"I want that, too. But I need to do something first."

"What?"

He rolled over and opened a drawer on the nightstand. "I planned to do this at dinner tomorrow, but the time feels right now."

Damaris looked down. Noah held a small box covered with crystals. "An early Christmas present?"

"Your belated birthday gift. Open it."

With eyes still on him, she lifted the lid. Inside, the box was lined with crushed black velvet surrounding a perfectly round four-carat blue diamond solitaire. Her hand slowly rose to her mouth.

"Noah, it's stunning. I've never seen anything more beautiful in my life."

"It will look even more beautiful on you." He pulled the ring from the box, lifted her left hand.

Her jaw dropped.

His eyes sparkled. In that moment Damaris knew a handsomer man did not exist in the world.

"Will you do it?"

"Wear that big rock? Absolutely."

The twinkle in Damaris's eyes proved she'd understood the question.

Noah became serious. "Damaris Glen, will you marry me?"

"Yes, Noah Breedlove. Of course, I will."

Noah pulled the sash from her robe to reveal her naked body. "Damn, you're beautiful. I love you, baby."

She reached for his belt buckle. "I love you, too."

"Baby, hold on. I can't think straight." He pulled the silk fabric together to cover her body, reached for her finger and took a deep breath. "This might seem crazy, even ill-planned. I've always gone with my gut. Now my heart's in it, too. Tumbling down that mountain, waking up unable to move, I would never have believed anything good could come from that. But something phenomenal did. The rest of my life started there. I'm so happy that you'll share the rest of it with me."

He slid the robe off her shoulders, ran his hands over her breasts, across her stomach, down her thighs. He slid a finger along the seam of her heat. Desire burned in his eyes.

"You want to practice a little physical therapy, see if I can feel anything?"

Damaris again reached for the buckle on his pants and undid it. She unzipped them, slid a hand inside his boxers and stroked his dick.

"I want to see if I feel anything."

"Oh, baby. You're so sexy. I'll make sure you feel all of this…as often as you'd like."

Damaris hissed as Noah guided them down and slid a finger inside her, his tongue swirling to the rhythm of that same lazy beat. He took her over the edge, and while she shivered, slowly, gently, eased into her wet and ready paradise. She cried out, before relaxing so that he could go further. With their bodies, minds and souls fully connected, the first phase of his Sin City seduction was over. Another more poignant, deeper healing had only just begun.

* * * * *

COMING SOON!

We really hope you enjoyed reading this book.
If you're looking for more romance, be sure to
head to the shops when new books are
available on

Thursday 6th August

MILLS & BOON